ELSIE'S GIRLHOOD

ELSIE'S GIRLHOOD

Martha Finley

An Imprint of
Holly Hall Publications, Inc.

Elsie's Girlhood
Book 3 of The Elsie Books
by Martha Finley

© 1997 Holly Hall Publications
ISBN 1-888306-33-5

Published by Holly Hall Publications
255 South Bridge Street
P.O. Box 254
Elkton, MD 21922-0254
Tel. (888)-669-4693

Send requests for information to the above address.

Cover & book design by Mark Dinsmore
Arkworks@aol.com

Printed in the United States of America.

PREFACE

Oh! Time of promise, hope, and innocence,
Of trust, and love, and happy ignorance!
Whose every dream is heaven, in whose fair joy,
Experience yet has thrown no black alloy.

—THOUGHTS OF A RECLUSE

SOME YEARS have now elapsed since my little heroine "Elsie Dinsmore" made her début into the great world. She was sent out with many an anxious thought regarding the reception that might await her there. But she was kindly welcomed, and such has been the favor shown her ever since, that Publishers and Author have felt encouraged to prepare a new volume in which will be found the story of those years that have carried Elsie on from childhood to womanhood—the years in which her character was developing, and mind and body were growing and strengthening for the real work and battle of life.

May my readers who have admired and loved her as a child find her still more charming in her fresh young girlhood; may she prove to all a pleasant companion and friend; and to those of them now treading the same portion of life's pathway a useful example also, particularly in her filial love and obedience.

—M.F.

CHAPTER FIRST

It is a busy, talking world.

—ROWE.

"I THINK I SHALL ENJOY the fortnight we are to spend here, papa. It seems such a very pleasant place," Elsie remarked, in a tone of great satisfaction.

"I am glad you are pleased with it, daughter," returned Mr. Dinsmore, opening the morning paper, which John had just brought up.

They—Mr. Dinsmore and Elsie, Rose and Edward Allison—were occupying very comfortable quarters in a large hotel at one of our fashionable watering-places. A bedroom for each, and a private parlor for the joint use of the party, had been secured in advance, and late the night before they had arrived and taken possession.

It was now early in the morning. Elsie and her papa were in his room, which was in the second story and opened upon a veranda, shaded by tall trees, and over-looking a large grassy yard at the side of the building. Beyond were green fields, woods, and hills.

"Papa," said Elsie, gazing longingly upon them, as she stood by the open window, "can't we take a walk?"

"When Miss Rose is ready to go with us."

"May I run to her door and ask if she is? And if she isn't, may I wait for her out here on the veranda?"

"Yes."

She skipped away, but was back again almost immediately. "Papa, what do you think? It's just too bad!"

"What is too bad, daughter? I think I never before saw so cross a look on my little girl's face," he said, peering at her over the top of his newspaper. "Come here, and tell me what it is all about."

She obeyed, hanging her head and blushing. "I think I have some reason to be cross, papa," she said. "I thought we were going to have such a delightful time here, and now it is all spoiled. You could never guess who has the rooms just opposite ours, on the other side of the hall."

"Miss Stevens?"

"Why, papa, did you know she was here?"

"I knew she was in the house, because I saw her name in the hotel book last night when I went to register ours."

"And it just spoils all our pleasure."

"I hope not, daughter. I think she will hardly annoy you when you are close at my side, and that is pretty much all the time, isn't it?"

"Yes, papa, and I'll stick closer than ever to you if that will make her let me alone," she cried, with a merry laugh, putting her arm round his neck and kissing him two or three times.

"Ah, now I have my own little girl again," he said, drawing her to his knee and returning her caresses with interest. "But there, I hear Miss Rose's step in the hall. Run to mammy and have your hat put on."

Miss Stevens' presence proved scarcely less annoying to Elsie than the child had anticipated. She tried to keep out of the lady's way, but it was quite impossible. She could scarcely step out on the veranda, go into the parlor, or take a turn in the garden by herself, but in a moment Miss Stevens was at her side fawning upon and flattering her—telling her how sweet and pretty and amiable she was, how dearly she loved her, and how much she thought of her papa too: he was so handsome and so good; everybody admired him and thought him such a fine-looking gentleman, so polished in his manners, so agreeable and entertaining in conversation.

Then she would press all sorts of dainties upon the little girl in such a way that it was next to impossible to decline them, and occasionally even went so far as to suggest improvements, or rather alterations, in her dress, which she said was entirely too plain.

"You ought to have more flounces on your skirts, my dear," she remarked one day. "Skirts flounced to the waist are so very pretty and dressy, and you would look sweetly in them, but I notice you don't wear them at all. Do ask your papa to let you get a new dress and have it made so. I am sure he would consent, for anyone can see that he is very fond of you. He doesn't think of it—we can't expect gentlemen to notice such little matters. You ought to have a mamma to attend to such things for you. Ah, if you were my child, I would dress you sweetly, you dear little thing!"

"Thank you, ma'am, I daresay you mean to be very kind," replied Elsie, trying not to look annoyed, "but I don't want a mamma, since my own dear mother has gone to heaven. Papa is enough for me, and I like the way he dresses me. He always buys my dresses himself and says how they are to be made. The dressmaker wanted to put more flounces on, but papa didn't want them and neither did I. He says he doesn't like to see little girls loaded with finery, and that my clothes shall be of the best material and nicely made, but neat and simple."

"Oh, yes, I know your dress is not cheap. I didn't mean that at all. It is quite expensive enough, and some of your white dresses are beautifully worked—but I would like a little more ornament. You wear so little jewelry, and your father could afford to cover you with it if he chose. A pair of gold bracelets, like mine for instance, would be very pretty, and look charming on your lovely white arms. Those pearl ones you wear sometimes are very handsome—anyone could tell that they are the real thing—but you ought to have gold ones too, with clasps set with diamonds. Couldn't you persuade your papa to buy some for you?"

"Indeed, Miss Stevens, I don't want them! I don't want anything but what papa chooses to buy for me of his own accord. Ah! There is Miss Rose looking for me. I must go," and the little girl, glad of an excuse to get away, ran joyfully to her friend who had come to the veranda, where she and Miss Stevens had been standing, to tell her that they were going out to walk, and her papa wished to take her along.

Elsie went in to get her hat, and Miss Stevens came towards Rose, saying, "I think I heard you say you were going to walk, and I believe, if you don't forbid me, I shall do myself the pleasure of accompanying you. I have just been waiting for pleasant company. I will be ready in one moment." And before Rose could recover from her astonishment sufficiently to reply she had disappeared through the hall door.

Elsie was out again in a moment, just as the gentlemen had joined Rose, who excited their surprise and disgust by a repetition of Miss Stevens' speech to her.

Mr. Dinsmore looked excessively annoyed, and Edward pshawed, and wished her "at the bottom of the sea."

"No, brother," said Rose, smiling, "you don't wish any such thing. On the contrary, you would be the very first to fly to the rescue if you saw her in danger of drowning."

But before there was time for anything more to be said Miss Stevens had returned, and walking straight up to Mr. Dinsmore, she put her arm through his, saying with a little laugh, and what was meant for a very arch expression, "You see I don't stand upon ceremony with old friends, Mr. Dinsmore. It isn't my way."

"No, Miss Stevens, I think it never was," he replied, offering the other arm to Rose.

She was going to decline it on the plea that the path was too narrow for three, but something in his look made her change her mind and accept, and they moved on, while Elsie, almost ready to cry with vexation, fell behind with Edward Allison for an escort.

Edward tried to entertain his young companion, but

was too much provoked at the turn things had taken to make himself very agreeable to anyone, and altogether it was quite an uncomfortable walk—no one seeming to enjoy it but Miss Stevens, who laughed and talked incessantly; addressing nearly all her conversation to Mr. Dinsmore, he answering her with studied politeness, but nothing more.

Miss Stevens had, from the first, conceived a great antipathy to Rose, whom she considered a dangerous rival, and generally avoided, excepting when Mr. Dinsmore was with her, but she always interrupted a tête-à-tête between them when it was in her power to do so without being guilty of very great rudeness. This, and the covert sneers with which she often addressed Miss Allison, had not escaped Mr. Dinsmore's notice, and it frequently cost him quite an effort to treat Miss Stevens with the respectful politeness which he considered due to her sex and to the daughter of his father's old friend.

"Was it not too provoking, papa?" exclaimed Elsie, as she followed him into his room on their return from their walk.

"What, my dear?"

"Why, papa, I thought we were going to have such a nice time and she just spoiled it all."

"She? Who, daughter?"

"Why, papa, surely you know I mean Miss Stevens!"

"Then why did you not mention her name, instead of speaking of her as she? That does not sound respectful in a child of your age, and I wish my little girl always to be respectful to those older than herself. I thought I heard you the other day mention some gentleman's name without the prefix of Mr., and I intended to reprove you for it at the time. Don't do it again."

"No, sir, I won't," Elsie answered with a blush. "But, papa," she added the next moment, "Miss Stevens does that constantly."

"That makes no difference, my daughter," he said gravely. "Miss Stevens is the very last person I would have you take for your model. The less you resemble her in dress, manners, or anything else, the better. If you wish to copy anyone let it be Miss Allison, for she is a perfect lady in every respect."

Elsie looked very much pleased. "Yes, indeed, papa," she said, "I should be glad if I could be just like Miss Rose, she is always kind and gentle to everybody, even the servants, whom Miss Stevens orders about so crossly."

"Elsie!"

"What, papa?" she asked, blushing again, for his tone was reproving.

"Come here and sit on my knee. I want to talk to you. I'm afraid my little daughter is growing censorious," he said, with a very grave look as he drew her to his side. "You forget that we ought not to speak of other people's faults."

"I will try not to do it anymore, papa," she replied, the tears springing to her eyes, "but you don't know how very annoying Miss Stevens is. I have been near telling her several times that I did wish she would let me alone."

"No, daughter, don't do that. You must behave in a lady-like manner whether she does or not. We must expect annoyances in this world, my child, and must try to bear them with patience, remembering that God sends the little trials as well as the great, and that He has commanded us to 'let patience have her perfect work.' I fear it is a lack of the spirit of forgiveness that makes it so difficult for us to bear these trifling vexations with equanimity. And you must remember too, dear, that the Bible bids us be courteous, and teaches us to treat others as we ourselves would wish to be treated."

"I think you always remember the command to be courteous, papa," she said, looking affectionately into his face. "I was wondering all the time how you could be so very polite to Miss Stevens, for I was quite sure you would rather not have had her along. And then, what right had she to take your arm without being asked?" and Elsie's face flushed with indignation.

Her father laughed a little. "And thus deprive my little girl of her rights," he said, softly kissing the glowing cheek. "Ah! I doubt if you would have been angry had it been Miss Rose," he added a little mischievously.

"Oh, papa, you know Miss Rose would never have done such a thing!" exclaimed the little girl warmly.

"Ah, well, dear," he said in a soothing tone, "we won't talk any more about it. I acknowledge that I do not find Miss Stevens the most agreeable company in the world, but I must treat her politely, and show her a little attention sometimes, both because she is a lady and because her father once saved my father's life, for which I owe a debt of gratitude to him and his children."

"Did he, papa? I am sure it was very good of him, and I will try to like Miss Stevens for that. But won't you tell me about it?"

"It was when they were both quite young men," said Mr. Dinsmore, "before either of them was married. They were skating together and your grandfather broke through the ice, and would have been drowned, but for the courage and presence of mind of Mr. Stevens, who saved him only by very great exertion, and at the risk of his own life."

A few days after this, Elsie was playing on the veranda with several other little girls. "Do you think you shall like your new mamma, Elsie?" asked one of them in a careless tone, as she tied on an apron she had just been making for her doll, and turned it around to see how it fitted.

"My new mamma!" exclaimed Elsie, with unfeigned astonishment, dropping the scissors with which she had been cutting paper dolls for some of the little ones. "What can you mean, Annie? I am not going to have any new mamma."

"Yes, indeed, but you are though," asserted Annie positively, "for I heard my mother say so only yesterday, and it must be so, for she said Miss Stevens told it herself."

"Miss Stevens! And what does she know about it? What has she to do with my papa's affairs?" asked Elsie indignantly, the color rushing over face, neck, and arms.

"Well, I should think she might know, when she is going to marry him," returned the other with a laugh.

"She isn't! It's false! My"—but Elsie checked herself and shut her teeth hard to keep down the emotion that was swelling in her breast.

"It's true, you may depend upon it," replied Annie. "Everybody in the house knows it, and they are all talking about what a splendid match Miss Stevens is going to make, and mamma was wondering if you knew it, and how you would like her, and papa said he thought Mr. Dinsmore wouldn't think much of her if he knew how she flirted and danced until he came, and now pretends not to approve of balls, just because he doesn't."

Elsie made no reply, but dropping scissors, paper, and everything, sprang up and ran swiftly along the veranda, through the hall, upstairs, and without pausing to take breath, rushed into her father's room, where he sat quietly reading.

"Why, Elsie, daughter, what is the matter?" he asked in a tone of surprise and concern, as he caught sight of her flushed and agitated face.

"Oh, papa, it's that hateful Miss Stevens. I can't bear her!" she cried, throwing herself upon his breast, and bursting into a fit of passionate weeping.

Mr. Dinsmore said nothing for a moment, but thinking tears would prove the best relief to her overwrought feelings, contented himself with simply stroking her hair in a soothing way, and once or twice pressing his lips gently to her forehead.

"You feel better now, dearest, do you not?" he asked presently, as she raised her head to wipe away her tears.

"Yes, papa."

"Now tell me what it was all about."

"Miss Stevens does say such hateful things, papa!"

He laid his finger upon her lips. "Don't use that word again. It does not sound at all like my usually gentle sweet-tempered little girl."

"I won't, papa," she murmured, blushing and hanging her head. Then hiding her face on his breast, she lay there for several minutes perfectly silent and still.

"What is my little girl thinking of?" he asked at length.

"How everybody talks about you, papa. Last evening I was out on the veranda, and I heard John and Miss Stevens' maid, Phillis, talking together. It was moonlight, you know, papa," she went on, turning her face toward him again, "and they were out under the trees and John had his arm around her and he was kissing her, and telling her how pretty she was, and then they began talking about Miss Stevens and you, and John told Phillis that he reckoned you were going to marry her—"

"Who? Phillis?" asked Mr. Dinsmore, looking excessively amused.

"Oh, papa, no! You know I mean Miss Stevens," Elsie answered in a tone of annoyance.

"Well dear, and what of it all?" he asked soothingly. "I don't think the silly nonsense of the servants need trouble you. John is a sad fellow, I know. He courts all the pretty colored girls wherever he goes. I shall have to read him a serious lecture on the subject. But it is very kind of you to be so concerned for Phillis."

"Oh papa, don't!" she said, turning away her face. "Please don't tease me so. You know I don't care for Phillis or John, but that isn't all." And then she repeated what had passed between Annie and herself.

He looked a good deal provoked as she went on with her story, then very grave indeed. He was quite silent for a moment after she had done. Then drawing her closer to him, he said tenderly, "My poor little girl. I am sorry you should be so annoyed, but you know it is not true, daughter, and why need you care what other people think and say?"

"I don't like them to talk so, papa! I can't bear to have them say such things about you!" she exclaimed indignantly.

He was silent again for a little, then said kindly, "I think I had better take you away from these troublesome talkers. What do you say to going home?"

"Oh yes, papa, do take me home," she answered eagerly. "I wish we were there now. I think it is the pleasantest place in the world and it seems such a long, long while since we came away. Let us start tomorrow, papa, can't we?"

"But you know you will have to leave Miss Rose."

"Ah! I forgot that," she said a little sadly, but brightening again, she asked, "Couldn't you invite her to go home with us and spend the winter? Ah papa, do! It would be so pleasant to have her."

"No, my dear, it wouldn't do," he replied with a grave shake of the head.

"Why papa?" she asked with a look of keen disappointment.

"You are too young to understand why," he said in the same grave tone, and then relapsed into silence, sitting there for some time stroking her hair in an absent way, with his eyes on the carpet.

At last he said, "Elsie!" in a soft, low tone that quite made the little girl start and look up into his face, for she, too, had been in a deep reverie.

"What, papa?" she asked, and she wondered to see how the color had spread over his face, and how bright his eyes looked.

"I have been thinking," he said, in a half hesitating way, "that though it would not do to invite Miss Rose to spend the winter with us, it might do very nicely to ask her to come and live at the Oaks."

Elsie looked at him for a moment with a bewildered expression. Then suddenly comprehending, her face lighted up.

"Would you like it, dearest?" he asked. "Or would you prefer to go on living just as we have been, you and I together? I would consult your happiness before my own, for it lies very near my heart, my precious one. I can never forgive myself for all I have made you suffer, and when you were restored to me almost from the grave, I made a vow to do all in my power to make your future life bright and happy."

His tones were full of deep feeling, and as he spoke he drew her closer and closer to him and kissed her tenderly again and again.

"Speak, daughter, and tell me what you wish," he said, as she still remained silent.

At last she spoke, and he bent down to catch the words. "Dear papa," she whispered, "would it make you happy? And do you think mamma knows, and that she would like it?"

"Your mamma loves us both too well not to be pleased with anything that would add to our happiness," he replied gently.

"Dear papa, you won't be angry if I ask another question?"

"No, darling. Ask as many as you wish."

"Then, papa, will I have to call her mamma? And do you think my own mamma would like it?"

"If Miss Allison consents to take a mother's place to you, I am sure your own mamma, if she could speak to you, would tell you she deserved to have the title, and it would hurt us both very much if you refused to give it. Indeed, my daughter, I cannot ask her to come to us unless you will promise to do so, and to love and obey her just as you do me. Will you?"

"I will try to obey her, papa; and I shall love her very dearly, for I do already. But I can not love anybody quite so well as I love you, my own dear, dear father!" she said, throwing her arms around his neck.

He returned her caress, saying tenderly, "That's all I can ask, dearest. I must reserve the first place in your heart for myself."

"Do you think she will come, papa?" she asked anxiously.

"I don't know, daughter. I have not asked her yet. But shall I tell her that it will add to your happiness if she will be your mamma?"

"Yes, sir, and that I will call her mamma, and obey her and love her dearly. Oh, papa, ask her very soon, won't you?"

"Perhaps, but don't set your heart too much on it, for she may not be quite so willing to take such a troublesome charge as Miss Stevens seems to be," he said, returning to his playful tone.

Elsie looked troubled and anxious.

"I hope she will, papa," she said. "I think she might be very glad to come and live with you, and in such a beautiful home, too."

"Ah! But everyone does not appreciate my society as highly as you do," he replied, laughing and pinching her cheek, "and besides, you forget about the troublesome little girl. I have heard ladies say they would not marry a man who had a child."

"But Miss Rose loves me, papa. I am sure she does," she said, flushing, and the tears starting to her eyes.

"Yes, darling, I know she does," he answered soothingly. "I am only afraid she loves you better than she does me."

A large party of equestrians were setting out from the hotel that evening soon after tea, and Elsie, in company with several other little girls, went out upon the veranda to watch them mount and ride away. She was absent but a few moments from the parlor, where she had left her father, but when she returned to it he was not there. Miss Rose, too, was gone, she found upon further search, and though she had not much difficulty in conjecturing why she had thus, for the first time, been left behind, she could not help feeling rather lonely and desolate.

She felt no disposition to renew the afternoon's conversation with Annie Hart, so she went quietly upstairs to their private parlor and sat down to amuse herself with a book until Chloe came in from eating her supper. Then the little girl brought a stool, and seating herself in the old posture with her head in her nurse's lap, she drew her mother's miniature from her bosom, and fixing her eyes lovingly upon it, said, as she had done hundreds of times before: "Now, mammy, please tell me about my dear, dear mamma."

The soft eyes were full of tears, for with all her joy at

the thought of Rose, mingled a strange sad feeling that she was getting farther away from that dear, precious, unknown mother, whose image had been, since her earliest recollection, enshrined in her very heart of hearts.

CHAPTER SECOND

O lady! there be many things
That seem right fair above;
But sure not one among them all
Is half so sweet as love;—
Let us not pay our vows alone,
But join two altars into one.

—O. W. HOLMES

Here still is the smile that no cloud can o'ercast,
And the heart, and the hand, all thy own to the last.

—MOORE

MR. HORACE DINSMORE was quite remarkable for his conversational powers, and Rose, who had always heretofore found him a most entertaining companion, wondered greatly at his silence on this particular evening. She waited in vain for him to start some topic of conversation, but as he did not seem disposed to do so, she at length made the attempt herself, and tried one subject after another. Finding, however, that she was answered only in monosyllables, she too grew silent and embarrassed, and heartily wished for the relief of Elsie's presence.

She had proposed summoning the child to accompany them as usual, but Mr. Dinsmore replied that she had already had sufficient exercise, and he would prefer having her remain at home.

They had walked some distance, and coming to a rustic seat where they had often rested, they sat down. The moon was shining softly down upon them, and all nature seemed hushed and still. For some moments neither of them spoke, but at length Mr. Dinsmore broke the silence.

"Miss Allison," he said, in his deep, rich tones," I would like to tell you a story, if you will do me the favor to listen."

It would have been quite impossible for Rose to tell why her heart beat so fast at this very commonplace remark, but so it was, and she could scarcely steady her voice to reply, "I always find your stories interesting, Mr. Dinsmore."

He began at once.

"Somewhere between ten and eleven years ago, a wild, reckless boy of seventeen, very much spoiled by the indulgence of a fond, doting father, who loved and petted him as the only son of his departed mother, was spending a few months in one of our large Southern cities, where he met, and soon fell desperately in love with, a beautiful orphan heiress, some two years his junior.

"The boy was of too ardent a temperament, and too madly in love, to brook for a moment the thought of waiting until parents and guardians should consider them of suitable age to marry, in addition to which he had good reason to fear that his father, with whom family pride was a ruling passion, would entirely refuse his consent upon learning that the father of the young lady had begun life as a poor, uneducated boy, and worked his way up to wealth and position by dint of hard labor and incessant application to business.

"The boy, it is true, was almost as proud himself, but it was not until the arrows of the boy god had entered into his heart too deeply to be extracted, that he learned the story of his charmer's antecedents. Yet I doubt if the result would have been different had he been abundantly forewarned, for oh, Miss Rose, if ever an angel walked the earth in human form it was she—so gentle, so good, so beautiful!"

He heaved a deep sigh, paused a moment, and then went on.

"Well, Miss Rose, as you have probably surmised, they were privately married. If that sweet girl had a fault, it was that she was too yielding to those she loved, and she did love her young husband with all the warmth of her young guileless heart, for she had neither parents nor kinsfolk, and he was the one object around which her affections might cling. They were all the world to each other, and for a few short months they were very happy.

"But it could not last. The marriage was discovered. Her guardian and the young man's father were both furious, and they were torn asunder—she carried away to a distant plantation, and he sent north to attend college.

"They were well-nigh distracted, but cherished the hope that when they should reach their majority and come into possession of their property, which was now unfortunately entirely in the hands of their guardians, they would be reunited.

"But—it is the old story—their letters were intercepted, and the first news the young husband received of his wife was that she had died a few days after giving birth to a little daughter."

Again Mr. Dinsmore paused, then continued:

"It was a terrible stroke! For months, reason seemed almost ready to desert her throne. But time does wonders, and in the course of years it did much to heal his wounds. You would perhaps suppose that he would at once—or at least as soon as he was his own master—have sought out his child, and lavished upon it the wealth of his affections. But no; he had conceived almost an aversion to it, for he looked upon it as the cause—innocent, it is true—but still the cause of his wife's death. He did not know till long years afterwards that her heart was broken by the false story of his desertion and subsequent death. Her guardian was a hard, cruel man, though faithful in his care of her property.

"With him the child remained until she was about four years old, when a change was made necessary by his death, and she, with her faithful nurse, was received into her paternal grandfather's family until her father, who had then gone abroad, should return. But my story is growing very long, and you will be weary of listening. I will try to be as brief as possible.

"The little girl, under the care of her nurse and the faithful instructions of a pious old Scotchwoman—who had come over with the child's maternal grandparents, and followed the fortunes of the daughter and grand-daughter, always living as housekeeper in the families where they resided—had grown to be a sweet engaging child, inheriting her mother's beauty and gentleness. She had also her mother's craving for affection, and was constantly looking and longing for the return of her unknown father, which was delayed from time to time until she was nearly eight years of age.

"At last he came, but ah, what a bitter disappointment awaited the poor child! His mind had been poisoned against her, and instead of the love and tenderness she had a right to expect, he met her with coldness—almost with aversion. Poor little one! She was nearly heartbroken, and for a time scarcely dared venture into her father's presence. She was gentle, submissive, and patient; he cold, haughty, and stern. But she would love him in spite of his sternness, and at length she succeed-ed in winning her way to his affections, and he learned to love her with passionate tenderness.

"Still her troubles were not over. She was sincerely pious, and conscientiously strict in many things which her father deemed of little importance. Especially was this the case in regard to the observance of the Sabbath. He was a man of iron will, and she, though perfectly sub-missive in other respects, had the firmness of a martyr in resisting any interference with her conscience.

"Well, their wills came in collision. He required her to

do what she considered a violation of God's law, although he could see no harm in it, and therefore considered her stubborn and disobedient. He was firm, but so was she. He tried persuasions, threats, punishments—all without effect. He banished her from his arms, from the family circle, deprived her of amusements, denied her to visitors, broke off her correspondence with a valued friend, sent away her nurse, and finding all these acts of severity ineffectual, he at length left her, telling her he would return only when she submitted, and even refusing her a parting caress, which she pleaded for with heart-breaking entreaties."

Mr. Dinsmore's voice trembled with emotion, but recovering himself, he went on:

"Don't think, Miss Allison, that all this time the father's heart was not bleeding. It was, at every pore, but he was determined to conquer, and mistook the child's motives and the source of her strength to resist his will.

"He had bought a beautiful estate. He caused the house to be handsomely fitted up and furnished, especially lavishing trouble and expense upon a suite of rooms for his little girl, and when all was completed, he wrote to her, bidding her go and see the lovely home he had prepared for her reception as soon as she would submit, and presenting, as the only alternative, banishment to a boarding-school or convent until her education was finished. This was the one drop which made the cup overflow. The poor suffering child was prostrated by a brain fever which brought her to the very gates of death. Then the father's eyes were opened: he saw his folly and his sin, and repented in sackcloth and ashes, and God, in his great mercy, was pleased to spare him the terrible crushing blow which seemed to have already fallen—for at one time they told him his child was dead. Oh, never, never can he forget the unutterable anguish of that moment!"

Mr. Dinsmore paused, unable to proceed. Rose had been weeping for some time. She well knew to whose story she was listening, and her gentle, loving heart was filled with pity for both him and for his child.

"I have but little more to tell," he resumed. "The child has at length entirely recovered her health. She is dearer to her father's heart than words can express, and is very happy in the knowledge that it is so, and that henceforward he will strive to assist her to walk in the narrow way, instead of endeavoring to lead her from it.

"Their home has been a very happy one, but it lacks one thing. The wife and mother's place is vacant. She who filled it once is gone—never to return! But there is a sweet, gentle lady who has won the hearts of both father and daughter, and whom they would fain persuade to fill the void in their affections and their home.

"Miss Rose, dare I hope that you would venture to trust your happiness in the hands of a man who has proved himself capable of such cruelty?"

Rose did not speak, and he seemed to read in her silence and her averted face a rejection of his suit.

"Ah, you cannot love or trust me!" he exclaimed bitterly. "I was indeed a fool to hope it. Forgive me for troubling you. Forgive my presumption in imagining for a moment that I might be able to win you. But oh, Rose, could you but guess how I love you—better than aught else upon earth save my precious child—and even as I love her better than life. I said that our home had been a happy one, but to me it can be so no longer if you refuse to share it with me!"

She turned her blushing face towards him for a single instant, and timidly placed her hand in his. The touch sent a thrill through her whole frame.

"And you will dare trust me?" he said in a low tone of intense joy. "Oh, Rose! I have not deserved such happiness as this! I am not worthy of one so pure and good. But I will do all that man can do to make your life bright and happy."

"Ah, Mr. Dinsmore! I am very unfit for the place you have asked me to fill," she murmured. "I am not old enough, or wise enough to be a mother to your little girl."

"I know you are young, dear Rose, but you are far from foolish," he said tenderly, "and my little girl is quite prepared to yield you a daughter's love and obedience. But I do not think she will be a care or trouble to you. I do not intend that she shall, but expect to take all that upon myself. Indeed, Rose, dearest, you shall never know any care or trouble that I can save you from. No words can tell how dear you are to me, and were it in my power I would shield you from every annoyance, and give you every joy that the human heart can know. I have loved you from the first day we met! Ah, I loved you even before that, for all your love and kindness to my darling child, but I scarcely dared hope that you could return my affection, or feel willing to trust your happiness to the keeping of one who had shown himself such a monster of cruelty in his treatment of his little gentle daughter. Are you not afraid of me, Rose?"

His arm was around her waist, and he was bending over her, gazing down into her face, and eagerly awaiting her answer.

Presently it came, in calm, gentle tones: "No, Horace, 'perfect love casteth out fear,' and I cannot judge you hardly for what may have been only a mistaken sense of duty, and has been so bitterly repented."

"Heaven bless you, dearest, for these words," he answered with emotion. "They have made me the happiest of men."

Horace Dinsmore wore upon his little finger a splendid diamond ring, which had attracted good deal of attention, especially among the ladies, who admired it extremely, and of which Miss Stevens had hoped to be one day the happy and envied possessor. Taking Rose's small white hand in his again, he placed it upon her slender finger.

"This seals our compact, and makes you mine forever," he said, pressing the hand to his lips.

"With the consent of my parents," murmured Rose, a soft blush mantling her cheek.

Elsie was still in her papa's private parlor, for though

it was long past her usual hour for retiring, she had not yet done so, her father having left a message with Chloe to the effect that she might, if she chose, stay up until his return.

Chloe had dropped asleep in her chair and the little girl was trying to while away the time with a book. But she did not seem much interested in it, for every now and then she laid it down to run to the door and listen. Then sighing to herself, "They are not coming yet," she would go back and take it up again. But at last she started from her seat with an exclamation of delight that awoke Chloe, for this time there could be no doubt: she had heard his well-known step upon the stairs.

She moved quickly towards the door—stopped—hesitated, and stood still in the middle of the room.

But the door opened, and her father entered with Miss Rose upon his arm. One look at his radiant countenance, and Rose's blushing, happy face, told the whole glad story. He held out his hand with a beaming smile, and Elsie sprang towards him.

"My darling," he said, stooping to give her a kiss, "I have brought you a mother."

Then taking Rose's hand, and placing one of Elsie's in it, while he held the other in a close, loving grasp, he added: "Rose, she is your daughter also. I give you a share in my choicest treasure."

Rose threw her arm around the little girl and kissed her tenderly, whispering, "Will you love me, Elsie, dearest? You know how dearly I love you."

"Indeed I will. I do love you very much, and I am very glad, dear, darling Miss Rose," Elsie replied, returning her caress.

Mr. Dinsmore was watching them with a heart swelling with joy and gratitude. He led Rose to a sofa, and seating himself by her side, drew Elsie in between his knees, and put an arm round each. "My two treasures," he said, looking affectionately from one to the other. "Rose, I feel myself the richest man in the Union."

Rose smiled, and Elsie laid her head on her father's shoulder with a happy sigh.

They sat a few moments thus, when Rose made a movement to go, remarking that it must be growing late. She felt a secret desire to be safe within the shelter of her own room before the return of the riding party should expose her to Miss Stevens' prying curiosity.

"It is not quite ten yet," said Mr. Dinsmore looking at his watch.

"Late enough though, is it not?" she answered with a smile. "I think I must go. Good-night, dear little Elsie." She rose, and Mr. Dinsmore, gently drawing her hand within his arm, led her to her room, bidding her good-night at the door, and adding a whispered request that she would wait for him to conduct her down to the breakfast room in the morning.

"Must I go to bed now, papa?" asked Elsie, as he returned to the parlor again.

"Not yet," he said, "I want you." And sitting down, he took her in his arms. "My darling, my dear little daughter!" he said. "Were you very lonely this evening?"

"No, papa, not very, though I missed you and Miss Rose."

He was gazing down into her face. Something in its expression seemed to strike him, and he suddenly turned her towards the light, and looking keenly at her, said, "You have been crying. What was the matter?"

Elsie's face flushed crimson, and the tears started to her eyes again. "Dear papa, don't be angry with me," she pleaded. "I couldn't help it, indeed I could not."

"I am not angry, darling, only pained that my little girl is not so happy as I expected. I hoped that your joy would be unclouded tonight, as mine has been. But will you not tell your father what troubles you, dearest?"

"I was looking at this, papa," she said, drawing her mother's miniature from her bosom, and putting it into his hand, "and mammy was telling me all about my own mamma again. And, papa, you know I love Miss Rose, and I am very glad she is coming to us, but it seems as

- 28 -

if—as if—" She burst into a flood of tears, and hiding her face on his breast, sobbed out, "Oh, papa, I can't help feeling as though mamma—my own dear mamma—is farther away from us now, as if she is going to be forgotten."

There were tears in his eyes, too, but gently raising her head, he pushed back the curls from her forehead, and kissing her tenderly, said, in low, soothing tones, "No, darling, it is only a feeling, and will soon pass away. Your own dear mother—my early love—can never be forgotten by either of us. Nor would Rose wish it. There is room in my heart for both of them, and I do not love the memory of Elsie less because I have given a place in it to Rose."

There was a momentary silence. Then she looked up, asking timidly, "You are not vexed with me, papa?"

"No, dearest, not at all. And I am very glad you have told me your feelings so freely," he said, folding her closer and closer to his heart. "I hope you will always come to me with your sorrows, and you need never fear that you will not find sympathy, and help too, as far as it is in my power to give it. Elsie, do you know that you are very like your mother? The resemblance grows stronger every day, and it would be quite impossible for me to forget her with this living image always before me."

"Am I like her, papa? I am so glad!" exclaimed the little girl eagerly, her face lighting up with a joyous smile.

It seemed as though Mr. Dinsmore could hardly bear to part with his child that night. He held her a long time in his arms, but at last, with another tender caress, and a fervent blessing, he bade her good-night and sent her away.

CHAPTER THIRD

She twin'd—and her mother's gaze brought back
Each hue of her childhood's faded track.
Oh, hush the song, and let her tears
Flow to the dream of her early years!
Holy and pure are the drops that fall
When the young bride goes from her father's hall;
She goes unto love yet untried and new—
She parts from love which hath still been true.

—MRS. HEMANS' POEMS

"HOW DID IT HAPPEN that Mr. Dinsmore was not of your party last night, Miss Stevens?" inquired one of the lady boarders the next morning at the breakfast table.

"He had been riding all the morning with his little girl, and I presume was too much fatigued to go again in the evening," Miss Stevens coolly replied, as she broke an egg into her cup, and proceeded very deliberately to season it.

"It seems he was not too much fatigued to walk," returned the other, a little maliciously, "or to take a lady upon his arm."

Miss Stevens started, and looked up hastily.

"I would advise you to be on your guard, and play your cards well, or that quiet Miss Allison may prove a serious rival," the lady continued. "He certainly pays her a good deal of attention."

"It is easy to account for that," remarked Miss

Stevens, with a scornful toss of the head. "He is very fond of his little girl, and takes her out walking or riding every day, and this Miss Allison—who is, I presume, a kind of governess—indeed, it is evident that she is, from the care she takes of the child—goes along as a matter of course. But if you think Horace Dinsmore would look at a governess, you are greatly mistaken, for he is as proud as Lucifer, as well as the rest of his family, though he does set up to be so very pious!"

"Excuse me, madam," observed a gentleman sitting near, "but you must be laboring under a misapprehension. I am well acquainted with the Allison family, and can assure you that the father is one of the wealthiest merchants in Philadelphia."

At this moment Mr. Dinsmore entered with Rose upon his arm, and leading Elsie with the other hand. They drew near the table, he handed Miss Allison to a seat and took his place beside her. A slight murmur of surprise ran round the table, and all eyes were turned upon Rose, who, feeling uncomfortably conscious of the fact, cast down her own in modest embarrassment, while Elsie, with a face all smiles and dimples, sent a triumphant glance across the table at Annie Hart, who was whispering to her mother, "See, mamma, she has Mr. Dinsmore's ring!"

That lady immediately called Miss Stevens' attention to it, which was quite unnecessary, as she was already burning with rage at the sight.

"They walked out alone last evening, and that ring explains what they were about," said Mrs. Hart, in an undertone. "I am really sorry for you, Miss Stevens, for your prize has certainly slipped through your fingers."

"I am much obliged to you," she replied, with a toss of her head, "but there are as good fish in the sea as ever were caught."

The next moment she rose and left the table, Mrs. Hart following her into the public parlor, and continuing the conversation by remarking, "I would sue him for breach of promise if I were you, Miss Stevens. I understood you were engaged to him."

"I never said so. So what right had you to suppose it?" returned Miss Stevens snappishly.

And upon reflecting a moment, Mrs. Hart could not remember that she had ever said so in plain terms, although she had hinted it many times—talking a great deal of Mr. Dinsmore's splendid establishment, and frequently speaking of the changes she thought would be desirable in Elsie's dress, just as though she expected someday to have it under her control. Then, too, she had always treated Mr. Dinsmore with so much familiarity that it was perfectly natural strangers should suppose they were engaged, even though he never reciprocated it, for that might be only because he was naturally reserved and undemonstrative, as indeed Miss Stevens frequently averred, seeming to regret it very deeply.

Presently she burst out, "I don't know why people are always so ready to talk! I don't care for Horace Dinsmore, and never did! There was never anything serious between us, though I must say he has paid me marked attentions, and given me every reason to suppose he meant something by them. I never gave him any encouragement, however, and so he has been taken in by that artful creature. I thought he had more sense, and could see through her maneuvers—coaxing and petting up the child to curry favor with the father! I thank my stars that I am above such mean tricks! I presume she thinks, now, she is making a splendid match, but if she doesn't repent of her bargain before she has been married a year, I miss my guess! She'll never have her own way—not a bit of it—I can tell her that. Everybody that knows him will tell you that he is high-tempered and tyrannical, and as obstinate as a mule."

"The grapes are very sour, I think," whispered Mrs. Hart to her next neighbor, who nodded and laughed.

"There is Elsie out on the veranda, now," said Annie. "I mean to go and ask her what Miss Allison had her father's ring for. May I, mamma?"

"Yes, go, child, if you want to. I should like to hear

what she will say, though, of course, everybody understands that there must be an engagement."

"Well, Elsie, what made you run away in such a hurry yesterday?" asked Annie, running up to our little friend. "Did you ask your papa about the new mamma?"

"I told him what you said, Annie, and it wasn't true," Elsie answered, with a glad look of joy. "I am going to have a new mother though, and papa said I might tell you, but it is Miss Allison instead of Miss Stevens, and I am very glad, because I love her dearly."

"Is she your governess?"

"No, indeed! What made you ask?"

"Miss Stevens said so," replied Annie, laughing and running away. And just then Elsie's papa called her, and bade her go upstairs and have her hat put on, as they were going out to walk.

Edward Allison had been talking with his sister in her room, and they came down together to the veranda, where Mr. Dinsmore and Elsie were waiting for them. Edward was looking very proud and happy, but Rose's face was half hidden by her veil. She took Mr. Dinsmore's offered arm, and Elsie asked, "Aren't you going with us, Mr. Edward?"

"Not this time," he answered, smiling. "I have an engagement to play a game of chess with one of the ladies in the parlor yonder."

"Then I shall have papa's other hand," she said, taking possession of it.

She was very merry and talkative, but neither of her companions seemed much disposed to answer her remarks. They were following the same path they had taken the night before, and the thoughts of both were very busy with the past and the future.

At length they reached the rustic seat where they had sat while Mr. Dinsmore told his story, and he inquired of Rose if she would like to stop and rest.

She assented, recognizing the place with a smile and a blush, and they sat down.

"Papa," said Elsie, "I am not tired. Mayn't I run on to

the top of that hill yonder?"

"Yes, if you will not go out of sight or hearing, so that I can see that you are safe, and within call when I want you," he replied, and she bounded away.

Rose was sitting thoughtfully, with her eyes upon the ground, while those of her companion were following the graceful figure of his little girl, as she tripped lightly along the road.

"Mr. Dinsmore," Rose began.

"I beg pardon, but were you speaking to me?" he asked, turning to her with a half smile.

"Certainly," she replied, smiling in return. "There is no one else here."

"Well then, Rose, dear, please to remember that I don't answer to that name from your lips, at least not when we are alone. I am not Mr. Dinsmore to you, unless you mean to be Miss Allison to me," he added, taking her hand and gazing tenderly into her blushing face.

"Oh, no, no! I would not have you call me that!"

"Well then, dear Rose, I want you to call me Horace. I would almost as soon think of being Mr. Dinsmore to Elsie, as to you. And now, what were you going to say to me?"

"Only that I wish to set out on my homeward way tonight, with Edward. I think it would be best, more especially as mamma has written complaining of our long absence, and urging a speedy return."

"Of course your mother's wishes are the first to be consulted, until you have given me a prior right," he said, in a playful tone. "And so I suppose Elsie and I will be obliged to continue our journey by ourselves. But when may I claim you for my own indeed? Let it be as soon as possible, dearest, for I feel that I ought to return to my home ere long, and I am not willing to do so without my wife."

"I must have a few weeks to prepare: you know a lady's wardrobe cannot be got ready in a day. What would you say to six weeks? I am afraid mamma would think it entirely too short."

"Six weeks, dear Rose? Why, that would bring us to the middle of November. Surely a month will be long enough to keep me waiting for my happiness, and give the dressmakers sufficient time for their work. Let us say one month from today."

Rose raised one objection after another, but he overruled them all and pleaded his cause so earnestly that he gained his point at last, and the wedding was fixed for that day month, provided the consent of her parents, to so sudden a parting with their daughter, could be obtained.

While Rose was at home making her preparations, Mr. Dinsmore and his daughter were visiting the great lakes, and traveling through Canada. He heard frequently from her, and there were always a few lines to Elsie, which her father allowed her to answer in a little note enclosed in his, and sometimes he read her a little of his own, or of Miss Rose's letter, which she always considered a very great treat.

New York City was their last halting place on their route, and there they spent nearly two weeks in shopping and sight-seeing. Mr. Dinsmore purchased an elegant set of furniture for his wife's boudoir, and sent it on to his home, with his orders to Mrs. Murray concerning its arrangement. To this he added a splendid set of diamonds as his wedding gift to his bride, while Elsie selected a pair of very costly bracelets as hers.

They arrived in Philadelphia on Tuesday afternoon, the next morning being the time appointed for the wedding. Mr. Dinsmore himself went to his hotel, but sent Elsie and her nurse to Mr. Allison's, as he had been urgently requested to do, the family being now in occupation of their town residence.

Elsie found the whole house in a bustle of preparation. Sophy met her at the door and carried her off at once to her own room, eager to display what she called "her wedding dress." She was quite satisfied with the admiration Elsie expressed. "But I suppose you bought ever so many new dresses, and lots of other pretty things, in New York?" she said inquiringly.

"Yes, papa and I together. And don't you think, Sophy, he let me help him choose some of his clothes, and he says he thinks I have very good taste in ladies' and gentlemen's dress too."

"That was right kind of him, but isn't it odd, and real nice too, that he and Rose are going to get married? I was so surprised. Do you like it, Elsie? And shall you call her mamma?"

"Oh, yes, of course. I should be quite wretched if papa were going to marry anyone else, but I love Miss Rose dearly, and I am very glad she is coming to us. I think it is very good of her, and papa thinks so too."

"Yes," replied Sophy honestly, "and so do I, for I am sure I shouldn't like to leave papa and mamma and go away off there to live, though I do like you very much, Elsie, and your papa too. Only think! He is going to be my brother. And then won't you be some sort of relation too? I guess I'll be your aunt, won't I?"

"I don't know. I haven't thought about it," said Elsie, while at the same instant Harold put his head in at the half-open door, saying,

"Of course you will. And I'll be her uncle." The little girls were quite startled at first, but seeing who it was, Elsie ran towards him, holding out her hand.

"How do you do, Harold?" she said. "I am glad to see you."

He had his satchel of books on his arm. "Thank you, how are you? I am rejoiced to see you looking so well, but, as for me, I am quite sick—of lessons," he replied in a melancholy tone, and putting on a comically doleful expression.

Elsie laughed and shook her head. "I thought you were a good boy and quite fond of your books."

"Commonly, I believe I am, but not in these wedding times. It's quite too bad of your father, Elsie, to be carrying off Rose, when he won't let us have you. But never mind, I'll be even with him some of these days," and he gave her a meaning look.

"Come in, Harold, and put your books down," said Sophy. "You can afford to spend a few minutes talking to Elsie, can't you?"

"I think I will!" he replied, accepting her invitation.

They chatted for some time, and then Adelaide came in. Elsie had heard that she was coming on to be first bridesmaid. "Elsie, dear, how glad I am to see you! And how well and happy you are looking!" she exclaimed, folding her little niece in her arms, and kissing her fondly. "But come," she added, taking her by the hand and leading her into the next room, "Miss Rose came in from her shopping only a few minutes ago, and she wants to see you."

Rose was standing by the toilet-table, gazing intently, with a blush and a smile, at something she held in her hand. She laid it down as they came in, and embracing the little girl affectionately, said how very glad she was to see her.

Then, turning to the table again, she took up what she had been looking at—which proved to be a miniature of Mr. Dinsmore—and handed it to Adelaide, saying, "Is it not excellent? And so kind and thoughtful of him to give it to me."

"It is indeed a most perfect likeness," Adelaide replied. "Horace is very thoughtful about these little matters. I hope he will make you very happy, dear Rose. I cannot tell you how glad I was when I heard you were to be my sister."

"You have seemed like a sister to me ever since the winter I spent with you," said Rose. And then she began questioning Elsie about her journey, and asking if she were not fatigued, and would not like to lie down and rest a little before tea.

"No thank you," Elsie said. "You know it is only a short trip from New York, and I am not at all tired."

Just then the tea-bell rang, and Rose laughed and said it was well Elsie had not accepted her invitation. On going down to tea they found Mr. Dinsmore and Mr. Travilla there. Elsie was delighted to meet her old friend, and it was evident that he had already made himself a favorite with all the children, from Harold down to little May.

The wedding was a really brilliant affair. The bride and her attendants were beautifully dressed and, as everyone remarked, looked very charming. At an early hour in the morning carriages were in waiting to convey the bridal party and the family to the church where the ceremony was to be performed. When it was over they returned to the house, where an elegant breakfast was provided for a large number of guests, after which there was a grand reception for several hours. Then, when the last guest had departed, Rose retired to her own room, appearing shortly afterwards at the family dinner-table in her pretty traveling dress, looking very sweet and engaging, but sober and thoughtful, as were also her father and brothers, while Mrs. Allison's eyes were constantly filling with tears at the thought of losing her daughter.

There was very little eating done, and the conversation flagged several times in spite of the efforts of the gentlemen to keep it up. At length all rose from the table, and gathered in the parlor for a few moments. Then came the parting, and they were gone. And Mrs. Allison, feeling almost as if she had buried her daughter, tried to forget her loss by setting herself vigorously to work overseeing the business of putting her house in order.

Rose's feelings were mingled. She wept for a time, but the soothing tenderness of her husband's manner, and Elsie's winning caresses, soon restored her to herself, and smiles chased away the tears.

They had a very pleasant journey, without accident or detention, and arrived in due time at their own home, where they were welcomed with every demonstration of delight.

Rose was charmed with the Oaks, thought it even more lovely than either Roselands or Elingrove, and Mr. Dinsmore and Elsie intensely enjoyed her pleasure and admiration.

Then came a round of parties, which Elsie thought extremely tiresome, as she could have no share in them, and was thus deprived of the company of her papa and mamma almost every evening for several weeks. But at last that too was over, and they settled down into a quiet home life, that suited them all much better, for neither Mr. Dinsmore nor Rose was very fond of gaiety.

And now Elsie resumed her studies regularly, reciting as before to her father, while Rose undertook to instruct her in the more feminine branches of housekeeping and needlework, and a master came from the city several times a week to give her lessons in music and drawing. She had been so long without regular employment that she found it very difficult at first to give her mind to her studies, as she had done in former days, but her father, though kind and considerate, was very firm with her, and she soon fell into the traces and worked as diligently as ever.

Elsie did not find that her father's marriage brought any uncomfortable change to her. There was no lessening of his love or care, she saw as much of him as before, had full possession of her seat upon his knee, and was caressed and fondled quite as often and as tenderly as ever.

And added to all this were Rose's love and sweet companionship, which were ever grateful to the little girl, whether they were alone or with her father. Elsie loved her new mamma dearly and was as respectful and obedient to her as to her father, though Rose never assumed any authority—which, however, was entirely unnecessary, as a wish or request from her was sure to be attended to as if it had been a command.

And Rose was very happy in her new home. Mr. Dinsmore's family were pleased with the match and treated her most kindly, while he was always affectionate, thoughtful, and attentive, not less devoted as a husband than as a father. They were well suited in taste and disposition, seldom had the slightest disagreement on any subject, and neither had ever cause to regret the step they had taken, for each day they lived together seemed but to increase their love for each other, and for their little daughter, as Mr. Dinsmore delighted to call her, always giving Rose a share in the ownership.

CHAPTER FOURTH

Of all the joys that brighten suffering earth,
What joy is welcomed like a new-born child?

—MRS. NORTON

"MASSA WANTS YOU for to come right along to him in de study, darlin', jis as soon as your ole mammy kin get you dressed," said Chloe, one morning to her nursling.

"What for, mammy?" Elsie asked curiously, for she noticed an odd expression on her nurse's face.

"Massa didn't tell me nuffin 'bout what he wanted, an' I spects you'll have to ax hisself," replied Chloe evasively.

Elsie's curiosity was excited, and she hastened to the study as soon as possible. Her father laid down his paper as she entered, and held out his hand with a smile as he bade her good morning, and it struck her that there was an odd twinkle in his eye also, while she was certain that she could not be mistaken in the unusually joyous expression of his countenance.

"Good morning, papa. But where is mamma?" she asked, glancing about the room in search of her.

"She is not up yet, but do you sit down here in your little rocking chair. I have something for you."

He left the room as he spoke, returning again in a moment, carrying what Elsie thought was a strange-looking bundle.

"There! Hold out your arms," he said. And placing it in them, he gently raised one corner of the blanket, displaying to her astonished view a tiny little face.

"A baby! Oh, the dear little thing!" she exclaimed in tones of rapturous delight. Then looking up into his face, "Did you say I might have it, papa? Whose baby is it?"

"Ours; your mamma's and my son, and your brother," he answered, gazing down with intense pleasure at her bright, happy face, sparkling all over with delight.

"My little brother! My darling little brother," she murmured, looking down at it again, and venturing to press her lips gently to its soft velvet cheek. "Oh, papa, I am so glad, so glad! I have so wanted a little brother or sister. Is not God very good to give him to us, papa?" And happy grateful tears were trembling in the soft eyes as she raised them to his face again.

"Yes," he said, bending down and kissing first her cheek, and then the babe's. "I feel that God has indeed been very good to me in bestowing upon me two such treasures as these."

"What is his name, papa?" she asked.

"He has none yet, my dear."

"Then, papa, do let him be named Horace, for you. Won't you, if mama is willing? And then I hope he will grow up to be just like you, as handsome and as good."

"I should like him to be a great deal better, daughter," he answered with a grave smile, "and about the name—I don't know yet. I should prefer some other, but your mamma seems to want that, and I suppose she has the best right to name him. But we will see about it."

"Better give little marster to me now, Miss Elsie," remarked his nurse, stepping up. "I reckon your little arms begin to feel tired." And taking the babe she carried him from the room.

Nothing could have better pleased Mr. Dinsmore than Elsie's joyous welcome to her little brother, though it was scarcely more than he had expected.

"My own darling child, my dear, dear little daughter," he said, taking her in his arms and kissing her again and again. "Elsie, dearest, you are very precious to your father's heart."

"Yes, papa, I know it," she replied, twining her arms about his neck, and laying her cheek to his. "I know you love me dearly, and it makes me so very happy."

"May I go in to see mamma?" she asked presently.

"No, darling, not yet. She is not able to see you, but she sends her love, and hopes she may be well enough to receive a visit from you tomorrow."

"Poor mamma! I am sorry she is ill," she said sorrowfully, "but I will try to keep everything very quiet that she may not be disturbed."

That evening, after tea, Elsie was told that she would be allowed to speak to her mamma for a moment if she chose, and she gladly availed herself of the privilege.

"Dear Elsie," Rose whispered, drawing her down to kiss her cheek. "I am so glad you are pleased with your little brother."

"Oh, mamma, he is such a dear little fellow!" Elsie answered eagerly. "And now, if you will only get well we will be happier than ever."

Rose smiled and said she hoped soon to be quite well again, and then Mr. Dinsmore led Elsie from the room.

Rose was soon about again and in the enjoyment of her usual health and strength. Elsie's delight knew no bounds the first time her mamma was able to leave her room, and take her place at the table with her father and herself. She doted on her little brother, and, if allowed, would have had him in her arms more than half the time, but he was a plump little fellow, and soon grew so large and heavy that her father forbade her carrying him lest she should injure herself. But she would romp and play with him by the hour while he was in the nurse's arms, or seated on the bed, and when any of her little friends called, she could not be satisfied to let them go away without seeing the baby.

The first time Mr. Travilla called, after little Horace's arrival, she exhibited her treasure to him with a great deal of pride, asking if he did not envy her papa.

"Yes," he said, looking admiringly at her, and then turning away with a half sigh.

A few minutes afterwards he caught hold of her, set her on his knee, and giving her a kiss, said, "I wish you were ten years older, Elsie, or I ten years younger."

"Why, Mr. Travilla?" she asked rather wonderingly.

"Oh, because we would then be nearer of an age, and maybe you would like me better."

"No, I wouldn't, not a bit," she said, putting her arm round his neck, "for I like you now just as well as I could like any gentleman but papa."

The elder Mr. Dinsmore was very proud of his little grandson and made a great pet of him, coming to the Oaks much more frequently after his birth than before.

Once he spoke of him as his first grandchild.

"You forget Elsie, father," said Horace, putting his arm round his little girl, who happened to be standing by his side, and giving her a tender, loving look.

He greatly feared that the marked difference his father made between the two would wound Elsie's sensitive spirit, and perhaps even arouse a feeling of jealousy towards her little brother. Therefore, when his father was present, he was even more than usually affectionate in his manner towards her, if that were possible.

But Elsie had no feeling of the kind. She had long ceased to expect any manifestation of affection from her grandfather towards herself, but was very glad indeed that he could love her dear little brother.

"Ah, yes! To be sure, I did forget Elsie," replied the old gentleman carelessly. "She is the first grandchild of course; but this fellow is the first grandson, and quite proud of him I am. He is a pretty boy, and is going to be the very image of his father."

"I hope he will, father," said Rose, looking proudly at her husband. And then she added, with an affectionate glance at Elsie: "If he is only as good and obedient as his sister, I shall be quite satisfied with him. We could not ask a better child than our dear little daughter, nor love one more than we do her. She is a great comfort and blessing to us both."

The color mounted to Elsie's cheek, and her eyes

beamed with pleasure. Mr. Dinsmore, too, looked very much gratified, and the old gentleman could not fail to perceive that the difference he made between the children was quite distasteful to both parents.

Chapter Fifth

A lovely being, scarcely formed or moulded,
A rose with all its sweetest leaves yet folded.

—Byron

ELSIE WAS NEARLY twelve when her little brother was born. During the next three years she led a life of quiet happiness, unmarked by any striking event. There were no changes in the little family at the Oaks but such as time must bring to all. Mr. and Mrs. Dinsmore perhaps looked a trifle older than when they married, Elsie was budding into womanhood as fair and sweet a flower as ever was seen, and the baby had grown into a healthy romping boy.

At Roselands, on the contrary, there had been many and important changes. Louise and Lora were both married, the former to a resident of another State, who had taken her to his distant home, the latter to Edward Howard, an older brother of Elsie's friend Carrie. They had not left the neighborhood, but were residing with his parents.

For the last two or three years Arthur Dinsmore had spent his vacations at home; he was doing so now, having just completed his freshman year at Princeton. On his return Walter was to accompany him and begin his college career. Miss Day left soon after Lora's marriage and no effort had been made to fill her place, Adelaide having undertaken to act as governess to Enna, now the only remaining occupant of the school room.

Taking advantage of an unusually cool breezy afternoon, Elsie rode over to Tinesgrove, Mr. Howard's plantation—to make a call. She found the family at home and was urged to stay to tea, but declined, saying she could not without permission, and had not asked it.

"You will at least take off your hat," said Carrie.

"No, thank you," Elsie answered. "It is not worth while, as I must go so soon. If you will excuse me, I can talk quite as well with it on."

They had not met for several weeks and found a good deal to say to each other. At length Elsie drew out her watch.

"Ah!" she exclaimed. "I have overstayed my time! I had no idea it was so late—you have been so entertaining. But I must go now." And she rose hastily to take leave.

"Nonsense!" said her Aunt Lora, in whose boudoir they were sitting. "There is no such great hurry, I am sure. You'll get home long before dark."

"Yes, and might just as well stay another five or ten minutes. I wish you would, for I have ever so much to say to you," urged Carrie.

"It would be very pleasant, thank you, but indeed I must not. See how the shadows are lengthening, and papa does not at all like to have me out after sunset unless he is with me."

"He always was overcareful of you, erring on the right side, I suppose, if that be an allowable expression," laughed Lora, as she and Carrie followed Elsie to the door to see her mount her horse.

The adieus were quickly spoken and the young girl, just touching the whip to the sleek side of her pony, set off at a gallop, closely followed by her faithful attendant Jim.

Several miles of rather a lonely road lay between them and home, and no time was to be lost, if they would reach the Oaks while the sun was still above the horizon.

They were hardly more than half a mile from the

entrance to the grounds, when Elsie caught sight of a well-known form slowly moving down the road a few paces ahead of them. It was Arthur, and she soon perceived that it was his intention to intercept her. He stopped, turning his face toward her, sprang forward as she came up, and seized her bridle. "Stay a moment, Elsie," he said. "I want to speak to you."

"Then come on to the Oaks, and let us talk there. Please do, for I am in a hurry."

"No, I prefer to say my say where I am. I'll not detain you long. You keep out of earshot, Jim. I want to borrow a little money, Elsie, a trifle of fifty dollars or so. Can you accommodate me?"

"Not without papa's knowledge, Arthur. So I hope you do not wish to conceal the matter from him."

"I do. I see no reason why he should know all about my private affairs. Can't you raise that much without applying to him? Isn't your allowance very large now?"

"Fifty dollars a month, Arthur, but subject to the same conditions as of old. I must account to papa for every cent."

"Haven't you more than that in hand now?"

"Yes, but what do you want it for?"

"That's neither your business nor his. Let me have it for two weeks, I'll pay it back then, and in the meantime he need know nothing about it."

"I cannot. I never have any concealments from papa, and I must give in my account in less than a week."

"Nonsense! You are and always were the most disobliging creature alive!" returned Arthur with an oath.

"Oh, Arthur, how can you say such wicked words," she said, recoiling from him with a shudder. "And you quite misjudge me. I would be glad to do anything for you that is right. If you will let me tell papa your wish, and he gives consent, you shall have the money at once. Now please let me go. The sun has set and I shall be so late that papa will be anxious and much displeased."

"Who cares if he is!" he answered roughly, still retaining his hold upon her bridle, and compelling her to listen while he continued to urge his request, enforcing it with arguments and threats.

They were alike vain, she steadfastly refused to grant it except on the conditions she had named, and which he determinately rejected—and insisted being left free to pursue her homeward way.

He grew furious, and at length with a shocking oath released her bridle, but at the same instant struck her pony a severe blow upon his haunches, with a stout stick he held in his hand.

The terrified animal, smarting with the pain, started aside, reared and plunged in a way that would have unseated a less skillful rider, and had nearly thrown Elsie from the saddle, then darted off at the top of its speed, but fortunately turned in at the gate held open by Jim, who had ridden on ahead and dismounted for that purpose.

"Whoa, you Glossy! Whoa dere!" he cried, springing to the head of the excited animal, and catching its bridle in his powerful grasp.

"Just lead her for a little, Jim," said Elsie "There, there! My poor pretty Glossy, be quiet now. It was too cruel to serve you so, but it shan't happen again if your mistress can help it," she added in a voice tremulous with sympathy and indignation, patting and stroking her pony caressingly as she spoke.

Jim obeyed, walking on at a brisk pace, leading Glossy with his right hand, and keeping the bridle of the other horse over his left arm.

"I'll walk the rest of the way, Jim," said Elsie presently. "Just stop her and let me get down. There," springing lightly to the ground, "you may lead them both to the stable now."

She hurried forward along the broad, graveled winding carriage road that led to the house. The next turn brought her face to face with her father.

"What, Elsie! Alone and on foot at this late hour?" he said in a tone of mingled surprise and reproof.

"I have been riding, papa, and only a moment since

dismounted and let Jim lead the horses down the other road to the stables."

"Ah, but how did you come to be so late?" he asked, drawing her hand within his arm and leading her onward.

"I have been to Tinesgrove, sir, and Aunt Lora, Carrie, and I found so much to say to each other, that the time slipped away before I knew it."

"It must not happen again, Elsie."

"I do not mean it shall, papa, and I am very sorry."

"Then I excuse you this once, daughter. It is not often you give me occasion to reprove you."

"Thank you, papa," she said with a grateful, loving look. "Did you come out in search of me?"

"Yes, your mamma and I had begun to grow anxious lest some accident had befallen you. Our little daughter is such a precious treasure that we must needs watch over her very carefully," he added in a tone that was half playful, half tender, while he pressed the little gloved hand in his, and his eyes rested upon the sweet fair face with an expression of proud fatherly affection.

Her answering look was full of filial reverence and love. "Dear papa, it is so nice to be so loved and cared for, so sweet to hear such words from your lips. I do believe I'm the very happiest girl in the land." She had already almost forgotten Arthur and his rudeness and brutality.

"And I the happiest father," he said with a pleased smile. "Ah, here comes mamma to meet us with little Horace." The child ran forward with a glad shout to meet his sister. Rose met her with loving words and a fond caress. One might have thought from their joyous welcome, that she was returning after an absence of weeks or months instead of hours. Letting go her father's arm as they stepped upon the piazza, Elsie began a romping play with her little brother, but at a gentle reminder from her mamma that the tea-bell would soon ring, ran away to her own apartments to have her riding habit changed for something more suitable for the drawing room.

Chloe was in waiting and her skillful hands made rapid work, putting the last touches to her nursling's dress just as the summons to the supper table was given.

Mr. Dinsmore was quite as fastidious as in former days in regard to the neatness and tastefulness of Elsie's attire.

"Will I do, papa?" she asked, presenting herself before him, looking very sweet and fair in a simple white dress with blue sash and ribbon.

"Yes," he said with a satisfied smile. "I see nothing amiss with dress, hair, or face."

"Nor do I," said Rose, leading the way to the supper room. "Aunt Chloe is an accomplished tirewoman. But come, let us sit down to our meal and have it over."

On their return to the drawing room they found Mr. Travilla comfortably ensconced in an easy chair, reading the evening paper. He was an almost daily visitor at the Oaks, and seldom came without some little gift for one or both of his friend's children. It was for Elsie tonight. When the usual greetings had been exchanged, he turned to her, saying, "I have brought you treat. Can you guess what it is?"

"A book!"

"Ah, there must be something of the Yankee about you," he answered, laughing. "Yes, it is a book in two volumes, just published, and a most delightful, charming story," he went on, drawing them from his pockets, and handing them to her as he spoke.

"Oh, thank you, sir!" she cried with eager gratitude. "I'm so glad, if—if only papa will allow me to read it. May I, papa?"

"I can tell better when I have examined it, my child," Mr. Dinsmore answered, taking one of the volumes from her hands and looking at the title on the back. *The Wide, Wide World!* What sort of a book is it, Travilla?"

"A very good sort, I think. Just glance through it or read a few pages, and I'm pretty sure it will be sufficient to satisfy you of, not only its harmlessness, but that its perusal would be a benefit to almost anyone."

Mr. Dinsmore did so, Elsie standing beside him, her hand upon his arm, and her eyes on his face—anxiously watching its changes of expression as he read. They grew more and more satisfactory. The book was evidently approving itself to his taste and judgment, and presently he returned it to her, saying, with a kind fatherly smile, "Yes, my child, you may read it. I have no doubt it deserves all the praise Mr. Travilla has given it."

"Oh, thank you, papa, I'm very glad," she answered joyously. "I am just hungry for a nice story." And seating herself near the light, she was soon lost to everything about her in the deep interest with which she was following Ellen Montgomery through her troubles and trials.

She was loath to lay the book aside when at the usual hour—a quarter before nine—the bell rang for prayers. She hardly heeded the summons till her papa laid his hand on her shoulder, saying, "Come, daughter, you must not be left behind."

She started up then, hastily closing the book, and followed the others to the dining room, where the servants were already assembled to take part in the family devotions.

Mr. Travilla went away immediately after and now it was Elsie's bed-time. Her father reminded her of it as, on coming back from seeing his friend to the door, he found her again poring over the book.

"Oh, papa, it is so interesting! Could you let me finish this chapter?" she asked with a very entreating look up into his face as he stood at her side.

"I suppose I could if I should make a great effort," he answered laughingly. "Yes, you may, for once, but don't expect always to be allowed to do so."

"No, sir, oh, no. Thank you, sir."

"Well, have you come to a good stopping place?" he asked, as she presently closed the book and put it aside with a slight sigh.

"No, sir, it is just as bad a one as the other. Papa, I wish I was grown up enough to read another hour before going to bed."

"I don't," he said, drawing her to a seat upon his knee, and passing his arm about her waist. "I'm not ready to part with my little girl yet."

"Wouldn't a fine young lady daughter be just as good or better?" she asked, giving him a hug.

"No, not now. Some of these days I may think so."

"But mayn't I stay up and read till ten tonight?"

He shook his head. "Till half-past nine, then?"

"No, not even till quarter past. Ah, it is that now," he added, consulting his watch.

"You must say good-night and go. Early hours and plenty of sleep for my little girl, that she may grow up to healthful, vigorous womanhood, capable of enjoying life and being very useful in the church and the world." He kissed her with grave tenderness as he spoke.

"Good-night then, you dear father," she said, returning the caress. "I know you would indulge me if you thought it for my good."

"Indeed I would, pet. Would it help to reconcile you to the denial of your wish to know that I shall be reading the book, and probably enjoying it as much as you would?"

"Ah yes, indeed, papa! It is a real pleasure to resign it to you," she answered with a look of delight. "It's just the nicest story! At least as far as I've read. Read it aloud to mamma, won't you?"

"Yes, if she wishes to hear it. Now away with you to your room and your bed."

Only waiting to bid her mamma an affectionate good-night, Elsie obeyed, leaving the room with a light step, and a cheerful, happy face.

"Dear unselfish child!" her father said, looking after her.

"She is that indeed," said Rose. "How happy shall I be if Horace grows up to be as good and lovable."

Elsie was a fearless horsewoman, accustomed to the saddle from her very early years. Thus Arthur's wanton attack upon her pony had failed to give her nerves the severe shock it might have caused to those of most young girls of her age. Her feeling was more of excitement, and of indignation at the uncalled-for cruelty to a dumb animal, especially her own pet horse, than of fright at the danger to herself. But she well knew that the latter was what her father would think of first, and that he would be very angry with Arthur, therefore she had tried, and successfully, to control herself and suppress all signs of agitation on meeting him upon her return.

She felt glad now as the affair recurred to her recollection while preparing for the night's rest, that she had been able to do so. For a moment she questioned with herself whether she was quite right to have this concealment from her father, but quickly decided that she was. Had the wrong-doing been her own—that would have made it altogether another matter. She was shocked at Arthur's wickedness, troubled and anxious about his future, but freely forgave his crime against her pony and herself, and mingled with her nightly petitions an earnest prayer for his conversion, and his welfare temporal and spiritual.

CHAPTER SIXTH

O love! thou sternly dost thy power maintain,
And wilt not bear a rival in thy reign.

—DRYDEN.

IT WAS THE MIDDLE of the forenoon, and Elsie in her own pretty little sitting room was busied with her books, so deep in study indeed, that she never noticed a slight girlish figure as it glided in at the glass doors opening upon the lawn, today set wide to admit the air coming fresh and cool with a faint odor of the far-off sea, pleasantly mingling with that of the flowers in the garden, on the other side of the house.

"Buried alive in her books! Dear me! What a perfect paragon of industry you are," cried the intruder in a lively tone. "I wish you would imbue me with some of your love of study."

"Why, Lucy Carrington! How did you get here?" And Elsie pushed her books away, rose hastily and greeted her friend with an affectionate embrace.

"How? I came in through yonder door, miss, after riding my pony from Ashlands to the front entrance of this mansion," replied Lucy, curtsying low in mock reverence. "I hope your ladyship will excuse the liberty I have taken in venturing uninvited into your sanctum."

"Provided your repentance is deep and sincere," returned Elsie in the same jesting tone.

"Certainly, I solemnly pledge myself never to do it

again till the next time."

"Sit down, won't you?" and Elsie pushed forward a low rocking chair. "It's so pleasant to see you. But if I had thought about it at all I should have supposed you were at home, and as busy over books and lessons as I."

"No; my respected governess, Miss Warren, not feeling very well, has taken a week's holiday, and left me to do the same. Fancy my afflicted state at the thought of laying aside my beloved books for seven or eight whole days."

"You poor creature! How I pity you," said Elsie, laughing. "Suppose you stay here and share the instructions of my tutor. I have no doubt I could persuade him to receive you as a pupil."

"Horrors! I'm much obliged, very much, but I should die of fright the first time I had to recite. There, I declare I'm growing poetical, talking in rhyme all the time."

"Let mammy take your hat and scarf," said Elsie. "You'll stay and spend the day with me, won't you?"

"Thank you, no. I came to carry you off to Ashlands to spend a week. Will you come?"

"I should like to, dearly well, if papa gives permission."

"Well, run and ask him."

"I can't. Unfortunately he is out, and not expected to return till tea-time."

"Oh, pshaw! How provoking! But can't your mamma give permission just as well?"

"If it were only for a day she might, but I know she would say the question of a longer visit must be referred to papa."

"Dear me! I wouldn't be you for something. Why, I never ask leave of anybody when I want to pay a visit anywhere in the neighborhood. I tell mamma I'm going, and that's all-sufficient. I don't see how you stand being ordered about and controlled so."

"If you'll believe me," said Elsie, laughing a gay, sweet, silvery laugh, "I really enjoy being controlled by papa. It saves me a deal of trouble and responsibility in the way of deciding for myself; and then I love him so dearly that I almost always feel it my greatest pleasure to do whatever pleases him."

"And he always was so strict with you."

"Yes, he is strict, but oh, so kind."

"But that's just because you're so good. He'd have an awful time ruling me. I'd be in a chronic state of disgrace and punishment, and he obliged to be so constantly reproving me and frowning sternly upon my delinquencies that he'd never be able to don a smile of approval or slip in a word of praise edgewise."

"Indeed you're not half so bad as you pretend," said Elsie, laughing again, "nor I half so good as you seem determined to believe me."

"No, I've no doubt that you're an arch hypocrite, and we shall find out one of these days that you are really worse than any of the rest of us. But now I must finish my errand and go, for I know you're longing to be at those books. Do you get a feruling every time you miss a word? And enjoy the pain because it pleases papa to inflict it?"

"Oh, Lucy, how can you be so ridiculous?" and a quick, vivid blush mounted to Elsie's very hair.

"I beg your pardon, Elsie, dear, I had no business to say such a thing," cried Lucy, springing up to throw her arms round her friend and kiss her warmly, "but of course it was nothing but the merest nonsense. I know well enough your papa never does anything of the kind."

"No, if my lessons are not well prepared they have to be learned over again, that is all, and if I see that papa is displeased with me, I assure you it is punishment enough."

"Do you think he'll let you accept my invitation?"

"I don't know, indeed, Lucy. I think he will hardly like to have me give up my studies for that length of time, and in fact I hardly like to do so myself."

"Oh, you must come. You can practice on my piano every day for an hour or two, if you like. We'll learn some duets. And you can bring your sketch-book and carry it along when we walk or ride, as we shall every day. And we might read some improving books together—you and Herbert, and I. He is worse again, poor fellow, so that some days he hardly leaves his couch even to limp across the room, and it's partly to cheer him up that we want you to come. There's nothing puts him into better spirits than a sight of your face."

"You don't expect other company?"

"No, except on our birthday. But then we're going to have a little party, just of our own set, we boys and girls that have grown up—or are growing up—together, as one may say. Oh, yes, I want to have Carrie Howard, Mary Leslie, and Enna stay a day or two after the party. Now coax your papa hard, for we must have you," she added, rising to go.

"That would be a sure way to make him say no," said Elsie, smiling. "He never allows me to coax or tease, at least, not after he has once answered my request."

"Then don't think of it. Good-bye. No, don't waste time in coming to see me off, but go back to your books like a good child. I mean to have a little chat with your mamma before I go."

Elsie returned to her lessons with redoubled energy. She was longing to become more intimately acquainted with Ellen Montgomery, but resolutely denied herself even so much as a peep at the pages of the fascinating story-book until her allotted tasks should be faithfully performed.

These, with her regular daily exercise in the open air, filled up the morning. There was a half hour before, and another after dinner, which she could call her own, then two hours for needlework, music, and drawing, and she was free to employ herself as she would till bed-time.

That was very apt to be in reading, and if the weather was fine she usually carried her book to an arbor at some distance from the house. It was reached by a long shaded walk that led to it from the lawn, on which the glass doors of her pretty boudoir opened. It was a cool, breezy, quiet spot, on a terraced hillside, commanding a lovely view of vale, river, and woodland, and from being so constantly frequented by our heroine, had come to be called by her name—"Elsie's Arbor." Arthur, well acquainted with these tastes and habits, sought and found her here on the afternoon of this day—found her so deeply absorbed in Miss Warner's sweet story that she was not aware of his approach—so full of sympathy for little Ellen that her tears were dropping upon the page as she read.

"What, crying, eh?" he said with a sneer, as he seated himself by her side, and rudely pulled one of her curls, very much as he had been used to do years ago. "Well, I needn't be surprised, for you always were the greatest baby I ever saw."

"Please let my hair alone, Arthur. You are not very polite in either speech or action," she answered, brushing away her tears and moving a little farther from him.

"It's not worth while to waste politeness on you. What's that you're reading?"

"A new book Mr. Travilla gave me."

"Has no name, eh?"

"Yes, *Wide, Wide World.*"

"Some namby-pamby girl's story, I s'pose, since you're allowed to read it. Or are you doing it on the sly?"

"No, I never do such things, and hope I never shall. Papa gave me permission."

"Oh! Ah, then I haven't got you in my power—wish I had."

"Why?"

"Because I might turn it to good account. I know you are as afraid as death of Horace."

"No, I am not!" cried Elsie indignantly, the rich color rushing all over her fair face and neck. "For I know that he loves me dearly, and if I had been disobeying or deceiving him I would far sooner throw myself on his mercy than on yours."

"You would, eh? How mad you are—your face is as red as a beet. A pretty sort of Christian you are, aren't you?"

"I am not perfect, Arthur, but you mustn't judge of

religion by me."

"I shall, though. Don't you wish I'd go away?" he added teasingly, again snatching at her curls.

But she eluded his grasp, and rising, stood before him with an air of gentle dignity. "Yes," she said, " since you ask me, I'll own that I do. I don't know why it is that, though your manners are polished when you choose to make them so, you are always rude and ungentlemanly to me when you find me alone. So I shall be very glad if you'll just go away and leave me to solitude and the enjoyment of my book."

"I'll do so when I get ready, not a minute sooner. But you can get rid of me just as soon as you like. I see you take. Yes, I want that money I asked you for yesterday, and I am bound to have it."

"Arthur, my answer must be just the same that it was then. I can give you no other."

"You're the meanest girl alive! To my certain knowledge you are worth at least a million and a half, and yet you refuse to lend me the pitiful sum of fifty dollars."

"Arthur, you know I have no choice in the matter. Papa has forbidden me to lend you money without his knowledge and consent, and I cannot disobey him."

"When did he forbid you?"

"A long while ago, and though he has said nothing about it lately, he has told me again and again that his commands are always binding until he revokes them."

"Fifteen years old, and not allowed to do as you please even with your pocket money!" he said contemptuously. "Do you expect to be in leading-strings all your life?"

"I shall of course have control of my own money matters on coming of age, but I expect to obey my father as long as we both live," she answered, with gentle but firm decision.

"Do you have to show your balance in hand when you give in your account?"

"No. Do you suppose papa cannot trust my word?" she answered, somewhat indignantly.

"Then you could manage it just as easily as not. There's no occasion for him to know whether your balance in hand is at that moment in your possession or mine. As I told you before, I only want to borrow it for two weeks. Come, let me have it. If you don't, the day will come when you'll wish you had."

She repeated her refusal. He grew very angry and abusive, and at length went so far as to strike her.

A quick step sounded on the gravel walk, a strong grasp was laid on Arthur's arm, he felt himself suddenly jerked aside and flung upon his knees, while a perfect rain of stinging, smarting blows descended rapidly upon his back and shoulders.

"There, you unmitigated scoundrel, you mean, miserable caitiff. Lay your hand upon her again if you dare!" cried Mr. Travilla, finishing the castigation by applying the toe of his boot to Arthur's nether parts with a force that sent him reeling some distance down the walk, to fall with a heavy thud upon the ground.

The lad rose, white with rage, and shook his fist at his antagonist. "I'll strike her when I please," he said with an oath, "and not be called to account by you for it either. She's my niece, and nothing to you."

"I'll defend her nevertheless, and see to it that you come to grief if you attempt to harm her in any way whatever. Did he hurt you much, my child?" And Mr. Travilla's tone changed to one of tender concern as he turned and addressed Elsie, who had sunk pale and trembling upon the rustic seat where Arthur had found her.

"No, sir, but I fear you have hurt him a good deal, in your kind zeal for my defense," she answered, looking after Arthur, as he limped away down the path.

"I have broken my cane, that is the worst of it," said her protector coolly, looking regretfully down at the fragment he still held in his hand.

"You must have struck very hard, and oh, Mr. Travilla, what if he should take it into his head to challenge you?" And Elsie turned pale with terror.

"Never fear, he is too arrant a coward for that. He

- 61 -

knows I am a good shot, and that, as the challenged party, I would have the right to the choice of weapons."

"But you wouldn't fight, Mr. Travilla? You do not approve of dueling?"

"No, no indeed, Elsie. Both the laws of God and of the land are against it, and I could not engage in it either as a good citizen or a Christian."

"Oh, I am so glad of that, and that you came to my rescue, for I was really growing frightened. Arthur seemed in such a fury with me."

"What was it about?"

Elsie explained, then asked how he had happened to come to her aid.

"I had learned from the servants that your father and mother were both out, so came here in search of you," he said. "As I drew near I saw that Arthur was with you, and not wishing to overhear your talk, I waited at a little distance up there on the bank, watching you through the trees. I perceived at once that he was in a towering passion, and fearing he would ill-treat you in some way, I held myself in readiness to come to your rescue. And when I saw him strike you, such a fury suddenly came over me that I could not possibly refrain from thrashing him for it."

"Mr. Travilla, you will not tell papa?" she said entreatingly.

"My child, I am inclined to think he ought to hear of it."

"Oh, why need he? It would make him very angry with Arthur."

"Which Arthur richly deserves. I think your father should know, in order that he may take measures for your protection. Still, if you promise not to ride or walk out alone until Arthur has left the neighborhood, it shall be as you wish. But you must try to recover your composure, or your papa will be sure to ask the cause of your agitation. You are trembling very much, and the color has quite forsaken your cheeks."

"I'll try," she said, making a great effort to control herself, "and I give you the promise."

"This is a very pleasant place to sit with book or work," he remarked, "but I would advise you not even to come here alone again till Arthur has gone."

"Thank you, sir, I think I shall follow your advice. It will be only a few weeks now till he and Walter both go North to college."

"I see you have your book with you," he said, taking it up from the seat where it lay. "How do you like it?"

"Oh, so much! How I pity poor Ellen for having such a father, so different from my dear papa, and because she had to be separated from her mamma, whom she loved so dearly. I can't read about her troubles without crying, Mr. Travilla."

"Shall I tell you a secret," he said, smiling; "I shed some tears over it myself." Then he went on talking with her about the different characters of the story, thus helping her to recover her composure by turning her thoughts from herself and Arthur.

When, half an hour later, a servant came to summon her to the house, with the announcement that her father had returned and was ready to hear her recitations, all signs of agitation had disappeared. She had ceased to tremble, and her fair face was as sweet, bright, and rosy as its wont.

She rose instantly on hearing the summons. "You'll excuse me, I know, Mr. Travilla. But will you not go in with me? We are always glad to have you with us. I have no need to tell you that, I am sure."

"Thank you," he said, "but I must return to Ion now. I shall walk to the house with you though, if you will permit me," he added, thinking that Arthur might be still lurking somewhere within the grounds.

She answered gaily that she would be very glad of his company. She had lost none of her old liking for her father's friend, and was wont to treat him with the easy and affectionate familiarity she might have used had he been her uncle.

They continued their talk till they had reached the lawn at the side of the house on which her apartments were; then he turned to bid her good bye.

"I'm much obliged!" she said, taking his offered hand, and looking up brightly into his face.

"Welcome, fair lady. But am I to be dismissed without any reward for my poor services?"

"I have none to offer, sir knight, but you may help yourself if you choose," she said, laughing and blushing, for she knew very well what he meant.

He stooped and snatched a kiss from her ruby lips, then walked away sighing softly to himself, "Ah, little Elsie, if I were but ten years younger!"

She tripped across the lawn, and entering the open door of her boudoir, found herself in her father's arms. He had witnessed the little scene just enacted between Mr. Travilla and herself, had noticed something in his friend's look and manner that had never struck him before. He folded his child close to his heart for an instant, then held her off a little, gazing fondly into her face.

"You are mine, you belong to me. No other earthly creature has the least shadow of a right or title in you. Do you know that?"

"Yes, papa, and rejoice to know it," she murmured, putting her arms about his neck and laying her head against his breast.

"Ah!" he said, sighing. "You will not always be able to say that, I fear. One of these days you will—" He broke off abruptly, without finishing his sentence.

She looked up inquiringly into his face.

He answered her look with a smile and a tender caress. "I had better not put the nonsense into your head. It will get there soon enough without my help. Come now, let us have the lessons. I expect to find them well prepared, as usual."

"I hope so, papa," she answered, bringing her books and seating herself on a stool at his feet, he having taken possession of an easy-chair.

The recitations seemed a source of keen enjoyment to both, the one loving to impart, and the other to receive, knowledge.

Mr. Dinsmore gave the deserved meed of warm praise for the faithful preparation of each allotted task, prescribed those for the coming day, and the books were laid aside.

"Come here, daughter," he said, as she closed her desk upon them, "I have something to say to you."

"What is it, papa?" she asked, seating herself upon his knee. "How very grave you look." But there was not a touch of the old fear in her face or voice, as there had been none in his of the old sternness.

"Yes, for I am about to speak of a serious matter," he answered, gently smoothing back the clustering curls from her fair brow, while he looked earnestly into the soft brown eyes. "You have not been lending money to Arthur, Elsie?"

The abrupt, unexpected question startled her, and a crimson tide rushed over her face and neck, but she returned her father's gaze steadily: "No, papa. How could you think I would disobey you so?"

"I did not, darling, and yet I felt that I must ask the question and repeat my warning, my command to you— never to do so without my knowledge and consent. Your grandfather and I are much troubled about the boy."

"I am so sorry, papa. I hope he has not been doing anything very bad."

"He seems to have sufficient cunning to hide many of his evil deeds," Mr. Dinsmore said, with a sigh, "yet enough has come to light to convince us that he is very likely to become a shame and disgrace to his family. We know that he is profane, and to some extent, at least, intemperate and a gambler. A sad, sad beginning for a boy of seventeen. And to furnish him with money, Elsie, would be only to assist him in his downward course."

"Yes, papa, I see that. Poor grandpa, I'm so sorry for him! But, papa, God can change Arthur's heart, and make him all we could wish."

"Yes, daughter, and we will agree together to ask him to do this great work, so impossible to any human power, shall we not?"

"Yes, papa." They were silent a moment, then she turned to him again, told of Lucy Carrington's call and its object, and asked if she might accept the invitation.

He considered a moment. "Yes," he said kindly, "you may if you wish. You quite deserve a holiday, and I think perhaps would really be the better of a week's rest from study. Go and enjoy yourself as much as you can, my darling."

"Thank you, you dearest, kindest, and best of papas," she said, giving him a hug and kiss." But I think you look a little bit sorry. You would rather I should stay at home, if I could content myself to do so, and it would be a strange thing if I could not."

"No, my pet, I shall miss you, I know. The house always seems lonely without you, but I can spare you for a week, and would rather have you go, because I think the change will do you good. Besides, I am willing to lend my treasure for a few days to our friends at Ashlands. I would gladly do more than that, if I could, for that poor suffering Herbert."

CHAPTER SEVENTH

How many pleasant faces shed their light on every side.

—TUPPER

"REMEMBER it is for only one week. You must be back again next Wednesday by ten o'clock. I can't spare you an hour longer," Mr. Dinsmore said, as the next morning, shortly after breakfast, he assisted his daughter to mount her pony.

"Ten o'clock at night, papa?" asked Elsie in a gay, jesting tone, as she settled herself in the saddle, and took a little gold-mounted riding whip from his hand.

"No, ten A.M., precisely."

"But what if it should be storming, sir?"

"Then come as soon as the storm is over."

"Yes, sir. And may I come sooner if I get homesick?"

"Just as soon as you please. Now, good-bye, my darling. Don't go into any danger. I know I need not remind you to do nothing your father would disapprove."

"I hope not, papa," she said, with a loving look into the eyes that were gazing so fondly upon her. Then kissing her hand to him and her mamma and little Horace, who stood on the veranda to see her off, she turned her horse's head and cantered merrily away, taking the road to Ashlands on passing out at the gate.

It was a bright, breezy morning, and her heart felt so light and gay that a snatch of glad song rose to her lips. She warbled a few bird-like notes, then fell to humming softly to herself.

At a little distance down the road a light wagon was rumbling along, driven by one of the man-servants from the Oaks, and carrying Aunt Chloe and her young mistress' trunks.

"Come, Jim," said Elsie, glancing over her shoulder at her attendant satellite, "we must pass them. Glossy and I are in haste today. Ah, mammy, are you enjoying your ride?" she called to her old nurse as she cantered swiftly by.

"Yes, dat I is, honey!" returned the old woman. Then sending a loving, admiring look after the retreating form so full of symmetry and grace, "My bressed chile!" she murmured. "You's beautiful as de mornin', your ole mammy tinks, an' sweet as de finest rose in de garden, bright an' happy as de day am long, too."

"De beautifullest in all de country, an' de finest," chimed in her charioteer.

The young people at Ashlands were all out on the veranda enjoying the fresh morning air—Herbert lying on a lounge with a book in his hand, Harry and Lucy seated on opposite sides of a small round table and deep in a game of chess. Two little fellows of six and eight— John and Archie by name—were spinning a top.

"There she is! I had almost given her up, for I didn't believe that old father of hers would let her come," cried Lucy, catching sight of Glossy and her rider just entering the avenue, and she sprang up in such haste as to upset half the men upon the board.

"Hello! See what you've done!" exclaimed Harry. "Why, it's Elsie, sure enough!" And he hastily followed in the wake of his sister, who had already flown to meet and welcome her friend, while Herbert started up to a sitting posture, and looked enviously after them.

"Archie, John," he called, "one of you please be good enough to hand me my crutch and cane. Dear me, what a thing it is to be a cripple!"

"I'll get 'em, Herbie, this minute! Don't you try to step without 'em," said Archie, jumping up to hand them.

But Elsie had already alighted from her horse with Harry's assistance, and shaken hands with him, returned Lucy's rapturous embrace as warmly as it was given, and stepped upon the veranda with her before Herbert was fairly upon his feet. As she caught sight of him she hurried forward, her sweet face full of tender pity.

"Oh, don't try to come to meet me, Herbert," she said, holding out her little gloved hand. "I know your poor limb is worse than usual, and you must not exert yourself for an old friend like me."

"Ah," he said, taking the offered hand, and looking at its owner with a glad light in his eyes. "How like you that is, Elsie! You always were more thoughtful of others than anyone else I ever knew. Yes, my limb is pretty bad just now, but the doctor thinks he'll conquer the disease yet—at least so far as to relieve me of the pain I suffer."

"I hope so, indeed. How patiently you have borne it all these long years," she answered with earnest sympathy of tone and look.

"So he has. He deserves the greatest amount of credit for it," said Lucy, as John and Archie in turn claimed Elsie's attention for a moment. "But come now, let me take you to mamma and grandma, and then to your own room. Aunt Chloe and your luggage will be along presently, I suppose."

"Yes, they are coming up the avenue now."

Lucy led the way to a large, pleasant, airy apartment in one of the wings of the building, where they found Mrs. Carrington busily occupied in cutting out garments for her servants, her parents Mr. and Mrs. Norris with her, the one reading a newspaper, the other knitting. All three gave the young guest a very warm welcome. She was evidently a great favorite with the whole family.

These greetings and the usual mutual inquiries in regard to the health of friends and relatives having been exchanged, Elsie was next carried off by Lucy to the room prepared for her special use during her stay at Ashlands. It also was large, airy, and cheerful, on the second floor—opening upon a veranda on one side, on the other into a similar apartment occupied by Lucy herself. Fine India matting, furniture of some kind of yellow grained wood, snowy counterpanes, curtains and toilet covers gave them both an air of coolness and simple elegance, while vases of fresh flowers upon the mantels shed around a slight but delicious perfume.

Of course the two girls were full of lively, innocent chat. In the midst of it Elsie exclaimed, "Oh, Lucy! I have just the loveliest book you ever read—a present from Mr. Travilla the other day, and I've brought it along. Papa had begun it, but he is so kind he insisted I should bring it with me, and so I did."

"Oh, I'm glad! We haven't had anything new in the story-book line for some time. Have you read it yourself?"

"Partly, but it is worth reading several times, and I thought we would enjoy it all together—one reading aloud."

"Oh, 'tis just the thing! I'm going to help mamma today with the sewing, and a nice book read aloud will make it quite enjoyable. We'll have you for reader, Elsie, if you are agreed."

"Suppose we take turns sewing and reading? I'd like to help your mamma, too."

"Thank you. Well, we'll see. Herbert's a good reader, and I daresay will be glad to take his turn at it too. Ah, here comes your baggage and Aunt Chloe following it. Here, Bob and Jack,"—to the two stalwart black fellows who were carrying the trunk—"set it in this corner. How d'ye do, Aunt Chloe?"

"Berry well, tank you, missy," replied the old nurse, dropping a courtesy. "I'se berry glad to see you lookin' so bright dis here mornin'."

"Thank you. Now make yourself at home and take good care of your young mistress."

"Dat I will, missy, best I knows how. Trus' dis chile for dat."

Elsie's riding habit was quickly exchanged for a house dress, her hair made smooth and shining as its wont, and securing her book she returned with Lucy to the lower veranda, where they found Herbert still extended upon his sofa.

His face brightened at sight of Elsie. He had laid aside his book, and was at work with his knife upon a bit of soft pine wood. He whiled away many a tedious hour by fashioning in this manner little boxes, whistles, sets of baby-house furniture, etc., etc., for one and another of his small friends. Books, magazines, and newspapers filled up the larger portion of his time, but could not occupy it all, for, as he said, he must digest his mental food, and he liked to have employment for his fingers while doing so.

"Please be good enough to sit where I can look at you without too great an effort, won't you?" he said, smiling up into Elsie's face.

"Yes, if that will afford you any pleasure," she answered lightly, as Lucy beckoned to a colored girl, who stepped forward and placed a low rocking chair at the side of the couch.

"There, that is just right. I can have a full view of your face by merely raising my eyes," Herbert said with satisfaction, as Elsie seated herself in it. "What, you have brought a book?"

"Yes." And while Elsie went on to repeat the substance of what she had told Lucy, the latter slipped away to her mamma's room to make arrangements about the work, and ask if they would not all like to come and listen to the reading.

"Is it the kind of book to interest an old body like me?" asked Mrs. Norris.

"I don't know, grandma, but Elsie says Mr. Travilla and her papa were both delighted with it. Mr. Dinsmore, though, had not read the whole of it."

"Suppose we go and try it for a while then," said Mr. Norris, laying down his paper. "If our little Elsie is to be the reader, I for one am pretty sure to enjoy listening. Her voice is so sweet-toned and her enunciation so clear and distinct."

"That's you, grandpa!" cried Lucy, clapping her

hands in applause. "Yes, you'd better all come. Elsie is to be the reader at the start. She says she does not mind beginning the story over again."

Mrs. Carrington began gathering up her work, laying the garments already cut out in a large basket, which was then carried by her maid to the veranda. In a few moments Elsie had quite an audience gathered about her, ere long a deeply interested one. Scissors or needle had now and again to be dropped to wipe away a falling tear, and the voice of the reader needed steadying more than once or twice. Then Herbert took his turn at the book, Elsie hers with the needle, Mrs. Carrington half reluctantly yielding to her urgent request to be allowed to assist them.

So the morning, and much of the afternoon also, passed most pleasantly, and not unprofitably either. A walk toward sundown, and afterward a delightful moonlight ride with Harry Carrington and Winthrop Lansing, the son of a neighboring planter, finished the day, and Elsie retired to her own room at her usual early hour. Lucy followed and kept her chatting quite a while—for which Elsie's tender conscience reproached her somewhat—yet she was not long in falling asleep after her head had once touched her pillow.

The next day was passed in a similar manner, still more time being given to the reading—as they were able to begin it earlier—yet the book was not finished. But on the morning of the next day, which was Friday, Lucy proposed that, if the plan was agreeable to Elsie, they should spend an hour or two in a new amusement, which was no other than going into the dominions of Aunt Viney, the cook, and assisting in beating eggs and making cake.

Elsie was charmed with the idea, and it was immediately carried out, to the great astonishment of Chloe, Aunt Viney, and all her sable tribe.

"Sho, Miss Lucy! What fo' you go for to fotch de company right yere into dis yere ole dirty kitchen?" cried Aunt Viney, dropping a hasty courtesy to Elsie, then hurrying hither and thither in the vain effort to set everything to rights in a moment of time. "Clar out o' yere, you, Han an' Scip," she cried, addressing two small urchins of dusky hue and driving them before her as she spoke. "Dere ain't no room yere fo' you, an' kitchens ain't no place for darkies o' your size or sect. I'll fling de dishcloth at yo' brack faces ef yo' comes in agin fo' you sent for. I 'clare Miss Elsie, an' Miss Lucy, dose dirty niggahs make sich a muss in yere, dere ain't a char fit for you to set down in," she continued, hastily cleaning two, and wiping them with her apron. "I'se glad to see you, ladies, but ef I'd knowed you was a-comin' dis kitchen shu'd had a cleanin' up fo' shuah."

"You see, Aunt Viney, you ought to keep it in order, and then you would be ready for visitors whenever they happened to come," said Lucy laughingly. "Why, you're really quite out of breath with whisking about so fast. We've come to help you."

The fat old negress, still panting from her unwonted exertions, straightened herself, pushed back her turban, and gazed in round-eyed wonder upon her young mistress.

"What! Missy help ole Aunt Viney wid dose lily-white hands? Oh, go 'long! You's jokin' dis time fo' shuah."

"No indeed. We want the fun of helping to make some of the cake for tomorrow. You know we want ever so many kinds to celebrate our two birthdays."

"Two birthdays, Miss Lucy? Yo's and Massa Herbert's? Yes, dat's it. I don't disremember de day, but I do disremember de age."

"Sixteen, and now we're going to have a nice party to celebrate the day, and you must see that the refreshments are got up in your very best style."

"So I will, Miss Lucy, an' no 'casion for you and Miss Elsie to trouble yo' young heads 'bout de makin' ob de cakes an' jellies an' custards an' sich. Ole Aunt Vincy can 'tend to it all."

"But we want the fun of it," persisted Lucy. "We want to try our hands at beating eggs, rolling sugar, sifting flour, etc., etc. I've got a grand new receipt book here, and we'll read out the recipes to you, and measure and weigh the materials, and you can do the mixing and baking."

"Yes, missy, you' lily hands no' hab strength to stir, an' de fire spoil yo' buful 'plexions for shuah."

"I've brought mamma's keys," said Lucy. "Come along with us to the store-room, Aunt Viney, and I'll deal out the sugar, spices, and whatever else you want."

"Yes, Miss Lucy, but 'deed I don't need no help. You's berry kind, but ole Viney kin do it all, an' she'll have eberything fus'-rate fo' de young gemmen an' ladies."

"But that isn't the thing, auntie. You don't seem to understand. Miss Elsie and I want the fun, and to learn to cook, too. Who knows but we may someday have to do our own work?"

"Bress de Lord, Miss Lucy, how you talk, honey!" cried the old negress, rolling up her eyes in horror at the thought.

"Take care. Miss Elsie will think you very wicked if you use such exclamations as that."

"Dat wrong, you t'ink, missy?" asked Aunt Viney, turning to the young visitor, who had gone with them to the store-room, and was assisting Lucy in the work of measuring and weighing the needed articles.

"I think it is," she answered gently. "We should be very careful not to use the sacred name lightly. To do so is to break the third commandment."

"Den, missy, dis ole gal won't neber do it no more."

Chloe had been an excellent cook in her young days, and had not forgotten or lost her former skill in the preparation of toothsome dainties. She, too, came with offers of assistance, and the four were soon deep in the mysteries of pastry, sweetmeats, and confections. Novelty gave it an especial charm to the young ladies, and they grew very merry and talkative, while their ignorance of the business in hand, the odd mistakes they fell into in consequence, and the comical questions they asked, gave much secret amusement to the two old servants.

"What's this pound cake to be mixed up in, Aunt

Viney?" asked Lucy.

"In dis yere tin pan, missy."

"Is it clean?"

"Yes, missy, it's clean, but maybe 'taint suffishently clean. I'll wash it agin."

"How many kinds of cake shall we make?" asked Elsie.

"Every kind that Chloe and Aunt Viney can think of and know how to make well. Let me see—delicate cake, gold, silver and clove, fruitcake, sponge, and what else?"

"Mammy makes delicious jumbles."

"Will you make us some, Aunt Chloe?"

Chloe signified her readiness to do whatever was desired, and began at once to collect her implements.

"Got a rollin' pin, Aunt Viney?" she asked.

"Yes, to be shuah, a revoltin' roller, de very bes' kind. No, Miss Elsie, don' mix de eggs dat way, you spile 'em ef you mix de yaller all up wid de whites. An' Miss Lucy, butter an' sugar mus' be worked up togedder fus', till de butter resolve de sugah, 'fore we puts de udder gredinents in."

"Ah, I see we have a good deal to learn before we can hope to rival you as cooks, Aunt Viney," laughed Lucy.

"I spec' so, missy. You throw all de gredinents in togedder, an' tumble your flouah in all at once, an' you nebber get your cake nice an light."

They had nearly reached the end of their labors when sounds as of scuffling, mingled with loud boyish laughter, and cries of "That's it, Scip, hit him again! Pitch into him, Han, and pay him off well for it!" drew them all in haste to the window and door.

The two little darkies who had been ejected from the kitchen were tussling in the yard, while their young masters, John and Archie, looked on, shaking with laughter, and clapping their hands in noisy glee.

"What's all this racket about?" asked Grandpa Norris, coming out upon the veranda, newspaper in hand, Herbert limping along by his side.

"The old feud between Roman and Carthaginian,

sir," replied John.

"Why, what do you mean, child?"

"Hannah Ball waging a war on Skipio, you know, sir."

"History repeating itself, eh?" laughed Herbert.

"Ah, that's an old joke, Archie," said his grandfather, "and you're too big a rogue to set them at such work. Han and Scip, stop that at once."

CHAPTER EIGHTH

All your attempts
Shall fall on me like brittle shafts on armor.

LUCY CAME into Elsie's room early the next morning to show her birthday gifts, of which she had received one or more from every member of her family. They consisted of articles of jewelry, toilet ornaments, and handsomely-bound books.

They learned on meeting Herbert at breakfast that he had fared quite as well as his sister. Elsie slipped a valuable ring on Lucy's finger and laid a gold pencil-case beside Herbert's plate.

"Oh, charming! A thousand thanks, mon ami!" cried Lucy, her eyes sparkling with pleasure.

"Thank you, I shall value it most highly, especially for the giver's sake," said Herbert, examining his with a pleased look, then turning to her with a blush and joyous smile. "I am so much better this morning that I am going out for a drive. Won't you and Lucy give me the added pleasure of your company?"

"Thank you. I can answer for myself that I'll be very happy to do so."

"I, too," said Lucy. "It's a lovely morning for a ride. We'll make up a party and go, but we must be home again in good season, for Carrie and Enna promised to come to dinner. So I'm glad we finished the book yesterday, though we were all so sorry to part from little Ellen."

They turned out quite a strong party, Herbert and the

ladies filling up the family carriage, while Harry on horseback—and John and Archie each mounted upon a pony—accompanied it, now riding alongside, now speeding on ahead, or per chance dropping behind for a time as suited their fancy.

They traveled some miles, and alighting in a beautiful grove, partook of a delicate lunch they had brought with them. Then, while Herbert rested upon the grass the others wandered hither and thither until it was time to return. They reached home just in season to receive their expected guests.

Carrie Howard was growing up very pretty and graceful. Womanly in her ways, yet quite unassuming in manner, frank and sweet in disposition, she was a general favorite with old and young, and could already boast of several suitors for her hand.

Enna Dinsmore, now in her fourteenth year, though by some considered even prettier, was far less pleasing—pert, forward, and conceited as she had been in her early childhood. She was tall for her age, and with her perfect self-possession and grown-up air and manner might be easily mistaken for seventeen. She had already more worldly wisdom than her sweet, fair niece would ever be able to attain, and was, in her own estimation at least, a very stylish and fashionable young lady. She assumed very superior airs toward Elsie when her brother Horace was not by—reproving, exhorting, or directing her—and was very proud of being usually taken by strangers for the elder of the two. Some day she would not think that a feather in her cap.

Elsie had lost none of the childlike simplicity of five years ago. It still showed itself in the sweet, gentle countenance, the quiet graceful carriage, equally removed from forwardness on the one hand, and timid self-consciousness on the other. She did not consider herself a personage of importance, yet was not troubled by her supposed insignificance—in fact seldom thought of self at all, so engaged was she in adding to the happiness of others.

The four girls were gathered in Lucy's room. She had been showing her birthday presents to Carrie and Enna.

"How do you like this style of arranging the hair, girls?" asked the latter, standing before a mirror, smoothing and patting, and pulling out her puffs and braids. "It's the newest thing out. Isabel Carleton just brought it from New York. I saw her with hers dressed so, and sent Delia over to learn how."

Delia was Miss Enna's maid, and had been brought along to Ashlands that she might dress her young lady's hair in this new style for the party.

"It's pretty," said Lucy. "I think I'll have Minerva dress mine so for tonight, and see how it becomes me."

"Delia can show her how," said Enna. "Don't you like it, Carrie?"

"Pretty well, but if you'll excuse me for saying so, it strikes me as rather grown up for a young lady of thirteen," answered Carrie in a good-naturedly bantering tone.

Enna colored and looked vexed. "I'm nearly fourteen," she replied with a slight toss of the head, "and I overheard Mrs. Carleton saying to mamma the other day, that with my height and finished manners I might pass anywhere for seventeen."

"Perhaps so. Of course, knowing your age, I can't judge so well how it would strike a stranger."

"I see you have gone back to the old childish way of arranging your hair. What's that for?" asked Enna, turning to Elsie. "I should think it was about time you were beginning to be a little womanly in something."

"Yes, but not in dress or the arrangement of my hair. So papa says, and of course I know he is right."

"He would not let you have it up in a comb?"

"No," Elsie answered with a quiet smile.

"Why do you smile? Did he say anything funny when you showed yourself that day?"

"Oh, Elsie, have you tried putting up your hair?" asked Carrie, while Lucy exclaimed,

"Try it again tonight, Elsie, I should like to see how you would look."

"Yes," said Elsie, answering Carrie's query first. "Enna persuaded me one day to have mammy do it up in young-lady fashion. I liked it right well for a change, and that was just what mamma said when I went into the drawing-room and showed myself to her. But when papa came in, he looked at me with a comical sort of surprise in his face, and said: 'Come here. What have you been doing to yourself?' I went to him and he pulled out my comb, and ordered me off to mammy to have my hair arranged again in the usual way, saying, 'I'm not going to have you aping the woman already. Don't alter the style of wearing your hair again, till I give you permission.'"

"And you walked off as meek as Moses, and did his bidding," said Enna sarcastically. "No man shall ever rule me so. If papa should undertake to give me such an order, I'd just inform him that my hair was my own, and I should arrange it as suited my own fancy."

"I think you are making yourself out worse than you really are, Enna," said Elsie gravely. "I am sure you could never say anything so extremely impertinent as that to grandpa."

"Impertinent! Well, if you believe it necessary to be so very respectful, consistency should lead you to refrain from reproving your aunt."

"I did not exactly mean to reprove you, Enna, and you are younger than I."

"Nobody would think it," remarked Enna superciliously and with a second toss of her head, as she turned from the glass. "You are so extremely childish in every way, while, as mamma says, I grow more womanly in appearance and manner every day."

"Elsie's manners are quite perfect, I think," said Carrie, "and her hair is so beautiful, I don't believe any other style of arrangement could improve its appearance in the least."

"But it's so childish, so absurdly childish! Just that great mass of ringlets hanging about her neck and shoulders. Come, Elsie, I want you to have it dressed in this new style for tonight."

"No, Enna, I am perfectly satisfied to wear it in this childish fashion, and if I were not, still I could not disobey papa."

Enna turned away with a contemptuous sniff, and Lucy proposed that they should go down to the drawing-room, and try some new music she had just received, until it should be time to dress for the evening.

Herbert lay on a sofa listening to their playing. "Lucy," he said in one of the pauses, "what amusements are we to have tonight? Anything beside the harp, piano, and conversation?"

"Dancing, of course. Cad's fiddle will provide as good music as anyone need care for, and this room is large enough for all who will be here. Our party is not to be very large, you know."

"And Elsie, for one, is too pious to dance," sneered Enna.

Elsie colored, but remained silent.

"Oh! I did not think of that!" cried Lucy. "Elsie, do you really think it is a sinful amusement?"

"I think it wrong to go to balls, at least that it would be wrong for me, a professed Christian, Lucy."

"But this will not be a ball, and we'll have nothing but quiet country dances, or something of that sort, no waltzing or anything at all objectionable. What harm can there be in jumping about in that way more than in another?"

"None that I know of," answered Elsie, smiling. "And I certainly shall not object to others doing as they like, provided I am not asked to take part in it."

"But why not take part, if it is not wrong?" asked Harry, coming in from the veranda.

"Why, don't you know she never does anything without asking the permission of papa?" queried Enna tauntingly. "But where's the use of consulting her wishes in the matter, or urging her to take part in the wicked amusement? She'll have to go to bed at nine o'clock, like any other well-trained child, and we'll have time enough for our dancing after that."

"Oh, Elsie, must you? Must you really leave us at that early hour? Why, that's entirely too bad!" cried the others in excited chorus.

"I shall stay up till ten," answered Elsie quietly, while a deep flush suffused her cheek.

"That is better, but we shall not know how to spare you even that soon," said Harry. "Couldn't you make it eleven? That would not be so very late just for once."

"No, for she can't break her rules, or disobey orders. If she did, papa would be sure to find it out and punish her when she gets home."

"For shame, Enna! That's quite too bad!" cried Carrie and Lucy in a breath.

Elsie's color deepened, and there was a flash of anger and scorn in her eyes as she turned for an instant upon Enna. Then she replied firmly, though with a slight tremble of indignation in her tones: "I am not ashamed to own that I do find it both a duty and a pleasure to obey my father, whether he be present or absent. I have confidence, too, in both his wisdom and his love for me. He thinks early hours of great importance, especially to those who are young and growing, and therefore he made it a rule that I shall retire to my room and begin my preparations for bed by nine o'clock. But he gave me leave to stay up an hour later tonight, and I intend to do so."

"I think you are a very good girl, and feel just right about it," said Carrie.

"I wish he had said eleven, I think he might this once," remarked Lucy. "Why, don't you remember he let you stay up till ten Christmas Eve that time we all spent the holidays at Roselands, which was five years ago?"

"Yes," said Elsie, "but this is Saturday night, and as tomorrow is the Sabbath, I should not feel it to be right to stay up later, even if I had permission."

"Why not? It isn't Sunday till twelve," said Herbert.

"No, but I should be apt to oversleep myself, and be dull and drowsy in church next morning."

"Quite a saint!" muttered Enna, shrugging her shoulders and marching off to the other side of the room.

"Suppose we go and select some flowers for our hair," said Lucy, looking at her watch. "'Twill be tea-time presently, and we'll want to dress directly after."

"You always were such a dear good girl," whispered Carrie Howard, putting her arm about Elsie's waist as they left the room.

Enna was quite gorgeous that evening, in a bright-colored silk, trimmed with multitudinous flounces and many yards of ribbon and gimp. The young damsel had a decidedly gay taste, and glanced somewhat contemptuously at Elsie's dress of simple white, albeit 'twas of the finest India muslin and trimmed with costly lace. She wore her pearl necklace and bracelets, a broad sash of rich white ribbon—no other ornaments save a half-blown moss rosebud at her bosom, and another amid the glossy ringlets of her hair, their green leaves the only bit of color about her.

"You look like a bride," said Herbert, gazing admiringly upon her.

"Do I?" she answered smiling, as she turned and tripped lightly away—for Lucy was calling to her from the next room.

Herbert's eyes followed her with a wistful, longing look in them, and he sighed sadly to himself as she disappeared from his view.

Most of the guests came early, among them, Walter and Arthur Dinsmore. Elsie had not seen the latter since his encounter with Mr. Travilla. He gave her a sullen nod on entering the room, but took no further notice of her.

Chit-chat, promenading and the music of the piano and harp were the order of the evening for a time. Then games were proposed, and "Consequences," "How do you like it " and "Genteel lady, always genteel," afforded much amusement. Herbert could join in these, and did with much spirit. But dancing was a favorite pastime with the young people of the neighborhood, and the clock had hardly struck nine when Cadmus and his fiddle were summoned to their aid, chairs and tables were put out of the way, and sets began to form.

Elsie was in great request. The young gentlemen flocked about her, with urgent entreaties that she would join in the amusement, each claiming the honor of her hand in one or more sets, but she steadily declined.

A glad smile lighted up Herbert's countenance, as he saw one and another turn and walk away with a look of chagrin and disappointment.

"Since my misfortune compels me to act the part of a wallflower, I am selfish enough, I own, to rejoice in your decision to be one also," he said gleefully. "Will you take a seat with me on this sofa? I presume your conscience does not forbid you to watch the dancers?"

"No, not at all," she answered, accepting his invitation.

Elsie's eyes followed with eager interest the swiftly moving forms, but Herbert's were often turned admiringly upon her. At length he asked if she did not find the room rather warm and close, and proposed that they should go out upon the veranda. She gave a willing assent and they passed quietly out and sat down side by side on a rustic seat.

The full moon shone upon them from a beautiful blue sky, while a refreshing breeze, fragrant with the odor of flowers and pines, gently fanned their cheeks and played among the rich masses of Elsie's hair.

They found a good deal to talk about. They always did, for they were kindred spirits. Their chat was now grave, now gay—generally the latter, for Cad's music was inspiriting—but whatever the theme of their discourse, Herbert's eyes were constantly seeking the face of his companion.

"How beautiful you are, Elsie!" he exclaimed at length, in a tone of such earnest sincerity that it made her laugh. The words seemed to rush spontaneously from his lips. "You are always lovely, but tonight especially so."

"It's the moonlight, Herbert. There's a sort of witchery about it, that lends beauty to many an object which can boast none of itself."

"Ah, but broad daylight never robs you of yours. You always wear it wherever you are, and however dressed. You look like a bride tonight. I wish you were, and that I were the groom."

Elsie laughed again, this time more merrily than before. "Ah, what nonsense we are talking—we two children," she said. Then starting to her feet as the clock struck ten—"There, it is my bed-time, and I must bid you good-night, pleasant dreams, and a happy awaking."

"Oh, don't go yet!" he cried, but she was already gone, the skirt of her white dress just disappearing through the open hall door.

She encountered Mrs. Carrington at the foot of the stairs. "My dear child, you are not leaving us already?" she cried.

"Yes, madam, the clock has struck ten."

"Why, you are a second Cinderella."

"I hope not," replied Elsie, laughing. "See, my dress has not changed in the least, but is quite as fresh and nice as ever."

"Ah, true enough! There the resemblance fails entirely. But, my dear child, the refreshments are just coming in, and you must have your share. I had ordered them an hour earlier, but the servants were slow and dilatory, and then the dancing began. Come, can you not wait long enough to partake with us? Surely, ten o'clock is not late."

"No, madam, not for another night of the week, but tomorrow's the Sabbath, you know, and if I should stay up late tonight I would be likely to find myself unfitted for its duties. Besides, papa bade me retire at this hour, and he does not approve of my eating at night. He thinks it is apt to cause dyspepsia."

"Ah, that is too bad! Well, I shall see that something is set away for you, and hope you will enjoy it tomorrow. Good-night, dear. I must hurry away now to see the rest of my guests, and will not detain you longer," she added, drawing the fair girl toward her and kissing her affectionately, then hastening away to the supper-room.

Elsie tripped up the stairs and entered her room. A lamp burned low on the toilet table. She went to it, turned up the wick, and as she did so a slight noise on the veranda without startled her. The windows reached to the floor and were wide open.

"Who's there?" she asked.

"I," was answered, in a rough, surly tone, and Arthur stepped in.

"Is it you?" she asked in surprise and indignation. "Why do you come here? It is not fit you should, especially at this hour."

"It is not fit you should set yourself up to reprove and instruct your uncle. I've come for that money you are going to lend me."

"I am not going to lend you any money."

"Give it then—that will be all the better for my pocket."

"I have none to give you either, Arthur. Papa has positively forbidden me to supply you with money."

"How much have you here?"

"That is a question you have no right to ask."

"Well, I know you are never without a pretty good supply of the needful, and I'm needy. So hand it over without any more ado, otherwise I shall be very apt to help myself."

"No, you will not," she said, with dignity. "If you attempt to rob me, I shall call for assistance."

"And disgrace the family by giving the tattlers a precious bit of scandal to retail in regard to us."

"If you care for the family credit you will go away at once and leave me in peace."

"I will, eh? I'll go when I get what I came for, and not before."

Elsie moved toward the bell rope, but anticipating her intention, he stepped before it, saying with a jeering laugh, "No, you don't!"

"Arthur," she said, drawing herself up, and speaking with great firmness and dignity, "leave this room. I wish to be alone."

"Hoity-toity, Miss Dinsmore! Do you suppose I'm to

be ordered about by you? No, indeed! And I've an old score to pay off. One of these days I'll be revenged on you and old Travilla, too. Nobody shall insult and abuse me with impunity. Now hand over that cash!"

"Leave this room!" she repeated.

"None of your——impudence!" he cried fiercely, catching her by the arm with a grasp that wrung from her a low, half-smothered cry of pain.

But footsteps and voices were heard on the stairs, and he hastily withdrew by the window through which he had entered.

Elsie pulled up her sleeve and looked at her arm. Each finger of Arthur's hand had left its mark. "Oh, how angry papa would be!" she murmured to herself, hastily drawing down her sleeve again as the door opened and Chloe came in, followed by another servant bearing a small silver waiter loaded with dainties.

"Missus tole me fotch 'em up with her compliments, an' hopes de young lady'll try to eat some," she said, setting it down on a table.

"Mrs. Carrington is very kind. Please return her my thanks, Minerva," said Elsie, making a strong effort to steady her voice.

The girl, taken up with the excitement of what was going on downstairs, failed to notice the slight tremble in its tones. But not so with Chloe. As the other hurried from the room, she took her nursling in her arms, and gazing into the sweet face with earnest, loving scrutiny, asked, "What de matter, darlin'? What hab resturbed you so, honey?"

"You mustn't leave me alone, tonight, mammy," Elsie whispered, clinging to her, and half hiding her face on her breast. "Don't go out of the room at all, unless it is to step on the veranda."

Chloe was much surprised, for Elsie had never been cowardly.

"'Deed I won't, darlin'," she answered, caressing the shining hair, and softly rounded cheek. "But what my bressed chile 'fraid of?"

"Mr. Arthur, mammy," Elsie answered scarcely above her breath. "He was in here a moment since, and if I were alone again he might come back."

"An' what Marse Arthur doin' yer dis time ob night, I like ter know? What he want frightenin' my chile like dis?"

"Money, mammy, and papa has forbidden me to let him have any, because he makes a bad use of it." Elsie knew to whom she spoke. Chloe was no ordinary servant, and could be trusted.

"Dear, dear, it's drefful that Marse Arthur takes to dem bad ways! But don't go for to fret, honey. We'll 'gree together to ask de Lord to turn him to de right."

"Yes, mammy, you must help me to pray for him. But now I must get ready for bed. I have stayed up longer than papa said I might."

"Won't you take some of de 'freshments fust, honey?"

Elsie shook her head. "Eat what you want of them, mammy. I know I am better without."

Chapter Ninth

There's not a look, a word of thine
My soul hath e'er forgot;
Thou ne'er hast bid a ringlet shine,
Nor given thy locks one graceful twine,
Which I remember not.

—MOORE

THE CLOCK on the stairway was just striking nine, as someone tapped lightly on the door of Elsie's room, leading into the hall. Chloe rose and opened it. "Dat you, Scip?"

"Yes, Aunt Chloe. De missis say breakop's is ready, an' will Miss Dinsmore please for to come if she's ready. We don't ring de bell fear wakin' up de odder young ladies an' gemmen."

Elsie had been up and dressed for the last hour, which she had spent in reading her Bible—a book not less dear and beautiful in her esteem now than it was in the days of her childhood. She rose and followed Scip to the dining-room, where she found the older members of the family already assembled, and about to sit down to the table.

"Ah, my dear, good-morning," said Mrs. Carrington. "I was sure you would be up and dressed, but the others were so late getting to bed that I mean they shall be allowed to sleep as long as they will. Ah! And here comes Herbert, too. We have quite a party after all."

"I should think you would need a long nap this morning more than anyone else," Elsie said, addressing Herbert.

"No," he answered, coloring. "I took advantage of my semi-invalidism, and retired very shortly after you left us."

"You must not think it is usual for us to be quite so late on Sunday morning, Elsie," observed Mr. Carrington as he sent her her plate, "though I'm afraid we are hardly as early risers, even on ordinary occasions, as you are at the Oaks. I don't think it's a good plan to have Saturday-night parties," he added, looking across the table at his wife.

"No," she said lightly, "but we must blame it all on the birthday, for coming when it did. And though we are late, we shall still be in time to get to church. Elsie, will you go with us?"

"In the carriage with mother and me?" added Herbert.

Elsie, had she consulted her own inclination merely, would have greatly preferred to ride her pony, but seeing the eager look in Herbert's eyes, she answered smilingly that she should accept the invitation with pleasure, if there was a seat in the carriage which no one else cared to occupy.

"There will be plenty of room, my dear," said Mr. Carrington. "Father and mother always go by themselves, driving an ancient mare we call old Bess, who is so very quiet and slow that no one else can bear to ride behind her, and the boys and I either walk or ride our horses."

It was time to set out almost immediately upon leaving the table. They had a quiet drive through beautiful pine woods, heard an excellent gospel sermon, and returned by another and equally beautiful route.

Elsie's mind was full of the truth to which she had been listening, and she had very little to say. Mrs. Carrington and Herbert, too, were unusually silent, the latter feeling it enjoyment enough just to sit by Elsie's side. He had known and loved her from their very early childhood, with a love that had grown and strengthened year by year.

"You seem much fatigued, Herbert," his mother said to him, as a servant assisted him from the carriage, and up the steps of the veranda. "I am almost sorry you went."

"Oh, no, mother, I'm not at all sorry," he answered cheerfully. "I shall have to spend the rest of the day on my couch, but that sermon was enough to repay me for the exertion it cost me to go to hear it." Then he added in an undertone to Elsie, who stood near, looking at him with pitying eyes, "I shan't mind having to lie still if you will give me your company for even a part of the time."

"Certainly you shall have it, if it will be any comfort to you," she answered, with her own sweet smile.

"You must not be too exacting towards Elsie, my son," said his mother, shaking up his pillows for him, and settling him comfortably on them. "She is always so ready to sacrifice herself for others that she would not, I fear, refuse such a request, however much it might cost her to grant it. And no doubt she will want to be with the other girls."

"Yes, it was just like my selfishness to ask it, Elsie, and never think how distasteful it might be to you. I take it all back," he said, blushing, but with a wistful look in his eyes that she could never have withstood, had she wished to do so.

"It's too late for that, since I have already accepted," she said with an arch look as she turned away. "But don't worry yourself about me. I shall follow my own inclination in regard to the length of my visit, making it very short if I find your society irksome or disagreeable."

The other girls were promenading on the upper veranda in full dinner dress.

Carrie hailed Elsie in a lively tone. "So you've been to church, like a good Christian, leaving us three lazy sinners taking our ease at home. We took our breakfasts in bed, and have only just finished our toilets."

"Well, and why shouldn't we?" said Enna. "We don't

profess to be saints."

"No, I just said we were sinners. But don't think too ill of us, Elsie. It was so late—or rather early—well on into the small hours—when we retired, that a long morning nap became a necessity."

"I don't pretend to judge you, Carrie," Elsie answered gently. "It is not for me to do so. And I acknowledge that though I retired much earlier than you, I slept a full hour past my usual time for rising."

"You'll surely have to do penance for that," sneered Enna.

"No, she shan't," said Lucy, putting her arm around her friend's slender waist. "Come, promenade with me till the dinner-bell rings. The exercise will do you good."

The lively chat of the girls seemed to our heroine so unsuited to the sacredness of the day that she rejoiced in the excuse Herbert's invitation gave her for withdrawing herself from their society for the greater part of the afternoon. She found him alone, lying on his sofa, apparently asleep, but at the sound of her light footstep he opened his eyes and looked up with a joyous smile. "I'm so glad to see you! How good of you to come!" he cried delightedly. "It's abominably selfish of me, though. Don't let me keep you from having a good time with the rest."

"The Sabbath is hardly the day for what people usually mean by a good time, is it?" she said, taking possession of a low rocking-chair that stood by the side of his couch.

"No, but it is the day of days for real good, happy times. Everything is so quiet and still that it is easier than on other days to lift one's thoughts to God and Heaven. Oh, Elsie, I owe you a great debt of gratitude, that I can never repay."

"For what, Herbert?"

"Ah, don't you know it was you who first taught me the sweetness of carrying all my trials and troubles to Jesus? Years ago, when we were very little children, you told me what comfort and happiness you found in so doing, and begged me to try it for myself."

"And you did?"

"Yes, and have continued to do so ever since."

"And that is what enables you to be so patient and uncomplaining."

"If I am. But ah, you don't know the dreadfully rebellious feelings that sometimes will take possession of me, especially when, after the disease has seemed almost eradicated from my system, it suddenly returns to make me as helpless and full of pain as ever. Nobody knows how hard it is to endure it, how weary I grow of life, how unendurably heavy my burden seems."

"Yes, he knows," she murmured softly. "In all their afflictions he was afflicted; and the angel of his presence saved them."

"Yes, he is touched with the feeling of our infirmities. Oh, how sweet and comforting it is!"

They were silent for a moment. Then turning to her, he asked, "Are you ever afraid that your troubles and cares are too trifling for his notice? That you will weary and disgust him with your continual coming?"

"I asked papa about that once, and I shall never forget the tender, loving look he gave me as he said: 'Daughter, do I ever seem to feel that anything which affects your comfort or happiness one way or the other, is too trifling to interest and concern me?' 'Oh, no, no, papa,' I said, 'you have often told me you would be glad to know that I had not a thought or feeling concealed from you, and you always seem to like to have me come to you with every little thing that makes me either glad or sorry.' 'I am, my darling,' he answered, 'just because you are so very near and dear to me. And what does the Bible tell us? *Like as a father pitieth his children, so the Lord pitieth them that fear Him!*' "

"Yes," said Herbert, musingly. "Then that text somewhere in Isaiah about his love being greater than a mother's for her little helpless babe."

"And what Jesus said: 'Are not two sparrows sold for a farthing? And not one of them shall fall to the ground

- 93 -

without your Father. But the very hairs of your head are all numbered. Fear ye not therefore, ye are of more value than many sparrows.' And then the command: 'In everything by prayer and supplication, with thanksgiving let your requests be made known unto God.' Papa reminded me, too, of God's infinite wisdom and power, of the great worlds, countless in number, that he keeps in motion—the sun and planets of many solar systems besides our own—and then the myriads upon myriads of tiny insects that crowd earth, air, and water, God's care and providence ever over them all. Oh, one does not know how to take it in! One cannot realize the half of it. God does not know the distinctions that we do between great and small, and it costs him no effort to attend at one and the same time to all his creatures and all their affairs."

"No, that is true. Oh, how great and how good he is! And how sweet to know of his goodness and love, to feel that he hears and answers prayer! I would not give that up for perfect health and vigor, and all the wealth of the world beside."

"I think I would give up everything else first, and oh, I am so glad for you, Herbert," she said softly.

Then they opened their Bibles and read several chapters together, to converse about, pausing now and then to compare notes, as to their understanding of the exact meaning of some particular passage, or to look out a reference, or consult a commentary.

"I'm excessively tired of the house. Do let's take a walk," said Enna, as they stood or sat about the veranda after tea.

"Do you second the motion, Miss Howard?" asked Harry.

"Yes," she said, rising and taking his offered arm. "Elsie, you'll go too?"

"Oh, there's no use in asking her!" cried Enna. "She is much too good to do anything pleasant on Sunday."

"Indeed! I was not aware of that." And Harry shrugged his shoulders, and threw a comical look at Elsie. "What is your objection to pleasant things, Miss

Dinsmore? To be quite consistent you should object to yourself."

Elsie smiled. "Enna must excuse me for saying that she makes a slight mistake, for while it is true my conscience would not permit me to go pleasuring on the Sabbath, yet it does not object to many things that I find very pleasant."

"Such as saying your prayers, reading the Bible, and going to church?"

"Yes, Enna. Those are real pleasures to me."

"But to come to the point, will you walk with us?" asked Lucy.

"Thank you, no, not tonight. But please don't mind me. I have no right, and don't presume to decide such questions for anyone but myself."

"Then, if you'll excuse us, we'll leave mamma and Herbert to entertain you for a short time."

The short time proved to be two hours or more, and long before the return of the little party, Mrs. Carrington went into the house, leaving the two on the veranda alone.

They sang hymns together for a while, then fell to silent musing. Herbert was the first to speak. He still lay upon his sofa, Elsie sitting near, her face at that moment upturned to the sky, where the full moon was shining, and looking wondrous sweet and fair in the soft silvery light. Her thoughts seemed far away, and she started and turned quickly toward him as he softly breathed her name.

"Oh, Elsie, this has been such a happy day to me! What joy, what bliss, if we could be always together!"

"If you were only my brother! I wish you were, Herbert."

"No, no, I do not, for I would be something much nearer and dearer. Oh, Elsie, if you only would!" he went on, speaking very fast and excitedly. "You thought I was joking last night, but I was not, I was in earnest—never more so in my life. Oh, do you think you could like me, Elsie?"

"Why, yes, Herbert, I do, and always have ever since

we first became acquainted."

"No, I didn't mean like, I meant love. Elsie, could you love me—love me well enough to marry me?"

"Why, Herbert, what an idea!" she stammered, her face flushing visibly in the moonlight. "You don't know how you surprise me. Surely we are both too young to be thinking of such things. Papa says I am not even to consider myself a young lady for three or four years yet. I'm nothing but a child. And you, Herbert, are not much older."

"Six months, but that's quite enough difference. And your father needn't object on the score of our youth. You are as old now as I've been told your mother was when he married her, and another year will make me as old as he was. And your Aunts Louisa and Lora were both engaged before they were sixteen. It's not at all uncommon for girls in this part of the country to marry before they are that old. But I know I'm not half good enough for you, Elsie. A king might be proud to win you for his bride, and I'm only a poor, good-for-nothing cripple, not worth anybody's acceptance." And he turned away his face, with something that sounded very like a sob.

Elsie's kind heart was touched. "No, Herbert, you must not talk so. You are a dear, good, noble fellow, worthy of any lady in the land," she said, half playfully, half tenderly and laying her little soft white hand over his mouth.

He caught it in his and pressed it passionately to his lips, there holding it fast. "Oh, Elsie, if it were only mine to keep!" he cried. "I'd be the happiest fellow in the world."

She looked at his pale, thin face, worn with suffering, into his eyes so full of passionate entreaty, thought what a dear lovable fellow he had always been, and forgot herself entirely—forgot everything but the desire to relieve and comfort him, and make him happy.

"Only tell me that you care for me, darling, and that you are willing someday to belong to me! Only give me a little hope. I shall die if you don't!"

"I do care for you, Herbert. I would do any thing in my power to make you happy."

"Then I may call you my own! Oh, darling, God bless you for your goodness!"

But the clock was striking nine, and with the sound, a sudden recollection came to Elsie. "It is my bed-time, and—and, Herbert, it will all have to be just as papa says. I belong to him, and cannot give myself away without his permission. Good-night." She hastily withdrew the hand he still held, and was gone ere he had time to reply.

What had she done—something of which papa would highly disapprove? Would he be very much vexed with her? Elsie asked herself half-tremblingly, as she sat passively under her old mammy's hands, for her father's displeasure was the one thing she dreaded above all others.

She was just ready for bed when a light tap on the door was followed by the entrance of Mrs. Carrington.

"I wish to see your young mistress alone for a few moments, Aunt Chloe," she said, and the faithful creature went from the room at once.

Mrs. Carrington threw her arms around Elsie, folded her in close, loving embrace, and kissed her fondly again and again. "My dear child, how happy you have made me!" she whispered at last. "Herbert has told me all. Dear boy, he could not keep such good news from his mother. I know of nothing that could have brought me deeper joy and thankfulness, for I have always had a mother's love for you."

Elsie felt bewildered, almost stunned. "I—I'm afraid you—he has misunderstood me. It— it must be as papa says," she stammered. "I cannot decide it for myself, I have no right."

"Certainly, my dear, that is all very right, very proper. Parents should always be consulted in these matters. But your papa loves you too well to raise any objection when he sees that your heart is interested. And Herbert is worthy of you, though his mother says it. He is a noble, true-hearted fellow, well-educated, handsome, talented, polished in manners, indeed all that anybody could ask, if he were but well, and we do not despair of seeing him eventually quite restored to health. But I am keeping you up, and I know that your papa is very strict and particular about your observance of his rules, so good night." And, with another caress, she left her.

Thought was very busy in Elsie's brain as she laid her head upon her pillow. It was delightful to have given such joy and happiness to Herbert and his mother. Lucy, too, she felt sure would be very glad to learn that they were to be sisters. But her own papa, how would he feel—what would he say? Only the other day he had reminded her how entirely she belonged to him—that no other had the slightest claim upon her, and as he spoke, the clasp of his arms seemed to say that he would defy the whole world to take her from him. No, he would never give her up. And somehow she was not at all miserable at the thought, but on the contrary it sent a thrill of joy to her heart. It was so sweet to be so loved and cherished by him, her own "dear, dear papa!"

But then another thing came to her remembrance— his pity for poor suffering Herbert, his expressed willingness to do anything he could to make him happy— and again she doubted whether he would accept or reject the boy's suit for her hand.

Carrie and Enna were to leave at an early hour on Monday morning. They came into Elsie's room for a parting chat while waiting for the ringing of the breakfast bell, so the three went down together to answer its summons, and thus she was spared the necessity of entering the dining room alone—an ordeal she had really dreaded—a strange and painful shyness toward the whole family at Ashlands having suddenly come over her. She managed to conceal it pretty well, but carefully avoided meeting Herbert's eye, or those of his parents.

The girls left directly on the conclusion of the meal, and having seen them off, Elsie slipped away to her own room. But Lucy followed her almost immediately, fairly wild with delight at the news Herbert had just been giving her.

"Oh, you darling!" she cried, hugging her friend with all her might. "I never was so glad in all my life! To think that I'm to have you for a sister! I could just eat you up!"

"I hope you won't," said Elsie, laughing and blushing, as she returned the embrace as heartily as it was given. "But we must not be too sure. I'm not at all certain of papa's consent."

"No, I just expect he'll object to Herbie on account of his lameness, and his ill health. I don't think we ought to blame him if he does either." And Lucy suddenly sobered down to more than her ordinary gravity. "Ah, I forgot," she said, a moment after, "Herbert begs that you will come down and let him talk with you a little if you are not particularly engaged."

Elsie answering that she had nothing to do, her time was quite at his disposal, the two tripped downstairs, each with an arm about the other's waist, as they had done so often in the days of their childhood.

They found Herbert on the veranda, not lying down, but seated on his sofa. "You are better this morning?" Elsie said with a glad look up into his face, as he rose, leaning on his crutch, and gave her the other hand.

"Yes, thank you, much better. Joy has proved so great a cordial that I begin to hope it may work a complete cure." He drew her to a seat by his side, and Lucy considerately went away and left them alone.

"You have not changed your mind, Elsie?" His tone was low and half tremulous in its eagerness.

"No, Herbert, but it all rests with papa, you know."

"I hardly dare ask him for you, it seems like such presumption in a—a cripple like me."

"Don't say that, Herbert. Would you love me less if I should become lame or ill?"

"No, no, never! But I couldn't bear to have any such calamity come upon you. I can hardly bear that you should have a lame husband. The thought of it makes my trial harder to bear than ever."

"It is God's will, and we must not fight against it," she

said softly.

They conversed for some time longer. He was very anxious to gain Mr. Dinsmore's consent to their engagement, yet shrank from asking it, fearing an indignant refusal. Most of all, he dreaded a personal interview, and, but ill able to take the ride to the Oaks, it was finally decided between them that he should make his application by letter, doing so at once.

A servant was summoned to bring him his writing materials, and Elsie left him to his trying task, while she and Lucy and Harry mounted their horses and were away for a brisk, delightful ride through the woods and over the hills.

"It's gone, Elsie," Herbert whispered, when she came down dressed for dinner. "I wrote it twice. It didn't suit me then, but my strength was quite exhausted, so it had to go. I hope the answer will come soon, but oh, I shall be almost afraid to open it."

"Don't feel so. Papa is very good and kind. He pities you so much, too," and she repeated what he had said about being willing to do any thing he could for him.

Herbert's face grew bright with hope as he listened. "And do you think he'll answer at once?" he asked.

"Yes, papa is always very prompt and decided, never keeps one long in suspense."

Mr. Carrington met our heroine at the dinner table with such a bright, glad smile, and treated her in so kind and fatherly a manner that she felt sure he knew all, and was much pleased with the prospect before them. But she was afraid Harry did not like it—did not want her for a sister. He was usually very gay and talkative, full of fun and frolic. He had been so during their ride, but now his manner seemed strangely altered; he was moody and taciturn, almost cross.

Chapter Tenth

Keen are the pangs
Of hapless love and passion unapproved.

—Smollett's Regicide

Hardly anything could have been more distasteful to Horace Dinsmore than the state of affairs revealed to him by Herbert Carrington's note. He was greatly vexed, not at the lad's manner of preferring his request, but that it should have been made at all. He was not ready yet to listen to such a proposal coming from any person, however eligible, much less from one so sadly afflicted as poor Herbert. He sought his wife's presence with the missive in his hand.

"What is the matter, my dear?" she asked. "I have seldom seen you so disturbed."

"The most absurd nonsense! The most ridiculously provoking affair! Herbert Carrington asking me to give him my daughter! I don't wonder at your astonished look, Rose—a couple of silly children. I should have given either of them credit for more sense."

"It has certainly taken me very much by surprise," said Rose, smiling. "I cannot realize that Elsie is grown up enough to be beginning with such things, yet you know she has passed her fifteenth birthday, and that half the girls about here become engaged before they are sixteen."

"But Elsie shall not. I'll have no nonsense of the kind for years to come. She shall not marry a day before she is twenty-one—I had nearly said twenty-five, and I don't think I'll allow it before then."

Rose laughed. "My dear, do you know what my age was when you married me?"

"Twenty-one, you told me."

"Don't you think my father ought then to have kept us waiting four years longer?"

"No," he answered, stooping to stroke her hair, and snatch a kiss from her rich red lips.

She looked up smilingly into his face. "Ah, consistency is a jewel! And pray how old were you when you married the first time? And what was then the age of Elsie's mother?"

"Your arguments are not unanswerable, Mrs. Dinsmore. Your father could spare you, having several other daughters. I have but one, and can't spare her. Elsie's mother was not older when I married her, it is true, than Elsie is now, but was much more mature, and had neither the happy home nor the doting father her daughter has. And as for myself, though much too young to marry, I was a year older than this Herbert Carrington, and I was in sound and vigorous health, while he, poor fellow, is sadly crippled, and likely always to be an invalid, and very unlikely to live to so much as see his majority. Do you think I ought for a moment to contemplate allowing Elsie to sacrifice herself to him?

"It would seem a terrible sacrifice, and yet after all it will depend very much upon the state of her own feelings."

"If she were five or six years older, I should say yes to that, but girls of her age are not fit to choose a companion for life. Taste and judgment are not matured, and the man who pleases them now may be utterly repugnant to them in after years. Is not that so?"

"Yes, and I think your decision is wise and kind. Still, I am sorry for the poor boy, and hope you will deal very gently and kindly with him."

"I shall certainly try to do so. I pity him, and cannot blame him for fancying my lovely daughter—I really don't see how he or any young fellow can help it. But he can't have her, and of course I must tell him so. I must see Elsie first however, and have already sent her a note ordering her home immediately."

"Come into my room for a little, dear," Mrs. Norris whispered to Elsie as they rose from the dinner table. "Herbert must not expect to monopolize all your time."

It turned out that all the old lady wanted was an opportunity to express her delight in the prospect of someday claiming Elsie as her granddaughter, and to pet and fondle her a little. Mr. Norris did his share of that also, and when at length they let her go she encountered Mr. Carrington in the hall, and had to submit to something more of the same sort from him.

"We are all heartily rejoiced, little Elsie," he said, "all of us who know the secret. It is to be kept from the children, of course, till your father's consent has made all certain. But there is Lucy looking for you, Herbert has sent her, I daresay. No doubt he grudges every moment that you are out of his sight."

That was true, and his glad look, as she took her accustomed place by the side of his couch, was pleasant to see. But he was not selfish in his happiness, and seemed well satisfied to share Elsie's society with his sister.

The three were making very merry together, when a servant from the Oaks was seen riding leisurely up the avenue. He had some small white object in his hand which he began waving about his head the moment he saw that he had attracted their attention.

"It's a letter!" exclaimed Lucy. "Han, Scip,"—to the two little blacks who, as usual, were tumbling over each other on the grass nearby,—"run, one of you and get it, quick now!"

"What—who—Miss Lucy?" they cried, jumping up.

"Yonder. Don't you see Mr. Dinsmore's man with a letter? Run and get it, quick!"

"Yes'm!" and both scampered off in the direction of the horseman, who, suddenly urging on his steed, was now rapidly nearing the house.

"Hollo! Dar now, you ole Jim!" shouted Scip, making a dash at the horse. "Who dat lettah fur? You gub um to me."

A contemptuous sniff was the only answer, and dashing by them, Jim drew rein close to the veranda. "Massa he send dis for you, Miss Elsie," he said, holding out the letter to her.

She sprang forward, took it from his hand and hastily tore open the envelope, the rich color coming and going in her cheek. A glance was sufficient, and turning her flushed face to the anxious, expectant Herbert: "Papa has sent for me to return home immediately," she said. "I must go."

"Oh, Elsie, must you indeed? And is there no word for me—none at all?"

"Yes, he says you shall hear from him today or tomorrow."

She had gone close to him and was speaking in a low tone that the servants might not hear. Herbert took both her hands in his. "Oh, I am so sorry ! You were to have stayed two days longer. I fear this sudden recall does not argue well for me. Is he angry, do you think?"

"I don't know, I can't tell. The note is simply an order for me to come home at once and the message to you that I have given—nothing more at all. Jim is to see me safely to the Oaks." Then turning to the messenger, "Go and saddle Glossy, and bring her round at once, Jim," she said.

"Yes, Miss Elsie, hab her roun' in less dan no time."

"Go with Jim to the stables, Han," said Herbert, sighing as he spoke.

"Elsie? I can't bear to have you leave us so suddenly," cried Lucy. "It does seem too bad of your father, after giving you permission to stay a whole week, to go and dock off two days."

"But papa has a right, and I can't complain. I've nothing to do but obey. I'll go up and have my riding-habit put on, while Glossy is being saddled."

"Miss Elsie," said Jim, leisurely dismounting, "massa say de wagon be here in 'bout an hour for de trunk, an'

Aunt Chloe mus' hab 'em ready by dat time, herself too."

"Very well, she shall do so," and with another whispered word to Herbert, Elsie went into the house, Lucy going with her.

"Why, my dear, this is very sudden, is it not?" exclaimed Mrs. Carrington, meeting her young guest as she came down dressed for her ride. "I thought you were to stay a week, and hoped you were enjoying your visit as much as we were."

"Thank you, dear Mrs. Carrington. I have had a delightful time, but papa has sent for me."

"And like a good child, you obey at once."

"My father's daughter would never dare to do otherwise," replied Elsie, smiling, "though I hope I should not, if I did dare."

"You'll come again soon—often, till I can get strength to go to you?" Herbert said entreatingly, as he held her hand in parting. "And we'll correspond, won't we? I should like to write and receive a note every day when we do not meet."

"I don't know. I can promise nothing till I have asked permission of papa."

"But if he allows it?"

"If he allows it, yes. Good-bye."

Dearly as Elsie loved her father, she more than half dreaded the meeting with him now, so entirely uncertain was she how he would feel in regard to this matter.

He was on the veranda, watching for her. Lifting her from her horse, he led her into his study. Then putting an arm about her waist, his other hand under her chin so that her blushing, downcast face was fully exposed to his gaze, "What does all this mean?" he asked. "Look up into my face and tell me if it is really true that you want me to give you away? If it is possible that you love that boy better than your father?"

She lifted her eyes as he bade her, but dropped them again instantly. Then as he finished his sentence, "Oh, no, no, papa! Not half so well. How could you think it?" she cried, throwing her arms about his neck, and hiding her face on his breast.

"Ah, is that so?" he said, with a low, gleeful laugh, as he held her close to his heart. "But he says you accepted him on condition that papa would give consent, that you owned you cared for him."

"And so I do, papa. I've always loved him as if he were my brother, and I'm so sorry for all he suffers, that I would do anything I could to make him happy."

"Even to sacrificing yourself? It is well indeed for you that you have a father to take care of you."

"Are you going to say 'No' to him, papa?" she asked, looking up half beseechingly.

"Indeed I am."

"Ah, papa, he said it would kill him if you did."

"I don't believe it. People don't die so easily. And I have several reasons for my refusal, each one of which would be quite sufficient of itself. But .you just acknowledged to me that you don't love him at all as you ought. Why, my child, when you meet the right person you will find that your love for him is far greater than what you feel for me."

"Papa, I don't think that could be possible," she said, clinging closer to him than before.

"But you'll be convinced when the time comes, though I hope that will not be for many a long year yet. Then Herbert's ill health and lameness are two insuperable objections. Lastly, you are both entirely too young to be thinking of such matters."

"He didn't mean to ask you to give me to him now, papa, not for a year or two at the very least."

"But I won't have you engaging yourself while you are such a mere child. I don't approve of long engagements, or intend to let you marry for six or seven years to come. So you may as well dismiss all thoughts on the subject, and if any other boy or man attempts to talk to you as Herbert has, just tell him that your father utterly forbids you to listen to anything of the kind. What! Crying! I hope these are not rebellious tears ?"

"No, papa, please don't be angry. It is only that I feel

so sorry for poor Herbert. He suffers so, and is so patient and good."

"I am sorry for him too, but it cannot be helped. I must take care of you first, and not allow anything which I think will interfere with your happiness or well being."

"Papa, he wants to correspond with me."

"I shall not allow it."

"May we see each other often?"

"No, not at all for some time. He must get over this foolish fancy first. It cannot be anything more, and there is great danger that he will not unless you are kept entirely apart."

Elsie sighed softly, but said not a word. There was no appeal from her father's decisions, no argument or entreaty allowed after they were once announced.

Little feet were heard running down the hall. Then there was the sound of a tiny fist thumping on the door, and the voice of little Horace calling, "Elsie, Elsie, tum out! Me wants to see you!"

"There, you may go now," her father said, releasing her with a kiss, "and leave me to write that note. Well, what is it?" for she lingered, looking up wistfully into his face.

"Dear papa, be kind to him for my sake," she murmured softly, putting her arm about his neck again. "He is such a sufferer, so patient and good, and it quite makes my heart ache to think how grievously your refusal will pain him."

"My own sweet child! Always unselfish, always concerned for the happiness of others," thought the father as he looked down into the pleading face. But he only stroked her hair, and kissed her more tenderly than before, saying, "I shall try to be as kind as circumstances will allow, daughter. You shall read the letter when it is done, and if you think it is not kind enough it shall not be sent."

She thanked him with a very grateful look, then hurried away, for the tiny fists were redoubling their blows upon the door, while the baby voice called more and more clamorously for "sister Elsie."

She stooped to hug and kiss the little fellow, then was led off in triumph to "mamma," whose greeting, though less noisy, was quite as joyous and affectionate.

"Oh, how nice it is to get home!" cried Elsie, and wondered within herself how she had been contented to stay away so long. She had hardly finished giving Rose an animated account of her visit, including a minute description of the birthday party, when her father's voice summoned her to the study again.

"Does it satisfy you?" he asked when she had read the note.

"Yes, papa. I think it is as kind as a refusal could possibly be made."

"Then I shall send it at once. And now this settles the matter, and I bid you put the whole affair out of your mind as completely as possible, Elsie."

"I shall try, papa," she answered in a submissive and even cheerful tone.

That note, kindly worded though it was, caused great distress to Herbert Carrington. He passed an almost sleepless night, and the next morning, finding himself quite unable to rise from his couch, he sent an urgent entreaty that Mr. Dinsmore would call at Ashlands at his earliest convenience.

His request was granted at once, and the lad pleaded with all the eloquence of which he was master for a more favorable reception of his suit.

Had he been as well acquainted with Horace Dinsmore's character as Elsie was, he would have known the utter uselessness of such a proceeding. He received a patient hearing, then a firm, though kind denial. Elsie was entirely too young to be allowed even to think of love or matrimony, her father said. He was extremely sorry the subject had been broached to her; it must not be again for years. He would not permit any engagement, correspondence, or, for the present at least, any exchange of visits, because he wished the matter to be dropped entirely, and, if possible, forgotten. Nor would he hold out the slightest hope for the future, answering

Herbert's petition for that by a gentle hint that one in his ill health should be content to remain single.

"Yes, you are right, Mr. Dinsmore, and I don't blame you for refusing to give me your lovely daughter. I'm entirely unworthy of such a treasure," said the poor boy in a broken voice.

"Not in character, my dear boy," said Mr. Dinsmore, almost tenderly. "In that you are all I could ask or desire, and it is all that you are responsible for. And now while she is such a mere child, I should reject any other suitor for her hand, quite as decidedly as I do you."

"You don't blame me for loving her?"

"No, oh, no!"

"I can't help it. I've loved her ever since I first saw her, and that was before I was five years old."

"Well, I don't object to a brotherly affection, and when you can tone it down to that, shall not forbid occasional intercourse. And now, with the best wishes for your health and happiness, I must bid you good-bye."

"Good-bye, sir, and thank you for your kindness in coming," the boy answered with a quivering lip. Then, turning to his mother, as Mr. Dinsmore left the room, "I shall never get over it," he said. "I shall not live long, and I don't want to. Life without her isn't worth having."

Her heart ached for him, but she answered cheerily: "Why, my dear child, don't be so despondent. I think you may take hope and courage from some things that Mr. Dinsmore said. It is quite in your favor that he will not allow Elsie to receive proposals from anyone at present, for who knows but by the time he considers her old enough, you may be well and strong."

Mrs. Carrington's words had a very different effect from what she intended. The next time Herbert saw his physician, he insisted so strongly on knowing exactly what he might look forward to that there was no evading the demand, and on learning that he was hopelessly crippled for life, he sank into a state of utter despondency, and from that moment grew rapidly worse, failing visibly day by day.

Elsie, dutifully abstaining from holding any communication with Ashlands, and giving all her thoughts as far as possible to home duties and pleasures, knew nothing of it till one day Enna came in, asking, "Have you heard the news?"

"No," said Elsie, pausing in a game of romps with her little brother. "What is it?"

"It! You should rather say they. There's more than one item of importance." And Enna straightened herself and smoothed out her dress with a very consequential air. "In the first place Arthur has been found out in his evil courses. He's been betting and gambling till he's got himself over head and ears in debt. Papa was so angry, I almost thought he would kill him. But he seemed to cool down after he'd paid off the debts, and Arthur is, or pretends to be, very penitent, promises never to do the like again, and so he's got forgiven, and he and Walter are to start for college early next week. They've both gone to the city today with papa. Arthur seems to be mad at you. He says that you could have saved him from being found out, but didn't choose to, and someday he'll have his revenge. Now, what was it you did, or didn't do?"

"He wanted money, and I refused to lend it because papa had forbidden me."

"You're good at minding and always were," was Enna's sneering comment. "No, I'll take that back. I forgot that time when you nearly died rather than mind."

An indignant flush suffused Elsie's fair face for an instant, but the sneer was borne in utter silence. Rose entered the room at that moment, and, having returned her greeting, Enna proceeded to give another important bit of news.

"Herbert Carrington is very ill—not confined to his bed, but failing very fast. The doctors advised them to take him from home, because they said they thought he had something on his mind, and taking him into new scenes might help him to forget it. They think he's not likely to live long anyhow, but that is the last hope. His mother and Lucy started North with him this morning."

Elsie suddenly dropped the ball she was tossing for Horace and ran out of the room.

"Why, what did she do that for?" asked Enna, in a tone of surprise, turning to Rose for an explanation. "Is she in love with him, do you suppose?"

"No, I know she is not, but I think she has a strong sisterly regard for him, and I am sorry the news of his increased illness was told her so abruptly."

"Such a baby, as she always was," muttered Enna, "crying her eyes out about the least little thing."

"If she lacks sufficient control over her feelings it is almost the only fault she has," replied Rose warmly. "And I think, Enna, you are hardly capable of appreciating her delicately sensitive nature, and warm, loving heart, else you would not wound her as you do. She certainly controls her temper well, and puts up with more from you than I should."

"Pray, what do you mean, Mrs. Dinsmore? What have I done to your pet?" asked the young lady angrily.

"She is older than you, yet you treat her as if she were much younger. Your manner toward her is often very contemptuous, and I have frequently heard you sneer at her principles and taunt her with her willing subjection to her father's strict rule, for which she deserves nothing but the highest praise."

"Nobody could ever rule me the way Horace does her!" cried Enna, with a toss of her head. "And as to her being older than I am, I'm sure no one would think it, she is so absurdly childish in her way—not half so mature as I, mamma says."

"I'm glad and thankful that she is not," answered Rose, with spirit. "Her sweet childish simplicity and perfect naturalness are very charming in these days, when they are so rarely found in a girl who has entered her teens."

Little Horace, standing by the window, uttered a joyous shout," Oh, papa tumin'!" and rushed from the room to return the next moment clinging to his father's hand, announcing as they came in together, "Here papa is! Me found him!"

Mr. Dinsmore shook hands with his sister, addressed a remark to his wife, then, glancing about the room, asked, "Where is Elsie?"

"She left us a moment since, but did not say where she was going," said Rose.

"I presume you'll find her crying in her boudoir or dressing room," added Enna.

"Crying! Why, what is wrong with her?"

"Nothing that I know of, except that I told her of Herbert Carrington's being so much worse that they've taken him North as a last hope."

"Is that so?" and Mr. Dinsmore looked much concerned.

"Yes, there can be no doubt about it, for I heard it from Harry himself this morning."

Mr. Dinsmore rose, and, putting his little son gently aside, left the room.

Elsie was not in her own apartments. He passed through the whole suite, looking for her, then, going on into the grounds, found her at last in her favorite arbor. She was crying bitterly, but at the sound of his step checked her sobs, and hastily wiped away her tears. She thought he would reprove her for indulging her grief, but instead he took her in his arms and soothed her tenderly.

"Oh, papa," she sobbed, "I feel as if I had done it—as if I had killed him."

"Darling, he is not past hope. He may recover, and in any event not the slightest blame belongs to you. I have taken the whole responsibility upon my shoulders."

She gave him a somewhat relieved and very grateful look, and he went on: "And even if I had allowed you to decide the matter for yourself, you would have done what was your duty in refusing to promise to belong to one whom you love less than you love your father."

Some months later there came news of Herbert's death. Elsie's grief was deep and lasting. She sorrowed as she might have done for the loss of a very dear brother, while added to that was a half-remorseful feeling which reason could not control or entirely relieve; and it was long ere she was quite her own bright, gladsome sunny self again.

CHAPTER ELEVENTH

The bloom of opening flowers' unsullied beauty—
Softness and sweetest innocence she wears,
And looks like nature in the world's first spring.

—ROWE'S TAMERLANE

"WHAT A VERY PECULIAR hand, papa—so stiff and cramped and old-fashioned," Elsie remarked, as her father laid down a letter he had just been reading.

"Yes. Did you ever hear me speak of Aunt Wealthy Stanhope?"

His glance seemed to direct the question to Rose, who answered, with a look of surprise and curiosity, "No, sir. Who is she?"

"A half-sister of my own mother. She was the daughter of my maternal grandfather by his first wife, my mother was the child of the second, and there were some five or ten years between them. Aunt Wealthy never married, would never live with any of her relatives, but has always kept up a cosy little establishment of her own."

"Do you know her, papa?" asked Elsie, who was listening with eager interest.

"I can hardly say that I do. I saw her once, nearly eighteen years ago, about the time you were born—but I was not capable of appreciating her then—indeed, was so unhappy and irritable as to be hardly in a condition to either make or receive favorable impressions. I now believe her to be a truly good and noble little woman, though decidedly an oddity in some respects. Then I called her a fidgety, fussy old maid."

"And your letter is from her?" Rose said inquiringly.

"Yes. She wants me to pay her a visit, taking Elsie with me, and leaving her there for the summer."

"There, papa! Where?"

"Lansdale, Ohio. Should you like to go?"

"Yes, I think I should like to go, papa, if you take me. But whether I should like to stay all summer I could hardly tell till I get there."

"You may read the letter," he said, handing it to her.

"It sounds as though it might be very pleasant, papa," she said, as she laid it down after an attentive perusal.

It spoke of Lansdale as a pretty, healthful village, surrounded by beautiful scenery, and boasting of some excellent society—of two lively young girls, living in the next house to her own, who would be charming companions for Elsie, etc.

"Your remark that your aunt was an oddity in some respects has excited my curiosity," said Rose.

"Ah! And I am to understand that you would like me to gratify it, eh?" returned her husband, smiling. "Her dress and the arrangement of her hair are in a style peculiarly her own—unless she has become more fashionable since I saw her, which is not likely—and she has an odd way of transposing her sentences and the names of those she addresses or introduces, or calling them by some other name suggested by some association with the real one. Miss Bell, for instance, she would probably call Miss Ring; Mr. Foot, Mr. Shoe, and so on."

"Does she do so intentionally, papa?" Elsie asked.

"No, not at all. Her mistakes are quite innocently made, and are therefore very amusing."

Mrs. Horace Dinsmore's parents had been urging her to visit them, and after some further consideration it was decided that the whole family should go North for the summer, Mr. Dinsmore see his wife and little son safe at her father's, then take Elsie on to visit his aunt—the length of the visit to be determined after their arrival.

It was a lovely morning early in May; the air was vocal with the songs of birds and redolent with the breath of flowers all bathed in dew. Delicate wreaths of snowy vapor rose slowly from the rippling surface of the river that threaded its way through the valley, and folded themselves about the richly-wooded hill-sides, behind which bright streaks of golden light were shooting upward, fair heralds of the coming of the king of day. On the outskirts of the pretty village of Lansdale, and in the midst of a well-kept garden and lawn, stood a tasteful dwelling, of Gothic architecture. Roses, honeysuckle, and Virginia creeper clambered over its walls, twined themselves about the pillars of its porticos and porches, or hung in graceful festoons from its many gables. The garden was gay with sweet spring flowers. The trees, the grass on the lawn, and the hedge that separated it from the road—all were liveried in that vivid green so refreshing to the eye.

"Phillis! Simon!" called a sweet-toned voice from the foot of the back staircase. "Are you up? It's high time—nearly five o'clock now—and the train's due at six."

"Coming, ma'am. I'll have time to do up all my chores and git to the depot 'fore de train, you neber fear," replied a colored lad of fifteen or sixteen, hurrying down as he spoke.

A matronly woman, belonging to the same race, followed close in his rear.

"You're smart dis mornin', missis," she said, speaking from the middle of the stairway. "I didn't 'spect you'd git ahead o' me, and de sun hardly showin' his face 'bove de hill-tops yit."

"I woke early, Phillis, as I always do when something's going to happen that I expect. Simon make haste to feed and water your horses and be sure you have old Joan in the carriage and at the gate by a quarter before six."

"Am I to drive her to the depot, ma'am?"

"No, Miss Lottie Prince will do that, and you are to take the one-horse wagon for the trunks. Did you go to Mr. Laugh's and engage it, as I told you yesterday?"

"I went to Mr. Grinn's and disengaged de one horse wagon, ma'am, yes'm."

"Very well. Now come into the sitting room and I'll show you the likenesses of the lady and gentleman, and the old colored woman they're going to bring with them," replied the mistress, leading the way into an apartment that, in spite of its plain, old-fashioned furniture, wore a very attractive appearance, it was so exquisitely neat, and the windows, reaching to the floor, opened upon one side into the conservatory and garden, on the other upon a porch that ran the whole length of the front of the house. Taking a photograph album from a side-table, she showed the three pictures to Simon, who pronounced the gentleman very handsome, the lady the prettiest he ever saw, and was sure he should recognize both them and their servant.

"Now, Phillis, we'll have to bestir ourselves," said Miss Stanhope, returning to the kitchen. "Do you think you can get breakfast in less than an hour? Such a breakfast as we should have this morning—one fit for a king."

"Yes, Miss Wealthy, but you don't want it that soon, do you? Folks is apt to like to wash and dress 'fore breakfast."

"Ah, yes! Sure enough. Well, we'll give them half an hour."

A few moments later, as Miss Stanhope was busy with broom and duster in the front part of the house, a young girl opened the gate, tripped gaily up the gravel walk that led from it across the lawn, and stepped upon the porch. She was a brunette with a very rich color in her dark cheek, raven hair, and sparkling, roguish black eyes. She wore a suit of plain brown linen, with snowy cuffs and collar, and a little straw hat. "Good-morning, Aunt Wealthy!" she cried, in a lively tone. "You see I'm in good time."

"Yes, Lottie, and looking as neat as a pin, too. It's very kind of you, because of course I want to be here to receive them as they come, to offer to introduce yourself and drive down to the depot for them."

"Of course I'm wonderfully clever, considering that I don't at all enjoy a drive in this sweet morning air, and ain't in a bit of a hurry to see your beautiful young heiress and her papa. Net wonders at my audacity in venturing to face them alone, but I tell her I'm too staunch a republican to quail before any amount of wealth or consequence, and if Mr. and Miss Dinsmore see fit to turn up their aristocratic noses at me, why—I'll just return the compliment."

"I hope they're not of that sort, Lottie, but if they are, you will serve them right."

"She does not look like it," observed the young girl, taking the album from the table and gazing earnestly upon Elsie's lovely countenance. "What a sweet, gentle, lovable face it is! I'm sure I shall dote on her, and if I can only persuade her to return my penchant, won't we have grand good times while she's here? But there's Simon with old Joan and the carriage. He'll hunt them up for me at the depot, won't he, Aunt Wealthy?"

"Yes, I told him to."

The shrill whistle of the locomotive echoed and re-echoed among the hills.

"Lansdale!" shouted the conductor, throwing open the car door.

"So we are at our destination at last, and I am very glad for your sake, daughter, for you are looking weary," said Mr. Dinsmore, drawing Elsie's shawl more closely about her shoulders.

"Oh, I'm not so very tired, papa," she answered, with a loving look and smile, "not more so than you are, I presume. Oh, see, papa, what a pretty girl in that carriage there!"

"Yes, yes! Come to meet some friend, doubtless. Come, the train has stopped. Keep close to me," he said. "Aunt Chloe, see that you have all the parcels."

"Dis de gentleman and lady from de South, what Miss Stanhope's 'spectin'?" asked a colored lad, stepping up to our little party as they alighted.

"Yes."

"Dis way den, sah, if you please, sah. Here's de carriage. De lady will drive you up to de house, and I'll take your luggage in de little wagon."

"Very well. Here are the checks. You will bring it up at once?"

"Yes, sah, have it dar soon as yourself, sah. Dis cullad person better ride wid me and de trunks."

They were nearing the carriage and the pretty girl Elsie had noticed from the car window. "Good-morning! Mr. and Miss Dinsmore, I presume?" she said with a bow and smile. "Will you get in? Let me give you a hand, Miss Dinsmore. I am Lottie King, a distant relative and near neighbor of your aunt, Miss Stanhope."

"And have kindly driven down for us. We are much obliged, Miss King," Mr. Dinsmore answered, as he followed his daughter into the vehicle. "Shall I not relieve you of the reins?"

"Oh, no, thank you. I'm used to driving, and fond of it. And, besides, you don't know the way."

"True. How is my aunt?"

"Quite well. She has been looking forward with great delight to this visit, as have my sister Nettie and I also," Lottie answered, with a backward glance of admiring curiosity at Elsie. "I hope you will be pleased with Lansdale, Miss Dinsmore—sufficiently so to decide to stay all summer."

"Thank you. I think it is looking lovely this morning. Does my aunt live far from the depot ?"

"Not very—about a quarter of a mile."

"Oh, what a pretty place, and what a quaint-looking little old lady on its porch!" Elsie presently cried out. "See, papa!"

"Yes, that's Aunt Wealthy, and doesn't she make a picture standing there under the vines in her odd dress?" said Miss King, driving up to the gate. "She's the very oddest, and the very dearest and sweetest little old lady in the world."

Elsie listened and looked again, this time with eager interest and curiosity.

Certainly, Aunt Wealthy was no slave to fashion. The tyrannical dame at that time prescribed gaiter boots, a plain pointed waist and straight skirt, worn very long and full. Miss Stanhope wore a full waist made with a yoke and belt, a gored skirt, extremely scant, and so short as to afford a very distinct view of a well-turned ankle and small, shapely foot encased in snowy stocking and low-heeled black kid slipper. The material of her dress was chintz—white ground with a tiny brown figure—finished at the neck with a wide white ruffle. She had black silk mitts on her hands, and her hair, which was very gray, was worn in a little knot almost on the top of her head, and one thick, short curl, held in place by a puff-comb, on each side of her face.

At sight of the carriage and its occupants, she came hurrying down the gravel walk, meeting them as they entered the gate. She took Mr. Dinsmore's hand, saying, "I am glad to see you, nephew Horace," and held up her face for a kiss. Then turning to Elsie, gave her a very warm embrace. "So, dear, you've come to see your old auntie? That's right. Come into the house."

Elsie was charmed with her and with all she saw—all without was so fresh and bright, everything within so exquisitely neat and clean. The furniture of the whole house was very plain and old-fashioned, but Miss Stanhope never thought of apologizing for what to her wore the double charm of ownership, and of association with the happy days of childhood and youth, and loved ones gone. Nor did her guests deem anything of the kind called for in the very least. House and mistress seemed well suited the one to the other and Elsie thought it not unpleasant to exchange, for a time, the luxurious furnishing of her home apartments for the simple adornments of the one assigned her here. The snowy drapery of its bed and toilet-table, its wide-open casements giving glimpses of garden, lawn, and shrubbery, and the beautiful hills beyond, looked very inviting. There were vases of fresh flowers too, on mantel and bureau, and green vines peeping in at the windows. It seemed a haven of rest after the long, fatiguing journey.

"The child is sweet and fair to look upon, Horace, but I see nothing of you or my sister in her face," observed Miss Stanhope, as her nephew entered the breakfast-room, preceding his daughter by a moment or two. "Whom does she resemble?"

"Elsie is almost the exact counterpart of her own mother, Aunt Wealthy, and looks like no one else," he answered, with a glance of proud fatherly affection at the young creature as she entered and took her place at the table.

"Now my daughter," he said, at the conclusion of the meal, "you must go and lie down until near dinner-time, if possible."

"Yes, that is excellent advice," said Miss Stanhope. "I see, and I'm glad, she's worth taking care of, as you are sensible, Horace. You shall be called in season, dear. So take a good nap."

Elsie obeyed, retired to her room, slept several hours, and woke feeling greatly refreshed. Chloe was in waiting to dress her for dinner.

"Had you a nap too, my poor old mammy?" asked her young mistress.

"Yes, darlin', I've been lying on that couch, and feel good as ever now. Hark! What dat?"

"It sounds like a dog in distress," said Elsie, as they both ran to the window and looked out.

A fat poodle had nearly forced his plump body between the palings of the front gate in the effort to get into the street, and sticking fast, was yelping in distress. As they looked Miss Stanhope ran quickly down the path, seized him by the tail, and jerked him back, he uttering a louder yelp than before.

"There, Albert," she said, stroking and patting him, "I don't like to hurt you, but how was I to get you out, or in? You must be taught that you're to stay at home, sir. Thomas! Thomas! Come home, Thomas!" she called, and a large cat came running from the opposite side of the street.

"So those are Aunt Wealthy's pets. What an odd name for a cat," said Elsie, laughing.

"Yes, Miss Elsie, dey's pets, sure nuff. Phillis says Miss Wealthy's mighty good t'em."

"There, she is coming in with them, and, mammy, we must make haste. I'm afraid it's near dinner-time," said Elsie, turning away from the window.

Her toilet was just completed when there was a slight tap on the door, and her father's voice asked if she was ready to go down.

"Yes, papa," she answered, hurrying to him as Chloe opened the door.

"Ah, you are looking something like yourself again," he said, with a pleasant smile, as he drew her hand within his arm, and led her down the stairs. "You have had a good sleep?"

"A delicious rest. I must have slept at least four hours. And you, papa?"

"I took a nap of about the same length, and feel ready for almost anything in the shape of dinner, etc. And there is the bell."

Miss Stanhope cast many an admiring glance at nephew and niece during the progress of the meal.

"I'm thinking, Horace," she said at length, "that it's a great shame I've been left so many years a stranger to you both."

"I'm afraid it is, Aunt Wealthy, but the great distance that lies between our homes must be taken as some excuse. We would have been glad to see you at the Oaks, but you never came to visit us."

"Ah, it was much easier for you to come here," she replied, shaking her head. "I've been an old woman these many years. Come," she added, rising from the table, "come into the parlor, children, and let me show you the olden relics of time I have there—things that I value very highly, because they've been in the family for generations."

They followed her—Elsie unable to forbear a smile at hearing her father and herself coupled together as "children"—and looked with keen interest upon some half dozen old family portraits, an ancient cabinet of curiosities, a few musty time-worn volumes, a carpet that had been very expensive in its day, but was now somewhat faded and worn, and tables, sofas, and chairs of solid mahogany—each of the last-named covered with a heavily-embroidered silken cushion.

"That sampler," said Aunt Wealthy, pointing to a large one with a wonderful landscape worked upon it, that, framed and glazed, hung between two of the windows, "is a specimen of my paternal grandmother's handiwork. These chair-cushions, too, she embroidered and filled with her own feathers, so that I value them more than their weight in gold."

"My great-grandmother kept a few geese, I presume," Mr. Dinsmore remarked aside to Elsie with a quiet smile.

Having finished their inspection of the parlor and its curiosities, they seated themselves upon the front porch, where trees and vines gave a pleasant shade. Miss Stanhope had her knitting, Mr. Dinsmore the morning paper, while Elsie sat with her pretty white hands lying idle in her lap, doing nothing but enjoy the beautiful prospect and a quiet chat with the sweet-voiced old lady.

The talk between them was quite brisk for a time, but gradually it slackened, till at length they had been silent for several minutes and Elsie, glancing at her aunt, saw her nodding over her work.

"Ah, you must excuse me, dear," the old lady said apologetically, waking with a start. "I'm not very well, and, deary, I woke unusually early this morning, and have been stirring about ever since."

"Can't you afford yourself a little nap, auntie" Elsie asked in return. "You mustn't make company of me, and besides, I have a book that I can amuse myself with."

"You would be quite alone, child for I see your father has gone in."

"I shall not mind that at all, auntie. Do go and lie down for at least a little while."

"Well, then, dear, I will just lie down on the sofa in the sitting room, and you must call me if anyone comes."

"Aunt Wealthy couldn't have meant for a child like that, unless she comes on some important errand," thought Elsie, as, a few moments later, a little girl came slowly across the lawn and stepped upon the porch.

The child looked clean and decent, in a neat calico dress and gingham sun-bonnet. At sight of Elsie she stood still, and, gazing with open-mouthed curiosity, asked, "Be you the rich young lady that was coming to see Miss Wealthy from 'way down south?"

"I have come from the South to see Miss Stanhope. What do you wish?"

"Nothin', I just come over 'cause I wanted to."

"Will you take a seat?"

"Yes," taking possession of the low rocking chair Miss Stanhope had vacated.

"What's your name?" inquired Elsie.

"Lenwilla Ellawea Schilling," returned the child, straightening herself up with an air of importance. "Mother made it herself."

"I should think so," replied Elsie, with a sparkle of fun in her eye. "And your mother is Mrs. Schilling, is she?"

"Yes, and pap, he's dead, and my brother's named Corbinus."

"What do they call you for short?"

"Willy, and him Binus."

"Where do you live?"

"Over yonder," nodding her head towards the opposite side of the street. "Mother's comin' over to see you some time. I guess I'll be going now." And away she went.

"What did that child want?" asked Miss Stanhope, coming out just in time to see the little maiden pass through the gate.

"Nothing but to look at and question me, I believe," Elsie answered, with an amused smile.

"Ah! She generally comes to borrow some little thing or other. They're the sort of folks that always have something they're out of. Mrs. Sixpence is a very odd sixpence indeed."

"I think the little girl said her last name was Schilling."

"Ah, yes, so it is, but I'm always forgetting their exact commercial value," Aunt Wealthy laughed softly. "In fact, I've a very good forgetting of my own, and am more apt to get names wrong than right."

"Mrs. Schilling must have an odd taste for names," said Elsie.

"Yes, she's a manufacturer of them, and very proud of her success in that line."

Miss Stanhope was a great lover of flowers, very proud of hers, cultivated principally by her own hands. After tea she invited her nephew and niece to a stroll through her garden, while she exhibited her pets with a very excusable pride in their variety, beauty, and fragrance.

As they passed into the house again, Phillis was feeding the chickens in the back yard.

"You have quite a flock of poultry, aunt," remarked Mr. Dinsmore.

"Yes, I like to see them running about, and the eggs you lay yourself are so much better than any you can buy, and the chickens, too, have quite another taste. Phillis, what's the matter with that speckled hen?"

"Dunno, mistis. She's been crippled dat way all dis week."

"Well, well, I dare say it's the boys. One of them must have thrown a stone and hit her between her hind legs. They're great plagues. Poor thing! There, Albert, don't you dare to meddle with the fowls! Come away, Thomas. That cat and dog are nearly as bad and troublesome to the boys as the poultry."

Puss and the poodle followed their mistress into the house, where Albert lay down at her feet, while Thomas sprang into her lap, where he stood purring and rubbing his head against her arm.

"You seem to have a good many pets, auntie," Elsie remarked.

"Yes, I am fond of them. A childless old woman must

have something to love. I've another that I'm fonder of than any of these though—my grand-nephew, Harry Duncan. He's away at school now, but I hope to show him to you one of these days."

"I should like to see him. Is he a relative of ours?" Elsie asked, turning to her father.

"No, he belongs to the other side of the house."

"How soft and fine this cat's fur is, aunt. He's quite handsome," remarked Elsie, venturing to stroke Thomas very gently.

"Yes, I raised him, and his mother before him. My sister Beulah was first husband's child of Harry's grandmother twice married, and my mother. Yes, I think a great deal of him, but was near losing him last winter. A fellow in our town—he's two years old now—wanted a buffalo robe for his sleigh, and undertook to make it out of cat-skins. He advertised that he'd give ten cents for every cat-skin the boys would bring him. You know the old saying that you can't have more of a cat than its skin, and hardly anybody's was safe after that. They went about catching all they could lay hands on, even borrowing people's pets and killing them."

Elsie turned to her father with a very perplexed look, puzzled to understand who it was that had married twice, and whether her aunt had stated Harry's age or that of the cat.

But at that instant steps and voices were heard upon the porch, and the door-bell rang.

"It's Lottie and her father," said Miss Stanhope, pushing Thomas from her lap. "Come in, friends, and don't stand for ceremony." For both doors stood wide open.

"Good-evening," said the young lady, coming forward, leaning upon the arm of a middle-aged gentleman. "Mr. Dinsmore, 1 have brought my father, Dr. King, to see you."

The gentlemen shook hands, the doctor observing, "I am happy to make your acquaintance, Mr. Dinsmore. I brought my daughter along to introduce me, lest our good Aunt Wealthy here, in her want of appreciation of nobility and birth, should, as she sometimes does, give me a rank lower than my true one, making me to appear only a Prince, while I am really a King."

A general laugh followed this sally, Miss Stanhope insisting that that was a mistake she did not often make now. Then Elsie was introduced, and, all being seated again, Dr. King turned to his hostess with the laughing remark, "Well, Aunt Wealthy, by way of amends, I'll own up that my wife says that you're the better doctor of the two. That bran has done her a world of good."

"Bran?" said Mr. Dinsmore inquiringly.

"Yes, sir. Mrs. King was suffering from indigestion. Miss Stanhope advised her to try eating a tablespoonful or so of dry bran after her meals, and it has had an excellent effect."

"My father learnt it from an old sea-captain," said Miss Stanhope, "and it has helped a great many I've recommended it to. Some prefer to mix it with a little cream, or take a little water with it but the best plan's to take it dry if you can."

∼≫⋖∼

Chapter Twelfth

When to mischief mortals bend their will,
How soon they find fit instruments of ill.

—POPE'S RAPE OF THE LOCK

"WHAT, ART, are you going out?"

"Yes."

"Do you know it's after ten?"

"Yes, you just mind your own business, Wal. Learn your lessons, and go off to bed like a good boy when you get through. I'm old enough to take care of myself."

"Dear me! I'm awfully afraid he's gone back to his evil courses, as father says," muttered Walter Dinsmore to himself, as the door closed upon his reckless elder brother. "I wonder what I ought to do about it," he continued, leaning his head upon his hand, with a worried, irresolute look. "Ought I to report to the governor? No, I shan't, there then. I don't know anything, and I never will be a sneak or a tell-tale." And he drew the light nearer, returned to his book with redoubled diligence for some ten or fifteen minutes more, then, pushing it hastily aside, with a sigh of relief, started up, threw off his clothes, blew out the light, and tumbled into bed.

Meanwhile Arthur had stolen noiselessly from the college, and pursued his way into the heart of the town. On turning a corner he came suddenly upon another young man, who seemed to have been waiting for him. Simply remarking, "You're late tonight, Dinsmore," he faced about in the same direction, and the two walked on together.

"Of course. But how can a fellow help it when he's obliged to watch his opportunity till the Argus eyes are closed in sleep, or supposed to be so?" grumbled Arthur.

"True enough, old boy. But cheer up, your day of emancipation must come some time or other," remarked his companion, clapping him familiarly on the shoulder. "Of age soon, aren't you?"

"In about a year. But what good does that do me? I'm not so fortunate as my older brother—shall have nothing of my own till one or other of my respected parents sees fit to kick the bucket, and leave me a pile—a thing which at present neither of them seems to have any notion of doing."

"You forget your chances at the faro-table."

"My chances! You win everything from me, Jackson. I'm a lame duck now, and if my luck doesn't soon begin to turn, I'll—do something desperate, I believe."

The lad's tone was bitter, his look reckless and half despairing.

"Pooh, don't be a spooney! We all have our ups and downs, and you must take your turn at both, like the rest."

They had ascended a flight of steps, and Jackson rang the bell as he spoke. It was answered instantly by a colored waiter, who with a silent bow stepped back and held the door open for their entrance. They passed in and presently found themselves in a large, well-lighted, and handsomely-furnished room, where tables were set out with the choicest viands, rich wine, and trays of fine cigars.

They seated themselves, ate and drank their fill, then, each lighting a cigar, proceeded to a saloon, on the story above, where a number of men were engaged in playing cards—gambling, as was evident from the piles of gold, silver, and bank-notes lying here and there upon the tables about which they sat.

Here also costly furniture, bright light, and rich wines lent their attractions to the scene.

Arthur took possession of a velvet-cushioned chair on one side of an elegant marble-topped table, his companion placing himself in another directly opposite. Here, seated in the full blaze of the gas-light, each face was brought out into strong relief. Both were young, both handsome: Jackson, who was Arthur's senior by five or six years, remarkably so, yet his smile was sardonic, and there was often a sinister expression in his keen black eye as its glance fell upon his victim, for such Arthur Dinsmore was—no match for his cunning and unscrupulous antagonist, who was a gambler by profession.

Arthur's pretended reformation had lasted scarcely longer than until he was again exposed to temptation, and his face, as seen in that brilliant light, wore unmistakable signs of indulgence in debauchery and vice. He played in a wild, reckless way, dealing out his cards with a trembling hand, while his cheek burned and his eye flashed.

At first Jackson allowed him to win, and filled with a mad delight at the idea that "his luck had turned," the boy doubled and trebled his stakes.

Jackson chuckled inwardly, the game went on, and at length Arthur found all his gains suddenly swept away and himself many thousands of dollars in debt.

A ghastly pallor overspread his face, he threw himself back in his chair with a groan, then starting up with a bitter laugh, "Well, I see only one way out of this," he said. "A word in your ear, Tom. Come along with me. I've lost and you won enough for one night, haven't we, eh?"

"Well yes; I'm satisfied if you are." And the two hurried into the now dark and silent street, for it was long past midnight, and sober and respectable people generally had retired to their beds.

"Where are you going?" asked Jackson.

"Anywhere you like that we can talk without danger of being overheard."

"This way then, down this street. You see 'tis

absolutely silent and deserted."

They walked on, talking in an undertone.

"You'd like your money as soon as you can get it?" said Arthur.

"Of course. In fact I must have it before very long, for I'm hard pushed now."

"Suppose I could put you in the way of marrying a fortune, would you hold me quit of all your claims against me?"

"H'm, that would depend upon the success of the scheme."

"And that upon your own coolness and skill. I think I've heard you spoken of as a woman killer?"

"Ha, ha! Yes, I flatter myself that I have won some reputation in that line, and that not a few of the dear creatures have been very fond of me. It's really most too bad to break their soft little hearts, but then a man can't marry 'em all, unless he turns Mormon."

Arthur's lips curled with scorn and contempt, and he half turned away in disgust and aversion. But remembering that he was in the power of this man, whom, too late—alas!—he was discovering to be an unscrupulous villain, he checked himself, and answered in his usual tone, "No, certainly not. And so you have never yet run your neck into the matrimonial noose?"

"No, not I, and don't fancy doing so either, yet I own that a fortune would be a strong temptation. But, I say, lad, if it's a great chance, why do you hand it over to me? Why not try for it yourself? It's not your sister, surely?"

"No, indeed. You're not precisely the sort of brother-in-law I should choose," returned the boy, with a bitter, mocking laugh. "But stay, don't be insulted"—for his companion had drawn himself up with an air of offended pride—"the lady in question is but a step farther from me: she is my brother's daughter."

"Eh, you don't say? A mere child, then, I presume."

"Eighteen, handsome as a picture, as the saying is, and only too sweet-tempered for my taste."

"And rich, you say? That is, her father's wealthy, eh?"

"Yes, he's one of the richest men in our county, but she has a fortune in her own right—over a million at the very lowest computation."

"Whew! You expect me to swallow that?"

"It's true, true as preaching. You wonder that I should be so willing to help you to get her. Well, I owe her a grudge, I see no other way to get out of your clutches, and I shall put you in the way of making her acquaintance only on condition that if you succeed we share the spoils."

"Agreed. Now for the modus operandi. You tell me her whereabouts and provide me with a letter of introduction, eh?"

"No, on the contrary, you are carefully to conceal the fact that you have the slightest knowledge of me. The introduction must come from quite another quarter. Listen, and I'll communicate the facts and unfold my plan. It has been running in my head for weeks, ever since I heard that the girl was to spend the summer in the North with nobody but an old maiden aunt, half-cracked at that, to keep guard over her, but I couldn't quite make up my mind to it till tonight, for you must see, Tom," he added with a forced laugh, "that it can't be exactly delightful to my family pride to think of bringing such a dissipated fellow as you into the connection."

"Better look at home, lad. But you are right, one such scamp is, or ought to be, all-sufficient for one family."

Arthur said, "Certainly," but winced at the insinuation nevertheless. It was not a pleasant reflection that his vices had brought him down to a level with this man who lived by his wits—or perhaps more correctly speaking, his rascalities—of whose antecedents he knew nothing and whom, with his haughty Southern pride, he thoroughly despised.

But scorn and loathe him as he might in his secret soul, it was necessary that he should be conciliated, because it was now in his power to bring open disgrace and ruin upon his victim. So Arthur went on to explain matters and, with Jackson's assistance, to concoct a plan of getting Elsie and her fortune into their hands.

As he had said, the idea had been in his mind for weeks, yet it was not until that day that he could see clearly how to carry it out. Also, his family pride had stood in the way until the excitement of semi-intoxication and his heavy losses had enabled him to put it aside for the time. Tomorrow he would more than half regret the step he was taking, but now he plunged recklessly into the thing with small regard for consequences to himself or others.

"Can you imitate the chirography of others?" he asked.

"Perfectly, if I do say it that shouldn't."

"Then we can manage it. My brother Walter has kept up a correspondence with this niece ever since he left home. In a letter received yesterday she mentions that her father was about leaving her for the rest of the summer. Also that Miss Stanhope, the old aunt she's staying with, was formerly very intimate with Mrs. Waters of this city.

"It just flashed on me at once that a letter of introduction from her would be the very thing to put you at once on a footing of intimacy in Miss Stanhope's house, and that if you were good at imitating handwriting we might manage it by means of a note of invitation which I received from Mrs. Waters some time ago, and which, as good luck would have it, I threw into my table drawer instead of destroying."

"But who knows that it was written by the lady herself?"

"I do, for I heard Bob Waters say so."

"Good! Have you the note about you?"

"Yes, here it is." And Arthur drew it from his pocket. "Let's cross over to that lamp-post."

They did so, and Jackson held the note up to the light for a moment, scanning it attentively. "Ah, ha! The very thing! No trouble at all about that," he said, pocketing it with a chuckle of delight. "But," and a slight frown contracted his brows, "what if the old lady should take it into her head to open a correspondence on the subject with her old friend?"

"I've thought of that too, but fortunately for our scheme Mrs. Waters sails for Europe tomorrow; and by the way that should be mentioned in the letter of introduction."

"Yes, so it should. Come to my room at the Merchants' House tomorrow night, and you shall find it ready for your inspection. I suppose the sooner the ball's set in motion the better?" he added as they moved slowly on down the street.

"Yes, for there's no knowing how long it may take you to storm the citadel of her ladyship's heart, or how soon her father may come to the conclusion that he can't do without her, and go and carry her off home. And I tell you, Tom, you'd stand no chance with him, or with her if he were there. He'd see through you in five minutes."

"H'm! What sort is she?"

"The very pious!" sneered Arthur. "And you're bound to take your cue from that or you'll make no headway with her at all."

"A hard rôle for me, Dinsmore. I know nothing of cant."

"You'll have to learn it then. Let her once suspect your true character—a drinking, gambling, fortune-hunting rogue—and she'll turn from you with the same fear and loathing that she would feel for a venomous reptile."

"Ha, ha! You're in a complimentary mood tonight, Dinsmore. Well, well, such a fortune as you speak of is worth some sacrifice and effort, and I think I may venture the character of a perfectly moral and upright man with a high respect for religion. The rest I can learn by degrees from her, and come to think of it, it mightn't be a bad idea to let her imagine she'd converted me."

"Capital! The very thing, Tom! But good night. I must be off now to the college. I'll come to your room tomorrow night and we'll finish the arrangement of all preliminaries."

More than a fortnight had passed since the arrival of Miss Stanhope's guests. It had been a season of relaxation and keen enjoyment to them, to her, and to Dr. King's family, who had joined them in many a pleasant little excursion to points of interest in the vicinity, and several sociable family picnics among the surrounding hills and woods. A warm friendship had already sprung up between the three young girls, and had done much toward reconciling Elsie to the idea of spending the summer there away from her father.

She had finally consented to do so, yet as the time drew near her heart almost failed her. In all these years since they went to live together at the Oaks, they had never been far apart—except once or twice for a few days when he had gone to New Orleans to attend to business connected with the care of her property, and only on a very few occasions, when she paid a little visit in their own neighborhood, had they been separated for more than a day.

She could not keep back her tears as she hung about his neck on parting. "Ah, papa, how can I do without you for weeks and months?" she sighed.

"Or I without you, my darling?" he responded, straining her to his breast. "I don't know how I shall be able to stand it. You need not be surprised to see me again at any time, returning to claim my treasure, and in the mean-while we will write to each other every day. I shall want to know all you are doing, thinking, and feeling. You must tell me of all your pursuits and pleasures, your new acquaintances, too, if you form any. In that you must be guided by the advice of Aunt Wealthy, together with your father's known wishes. I am sure I can trust my daughter to obey those in my absence as carefully as in my presence."

"I think you may, papa. I shall try to do nothing that you would disapprove, and to attend faithfully to all your wishes."

Mr. Dinsmore left by the morning train, directly after breakfast. It was a bright, clear day, and Miss Stanhope, anxious to help Elsie to recover her spirits, proposed a little shopping expedition into the village.

"You have not seen our stores yet," she said, "and I think we'd better go now before the sun gets any hotter.

Should you like it, my dear?"

"Thank you, yes, auntie. I will go and get ready at once."

Elsie could hardly forbear smiling at the quaint little figure that met her in the porch a few moments later, and trotted with quick, short steps by her side across the lawn and up and down the village streets. The white muslin dress with its short and scanty skirt, an embroidered scarf of the same material, the close, old-fashioned leg-horn bonnet, trimmed with one broad strip of white mantua ribbon, put straight down over the top and tied under the chin, and the black mitts and morocco slippers of the same hue, formed a tout ensemble which, though odd, was not unpleasant to look upon. In one hand the little lady carried a very large parasol, in the other a gaily-colored silk reticule of corresponding size, this last not by a ribbon or string, but with its hem gathered up in her hand. All in singular contrast to Elsie with her slight, graceful form, fully a head taller, and her simple yet elegant costume. But the niece no more thought of feeling ashamed of her aunt, than her aunt of her.

They entered a store, and the smiling merchant asked, "What can I do for you today, ladies?"

"I will look at shirting muslin, if you please, Mr. Under," replied Miss Stanhope, laying parasol and reticule upon the counter.

"Over, if you please, Miss Stanhope," he answered with an amused look. "Just step this way, and I'll show you a piece that I think will suit."

"I beg your pardon, I'm always making mistakes in names," she said, doing as requested.

"Anything else today, ladies?" he asked when the muslin had been selected. "I have quite a lot of remnants of dress goods, Miss Stanhope. Would you like to look at them?"

"Yes," she answered almost eagerly, and he quickly spread them on the counter before her. She selected quite a number, Elsie wondering what she wanted with them.

"I'll send the package at once," said Mr. Over, as they

left the store.

They entered another where Miss Stanhope's first inquiry was for remnants, and the same thing was repeated till, as she assured Elsie, they had visited every dry-goods store in the place.

"Pretty nice ones, too, some of them are. Don't you think so, dear?"

"Yes, auntie, but do you know you have strongly excited my curiosity?"

"Ah! How so?"

"Why, I cannot imagine what you can want with all those remnants. I'm sure hardly one of them could be made into a dress for yourself or for Phillis, and you have no little folks to provide for."

"But other folks have, child, and I shall use some of the smallest for patchwork."

"Dere's a lady in de parlor, Miss Stanhope," said Chloe, meeting them at the gate, "kind of lady," she added with a very broad smile, "come to call on you, ma'am, and Miss Elsie too."

"We'll just go in without keeping her waiting to take off our bonnets," said Aunt Wealthy, leading the way.

They found a rather gaudily-dressed, and not very refined-looking woman, who rose and came forward to meet them with a boisterous manner, evidently assumed to cover a slight feeling of embarrassment. "Oh, I'm quite ashamed, Aunt Wealthy, to have been so long in calling to see your friends. You really must excuse me. It's not been for want of a strong disinclination, I do assure you; but you see I've been away a-nursing of a sick sister."

"Certainly, Mrs. Sixpence."

"Excuse me, Schilling."

"Oh no, not at all, it's my mistake. Elsie, Mrs. Schilling. My niece, Miss Dinsmore. Sit down, do. I'm sorry you got here before we were through our shopping."

"I'm afraid it's rather an early call," began Mrs. Schilling, her rubicund countenance growing redder than ever, "but—"

"Oh, aunt did not mean that," interposed Elsie, with gentle kindliness. "She was only regretting that you had been kept waiting."

"Certainly," said Miss Stanhope. "You know I'm a sad hand at talking, always getting the horse before the cart, as they say. But tell me about your sister. I hope she has recovered. What ailed her?"

"She had inflammation of the tonsils. She's better now, though. The tonsils are all gone, and I think she'll get along. She's weak yet, but that's all. There's been a good bit of sickness out there in that neighborhood, through the winter and spring. There were several cases of scarlet fever, and one of small-pox. That one died, and what do you think, Aunt Wealthy: they had a regular big funeral, took the corpse into the church, and asked everybody around to come to it."

"I think it was really wicked, and that if I'd been the congregation, every one of me would have staid away."

"So would I. There now, I'm bound to tell you something that happened while I was at father's. My sister had a little girl going on two years old, and one day the little thing took up a flat iron, and let it fall on her toe, and mashed it so we were really afraid 'twould have to be took off. We wrapped it up in some kind o' salve mother keeps for hurts, and she kept crying and screamin' with pain, and we couldn't peacify her nohow at all, till a lady that was visiting next door come in and said we'd better give her a few drops of laud'num. So we did, and would you believe it? It went right straight down into her toe, and she stopped cryin', and pretty soon dropped asleep. I thought it was the curiosest thing I ever heard of."

"It was a wise prescription, no doubt.", returned Miss Stanhope, with a quiet smile.

"Oh, aunt Wealthy, won't you tell me how you make that Farmer's fruit-cake?" asked the visitor, suddenly changing the subject. "Miss Dinsmore, it's the nicest thing you ever eat. You'd be sure it had raisins or currants in it."

"Certainly, Mrs. Schilling. You must soak three cups of dried apples in warm water over night, drain off the water through a sieve, chop the apples slightly, then simmer them for two hours in three cups of molasses. After that add two eggs, one cup of sugar, one cup of sweet milk or water, three-fourths of a cup of butter or lard, one-half teaspoonful of soda, flour to make a pretty stiff batter, cinnamon, cloves, and other spices to suit your taste."

"Oh, yes! But I'm afraid I'll hardly be able to remember all that."

"I'll write the receipt and send it over to you," said Elsie.

Mrs. Schilling returned her thanks, sat a little longer, conversing in the same lucid style, then rose and took leave, urging the ladies to call soon, and run in sociably as often as they could.

She was hardly out of the door before Aunt Wealthy was beating up her crushed chair-cushions to that state of perfect roundness and smoothness in which her heart delighted. It amused Elsie, who had noticed that such was her invariable custom after receiving a call in her parlor.

Lottie King and Mrs. Schilling passed each other on the porch, the one coming in as the other went out. Kind Aunt Wealthy, intent on preventing Elsie from grieving over the emptiness of her father's accustomed seat at the table, had invited her young friend to dinner. The hour of the meal had, however, not yet arrived, and the two girls repaired to Elsie's room to spend the intervening time.

Lottie, in her benevolent desire to be so entertaining to Elsie that her absent father should not be too sorely missed, seized upon the first topic of conversation which presented itself and rattled on in a very lively manner.

"So you have begun to make acquaintance with our peculiar currency, mon ami! An odd sixpence as Aunt Wealthy calls her. Two of them I should say, since it takes two sixpences to make a shilling."

"I don't know; I'm inclined to think Aunt Wealthy's arithmetic has the right of it, since she was never more than a shilling, and has lost her better half," returned Elsie, laughing.

"Better half, indeed! Fie on you, Miss Dinsmore! Have you so little regard for the honor of your sex as to own that the man is ever that? But I must tell you of the time when she sustained the aforesaid loss, and let me observe, sustained is really the proper—very properest of words to express my meaning, for it was very far from crushing her. While her husband was lying a corpse, mother went over with a pie, thinking it might be acceptable, as people are not apt to feel like cooking at such a time. She did not want to disturb the new-made widow in the midst of her grief, and did not ask for her, but Mrs. Schilling came to the door. 'Oh, I'm so much obliged to you for bringing that pie!' she said. 'It was so good of you. I hadn't any appetite to eat while he was sick, but now that he's dead, I feel as if I could eat something. You and your girls must come over and spend a day with me some time soon. He's left me full and plenty, and you needn't be afraid to take a meal's victuals off me!'"

"How odd! I don't think she could be quite broken-hearted."

"No, and she has apparently forgotten him, and bestowed her affections upon another—a widower named Wert. Mr. Was, Aunt Wealthy usually calls him. They both attend our church, and everybody notices how impossible it seems to be for her to keep her eyes off him, and you can never be five minutes in her company without hearing his name. Didn't she talk of him today?"

"Oh, yes, she spoke of Mr. Wert visiting some sick man, to talk and pray with him, and rejoiced that the man did not die till he gave evidence that he was repaired."

"Yes, that sounds like her," laughed Lottie. "She's always getting the wrong word. I told you she never could keep her eyes off Mr. Wert. Well, the other day—

three or four weeks ago—coming from church he was behind her. She kept looking back at him, and presently came bump up against a post. She made an outcry, of course everybody laughed, and she hurried off with a very red face. That put an idea into my head, and—" Lottie paused, laughing and blushing—

"I'm half ashamed to tell you, but I believe I will— Nettie and I wrote a letter in a sort of manly hand, signed his initials, and put it into an iron pot that she keeps standing near her back door. The letter requested that she would put her answer in the same place, and she did. Oh, it was rich! Such a rapture of delight, and such spelling and such grammar as were used to express it! It was such fun that we went on, and there have been half a dozen letters on each side. I daresay she is wondering why the proposal doesn't come. Ah, Elsie, I see you don't approve; you are as grave as a judge."

"I would prefer not to express an opinion, so please don't ask me."

"But you don't think it was quite right, now do you?"

"Since you have asked a direct question, Lottie, dear," Elsie answered, with some hesitation, "I'll own that it does not seem to me quite according to the golden rule."

"No," Lottie said, after a moment's pause, in which she sat with downcast eyes, and cheeks crimsoning with mortification. "I'm ashamed of myself, and I hope I shall never again allow my love of fun to carry me so far from what is true and kind.

"And so Aunt Wealthy took you out shopping, and secured the benefit of your taste and judgment in the choice of her remnants?" she exclaimed, with a sudden change to a lively, mirthful tone.

"How do you know that she bought remnants?" asked Elsie, in surprise.

"Oh, she always does. That's a particular hobby of the dear old body's. Two or three times in a season she goes around to all the stores, and buys up the most of their stock. They save the best of them for her, and always know what she's after the moment she shows her pleasant face. She gives them away, generally, to the minister's wife, telling her the largest are to be made into dresses for her little girls; and the poor lady is often in great tribulation, not knowing how to get the dresses out of such small patterns, and afraid to put them to any other use, lest Miss Stanhope should feel hurt or offended. By the way, what do you think of Aunt Wealthy's own dress?"

"That it is very quaint and odd, but suits her as no other would."

"I'm so glad! It's just what we all think, but before you came we were much afraid you would use your influence to induce her to adopt a more fashionable attire."

Chapter Thirteenth

Bear fair presence, though your heart be tainted;
Teach sin the carriage of a holy saint.

—Shakespeare's Comedy of Errors

"It's a very handsome present, child, very, and your old auntie will be reminded of you every time she uses it, or looks at it."

"Both beautiful and useful, like the giver," remarked Lottie.

"It" was a sewing-machine, Elsie's gift to Aunt Wealthy, forwarded from Cincinnati, by Mr. Dinsmore. The handsomest and the best to be found in the city, so Elsie had requested that it should be, and so he had written that it was.

"I am glad you like it, auntie, and you too, Lottie," was all she said in response to their praises, but her eyes sparkled with pleasure at the old lady's evident delight.

"It" had arrived half an hour before, on this the second morning after Mr. Dinsmore's departure, and now stood in front of one of the windows of Aunt Wealthy's bedroom—a delightfully shady, airy apartment on the ground floor, back of the parlor, and with window and door opening out upon a part of the lawn where the trees were thickest and a tiny fountain sent up its showers of spray.

Miss Stanhope stood at a table, cutting out shirts. Lottie was experimenting on the machine with a bit of muslin, and Elsie sat near by with her father's letter in her hand, her soft dark eyes now glancing over it for perhaps the twentieth time, now at the face of one or the other of her companions, as Lottie rattled on in her usual gay, flighty style, and Aunt Wealthy answered her sometimes with a straightforward sentence, and again with one so topsy-turvy that her listeners could not forbear a smile.

"For whom are you making shirts, aunt?" asked Elsie.

"For my boy Harry. He writes that his last set are going wonderfully fast, so I must send up another to make."

"You must let us help you, Lottie and I. We have agreed that it will be good fun for us."

"Thank you, dearie, but I didn't suppose plain sewing was among your accomplishments."

"Mamma says I am quite a good needle-woman," Elsie replied with a smile and a blush, "and if I am not, it is no fault of hers. She took great pains to teach me. I cut out a shirt for papa once, and made every stitch of it myself."

"And she can run the Machine too," said Lottie, "though her papa won't let her do so for more than half an hour at a time, lest she should hurt herself."

"He's very careful of her, and no wonder," Aunt Wealthy responded, with a loving look at the sweet, fair face. "You may help me a little, now and then, children, when it just suits your humor, but I want you to have all the rides and walks, the reading and recreation of every sort that you can enjoy."

"Here comes Lenwilla Ellawea Schilling," said Lottie, glancing from the window.

"What do you want, Willy?" asked Miss Stanhope, as the child appeared in the doorway with a teacup in her hand.

"Mother wants a little light'ning to raise her bread."

"Yeast? Oh, yes, just go round to Phillis, and she'll give you some."

The door-bell rang.

"It's a gentleman," said the child, "I seen him a-coming in at the gate."

Chloe answered the bell and entered the room the next moment with a letter, which she handed to Miss Stanhope.

The old lady adjusted her spectacles and broke the seal. "Ah, a letter of introduction, and from my old friend and schoolmate Anna Waters, wishes me to treat the young man with all the courtesy and kindness I would show to her own son, for she esteems him most highly, etc., etc. Aunt Chloe, what have you done with him?"

"Showed him into de parlor, mistis, and leff him a-sittin' dar."

"What's his name, auntie?" asked Lottie, as the old lady refolded the letter and took off her glasses.

"Bromly Egerton. Quite romantic, isn't it? Excuse me for a few minutes, dears. I must go and see what he wants."

Aunt Wealthy found a well-dressed, handsome young man seated on one of her softly-cushioned chairs. He rose and came forward to meet her with courtly ease and grace. "Miss Stanhope, I presume?"

"You are right, Mr. Ledgerfield. Pray be seated, sir."

"Thank you, madam, but let me first help you to a seat. Excuse the correction, but Egerton is my name."

"Ah, yes! For the sake of my friend, Mrs. Waters, I welcome you to Lansdale. Do you expect to make some stay in our town?"

"Well, madam, I hardly had such expectation before arriving here, but I find it so pretty a place that I begin to think I can scarcely do better. My health has been somewhat impaired by very strict and close attention to business, and my physician has ordered entire relaxation for a time, and fresh country air. Can you recommend a boarding-place in town? Some quiet, private hotel where drinking and things of that kind would not be going on. I'm not used to it, and should find it very disgusting."

"I'm glad to hear such sentiments, young man. They do you honor. I daresay Mrs. Sixpence—no, Mrs.

Schilling—just opposite here, would take you in. She told me some weeks ago that she would be glad to have one or two gentlemen boarders."

"Thank you, the location would suit me well, and you think she could give me comfortable accommodations?"

"I do. She has pleasant rooms and is a good cook."

"A widow?"

"Yes, not very young, and has two children But they are old enough not to be annoying to a boarder."

"What sort of woman is she?"

"A good manager, neat, industrious, honest, and obliging. Very suitable for a landlady, if you are not looking in the person of your hostess for an intellectual companion."

"Oh, not at all, Miss Stanhope, unless—unless you could find it in your benevolent heart to take me in yourself," and his smile was very insinuating. "In that case I should have the luxury of intellectual companionship superadded to the other advantages of which you have spoken."

The old lady smiled, but shook her head quite decidedly. "I have lived so long in the perfect house that I should not know how to give it up. I have come to think men a care and a trouble that I cannot take upon me in my old age."

"Excuse me, my dear madam, for the unwarrantable liberty I took in asking it," he said in an apologetic tone, and with a slightly embarrassed air. "I beg ten thousand pardons."

"That is a great many," she answered with a smile, "but you may consider them all granted. I hope you left my friend Mrs. Waters well? I must answer her letter directly."

"Ah, then you are not aware that she is already on her way to Europe?"

"No, is she indeed?"

"Yes, she sailed the day after that letter was written, which accounts for the date not being a very recent one. You see I did not leave immediately on receiving it from her."

She was beginning to wish that he would go, but he lingered for some time, vainly hoping for a glimpse of Elsie. On finally taking his leave, he asked her to point out Mrs. Schilling's house, and she noticed that he went directly there.

"Really, auntie, we began to think that your visitor must intend to spend the day," cried Lottie, as Miss Stanhope returned to her room and her interrupted employment.

"Ah, well! It was not my urging that kept him. I was very near telling him that he was making me waste a good deal of time," replied the old lady. Then seeing that Lottie was curious on the subject, she kindly went on to tell all that she had learned in regard to the stranger and his intentions.

Elsie was amusing herself with Thomas, trying to cajole him to return to the frolicsomeness of his long-forgotten kittenhood, and did not seem to hear or heed. What interest for her had this stranger, or his doings?

"Young and handsome, you say, Aunt Wealthy? And going to stay in Lansdale all summer? Would you advise me to set my cap for him?"

"No, Lottie, not I."

"You were not smitten with the gentleman, eh?"

"Not enough to spare him to you anyhow, but he may improve upon acquaintance."

"I don't approve of marrying, though, do you, auntie? Your practice certainly seems to speak disapproval."

"Perhaps everyone does not have the opportunity, my dear," answered the old lady, with a quiet smile.

"Oh, but you must have had plenty of them. Isn't that so? And why did you never accept?"

Elsie dropped the string she had been waving before the eyes of the cat, and looked up with eager interest.

"Yes, I had offers, and one of them I accepted," replied Aunt Wealthy, with a slight sigh, while a shade of sadness stole over her usually happy face. "But my friends interfered and the match was broken off. Don't follow my example, children, but marry if the right one comes along."

"Surely you don't mean if our parents refuse their consent, auntie?" Elsie's tone spoke both surprise and disapproval.

"No, no, child! It is to those who keep the fifth commandment God promises long life and prosperity."

"And love makes it so easy and pleasant to keep it," murmured Elsie, softly, and with a sweet, glad smile on her lips and in her eyes, thinking of her absent father, and almost unconsciously thinking aloud.

"Ah, child, it can sometimes make it very hard," said Miss Stanhope, with another little sigh, and shaking her head rather sadly.

"Elsie, you must have had lots of lovers before this, I am sure!" exclaimed Lottie, stopping her machine, and facing suddenly round upon her friend. "No girl as rich and beautiful as you are could have lived eighteen years without such an experience."

Elsie only smiled and blushed.

"Come now, am I not right?" persisted Lottie.

"I do assure you that I have actually lived to this mature age quite heart-whole," laughed Elsie. "If I have an idol, it is papa, and I don't believe anybody can ever succeed in displacing him."

"You have quite misunderstood me, wilfully or innocently. I asked of your worshippers, not of your idols. Haven't you had offers?"

"Several. Money has strong attractions for most men, papa tells me."

"May the Lord preserve you from the sad fate of a woman married for her money, dear child!" ejaculated Aunt Wealthy, with a glance of anxious affection at her lovely niece. "I'm sometimes tempted to think a large amount of it altogether a curse and an affliction."

"It is a great responsibility, auntie," replied Elsie, with a look of gravity beyond her years. Then after a moment's pause, her expression changing to one of gaiety and joy, "Now, if you and Lottie will excuse me for a little, I'll run up to my room, and answer papa's letter," she said, rising to her feet. "After which I shall be ready to make myself useful in the capacity of seamstress. Au revoir." And she tripped away with a light, free step, every movement as graceful as those of a young gazelle.

Mr. Bromly Egerton, alias Tom Jackson, was fortunate enough to find Mrs. Schilling at home. It was she who answered his knock.

"Good-day, sir," she said. "Will you walk in? Just step into the parlor here, and take a seat."

He accepted the invitation and stated his business without preface, or waiting to be questioned at all.

She seemed to be considering for a moment. "Well, yes, I can't say as I'd object to taking a few gentlemen boarders, but—I'd want to know who you be, and all about you."

"Certainly, ma'am, that's all right. I'm from the East, rather broken down with hard work—a business man, you see—and want to spend the summer here to recruit. Pitched upon your town because it strikes me as an uncommonly pretty place. I brought a letter of introduction to your neighbor, Miss Stanhope, and she recommended me to come here in search of board, saying you'd make a capital landlady."

"Well, if she recommends you, it's all right. Would you like to look at the rooms?"

She had two to dispose of—one at the back and the other in the front of the house, both cheerful, airy, of reasonable size, and neatly furnished. He preferred the latter, because it overlooked Miss Stanhope's house and grounds.

As he stood at the window, taking note of this, a young girl appeared at the one opposite. For one minute he had a distinct view of her face as she stood there and put out her hand to gather a blossom from the vine that had festooned itself so gracefully over the window.

He uttered an exclamation of delighted surprise, and turning to his companion asked, "Who is she?"

"Miss Dinsmore, Miss Stanhope's niece. She's here

on a visit to her aunt. She's from the South, and worth a mint of money, they say. Aint she handsome though? Handsome as a picture?"

"Posh! Handsome doesn't begin to express it! Why, she's angelic! But there! She's gone!" And he drew a long breath as he turned away.

"You'd better conclude to take this room if you like to look at her," artfully suggested Mrs. Schilling. "That's her bedroom window, and she's often at it. Besides, you can see the whole front of Miss Stanhope's place from here, and watch all the comings and goings o' the girls—Miss Dinsmore, and Miss Nettie and Lottie King."

"Who are they?"

"Kind o' fur-off cousins to Miss Stanhope. They live in that next house to hern, and are amazin' thick with her, runnin' in and out all times o' day. Nice, spry, likely girls they be too, not bad-lookin' neither, but hardly fit to hold a candle to Miss Dinsmore, as fur as beauty's concerned. Well, what do you say to the room, Mr. Egerton?"

"That I will take it, and would like to have immediate possession."

"All right, sir. Fetch your traps whenever you've a mind—right away, if you like."

There was no lack of good society in Lansdale. It had even more than the usual proportion of well-to-do, intelligent, educated, and refined people to be found in American villages of its size. They were hospitable folks, too, disposed to be kind to strangers tarrying in their midst, and, Miss Stanhope being an old resident, well known and highly esteemed, spite of her eccentricities, her friends had received a good deal of attention. Elsie had already become slightly acquainted with a number of pleasant families. A good many young girls, and also several young gentlemen had called upon her, and Lottie assured her there were many more to come.

"Some of the very nicest are apt to be slow about calling—we're such busy folks here," she said, laughing. "I've a notion, too, that several of the beaux stood rather in awe of your papa."

They were talking together over their sewing, after Elsie had come down from finishing her letter, and sent Chloe to the post-office with it.

"I don't wonder," she answered, looking up with a smile. "There was a time, a long while ago, when I was very much afraid of him myself, and even now I have such a wholesome dread of his displeasure as would keep me from any act of disobedience, if love was not sufficient to do that without help from any other motive."

"You are very fond of him, and he of you?"

"Yes, indeed! How could it be otherwise when for so many years each was all the other had? But I'm sure, quite sure that neither of us loves the other less because now we have mamma and darling little Horace."

"I should like to know them both," said Miss Stanhope. "I hope your father will bring them with him when he comes back for you."

"Oh, I hope he will! I want so much to have you know them. Mamma is so dear and sweet, almost as dear as papa himself. And Horace—well, I can't believe there ever was quite such another darling to be found," Elsie continued, with a light, joyous laugh.

"Ah!" said Aunt Wealthy with a sigh and a smile. "It is a good and pleasant thing to be young and full of life and gaiety, and to have kind, wise parents to look to for help and guidance. You will realize that when you grow old and have to be a prop for others to lean upon instead."

"Yes, dear auntie," Elsie answered, giving her a look of loving reverence, "but surely the passing years must have brought you so much wisdom and self-reliance that that can be no such very hard task to you."

"Ah, child!" replied the old lady, shaking her head. "I often feel that my stock of those is very small. But then how sweet it is to remember that I have a Father to whom I never shall grow old; never cease to be his little child, in constant need of his tender, watchful care to guard and guide. Though the gray hairs are on my head, the wrinkles of time, sorrow, and care upon my brow, he does not think me old enough to be left to take care of myself. No, he takes my hand in his and leads me tenderly and lovingly along, choosing each step for me, protecting me from harm, and providing for all my needs. What does he say? 'Even to your old age I am he; and even to hoar hairs will I carry you!'"

"Such sweet words! They almost reconcile one to growing old," murmured Lottie.

And Aunt Wealthy answered, with a subdued gladness in her tones, "You need not dread it, child, for does not every year bring us nearer home?"

The needles flew briskly until the dinner-bell sounded its welcome summons.

"We shall finish two at least this afternoon, I think," said Lottie, folding up her work.

"No, we've had sewing enough for today," replied Miss Stanhope. "I have ordered the carriage at two. We will have a drive this afternoon, and music this evening, if you and Elsie do not consider it too much of a task to play and sing for your old auntie."

"A task, Aunt Wealthy! It would be a double delight— giving you pleasure and ourselves enjoying the delicious tones of that splendid piano. Its fame has already spread over the whole town," she added, turning to Elsie, "and between its attractions and those of its owner, I know there'll be a great influx of visitors here."

Elsie was a very fine musician, and for her benefit during her stay in Lansdale, Mr. Dinsmore had had a grand piano sent on from the East, ordering it in season to have it arrive almost as soon as they themselves.

"Yes, Lottie is quite right about it, Aunt Wealthy, and you shall call for all the tunes you want," Elsie said, noticing her friend's prediction merely by a quiet smile.

"You don't know how I enjoy that piano," Lottie rattled on as they began their meal. "It must be vastly pleasant to have plenty of money and such an indulgent father as yours, Elsie. Not that I would depreciate my own at all—I wouldn't exchange him even for yours—but he, you see, has more children and less money."

"Yes, I think we are both blessed in our fathers," answered Elsie. "I admire yours very much, and mine is, indeed, very indulgent, though at the same time very strict. He never spares expense or trouble to give me pleasure. But the most delightful thing of all is to know that he loves me so very, very dearly," and the soft eyes shone with the light of love and joy.

It was nearly tea time when they returned from their drive, some lady callers having prevented them from setting out at the early hour intended.

"Now I must run right home," said Lottie, as they alighted. "Mother complains that she gets no good of me at all of late."

"Well, she has Nettie," returned Miss Stanhope, "and she told me Elsie and I might have all we wanted of you till the poor child gets a little used to her father's absence."

"Did she, Aunt Wealthy? There, I'll remind her of that, and also of the fact that Nettie is worth two of me any day."

"And you'll come back to spend the evening? Indeed you must, or how is Elsie to learn her visitors' names? You know I could never get them straight. But there's the tea-bell, so come in with us. No need to go home till bed-time, or till tomorrow, that I can see."

"Thank you, but of course, auntie, I want to primp a bit, just as you did in your young days, when the beaux were coming. So good-bye for the present," she cried, skipping away with a merry laugh, Miss Stanhope calling after her to bring Nettie along when she returned.

"We have so many odd names in this town, and I such an odd sort of memory, that I make a great many mistakes," said the old lady, leading the way to the house.

Elsie thought that was all very true, when in the course of the evening she was introduced to Mr. Comings, Mr. Tizard, Mr. Stop, Miss Lock, and Miss Over, and afterward heard her aunt address them variously as "Mr. In-and-out," "Mr. Wizard," "Mr. Lizard," "Mr. Quit," "Miss Under," and "Miss Key."

But the old lady's peculiarity was so well known that no one thought of taking offense, and her mistakes caused only mirth and amusement.

Lottie's prediction was so fully verified that Elsie seemed to be holding a sort of levee.

"What faultless features, exquisitely beautiful complexion, and sweet expression she has." "What a graceful form, what pleasant, affable manners, so entirely free from affectation or hauteur; no patronizing airs about her either, but perfect simplicity and kindliness." "And such a sweet, happy, intelligent face." "Such beautiful hair too; did you notice that? So abundant, soft and glossy, and such a lovely color." "Yes, and what simple elegance of dress." "She's an accomplished musician, too, and has a voice as sweet, rich, and full as a nightingale's," remarked one and another as they went away. The unanimous verdict seemed to be, that the young stranger was altogether charming.

Across the street, Mrs. Schilling's boarder paced to and fro, watching the coming and going, listening to the merry salutations, and gay adieu, the light laughter, and the sweet strains of music and song, till the desire to make one of the happy throng grew so strong upon him that it was no longer to be resisted.

"I will go in with those," he muttered, crossing over just in time to enter directly in the rear of a lady and gentleman, whom he saw coming up the street. "Miss Stanhope invited me to call again, without particularizing how soon, and I can turn my speedy acceptance into a compliment to their music, without even a white lie, for it does sound extremely attractive to a lonely, idle fellow like me."

Miss Stanhope met him at the door, would scarce listen to his apology, insisting that "none was needed," one who had come to her "with such an introduction from so valued a friend as Mrs. Waters, must always be a welcome guest" in her house, and ushering him into the parlor, introduced him to her niece, and all others present.

A nearer and more critical view of Elsie only increased his admiration. He thought her the loveliest creature he had ever seen. But it did not suit his tactics to show immediately any strong attraction toward her, or desire to win her regard. For this evening he devoted himself almost exclusively to Miss Stanhope, exerting all his powers to make a favorable impression upon her.

In this he was entirely successful. He had, when he chose, most agreeable and polished manners. Also he had seen much of the world, possessed a large fund of general information, and knew exactly how to use it to the best advantage. With these gifts, very fine, expressive eyes, regular features, and handsome person, no wonder he could boast himself "a woman-killer."

Aunt Wealthy, though old enough to be invulnerable to Cupid's arrows, showed by her warm praises, after he had left that evening, that she was not proof against his fascinations.

CHAPTER FOURTEENTH

Your noblest natures are most credulous.

—CHAPMAN

BROMLY EGERTON (we give him the name by which he had become known to our friends in Lansdale) considered it "a very lucky chance" that had provided him a boarding-place so near the temporary home of his intended victim. He felicitated himself greatly upon it, and lost no time in improving to the utmost all the advantages it conferred. It soon came to be a customary thing for him to drop in at Miss Stanhope's every day, or two or three times a day, and to join the young girls in their walks and drives, for, though at first paying court to no one but the mistress of the mansion, he gradually turned his attention more and more to her niece and Miss King.

As their ages were so much nearer his this seemed perfectly natural, and excited no suspicion or remark. Aunt Wealthy was quite willing to resign him to them, for—a very child in innocent trustfulness—she had no thought of any evil design on the part of the handsome, attractive young stranger so warmly recommended to her kindness and hospitality by an old and valued friend, and only rejoiced to see the young folks enjoying themselves so much together.

Before leaving Lansdale Mr. Dinsmore had provided his daughter with a gentle, but spirited and beautiful little pony, and bade her ride out every day when the weather was favorable, as was her custom at home. At the same time he cautioned her never to go alone, but always to have Simon riding in her rear, and, if possible, a lady friend at her side.

Dr. King was not wealthy, and having a large family to provide for, kept no horse except the one he used in his practice. But Elsie, with her well-filled purse, was more than content to furnish ponies for her friends Lottie and Nettie whenever they could accompany her, and matters were so arranged by their indulgent mother that one or both could do so every day.

It was not long before Mr. Egerton joined them in these excursions also, having made an arrangement with a livery-stable keeper for the daily use of a horse. And gradually his attention, in the beginning about equally divided between the two, or the three, were paid more and more exclusively to Elsie.

She was not pleased with him in their earlier interviews. She could scarcely have told why, but there was an intuitive feeling that he was not one to be trusted. That, however, gradually gave way under the fascinations of his fine person, agreeable manners, and intellectual conversation. He was very plausible and captivating, she full of charity and ready to believe the best of everybody, and so, little by little, he won her confidence and esteem so completely that at length she had almost forgotten that her first impression had not been favorable.

He went regularly to the church she, her aunt, and the Kings attended, appearing an interested listener, and devout worshipper, and that not on the Sabbath only, but also at the regular week-day evening service. He seemed also to choose his associates among good, Christian people. The natural inference from all this was that he too was a Christian, or at least a professor of religion, and thus all our friends soon came to look upon him as such, and to feel the greater friendship for, and confidence in him.

He found that Elsie's beauty would bear the closest

scrutiny, that her graces of person and mind were the more apparent the more thoroughly she was known, that she was highly educated and accomplished, possessed of a keen intellect, and talents of no common order, and a wonderful sweetness of disposition. He acknowledged to himself that, even leaving money out of the question, she was a prize any man might covet, yet that if she were poor, he would never try to win her. A more voluptuous woman would have suited him better. Elsie's very purity made her distasteful to him, his own character seeming so much blackened by contrast that at times he could but loathe and despise himself.

But her fortune was an irresistible attraction, and he resolved more firmly than ever to leave no stone unturned to make himself master of it.

He soon perceived that he had many rivals, but he possessed one advantage over them all in his entire leisure from business, leaving him at liberty to devote himself to her entertainment during the day as well as the evening.

For a while he greatly feared that he had a more dangerous rival at a distance, for, watching from his windows, he saw that every morning Simon brought one or more letters from the post, and that Elsie was usually on the front porch awaiting his coming; that she would often come flying across the lawn, meet her messenger at the gate, and snatching her letter with eager, joyful haste, rush back to the house with it, and disappear within the doorway. Then frequently he would see her half an hour later looking so rosy and happy, that he could hardly hope her correspondent was other than an accepted lover.

For weeks he tormented himself with this idea, the more convinced that he was right in his conjecture, because she almost always posted her reply with her own hands, when going out for her daily walk, or sent it by her faithful Chloe. But one day, venturing a jest upon the subject, she answered him, with a merry laugh, "Ah, you are no Yankee, Mr. Egerton, to make such a guess as that! I have a number of correspondents, it is true, but the daily letter I am so eager for comes from my father."

"Is it possible, Miss Dinsmore! Do you really receive and answer a letter from your father every day ?"

"We write every day, and each receives a letter from the other every day but Sunday. On that day we never go or send to the post-office, and we write only on such subjects as are suited to the sacredness of its Sabbath rest. I give papa the text and a synopsis of the sermon I have heard, and he does the same by me."

"You must be extremely strict Sabbath-keepers."

"We are, but not more so than the Bible teaches that we should be."

"But isn't it very irksome? Don't you find the day very long and tedious?"

"Not at all. I think no other day in the week is quite so short to me, none, I am sure, so delightful."

"Then it isn't only because your aunt is strict too, that you go on keeping your father's rules, while you are at a safe distance from him?" he queried in a half jesting tone.

Elsie turned her soft eyes full upon him, as she answered with gentle gravity: "I feel that the commands of both my earthly and my heavenly Father are binding upon me at all times, and in all places, and I hope I may ever be kept from becoming an eye-servant. Love makes it easy to obey and God's commands are not grievous to those who love him."

"I beg your pardon," he said, "but to go back to the letters, how can you fill one every day to your father? I can imagine that lovers might, in writing to each other, but fathers and daughters would not be apt to indulge in that sort of nonsense."

"But Mr. Dinsmore and Elsie are no common father and daughter," remarked Lottie, who had not spoken for the last ten minutes.

"And can find plenty to say to each other," added Elsie, with a bright look and smile. "Papa likes to hear just how I am spending my time, what I see in my walks, what new plants and flowers I find, etc., etc., what new acquaintances I make, what books I am reading, and what I think of them."

"The latter or the former?" he asked, resuming his jesting tone.

"Both. And I tell him almost everything. Papa is my confidant, more so than any other person in the world."

They were returning from a walk over the hills, and had just reached Miss Stanhope's gate. Mr. Egerton opened it for the ladies, closed it after them, bowed a good-morning and retired, wondering if he was mentioned in those letters to Mr. Dinsmore, and cautioning himself to be exceeding careful not to say or do a single thing which, if reported there, might be taken as a warning of danger to the heiress.

The girls ran into Miss Wealthy's room, and found her lamenting over a white muslin apron.

"What is it, auntie?" Elsie asked.

"Why, just look here, child, what a hole I have made in this! It had got an ink-stain on it, and Phillis had put one of Harry's new shirts into a tin basin, and iron-rusted it, so I thought I would try some citric acid on them both, and I did, but probably made it too strong, and this is how it served the apron."

"And the shirt?" asked Lottie, interested for the garment she had helped to make.

"Well, it's a comfort I handled it very gingerly, and it seems to be sound yet, after I saw what this has come to."

"It is quite a pity about the apron, for it really is a very pretty one," said Elsie. "The acid must have been very strong."

"Yes, and I am sorry to have the apron ruined, but after all, I shall not care so very much, if it only doesn't eat Harry's tail off, and it will make a little one for some child."

Both girls laughed. It was impossible to resist the inclination to do so.

"The shirt's tail I mean, of course, and a little apron," said Miss Wealthy, joining in the mirth. "That's where the spots all happen to be, which is a comfort in case a piece should have to be set in."

"There comes Lenwilla Ellawea, for some more light'ning, I suppose, as I see she carries a teacup in her hand," whispered Lottie, glancing from the window, as a step sounded upon the gravel walk. "Good-morning, little sixpence. What are you after now?" she added aloud, as the child appeared in the open doorway.

"Mother's out o' vinegar, and dinner's just ready, and the gentleman'll want some for his salad, and there ain't no time to send to the grocery. And mother says, will you lend her a teacupful, Aunt Wealthy? And she's goin' to have some folks there tonight, and she says you're all to come over."

"Tell her we're obliged, and she's welcome to the vinegar," said Miss Stanhope, taking the cup and giving it to Chloe to fill. "But what sort of company is it to be?"

"I dunno. Ladies and gentlemen, but no married folks, I heard her say. She's goin' to have nuts, and candies, and things to hand round, and you'd better come. I hope that pretty lady will," in a stage whisper, bending toward Miss Stanhope, as she spoke, and nodding at Elsie.

All three laughed.

"Well, I'll try to coax her," said Aunt Wealthy, as Chloe re-entered the room. "And here's your vinegar. You'd better hurry home with it."

"Aunt Wealthy, you can't want me to go there!" cried Elsie, as the child passed out of hearing. "Why, the woman is not a lady, and I am sure papa would be very unwilling to have me make an associate of her. He is very particular about such matters."

"She is not educated or very refined, it is true, my child; and I must acknowledge is a little silly, too, but she is a clever, kind-hearted woman, a member of the same church with myself, and a near neighbor whom I should feel sorry to hurt. And I am sure she would be much hurt if you should stay away, and deeply gratified by your attendance at her little party."

"I wouldn't miss it for anything!" cried Lottie, pirouetting about the room, laughing and clapping her hands. "She has such comical ways of talking and acting. I know it will be real fun. You won't think of staying away, Elsie?"

"I really do not believe your father would object, if he were here, my child," added Miss Stanhope, laying her hand on her niece's shoulder and looking at her with a kindly persuasive smile.

"Perhaps not, auntie; and he bade me obey you in his absence; so if you bid me, I will go," Elsie answered, returning the smile, and touching her ruby lips to the faded cheek.

"That's a dear," cried Lottie. "Hold her to her word, Aunt Wealthy. And now I must run home, and see if Nettie's had an invite, and what she's going to wear."

The ladies were just leaving the dinner-table, when Mrs. Schilling came rushing in. "Oh, excuse my informality in not waiting to ring, Miss Stanhope, but I'm in the biggest kind of a hurry. I've just put up my mind to make some sponge-cake for tonight, and I thought I'd best run over and get your prescription—you always have so much better luck than me. I don't know whether it's all in the luck though, or whether it's partly the difference in prescriptions—I know some follows one, and some another—and so, if you'll let me have yours, I'll be a thousand times obliged."

"Certainly, Mrs. Sixpence, you'll be as many times welcome," returned Aunt Wealthy, going for her receipt-book. "It's not to be a large party, is it?" she asked, coming back.

"No, ma'am, just a dozen or so of the young folks—such ladies and gentlemen which I thought would be agreeable to meet Miss Dinsmore. I hope you'll both be over and bright and early too, for I've heard say you don't never keep very late hours, Miss Dinsmore."

"No, papa does not approve of them, not for me at least. He is so careful of me, so anxious that I should keep my health."

"Well, I'm sure that's all right and kind. But you'll

come, both of you, won't you?" And receiving an assurance that such was their intention, she hurried away as fast as she had come.

"I wonder she cares to make a party when she must do all the work of preparing for it herself," said Elsie, looking after her as she sped across the lawn.

"She is strong and healthy, and used to work, and doubtless feels that it will be some honor and glory to be able to boast of having entertained the Southern heiress who is visiting Lansdale," Miss Stanhope answered in a half-jesting tone.

Elsie looked amused, then grave, as she replied: "It is rather humbling to one's pride to be valued merely or principally on account of one's wealth."

"Yes, but, dearie, those who know you don't value you for that, but for your own dear, lovable self. My darling, your old aunt is growing very fond of you, and can hardly bear to think how soon your father will be coming to carry you away again," she added, twinkling away a tear, as she took the soft, white hand, and pressed it affectionately in both her own.

"And I shall be so sorry to leave you, auntie. I wish we could carry you away with us. I have so often thought how happy my friend Lucy Carrington ought to be in having such a nice grandma. I have never had one, you know, for papa's stepmother would never own me for her grandchild; but you seem to be the very one I have always longed for."

"Thank you, dear," and Miss Stanhope sighed slightly. "Had your own grandmother, my sweet and dear sister Eva, been spared to this time, you would have had one to love and be proud of. Now, do you want to take a siesta? You must feel tired after this morning's long tramp, I should think, and I want you to be very bright and fresh tonight, that it may not harm you if you should happen to be kept up a little later than usual. You see I want to take such care of you, that when your father comes he can see only improvement in you, and feel willing to let me have you again someday."

"Thank you, you dear old auntie!" Elsie answered, giving her a hug. "I'm sure even he could hardly be more kindly careful of me than you are. But I am not very tired, and sitting in an easy-chair will give me all the rest I need. Haven't you some work for me? I've done nothing but enjoy myself in the most idle fashion all day."

"No, my sewing's all done now that the shirts are finished. But I must lie down whether you will or not. I can't do without my afternoon nap."

"Yes, do, auntie, and I shall begin tomorrow's letter to papa, finishing it in the morning with an account of the party."

She was busy with her writing when Lottie burst in upon her.

"I ran in," she said, "to propose that we all go over there together, and to ask you to come into our house when you're dressed. Nettie and I are going to try a new style of doing up our hair, and we want your opinion about its becomingness."

"I'll be happy to give it for what it is worth."

"By the way, I admire your style extremely. But of course no one could imitate it who was not blessed with a heavy suit of natural curls. You always wear it one way, don't you?"

"Yes, papa likes it so, but until within the last year, he would not let me have it in a comb at all."

She wore it now gathered into a loose knot behind, and falling over a comb, in a rich mass of shining curls, while in front it waved and rippled above her white forehead, or fell over it, in soft, tiny, golden brown rings.

"It is so beautiful!" continued Lottie, passing her hand caressingly over it. "And so is its wearer. Oh, if I were only a gentleman!"

"You don't wish it," said Elsie, laughing. "I don't believe a real, womanly woman ever does."

"You don't, hey? Well, I must go, for I've a lot to do to Lot King's wearing apparel. Adieu, mon cher. Nay, don't disturb yourself to come to the door."

Elsie came down to tea ready dressed for the evening,

in simple white, with a white rose in her hair.

"I like your taste in dress, child," said Aunt Wealthy, regarding her with affectionate admiration. "The rose in your hair is lovely, and you seem to me like a fresh, fair, sweet flower, yourself."

"Ah, how pleasant it is to be loved, auntie, for love always sees through rose-colored spectacles," answered the young girl gaily.

"I promised Lottie to run in there for a moment to give my opinion about their appearance," she said, as they rose from the table. "I'll not be gone long, and they're to come in and go with us."

She found her friends in the midst of their hair-dressing.

"Isn't it a bore?" cried Lottie. "How fortunate you are in never having to do this for yourself."

"Why," said Elsie," I was just admiring your independence, and feeling ashamed of my own helplessness."

"Did you ever try it, " asked Nettie, "doing your own hair, I mean?"

"No, never."

"Did you ever dress yourself?"

"No, I own that I have never so much as put on my own shoes and stockings," Elsie answered with a blush, really mortified at the thought.

"Well, it is rather nice to be able to help yourself," remarked Lottie complacently. "There! Mine's done; what do you think of it, Miss Dinsmore?"

"That it is very pretty and extremely becoming. Girls, mammy will dress your hair for you at any time, if you wish."

"Oh, a thousand thanks!" exclaimed Nettie. "Do you think she would be willing to come over and do mine now? I really can't get it to suit me, and I know Lot wants to put on her dress."

"Yes, I'll go back and send her."

"Oh, no; don't go yet; can't we send for her?"

"That would do; but I told Aunt Wealthy I wouldn't stay long, so I think I'd better go. Perhaps I can be of use to her."

"I don't believe she'll need any help with her toilet," said Lottie, "she does it all her own way. But I daresay she grudges every minute of your company. I know I should. Isn't she sweet and lovely, and good as she can be?" she added to her sister as Elsie left the room.

"Yes, and how tastefully she dresses. Everything is rich and beautiful, yet so simply elegant. What magnificent lace she wears, and what jewelry, yet not a bit too much of either."

"And she knows all about harmony of colors, and what suits her style, though I believe she would look well in anything."

There was a communicating gate between Dr. King's grounds and Miss Stanhope's, and Elsie gained her aunt's house by crossing the two gardens. As she stepped upon the porch, she saw Mr. Egerton standing before the door.

"Good-evening, Miss Dinsmore," he said, bowing and smiling. "I was just about to ring, but I presume that is not necessary now."

"No, not at all. Walk into the parlor, and help yourself to a seat. And if you will please excuse me I shall be there in a moment."

"I came to ask if I might have the pleasure of escorting you to the party," he said laughingly, as she returned from giving Chloe her directions, and asking if her aunt needed any assistance.

"Thank you, but you are taking unnecessary trouble," she answered gaily, "since it is only across the street, and there are four of us to keep each other company."

"The Misses King are going with you?"

"Yes. They are not quite ready yet, but it is surely too early to think of going?"

"A little, but Mrs. Schilling is anxious to see you as soon as possible, particularly as she understands there is no hope of keeping you after ten o'clock. Do you really always observe such early hours?"

"As a rule, yes. I believe the medical authorities agree that it is the way to retain one's youth and health."

"And beauty," he added, with an admiring glance at her blooming face.

"I do believe we shall be almost the first—very unfashionably early," remarked Nettie King, as their little party crossed the street.

"We are not the first, I have seen several go in," rejoined Aunt Wealthy, as Mr. Egerton held open the gate for them to pass in.

Mrs. Schilling in gay attire, streamers flying, cheeks glowing, and eyes beaming with delight, met them at the door, and invited them to enter.

"Oh, ladies, good-evening. How do you all do? I'm powerful glad you came so early. Walk right into the parlor."

She ushered them in as she spoke. Four or five young misses were standing about the centre-table, looking at prints, magazines, and photographs, while Lenwilla Ellawca, arrayed in her Sunday best, had ensconced herself in a large cushioned rocking-chair. She was leaning lazily back in it, and stretching out her feet in a way to show her shoes and stockings to full advantage. Mrs. Schilling had singular taste in dress. The child wore a Swiss muslin over a red flannel skirt, and her lower limbs were encased in black stockings and blue shoes.

"Daughter Lenwilla Ellawea, subside that chair!" exclaimed the mother, with a wave of her hand. "You should know better than to take the best seat, when ladies are standing. Miss Stanhope, do me the honor to take that chair. I assure you, you will find it most commodious. Take a seat on the sofy, Miss Dinsmore, and— ah, that is right, Mr. Egerton, you know how to attend to the ladies."

Greetings and introductions were exchanged. An uncomfortable pause followed, then a young lady, with a magazine open on the table before her, broke the silence by remarking: "What sweet verses these are!"

"Yes, " said Mrs. Schilling, looking over her shoulder. "I quite agree in that sentiment. Indeed, she's my favorite author."

"Who?" asked Mr. Egerton.

"Anon."

"Ah! Does she write much for that periodical?" he asked, with assumed gravity.

"Oh, yes, she has a piece in nearly every number, sometimes two of 'em."

"That's my pap, that is," said Lenwilla Ellawea, addressing a second young lady, who was slowly turning the leaves of a photograph album.

"Is it?"

"Yes, and we've got two or three other picters of him."

"Photographs, Lenwilla Ellawea," corrected her mother. "Yes, we've got several. Miss Stanhope, do you know there's a sculpture in town? And what do you think? He wants to make a basque relief out o' one o' them photo graphs of my 'Lijah. But I don't know as I'll let him. Would you?"

A smile trembled about the corners of Elsie's lips, and she carefully avoided the glance of Lottie's eyes, which she knew were dancing with fun while there was a half-suppressed titter from the girls at the table.

"I really can't say I understand exactly what it is," said Aunt Wealthy dubiously.

"What sort of looking creature is a sculpture, Mrs. Schilling?" asked Mr. Egerton.

"Excuse me, there's some more company coming," she answered, hurrying from the room.

"My good landlady is really quite an amusing person," he observed in an aside to Elsie, near to whom he had seated himself.

She made no response. The newly-arrived guests were being ushered in, and there were fresh greetings and introductions to be gone through with. Then conversation became quite brisk, and after a little, it seeming to be understood that all invited, or expected, were present, someone proposed playing games. They tried several of the quieter kind, then Lottie King proposed "Stage-coach."

"Lot likes that because she's a regular romp," said her sister.

"And because she tells the story so well. She's just splendid at it!" cried two or three voices. "Will you take that part if we agree to play it?"

"Yes, if no one else wants it."

"No danger of that. We'll play it. Miss Dinsmore, will you take part?"

"Thank you, I never heard of the game before, and should not know what to do."

"Oh, it's easy to understand. Each player—except the story-teller—takes the name of some part of the stage-coach, or something connected with it. One is the wheels, another the window, another the whip, another the horses, driver, and so on, and so on. After all are named and seated—leaving one of their number out, and no vacancy in the circle—the one left out stands in the centre, and begins a story, in which he or she introduces the names chosen by the others as often as possible. Each must be on the qui vive, and the instant his name is pronounced, jump up, turn round once and sit down again. If he neglects to do so, he has to pay a forfeit. If the word stage-coach is pronounced, all spring up and change seats, the story-teller securing one, if he can and leaving someone else to try his hand at that."

Lottie acquitted herself well. Mr. Egerton followed, doing even better. Then Aunt Wealthy was the one left out, and with her crooked sentences and backward or opposite rendering of names caused shouts of merriment. The selling of the forfeits which followed was no less mirth-provoking. Then the refreshments were brought in: first, several kinds of cake—the sponge and the farmers' fruit-cake, made after Miss Stanhope's prescription, as Mrs. Schilling informed her guests, and one or two other sorts. Elsie declined them all, saying that she never ate any thing in the evening.

"Oh, now that's too bad, Miss Dinsmore! Do take a little bit of something," urged her hostess. "I shall feel real hurt if you don't. It looks just as if you didn't think my victuals good enough for you to eat."

"Indeed you must not think that," replied Elsie,

blushing deeply. "Your cake looks very nice, but I always decline evening refreshments, and that solely because of the injury it would be to my health to indulge in them."

"Why, you ain't delicate, are you? You don't look so. You've as healthy a color as ever I see, not a bit like as though you had the dyspepsy."

"No, I have never had a touch of dyspepsia, and I think my freedom from it is largely owing to papa's care of me in regard to what I eat and when. He has never allowed me to eat cake in the evening."

"Well, I do say! You're the best girl to mind your pa that ever I see! But you're growed up now—'most of age, I should judge—and I reckon you've a sort o' right to decide such little matters for yourself. I don't believe a bit o' either of these would hurt you a mite, and if it should make you a little out o' sorts just you take a dose of spirits of pneumonia. That's my remedy for sick stomic, and it cures me right up, it does."

Elsie smiled, but again gently but firmly declined. "Please don't tempt me any more, Mrs. Schilling," she said, "for it is a temptation, I assure you."

"Well, p'raps you'll like the next course better," rejoined her hostess, moving on.

"She's a splendid cook and the cake is really nice," remarked Lottie King in a low tone, close at her friend's side.

"Yes, Miss Dinsmore, you'd better try a little of it. I don't believe it would hurt you, even so much as to call for the spirits of pneumonia," said Egerton, laughing.

"Oh, look!" whispered Lottie, her eyes twinkling with merriment. "Here comes the second course served up in the most original style."

Mrs. Schilling had disappeared for a moment, to return bearing a wooden bucket filled with a mixture of candies, raisins and almonds, and was passing it around among her guests, inviting each to take a handful.

"Now, Miss Dinsmore, you won't refuse to try a few of these?" she said persuasively, as she neared their corner. "I shall be real disappointed if you do."

"I am very sorry to decline your kind offer, even more for my own sake than yours," returned Elsie, laughing and blushing, "for I am extremely fond of confectionery. But I must say no, thank you."

"Mr. Egerton, do you think 'twas because my cakes and things wasn't good enough for her that she wouldn't taste 'em?" asked his landlady, in an aggrieved tone, as the last of the guests departed.

Elsie had gone an hour before, he having had the pleasure of escorting her and Miss Stanhope across the street, leaving them at their own door, but he did not need to ask whom Mrs. Schilling meant.

"Oh, no, not at all, my good woman!" he answered. "It was nothing but filial obedience joined to the fear of losing her exuberant health. Very wise, too, though your refreshments were remarkably nice."

"Poor Mrs. Sixpence," Lottie King was saying to her sister at that moment. "She whispered to me that though her party had gone off so splendidly, she had had two great disappointments: in Mr. Wert's absenting himself, and the refusal of the Southern heiress to so much as taste her carefully prepared dainties."

Chapter Fifteenth

A goodly apple rotten at the heart;
O what a goodly outside falsehood hath!

—Shakespeare's Merchant of Venice

IN MENTAL POWER, education, good looks, courtly manners, and general information Mr. Egerton was decidedly superior to any of the young men resident in Lansdale, and of this fact no one was better aware than himself. He did not confine his attentions to Elsie, and soon found himself a prime favorite among the ladies of the town. No female coquette ever coveted the admiration of the other sex more than he, or sought more assiduously to gain it. He carried on numerous small flirtations among the belles of the place, yet paid court to Elsie much oftener than to anyone else, using every art of which he was master in the determined effort to win her affection and to make himself necessary to her happiness.

He had read many books and seen much of life, having traveled all over our own country, and visited both Europe and South America; and possessing a retentive memory, fine descriptive powers, a fund of humor, and a decided talent for mimicry, was able, when he chose, to make his conversation exceedingly amusing and interesting, and very instructive. Also, he seemed all that was good and noble, and she soon gave him a very warm place in her regard, much warmer than she herself at first suspected.

According to his own account—and probably it was the truth—Bromly Egerton had had many hair-breadth escapes from sudden and violent death. He was telling of one of these in which he had risked and nearly lost his life from mere love of adventure. Elsie shuddered, and drew a long breath of relief, as the story reached its close.

"Does it frighten you to hear of such things?" he asked, with a smile.

"Yes, it seems to me a dreadful thing to risk the loss of one's life, when there is no good to ourselves or others to be gained by it."

"Ah, if you were a man or boy you would understand that more than half the charm of such adventures lies in the risk."

"But is it right, or wise?"

"A mere matter of taste, or choice, I should say—a long dull life, or a short and lively one."

Elsie's face had grown very grave. "Are those really your sentiments, Mr. Egerton?" she asked, in a pained, disappointed tone. "I had thought better of you."

"I do not understand. Have I said anything very dreadful?"

"Is it not a sin to throw away the life which God has given us to be used in his service?"

"Ah, perhaps that may be so, but I had not looked at it in precisely that way. I had only thought of the fact that life in this world is not so very delightful that one need be anxious to continue it for a hundred years. We grow tired of it at times, and are almost ready to throw it away; to use your expression."

"Ah, before doing that we should be very sure of going to a better place."

"But how can we be sure of that, or, indeed, of anything? What is there that we know absolutely, and beyond question? How can I be sure of even my own existence? How do I know that I am what I believe myself to be? There are crazy men who firmly believe themselves kings and princes, or something else quite as far from the truth, and how do I know that I am not as much mistaken as they?"

She gave him a look of grieved surprise, and he laughingly asked, "Well, now, Miss Dinsmore, is there anything of which you really are absolutely certain? Or you, Miss king?" as Lottie drew near the log on which the two were seated.

They had taken a long ramble through the woods that morning, and Egerton and Elsie had some ten minutes before sat down here to rest and wait for their companions, who had wandered a little from the path they were pursuing.

"Cogito, ergo sum," she answered gaily. "Also I am sure we have had a very pleasant walk. But isn't it time we were moving toward home?"

"Yes," Elsie answered, consulting her watch.

"That's a pretty little thing," observed Egerton. "May I look at it?" And he held out his hand.

"One of papa's birthday gifts to his petted only daughter," she said, with a smile, as she allowed him to take it. "I value it very highly on that account even more than for its intrinsic worth, though it is an excellent time-keeper."

"It must have cost a pretty penny; the pearls and diamonds alone must be worth quite a sum," he said, turning it about and examining it with eager interest. "I would be careful, Miss Dinsmore, how I let it be known that I carried any thing so valuable about me, or wore it into lonely places, such as these woods," he added, as he returned it to her.

"I never come out alone," she said, looking slightly anxious and troubled. "Papa laid his commands upon me never to do so. But I shall leave it at home in future."

"Riches bring cares, that's the way I comfort myself in my poverty," remarked Lottie, lightly. "But, Elsie, my dear, don't allow anxious fears to disturb you. We are a very moral people at Lansdale. I never heard of a robbery there yet."

"I believe I am naturally rather timid," said Elsie, "yet I seldom suffer from fear. I always feel very safe when papa is near to protect me, and our heavenly

Father's care is always about us."

"That reminds me that you have not answered my question," remarked Egerton, switching off the head of a clover-blossom with his cane. "Is the care you speak of one thing of which you feel certain?"

"Yes, and there are others."

"May I ask what?"

She turned her sweet, soft eyes full upon him as she answered in low, clear tones, "'I know that in me (that is, in my flesh) dwelleth no good thing.' 'I know that my Redeemer liveth.' 'I know that it shall be well with them that fear God.'"

"You are quoting?"

"Yes, from a book that I know is true. Do you doubt it, Mr. Egerton?"

"Why, Miss Dinsmore, you do not take me for an infidel, surely?"

"No, until today I had hoped you were a Christian."

Her eyes were downcast now, and there were tears in her voice as she spoke. He saw he had made a false step and lowered himself in her esteem, yet, remembering his talk with Arthur, he felt certain he could more than retrieve that error. And he grew exultant in the thought of the evident pain the discovery of his unbelief had caused her. "She does care for me. I believe the prize is even now almost within my reach," he said to himself, as they silently pursued their way into the town, no one speaking again until they parted at Miss Stanhope's gate.

Elsie, usually full of innocent mirth and gladness, was very quiet at dinner that day, and Aunt Wealthy, watching her furtively, thought she noticed an unwonted shade of sadness on the fair face.

"What is it, dear?" she asked at length. "Something seems to have gone wrong with you."

The young girl replied by repeating the substance of the morning's talk with Mr. Egerton, and expressing her disappointment at the discovery that he was not the Christian man she had taken him to be.

"Perhaps what you have taken in earnest, was but

spoken in jest, my child," said Miss Stanhope.

"Ah, auntie, but a Christian surely could not say such things even in jest," she answered, with a little sigh, and a look of sorrowful concern on her face.

Half an hour later, Elsie sat reading in the abode of the vine-covered porch, while her aunt enjoyed her customary after-dinner nap. She presently heard the gate swing to, and the next moment Mr. Egerton was helping himself to a seat by her side.

"I hope I don't intrude, Miss Dinsmore," he began, assuming a slightly embarrassed air.

"Oh, no, not at all," she answered, closing her book, "but aunt is lying down, and—"

"Ah, no matter. I wouldn't have her disturbed for the world, and in fact I am rather glad of the opportunity of seeing you alone. I—I have been thinking a good deal of that talk we had this morning, and—I am really quite shocked at the sentiments I then expressed, though they were spoken more than half in jest. Miss Dinsmore, I am not a Christian, but—but I want to be, and would, if I only knew how, and I've come to you to learn the way, for somehow I seem to feel that you could make the thing plainer to me than anyone else. What must I do first?"

Glad tears shone in the soft eyes she lifted to his face as she answered, "'Believe on the Lord Jesus Christ and thou shalt be saved.' Believe, 'only believe.'"

"But I must do something?"

"'Let the wicked forsake his way and the unrighteous man his thoughts, and let him return unto the Lord, and he will have mercy upon him, and to our God, for he will abundantly pardon.'"

The man was an arrant knave and hypocrite, simulating anxiety about his soul's salvation only for the purpose of ingratiating himself with Elsie, but "the sword of the spirit, which is the word of God," pricked him for the moment, as she wielded it in faith and prayer. What ways, what thoughts were his! Truly they had need to be forsaken if he would hope ever to see that holy city of which we are told "There shall in no wise enter it anything that defileth, neither whatsoever worketh abomination, or maketh a lie."

For a moment he sat silent and abashed before the gentle, earnest young Christian, feeling her very purity a reproach, and fearing that she must read his hypocrisy and the baseness of his motives in his countenance.

But hers was a most innocent and unsuspicious nature, apt to believe others as true and honest as herself. She went on presently. "It is so beautifully simple and easy—God's way of saving us poor sinners. It is its very simplicity that so stumbles wise men and women, while little children, in their sweet trustfulness, just taking God at his word, understand it without any difficulty." She spoke in a musing tone, not looking at Egerton at all, but with her eyes fixed meditatingly upon the floor.

He perceived that she had no doubts of his sincerity, and rallying from the thrust she had so unconsciously given him, went on with the rôle he had laid down for himself.

"I fear I am one of the wise ones you speak of, for I confess I do not see the way yet. Can you not explain it more fully?"

"I will try, " she said. "You believe that you are a sinner deserving of God's wrath?"

"Yes."

"You have broken his law, and his justice demands your punishment, but Jesus has kept its requirements and borne its penalty in your stead, and now offers you his righteousness and salvation as a free gift, 'without money and without price.'"

"But what am I to do?"

"Simply take the offered gift."

"But how? I fear I must seem very obtuse, but I really do not comprehend."

"Then ask for the teachings of the Spirit. Ask Jesus to give you repentance and faith. 'Ask, and it shall be given you; seek, and ye shall find; knock, and it shall be opened unto you; for every one that asketh receiveth; and he that seeketh, findeth; and to him that knocketh, it shall be opened.'"

Elsie's voice was low and pleading, her tones were tremulous with earnest entreaty, the eyes she lifted to his face were half filled with tears, for she felt that the eternal interests of her hearer were trembling in the balance.

He looked at her admiringly, and, lost in the contemplation of her beauty, had almost betrayed himself by his want of interest in what she was saying. But just then Miss Stanhope joined them, and shortly after he took his leave.

From this time Egerton played his part with consummate skill, deceiving Elsie so completely that she had not the slightest doubt of his being an humble, penitent, rejoicing believer. And great were her joy and thankfulness when he told her that she had been the means of leading him to Christ, that her words had made the way plain to him, as he had never been able to see it before. It seemed to her a very tender, strong tie between them, and he appeared to feel it to be so also.

She was not conscious of looking upon him in the light of a lover, but he saw with secret exultation that he was fast winning her heart. He read it in the flushing of her cheek and the brightening of her eye at his approach, and in many other unmistakable signs. He wrote to Arthur that the prize was nearly won, so nearly that he had no doubt of his ultimate success.

"And I'll not be long now about finishing up the job," he continued. "It's such precious hard work to be so good and pious all the time, that I can hardly wait till matters are fully ripe for action. I'm in constant danger of letting the mask slip aside in some unguarded moment, and so undoing the whole thing after the world of trouble it has cost me. It's no joke, I can assure you, for a man of my tastes and habits to lead the sort of life I've led for the last three months. I believe I'd give her up this minute, fortune and all, if the winning of them would lay me under the necessity of continuing it for the rest of my days, or even for any length of time. But once the knot is tied, and the property secured, there'll be an end of this farce. I'll let her know I'm done with cant, will neither talk it nor listen to it."

Arthur Dinsmore's face darkened as he read, and in a sudden burst of fury he tore the letter into fragments, then threw them into the empty grate. He was not yet so hardened as to feel willing to see Elsie in the power of such a heartless wretch, such a villain as he knew Tom Jackson to be. Many times already had he bitterly repented of having told him of her wealth, and helped him to an acquaintance with her. His family pride revolted against the connection, and some latent affection for his niece prompted him to save her from the life of misery that must be hers as the wife of one so utterly devoid of honor or integrity.

Yet Arthur lacked the moral courage to face the disagreeable consequences of a withdrawal from his compact with Jackson, and a confession to his father or Horace of the wretch's designs upon Elsie and his own disgraceful entanglement with him. He concluded to take a middle course. He wrote immediately to Jackson, somewhat haughtily, advising him at once to give up the whole thing.

"You will inevitably fail to accomplish your end," he said. "Elsie will never marry without her father's consent, and that you will find it utterly impossible to gain. Horace is too sharp to be hoodwinked or deceived, even by you. He will ferret out your whole past, lay bare the whole black record of your rascalities and hypocrisies, and forbid his daughter ever again to hold the slightest communication with you. And she will obey if it kills her on the spot."

"There's some comfort in that last reflection," muttered Arthur to himself, as he folded and sealed his epistle. "No danger of the rascal getting into the family."

Two days later, Egerton took this letter from the post-office in Lansdale. He read it with a scowl on his brow. "Ah! I see your game, young man," he muttered with an oath, "but you'll find that you've got hold of the wrong customer. My reply shall be short and sweet, and quite to the point."

It ran thus: "Your warning and advice come too late, my young friend. The mischief is already wrought, and however unworthy your humble servant may be deemed by yourself or others of its members to become connected with the illustrious D—family, they will find they cannot help themselves. The girl loves me, and believes in me, and I defy all the fathers and relations in creation to keep us apart." Then followed some guarded allusions to various sums of borrowed money, and so-called "debts of honor," and to some compact by which they were to be annulled, accompanied by a threat of exposure if that agreement were not kept to the very letter.

CHAPTER SIXTEENTH

Thou shalt not see me blush,
Nor change my countenance for this arrest.

—SHAKESPEARE'S HENRY VI, PART 1

IT WAS A SULTRY summer night. In the grounds of one of the largest and most beautiful of the many elegant country seats to be found in the suburbs of Cincinnati two gentlemen were pacing leisurely to and fro.

They were friends who had met that day for the first time in several years, strongly attached friends, spite of a very considerable difference in their ages. They had had much to say to each other for the first few hours, but it was now several minutes since either had spoken.

The silence was broken by the younger of the two exclaiming in a tone of hearty congratulation, "This is a magnificent place, Beresford! It does my heart good to see you so prosperous!"

"It is a fine place, Travilla, but," and he heaved a deep sigh, "I sometimes fear my wealth is to prove anything but a blessing to my children; that in fact my success in acquiring it is to be the ruin of my first-born."

"Ah, I hope not! Is Rudolph not doing well?"

"Well?" groaned the father, dropping his head upon his breast. "He seems to be rushing head-long to destruction. Have you not noticed his poor mother's sad and careworn look? Or mine? That boy is breaking our hearts. I could not speak of it to everyone, but to you, my long-tried friend, I feel that I may unburden myself, sure of genuine sympathy—" And he went on to tell how his son, becoming early imbued with the idea that his father's wealth precluded all necessity of exertion on his part, had grown up in habits of idleness that led to dissipation, and going on from bad to worse, was now a drunkard, a gambler, and frequenter of low haunts of vice.

"Day and night he is a heavy burden upon our hearts," continued the unhappy father. "When he is with us we find it most distressing to behold the utter wreck his excesses are making of him, and when he is out of our sight it is still worse, for we don't know what sin or danger he may be running into. Indeed at times we are almost distracted. Ah, Travilla, much as I love my wife and children, I am half tempted to envy your bachelor exemption from such care and sorrow!"

Mr. Travilla's kind heart was deeply moved. He felt painfully conscious of his own inability to comfort in such sorrow, but spoke of God's power to change the heart of the most hardened sinner, his willingness to save, and his promises to those who seek his aid in the time of trouble.

"Thank you. I knew you would feel for us. Your sympathy does me good," returned Mr. Beresford, grasping his friend's hand and pressing it between his own. "Your words too, for however well we know these truths we are apt to forget them, even when they are most needed.

"But it is growing late, and you must be weary after your journey. Let me show you to your room."

Three days passed in which Rudolph was not once seen in his home, and his parents were left in ignorance of his whereabouts. They exerted themselves for the pleasure and entertainment of their guest, but he could see plainly that they were enduring torture of anxiety and suspense.

Late in the evening of the third day, Mr. Beresford said to him, "My carriage is at the door. I must go into town and search for my boy. I have done so vainly several times since he last left his home, but I must try again tonight. Will you go with me?"

Travilla consented with alacrity, and they set out at once.

While on their way to the city Mr. Beresford explained that, for some time past, he had had reason to fear that his son was frequenting one of its gambling-hells, that thus far he had failed in his efforts to gain admittance, in order to search for him, but today, a professed gambler, well known in the house, had come to him and offered his assistance.

"As his convoy, I think we shall get in," added Mr. Beresford. "I cannot fathom the man's motives, but suspect he owes a grudge to a new-comer, who, he says, is winning large sums from Rudolph. I shall drive to Smith's livery stable, leave my horse and carriage there, then walk on to the place, which is only a few squares distant. Our guide is to meet us at the first corner from Smith's."

This programme was carried out. Their guide was in waiting at the appointed place, and at once conducted them to the gambling-house Mr. Beresford had spoken of. They were admitted without question or demur, and in another moment found themselves standing beside a table where a number of men were at play, nearly all so absorbed in their game as to seem entirely unconscious of the presence of spectators.

Two of them, pitted against each other, and both young, though there must have been several years' difference in their ages, particularly attracted Travilla's attention, and glancing at his friend, he saw that it was the same with him—that his eyes were fixed upon the face of the younger of the two, with an expression of keen distress, while he trembled with emotion, and almost gasped for breath, as he leaned toward him, and whispered, "It is he—my son."

At the same instant the young man's face grew deadly pale, he started up with a wild, ringing cry, "I am ruined!" drew a pistol from his breast, and placed the muzzle to his mouth.

But Mr. Travilla, springing forward, struck it from his

hand ere he could pull the trigger.

A scene of much excitement and confusion followed, in the midst of which young Beresford was led away by his father and Travilla.

A week later the latter gentleman reached Lansdale, arriving there in the early morning train. He put up at its principal hotel, and having refreshed himself by a few hours' sleep, a bath, and breakfast, inquired the way to Miss Stanhope's.

Elsie was just coming down the front stairway as he appeared before the open door, and was about to ring for admittance.

"Oh, Mr. Travilla, my dear old friend! Who would have expected to see you here?" she cried, in delighted surprise, as she bounded forward to meet him, with both hands extended in joyous greeting.

He took them in his, and kissed her first on one cheek, then on the other. "Still fresh and blooming as a rose, and with the same happy light in the sweet brown eyes," he said, gazing fondly into their tender depths.

"And you are the same old flatterer," she answered gaily, a rich color mantling her cheek. "Come in and sit down. But oh, tell me when did you see papa last? And mamma, and little Horace? Ah, the sight of you makes me homesick for them."

"I left them at Cape May, about a fortnight since, all well and happy, but missing you very much. I think papa will hardly be able to do without his darling much longer."

"Nor his darling without him. Oh, dear! Sometimes I get to wanting him so badly that I feel as if I should have to write to him to come for me at once. But excuse me while I go and call Aunt Wealthy."

"Not yet. Let us have a little chat together first."

Of course, after so long a separation, such old and tried friends would find a great deal to say to each other. The time slipped away very fast and half an hour afterward Mr. Egerton, coming in without ringing—a liberty he sometimes took of late—found them seated close together on the sofa, talking earnestly, Elsie with her hand in that of her friend, and a face even brighter and happier than its wont.

Mr. Travilla had one of those faces that often seem to come to a stand-still as regards age, and to scarcely know any change for many years. He was at this time thirty-four, but would have passed readily for twenty-five. Egerton thought him no more than that, and at once took him for a successful rival.

"Excuse me, Miss Dinsmore," he said, bowing stiffly. "I should have waited to ring, but—"

"Oh, never mind, Mr. Egerton," she said. "Let me introduce you to my old friend, Mr. Travilla—"

But she stopped in astonishment and dismay. Mr. Travilla had risen, and the two stood confronting each other like mortal foes.

Mr. Travilla was the first to speak. "I have met you before, sir!" he said with stern indignation.

"Indeed! That must be a mistake, sir, for upon my word and honor I never set eyes on you before."

"Your honor! The honor of a sharper, a black-leg, a—"

"Sir, do you mean to insult me? By what right do you apply such epithets to me? Pray where did you ever meet me?"

"In a gambling-hell in Cincinnati. The time, one week ago tonight, the occasion, the playing of a game of cards between young Beresford and yourself in which you were the winner—by what knavery you best know—the stakes so heavy that, on perceiving that he had lost, the young man cried out that he was ruined, and in his mad despair attempted self-destruction. It is quite possible that you may not have observed me in the crowd that gathered about your wretched victim, but I can never forget the face of the man who had wrought his ruin."

Egerton's countenance expressed the utmost astonishment and incredulity. "I have not been in Cincinnati for two months." he averred, "and all I know of that affair I have learned from the daily papers. But I shall not stay here to be insulted by you, sir. Good-afternoon,

Miss Dinsmore. I hope to be allowed an early opportunity to explain this, and to be able to do so to your entire satisfaction."

He bowed and withdrew, hastening from the house with the rapid step of one who is filled with a just indignation.

Mr. Travilla turned to Elsie. She was sitting there on the sofa, with her hands clasped in her lap, and a look of terror and anguish on her face, from which every trace of color had fled.

His own grew almost as pale, and his voice shook, as again sitting down beside her, and laying his hand on hers, he said, "My poor child! Can it be possible that you care for that wretch?"

"Oh, don't !" she whispered hoarsely and turning away her face. "I cannot believe it. There must be some dreadful mistake."

Then, recovering her composure by a mighty effort, she rose and introduced her aunt, who entered the room at that moment.

Mr. Travilla sat for some time conversing with her, Elsie joining in occasionally, but with a tone and manner from which all the brightness and vivacity had fled. Then he went away, declining a pressing invitation to stay to dinner but promising to be there to tea.

The moment he was gone Miss Stanhope was busied in beating up her cushions, and Elsie flew to her room, where she walked back and forth in a state of great agitation. But the dinner-bell rang, and composing herself as well as she could, she went down. Her cheeks were burning, and she seemed unnaturally gay, but ate very little as her aunt noticed with concern.

The meal was scarcely over, when a ring at the door-bell was followed by the sound of Mr. Egerton's voice asking for Miss Dinsmore.

"Ah!" said Miss Stanhope with an arch smile. "He does not ask this hour for me, knowing it's the time of my siesta."

Elsie found Egerton pacing the parlor floor to and fro. He took her hand, led her to the sofa, and sitting down by her side, began at once to defend himself against Mr. Travilla's charge. He told her he had never been guilty of gambling; he had "sowed some wild oats" years ago—getting slightly intoxicated on two or three occasions, and things of that sort—but it was all over and repented of, and surely she could not think it just and right that it should be brought up against him now.

As to Mr. Travilla's story—the only way he could account for the singular mistake was in the fact that he had a cousin who bore the same name as himself, and resembled him so closely that they had been frequently mistaken for each other. And that cousin, most unfortunately, especially on account of the likeness, did both drink and gamble. He was delighted by the look of relief that came over Elsie's face, as he told her this. She cared for him, then. Yet her confidence had been shaken.

"Ah, you doubted me, then?" he said in a tone of sorrowful reproach.

"Oh! I could not bear to think it possible. I was sure there must be a mistake somewhere," she said with a beautiful smile.

"But you are quite satisfied now?"

"Quite."

Then he told her he loved her very dearly, better than his own soul, that he found he could not live without her, life would not be worth having, unless she would consent to share it with him. Would she, oh, would she promise "someday to be his own precious little wife?"

Elsie listened with downcast, blushing face, and soft eyes beaming with joy, for the events of that day had revealed to her the fact that this man had made himself master of her heart.

"Will you not give to me a word of hope?" pleaded Egerton.

"I—I cannot, must not, without my father's permission," she faltered, "and oh! He forbade me to listen to anything of the kind. I am too young, he says."

"When was that?"

"Three years ago."

"Ah! But you are older now and you will let me write and ask his consent? I may say that you are not quite indifferent to me?"

"Yes," she murmured, turning her sweet, blushing face away from his ardent gaze.

"Thank you, dearest, a thousand thanks!" he cried, pressing her hand in his. "And now may I ask who and what that Mr. Travilla is?"

She explained, winding up by saying that he was much like a second father to her.

"Father!" he exclaimed. "He doesn't look a day over twenty-five."

"He is about two years younger than papa and doesn't look any younger, I think," she answered with a smile. "But strangers are very apt to take papa for my brother."

Egerton left an hour before Mr. Travilla came, and that hour Elsie spent in her own room in a state of great excitement—now full of the sweet joy of loving and being loved, now trembling with apprehension at the thought of the probable effect of Mr. Travilla's story upon her father. She was fully convinced of Egerton's truth and innocence, yet quite aware that his explanation might not prove so satisfactory to Mr. Dinsmore.

"Oh, papa, papa!" she murmured, as she paced restlessly to and fro. "How can I obey if you bid me give him up? And yet I must. I know it will be my duty, and that I must."

"What a color you hab in your cheeks, darlin'! An' how your eyes do shine. I'se 'fraid you's gettin' a fever," said Chloe, with an anxious, troubled gaze into her young lady's face, as she came in to dress her for the evening.

"Oh, no, mammy, I am perfectly well," Elsie answered with a slight laugh. Then seating herself before the glass, "Now do your best," she said gaily, "for we are to have company to tea. I doubt if you can guess whom?"

"Den 'spose my pet saves her ole mammy de trouble.

'Taint massa, for sure?"

"No, not quite so welcome a guest, but one you'll be delighted to see. Mr. Travilla."

"Ki, darlin'! He not here?"

"Yes, he came this morning. Ah! I knew you'd be delighted."

Elsie knew that it would require the very strongest proof to convince her father of the truth of Mr. Egerton's story, but hoped to find Mr. Travilla much more ready to give it credence. She was proportionably disappointed when, on hearing it from her, he scouted it as utterly unworthy of belief, or even examination.

"No, my child," he said, "the man's face is indelibly impressed upon my memory, and I can not be mistaken in his identity."

Elsie's face flushed crimson, and indignant tears sprang to her eyes and trembled in her voice as she answered, "I never knew you so uncharitable before, sir. I could not have believed it of my kind-hearted, generous old friend."

He gave her a very troubled, anxious look, as he replied, "Why should you take it so to heart, Elsie? Surely this man is nothing to you."

"He is to be someday, if papa will permit," she murmured, turning away her blushing face from his gaze.

Mr. Travilla uttered a groan, made two or three rapid turns across the room, and coming back to her side, laid his hand in an affectionate, fatherly manner upon her shoulder.

"My dear," he said with emotion, "I don't know when I have heard anything that distressed me so much, or that could give such pain and distress to your doting father."

"Mr. Travilla, you will not, you cannot be so unkind, so cruel, as to try to persuade papa to think as you do of—of Mr. Egerton?"

Her tone was half indignant, half imploring, and her eyes were lifted pleadingly to his face.

"My poor child," he said, "I could not be so cruel to

you as to leave him in ignorance of any of the facts, but I shall not attempt to bias his judgment, nor would it avail if I did. Your father is an independent thinker, and will make up his mind for himself."

"And against poor Bromly," thought Elsie, with an emotion of anguish, and something akin to rebellion rising in her heart.

Mr. Travilla read it all in her speaking countenance. "Do not fear your father's decision, my little friend," he said, sitting down beside her again. "He is very just, and you are as the apple of his eye. He will sift the matter thoroughly, and decide as he shall deem best for your happiness. Can you not trust his wisdom and his love?"

"I know he loves me very dearly, Mr. Travilla, but— he is only human, and may make a mistake."

"Then try to leave it all in the hands of your heavenly Father, who cannot err, who is infinite in wisdom, power, and in his love for you."

"I will try," she said with a quivering lip. "Now please talk to me of something else. Tell me of that young man. Did you say he shot himself?"

"Young Beresford, my friend's son? No, he was prevented." And he went on to tell of Rudolph's horror and remorse on account of that rash act, and of the excesses that led to it, also of the trembling hope his parents and friends were beginning to indulge that he was now truly penitent, and, clothed in his right mind, was sitting at the Saviour's feet.

Elsie listened with interest. They had had the parlor to themselves for an hour or more, Miss Stanhope having received an unexpected summons to the bedside of a sick neighbor.

She was with them at tea, and during most of the evening, but left them alone together for a moment just before Mr. Travilla took his leave, and he seized the opportunity to say to Elsie that he thought she ought to refrain from further intercourse with Egerton till she should learn her father's will in regard to the matter.

"I cannot promise—I will think of it," she said with a

look of distress.

"You write frequently to your papa?"

"Every day."

"I know you would not wish to deceive him in the least. Will you tell him what I conceive to be the facts in regard to Mr. Egerton? Or shall I?"

"I cannot, oh, I cannot!" she murmured, turning away her face.

"Then I shall spare you the painful task, by doing it myself, my poor child. I shall write tonight."

She was silent, but he could see the tumultuous heaving of her breast, and the tears glistening on the heavy drooping lashes that swept her pale cheek. His heart bled for her, while his indignation waxed hot against the hypocritical scoundrel who, he feared, had succeeded only too well in wrecking her happiness.

She had described to him Egerton's character as he had made it appear to her, telling of their conversations on religious subjects, his supposed conversion, etc., etc., thus unintentionally enabling Travilla to see clearly through the man's base designs. He silently resolved to stay in Lansdale and watch over her until her father's arrival.

"You ride out daily?" he inquired.

"Yes, sir."

"May I be your escort tomorrow?"

She cast down her eyes, which she had lifted to his face for an instant, blushing painfully. It seemed an effort for her to reply, and the words came slowly, and with hesitation. "I—should be glad to have you, sir. You know I have always valued your society, but—Mr. Egerton always goes with us—Lottie King and me—of late, and—and I can hardly suppose either of you would now find the company of the other agreeable."

"No, Elsie, but what do you think your father would wish?"

"I know he would be glad to have me under your care, and if you don't mind the unpleasantness."

"My dear, I would cheerfully endure far more than

that, to watch over your father's child. You will not let this unhappy circumstance turn you against your old friend? I could hardly bear that, little Elsie." And he drew her toward him caressingly.

"Oh, no, no! I don't think anything could do that. You've always been so good to me—almost a second father."

He released her hand with a slight involuntary sigh, as at that instant Miss Stanhope re-entered the room. The two were standing by the piano, Mr. Travilla having risen from one of the cushioned chairs to draw near to Elsie while talking to her. Miss Stanhope flew to the chair, caught up the cushion, shook it, laid it down again, and with two or three little loving pats restored it to its normal condition of perfect roundness. Mr. Travilla watched her with a surprised, puzzled look.

"Have I done any mischief, Elsie?" he asked in an undertone.

"Oh, no!" she answered with a faint smile. "It's only auntie's way."

Their visitor had gone, and Elsie turned to her aunt to say good-night.

"Something is wrong with you, child. Can't you tell the trouble to your old auntie and let her try to comfort you?" Miss Stanhope asked, putting an arm about the slender waist, and scanning the sweet face, usually so bright and rosy, now so pale and agitated, with a look of keen but loving scrutiny.

Then, in broken words, and with many a little half-sobbing sigh and one or two scalding tears, hastily brushed away, Elsie told the whole painful story, secure of warm sympathy from the kind heart to which she was so tenderly folded.

Miss Stanhope believed in Bromly Egerton almost as firmly as Elsie herself—what comfort there was in that! She believed too in the inspired assurances that "all things work together for good to them that love God" and that he is the hearer and answerer of prayer. She reminded her niece of them, bade her cast her burden on the Lord and leave it there, and cheered her with the hope that Bromly would be able to prove to her father that Mr. Travilla was entirely mistaken.

CHAPTER SEVENTEENTH

My heart has been like summer skies,
When they are fair to view;
But there never yet were heart or skies
Clouds might not wander through.

—Mrs. L.P. Smith

WALTER DINSMORE was doing well at college, studying hard, and keeping himself out of bad company. In this last he might not have been so successful but for his brother's assistance, for, though choosing his own associates from among the dissolute and vile, Arthur resolutely exerted himself to preserve this young brother from such contamination. "I've enough sins of my own to answer for, Wal," he would say, sometimes almost fiercely, "and I won't have any of yours added to 'em. Nobody shall say I led you into bad company, or initiated you into my own evil courses."

For months Arthur's spirits had been very variable, his frequent fits of gloom, alternating with unnatural gaiety, exciting Walter's wonder and sympathy.

"I cannot imagine what ails him," he said to himself again and again, for Arthur utterly refused to tell him the secret of his despondency.

It had been almost constant since the receipt of Egerton's last epistle, and Walter was debating in his own mind whether he ought not to speak of it in his next letter to their mother, when one night he was wakened by a sudden blow from Arthur's hand, and started up to find him rolling and tossing, throwing his arms about, and muttering incoherently in the delirium of fever.

It was the beginning of a very serious illness. It was pronounced such by the physician called in by Walter at an early hour the next morning, and the boy sat down with a heavy heart to write the sad tidings to his parents.

While doing so he was startled by hearing Arthur pronounce Elsie's name in connection with words that seemed to imply that some danger threatened her. He rose and went to the bedside, asking, "What's wrong with Elsie, Art?"

"I say, Tom Jackson, she'll never take you. Horace won't consent."

"I should think not, indeed!" muttered Walter. Then leaning over his brother, "Art, I say, Art ! What is it all about ? Has Tom Jackson gone to Lansdale?"

No answer, save an inarticulate murmur that might be either assent or dissent.

The doctor had promised to send a nurse and, as Walter now glanced about the room, the thought occurred to him that it would seem very disorderly to the woman. Arthur's clothes lay in a heap over the back of a chair, just as he had thrown them down on retiring.

"I can at least hang these in the closet," thought Walter, picking up the jacket.

A letter fell from the pocket upon the floor.

"Jackson's handwriting, I declare!" he exclaimed with a start of surprise, as he stooped to pick it up. It was without an envelope, written in a bold, legible hand, and unintentionally he read the date, "Lansdale, Ohio, Aug.— 185-," and farther down the page some parts of sentences connected with the "D—— family"... "can't help themselves"..."the girl loves me and believes in me."

He glanced at the bed. Arthur's eyes were closed. He looked down at the letter again. There was the signature "T. J, alias B. E."

"It's a conspiracy. There's mischief brewing, and I believe I ought to read it," he muttered, then, turning his back toward the bed, perused every word of it with close attention.

It was sufficient to give him a clear insight into the whole affair. Elsie's letters had of late spoken quite frequently of Mr. Bromly Egerton, and so he was the "T. J., alias B. E." of this epistle, the Tom Jackson who had been the ruin of Arthur.

"The wretch! The sneaking, hypocritical scoundrel!" muttered Walter between his teeth, and glancing again at the bed, though the epithet was meant to apply to Jackson and not to Arthur. "What can I do to circumvent him? Write to Horace, of course, and warn him of Elsie's danger." And though usually vacillating and infirm of purpose, on this occasion Walter showed himself both prompt and decided. The next mail carried the news of his discovery to Elsie's natural protector—her father, who with Rose, the Allison family, and little Horace, was still at Cape May.

This letter and the three from Lansdale were handed Mr. Dinsmore together. He opened Elsie's first. The contents puzzled, surprised, and alarmed him. They were merely a few hastily written lines of touching entreaty that he would not be angry, but would please forgive her for giving her heart to one of whom he knew nothing, and daring to let him speak to her of love, and that he would not believe anything against him until he had heard his defense.

With a murmured "My poor darling! You have been too long away from your father," Mr. Dinsmore laid it down and opened the one directed in a strange hand, rightly supposing it to come from the person to whom she alluded.

Egerton spoke in glowing terms of his admiration for Elsie's character and personal charms, and the ardent love with which they had inspired him and modestly of his own merits. Ignoring all knowledge of her fortune, he said that he had none, but was engaged in a flourishing business which would enable him to support her in comfort and to surround her with most of the elegancies and luxuries of life to which she had been accustomed. Lastly he alluded in a very pious strain to the deep debt of gratitude he owed her as the one who had been the means of his hopeful conversion, said she had acknowledged that she returned his affection, and earnestly begged for the gift of her hand.

Mr. Dinsmore gave this missive an attentive perusal, laid it aside, and opened Mr. Travilla's.

Rose was in the room, putting little Horace to bed. She had heard his little prayer, given him his good-night kiss, and now the child ran to his father to claim the same from him.

It was given mechanically, and Mr. Dinsmore returned to his letter. The child lingered a moment, gazing earnestly into his father's face, troubled by its paleness and the frown on his brow.

"Papa, " he said softly, leaning with confiding affection upon his knee, "dear papa, are you angry with me? Have I been a naughty boy, today ?"

"No, son, but I am reading. Don't disturb me now."

Mr. Dinsmore's hand rested caressingly on the curly head for an instant and the boy turned away satisfied. But Rose was not. Coming to her husband's side the next moment, and laying her hand affectionately on his shoulder, "What is it, dear?" she asked. "Has anything gone wrong with our darling, or at home?"

"Trouble for her, I fear, Rose. Read these," he answered with emotion, putting Elsie's, Egerton's, and Travilla's letters into her hands, then opening Walter's.

"Travilla is right! The man is an unmitigated scoundrel!" he cried, starting up with great excitement. "Rose, I must be off by the next train. It leaves in half an hour. I shall go alone and take only a portmanteau with me. Can it be got ready in season?"

"Yes, dear, I will pack it at once myself. But what is wrong? Where are you going? And how long will you be away?"

"To my brother's first—Arthur is seriously ill, and I must get hold of evidence that Walter can supply—then on to Lansdale with all speed to rescue Elsie from the wiles of a gambling, swindling, hypocritical, fortune-hunting rascal!"

At a very early hour of the next morning, Walter Dinsmore was roused from his slumbers by a knock at his door.

"Who's there?" he asked, starting up in bed.

"I, Walter," answered a well-known voice, and with a joyful exclamation he sprang to the door, and opened it.

"Horace! How glad I am to see you! I hardly dared hope you could get here so soon."

"Your news was of the sort to hasten a man's movements," returned Mr. Dinsmore, holding the lad's hand in a warm brotherly grasp. "How are you? And how's Arthur now?"

"About the same. Hark! You may hear him moaning and muttering. This is our study. I have had that cot-bed brought in here, and given up the bedroom to him and the nurse, though I'm with him a good deal too."

"You have a good nurse, and the best medical advice?"

"Yes."

"You must see that he has every comfort, Walter. Let no expense be spared, nothing left undone that may alleviate his sufferings or assist his recovery. What is the physician's opinion of the case?"

"He is not very communicative to me, may be more so to you. You'll stay and see him when he calls, won't you?"

"What time? I must be off again by the first train. I want to reach Lansdale tomorrow."

"It will give you time to do that. He calls early."

"Now take me to Arthur, and then I must see that letter, and hear all you have to tell me in regard to that matter."

"What does Elsie say?" asked Walter, with intense interest. "Do you think she cares for him?"

"I'm afraid she does," and Mr. Dinsmore shook his head sadly.

"Oh, dear! but you won't allow—"

"Certainly not. It would be to entail upon her a life of misery."

"It's her fortune he's after, that's evident, and indeed I would hurry to Lansdale, if I were you, lest they might take it into their heads to elope. Such a shame as it would be for him to get her—the dear, sweet darling!"

"I have no fear that Elsie could ever be so lost to her sense of filial duty, nor, I am sure, have you, Walter," answered Mr. Dinsmore gravely.

"No, Horace, and it's the greatest relief and comfort to me just now to know how truly obedient and affectionate she is to you."

Horace Dinsmore omitted nothing that he could do to add to the comfort of his brothers, saw the physician and learned from him that he had good hopes of a naturally vigorous constitution bringing Arthur safely through the attack from which he was suffering, examined the evidence Walter was able to furnish that Bromly Egerton and Tom Jackson were one and the same—a man in whom every vice abounded—found time to show an interest in Walter's studies and pastimes, and was ready to leave by the train of which he had spoken.

Jackson had not been wary enough to disguise his hand in either the letter that had fallen from Arthur's pocket, or the one written to Mr. Dinsmore, and a careful comparison of the two had proved conclusively that they were the work of the same person. The broken sentences that occasionally fell from Arthur's lips in his delirious ravings furnished another proof not less strong. Also Walter had managed to secure an excellent photograph of Jackson, which Mr. Dinsmore carried with him, safely bestowed in the breast pocket of his coat. He had studied it attentively and felt sure he should be able instantly to recognize the original.

Bromly Egerton lay awake most of the night following his passage at arms with Mr. Travilla, considering the situation, and how he would be most likely to secure the coveted prize. He remembered perfectly well all that Arthur Dinsmore had said about the difficulty of deceiving or outwitting his brother, and the impossibility of persuading Elsie to disobedience. Of the latter, he had had convincing proof that day, in her firm refusal to engage herself to him without first obtaining her father's consent. The conclusion he came to was, that should he remain inactive until Mr. Dinsmore's arrival, his chances of success were exceedingly small, in fact that his only hope lay in running away with Elsie, and afterwards persuading her into a clandestine marriage.

Their ride was to be taken shortly after an early breakfast, there being a sort of tacit understanding that he was to accompany the young ladies. But before Elsie had left her room, Chloe came up with a message. "Marse Egerton in de parlor, darlin', axin could he see my young missis for five minutes, just now."

Elsie went down at once. Her visitor stood with his back toward the door, apparently intently studying the pattern of her great-great-grand mother's sampler, but turning instantly at the sound of the light, quick footstep, came eagerly toward her with outstretched hand.

"Excuse this early call, dearest, but—ah, how lovely you are looking this morning!" and bending his head he drew her toward him.

But she stepped back, avoiding the intended caress, while a crimson tide rushed over the fair face and neck, and her eyes sought the carpet.

"We are not engaged, Mr. Egerton—cannot be till papa has given consent."

"I beg ten thousand pardons," he said, coloring violently in his turn, and feeling his hopes grow fainter.

"Will you not take a seat?" she asked, gently withdrawing her hand from his.

"Thank you, no. I have but a moment to stay. My errand was to ask if we could not so arrange it as, for once at least, to have our ride alone together? Miss Lottie is a very nice girl, but I would give much to have my darling all to myself today."

"I would like it much too, very much, but papa bade me always have a lady friend with me, and—and besides," she added with hesitation, and blushing more deeply than before, "papa's friend, Mr. Travilla, is to go with us. I—I have promised that he shall be my escort today."

Egerton was furious, and had much ado to conceal the fact, indeed, came very near uttering a horrible oath, and thus forever ruining his hopes. He bit his lips and kept silent, but Elsie saw that he was angry.

"Do not be offended or hurt," she said. "Do not suppose that I followed my own inclination in consenting to such an arrangement. No, I only acted from a sense of duty, knowing that it was what papa would wish."

"And you would put his wishes before mine? Love him best, I presume?"

"He is my father, and entitled to my obedience, whether present or absent."

"But what very strict ideas you must have on that subject! Do you really think it your duty to obey his wishes as well as his command?"

"I do. That is the kind of obedience he has taught me, that the Bible teaches, and that my love for him would dictate. I love my father very dearly, Mr. Egerton."

"I should think so, indeed, but you must pardon me if at present I am far more concerned about your love for me," he said, with a forced laugh. "As for this Travilla, I can hardly be expected to feel any great cordiality toward him after his attack upon me yesterday, and I am free to confess that it would not cause me great grief to learn that some sudden illness or accident had occurred to prevent his spoiling our ride today."

"Your feelings are perfectly natural, but, believe me, Mr. Travilla has the kindest of hearts, and when he learns his mistake will be most anxious to do all in his power to make amends for it. Will you stay and take breakfast with us?" For at that instant the bell rang.

"No, thank you," he said, moving toward the door. "But promise me, Elsie, that I shall be your escort after this until your father comes. Surely love may claim so small a concession from duty."

She could not resist his persuasive look and tone, but with a smile and a blush gave the promise for which he pleaded.

Procuring as fine a horse as his landlord could furnish, Mr. Travilla rode to Miss Stanhope's, and alighting at the gate, walked up to the house.

He found its mistress on the front porch, picking dead leaves from her vines. She had mounted a step ladder to reach some that otherwise were too high up for her small stature. Turning at the sound of his approach, "Good morning, sir," she said. "You see I'm like the sycamore tree that climbed into Zaccheus. Shortness is inconvenient at times. My, what a jar!" as she came down rather hard, missing the last step—"I feel it from the crown of my foot to the sole of my head. Here, Simon, take away this ladder-step. The next time I want it I think I'll do without. I'm growing so old in my clumsy age. Walk in and take a seat, Mr. Torville. Or shall we sit here? It's pleasanter than indoors I think."

"I agree with you," he said, accepting her invitation with a smile at the oddity of her address. "You have a fine view here."

They sat there conversing for some time before Elsie made her appearance, Mr. Travilla both charmed and amused with his companion, and she liking him better every moment. When Elsie did come down at last, looking wondrous sweet and fair in a pretty, coquettish riding hat and habit, her aunt informed her that she had been urging "Mr. Vanilla" to come and make his home with them while in town, and that he had consented to let her send Simon at once for his trunk.

"If it will be agreeable to my little friend to have me here?" Mr. Travilla said, taking her hand in his with the affectionate, fatherly manner she had always liked so much in him.

Her face flushed slightly, but she answered without an instant's hesitation that she hoped he would come.

The horses were already at the gate, Egerton was seen crossing the street, and Lottie came tripping in at a side entrance. She had heard a good deal of Mr. Travilla from Elsie, and seemed pleased to make his acquaintance.

Egerton came in, he and Mr. Travilla exchanged the coldest and most distant of salutations, and the party set off—Mr. Travilla riding by Elsie's side, Egerton and Lottie following a little in their rear.

Finding it almost a necessity to devote himself to Miss King for the time being, Egerton took a sudden resolution to make a partial confidante of her, hoping thus to secure a powerful ally. He told her of the state of affairs between Elsie and himself, of Mr. Travilla's "attack upon him," how "utterly mistaken" it was, and how he presumed "the mistake" had occurred, giving the story he had told Elsie of the cousin who bore so strong a likeness to him, and so bad a character. He professed the most ardent, devoted affection for Elsie, and the most torturing fears lest her father, crediting him with his cousin's vices, should forbid the match and crush all his hopes.

The warm-hearted, innocent girl believed every word, and rushing into her friend's room on their return, threw her arms about her, and hugging her close, told her she knew all, was so, so sorry for her, and for poor Egerton, and begged her not to allow anything to make her give him up and break his heart.

Elsie returned the embrace, shed a few tears, but answered not a word.

"You do believe in him? And won't give him up, will you?" persisted Lottie.

"I do believe in him, and will not give him up unless—unless papa commands it," Elsie answered in a choking voice.

"I wouldn't for that!" cried Lottie.

"'Children, obey your parents,'" repeated her friend, tears filling the soft brown eyes, and glistening on the drooping lashes. "It is God's command."

"But you're not a child any longer."

"I am papa's child. I always shall be. Oh, it would break my heart if ever he should disown me and say,

'You are no longer my child!'"

"How you do love him!"

"Better than my life!"

Mr. Travilla was already established at Miss Stanhope's, and very glad to be there, that he might keep the more careful and constant watch and ward over his "little friend." Thoroughly convinced of the vileness of the wretch who had won her unsuspicious heart, he could scarce brook the thought of leaving her alone with him, or of seeing him draw close to her side, touch her hand. or look into the soft, sweet eyes so full of purity and innocence. Yet these things no one but her father might forbid, and Mr. Travilla would not force his companionship upon Elsie when he saw or felt that it was distasteful to her. The lovers were frequently left to themselves in the parlor or upon the porch, though the friendly guardian, dreading he hardly knew what, took care always to be within call.

Elsie longed for, yet dreaded her father's coming. She knew he would not delay one moment longer than necessary after receiving their letters, yet he reached Lansdale almost a day sooner than she expected him.

Sitting alone in her room, she heard his voice and step in the hall below. She flew down to meet him.

"Oh, papa, dear, dear papa!"

"My darling, precious child!" And her arms were about his neck, his straining her to his heart. The next moment she lifted her face, and her eyes sought his with a wistful, pleading, questioning look. He drew her into the sitting-room, and Miss Stanhope closed the door, leaving them alone.

"My darling," he said, "you must give him up. He is utterly unworthy of you."

"Oh? Papa! Would you break my heart?"

"My precious one, I would save you from a life of misery."

"Ah, papa! You would never say that if you knew how—how I love him," she murmured, a deep blush suffusing her face.

"Hush! It horrifies me to hear you speak so of so vile a wretch—a drinking, swearing gambler, swindler, and rake, for I have learned that he is all these."

"Papa, it is not true! I will not hear such things said of him, even by you!" she cried, the hot blood dyeing her face and neck, and the soft eyes filling with indignant tears.

He put his finger upon her lips. "My daughter forgets to whom she is speaking," he said with something of the old sternness, though there was tender pity also in his tones.

"Oh, papa, I am so wretched!" she sobbed, hiding her face on his breast. "Oh, don't believe what they say. It isn't, it can't be true."

He caressed her silently, then taking the photograph from his pocket, asked, "Do you know that face?"

"Yes, it is his."

"I knew it, and it is also the face of the man whose character I have just described."

"Oh, no, papa!" and with breathless eagernes she repeated the story with which Egerton had swept away all her doubts. She read incredility in her father's face. "You do not believe it, papa?"

"No, my child, no more than I do black is white. See here!" and he produced Egerton's letter to him, and the one to Arthur, made her read and compare them, and gave her the further proofs Walter had furnished.

She grew deathly pale, but was no more ready to be convinced than he. "Oh, papa, there must be some dreadful mistake! I cannot believe he could be guilty of such things. The cousin has been personating him, has forged that letter, perhaps. And the photograph may be his also."

"You are not using your good common-sense, Elsie. The proof is very full and clear to my mind. The man is a fortune-hunter, seeking your wealth, not you—a scoundrel whose vices should shut him out of all decent society. I can hardly endure the thought that he has ever known you, or dared to address a word to you, and it must never be again."

"Must I give him up?" she asked with pale, quivering lips.

"You must, my daughter—at once and for ever."

A look of anguish swept over her face, then she started, flushed, and trembled, as a voice and step were heard on the porch without.

"It is he?" her father said inquiringly, and her look answered, "Yes."

He rose to his feet, for they had been sitting side by side on the sofa while they talked. She sprang up also, and clinging to his arm, looked beseechingly into his face, pleading in a hoarse whisper, "Papa, you will let me see him, speak to him once more? Just a few words—in your presence—oh, papa!"

"No, my darling, no. His touch, his breath, are contamination, his very look is pollution, and shall never rest upon you again if I can prevent it. Remember you are never to hold any communication with him again—by word, letter, or in any other way. I positively forbid it. You must never look at him or intentionally allow him a sight of your face. I must go now, and send him away." He held her to his heart as he spoke. His tone was affectionate, but very firm, and decided. He kissed her tenderly, two or three times, placed her in an easy-chair, saying, "Stay here till I come to you," and left the room.

For a moment she lay back against the cushions like one stunned by a heavy blow. Then, roused by the sound of the voices of the two she loved best on earth, started and leaned forward in a listening attitude, straining her ear to catch their words. Few of them reached her, but her father's tones were cold and haughty, Egerton's at first persuasive, then loud, angry, and defiant.

He was gone, she had heard the last echo of his departing footsteps, and again her father bent over her, his face full of tender pity. She lifted her sad face to his, with the very look that had haunted him for years, that he could never recall without a pang of regret and remorse—that pleading, mournful gaze with which she had parted from him in the time of their estrangement.

It almost unmanned him now, almost broke his heart. "Don't, my darling, don't look at me so," he said in low, moved tones, taking her cold hands in his. "You don't know, precious one, how willingly your father would bear all this pain for you if he could."

She threw herself upon his breast, and folding her close to his heart, he caressed her with exceeding tenderness, calling her by every fond, endearing name.

For many minutes she received it all passively, then suddenly raising her head, she returned one passionate embrace, withdrew herself from his arms, and hurried from the room.

He let her go unquestioned. He knew she went to seek comfort and support from One nearer and dearer, and better able to give it than himself. He rose and walked the room with a sad and troubled countenance, and a heart filled with grief for his child, with anger and indignation toward the wretch who had wrecked her happiness.

Miss Stanhope opened the door and looked in.

"You have had no dinner, Horace. It will be ready in a few moments."

"Thank you, aunt. I will go up to my room first and try to get rid of some of the dust and dirt I have brought with me."

"Stay a moment, nephew. I am sorely troubled for the child. You don't approve of her choice?"

"Very far from it. I have forbidden the man ever to come near her again."

"But you won't be hard with her, poor dear?"

"Hard with her, Aunt Wealthy? Hard and cruel to my darling whom I love better than my life? I trust not, but it would be the height of cruelty to allow this thing to go on. The man is a vile wretch guilty of almost every vice, and seeking my child for her wealth, not for herself. I have forbidden her to see or ever to hold the slightest communication with him again."

"Well, it is quite right if your opinion of him is correct,

and I hardly think she is likely to refuse submission."

"I have brought up my daughter to habits of strict, unquestioning obedience, Aunt Wealthy," he said, "and I think they will stand her in good stead now. I have no fear that she will rebel."

A half hour with her best Friend had done much to soothe and calm our sweet Elsie. She had cast her burden on the Lord and he sustained her. She knew that no trial could come to her without his will, that he had permitted this for her good, that in his own good time and way he would remove it, and she was willing to leave it all with him, for was he not all-wise, all-powerful, and full of tenderest, pitying love for her?

She had great faith in the wisdom and love of her earthly father also, and doubted not that he was doing what he sincerely believed to be for her happiness—giving her present pain only in order to save her from keener and more lasting distress and anguish in the future.

It was well for her that she had such trust in him and that their mutual love was so deep and strong, well too that she was troubled with no doubts of the duty of implicit obedience to parental authority when not opposed to the higher commands of God. Her heart still clung to Egerton, refusing to credit his utter unworthiness, and she felt it a bitter trial to be thus completely separated from him, yet hoped that at some future, and perhaps not distant day, he might be able to convince her father of his mistake.

Mr. Dinsmore felt it impossible to remain long away from his suffering child. After leaving the table, a few moments only were spent in conversation with his aunt and Mr. Travilla, and then he sought his darling in her room.

"My poor little pet, you have been too long away from your father," he said, taking her in his arms again. "I shall never forgive myself for allowing it. But, daughter, why was this thing suffered to go on? Your letters never spoke of this man in a way to lead me to suppose that he was paying you serious attention, and indeed I did not intend to permit that from anyone yet."

"Papa, I did not deceive you intentionally. I did not mean to be disobedient," she said imploringly. "Lottie and I were almost always together, and I did not think of him as a lover till he spoke."

"Well, dearest, I am not chiding you. Your father could never find it in his heart to add one needless pang to what you are already suffering." His tone was full of pitying tenderness.

She made no answer, only hid her face on his breast and wept silently. "Papa," she murmured at length. "I— I do so want to break one of your rules. Oh, if you would only let me, just this once!"

"A strange request, my darling," he said. "But which of them is it?"

"That when you have once decided a matter I must never ask you to reconsider. Oh, papa, do, do let me entreat you just this once!"

"I think it will be useless, daughter, only giving me the pain of refusing, and you of being refused, but you may say on."

"Papa, it is that I may write a little note to—to Mr. Egerton," she said, speaking eagerly and rapidly, yet half trembling at her own temerity the while, "just to tell him that I cannot do anything against your will, and that he must not come near me or try to hold any sort of intercourse with me till you give consent, but that I have not lost my faith in him, and if he is innocent and unjustly suspected, we need not be wretched and despairing, for God will surely someday cause it to be made apparent. Oh, papa, may I not? Please, please let me! I will bring it to you when written, and there shall not be one word in it that you do not approve." She had lifted her face, and the soft, beseeching eyes were looking pleadingly into his.

"My dearest child," he said, "it is hard to refuse you, but I cannot allow it. There, there! Do not cry so bitterly. Every tear I see you shed sends a pang to my heart. Listen to me, daughter. Believing what I do of that man,

I would not for a great deal have him in possession of a single line of your writing. Have you ever given him one?"

"No, papa, never," she sobbed.

"Or received one from him?"

"No, sir."

"It is well." Then as if a sudden thought had struck him, "Elsie, have you ever allowed him to touch your lips?" he asked almost sternly.

"No, papa, not even my cheek. I would not while we were not engaged, and that could not be without your consent."

"I am truly thankful for that!" he exclaimed in a tone of relief. "To know that he had—that these sweet lips had been polluted by contact with his—would be worse to me than the loss of half my fortune." And lifting her face as he spoke, he pressed his own to them again and again.

But for the first time in her life she turned from him as if almost loathing his caresses, and struggled to release herself from the clasp of his arm.

He let her go, and hurrying to the farther side of the room, she stood leaning against the window-frame, with her back toward him, shedding very bitter tears of mingled grief and anger.

But in the pauses of her sobbing a deep sigh struck upon her ear. Her heart smote her at the sound; still more as she glanced back at her father and noted the pained expression of his eye as it met hers. In a moment she was at his side again, down upon the carpet, with her head laid lovingly on his knee.

"Papa, I am sorry." The low, sweet voice was tremulous with grief and penitence.

"My poor darling, my poor little pet!" he said, passing his hand with soft, caressing movement over her hair and cheek. "Try to keep your love for your father and your faith in his for you, however hard this rule may seem."

"Ah, papa, my heart would break if I lost either," she

sobbed. Then lifting her tear-dimmed eyes with tender concern to his face, which was very pale and sad, "Dear papa," she said, "how tired you look! You were up all night, were you not?"

"Last night and the one before it."

"That you might hasten here to take care of me," she murmured in a tone of mingled regret and gratitude. "Do lie down now and take a nap. This couch is soft and pleasant, and I will close the blinds and sit by your side to keep off the flies."

He yielded to her persuasions, saying as he closed his eyes, "Don't leave the room without waking me."

She was still there when he woke, close at his side and ready to greet him with an affectionate look and smile, though the latter was touchingly sad and there were traces of tears on her cheeks."

"How long have I slept?" he asked.

"Two hours," she answered, holding up her watch, "and there is the tea-bell."

CHAPTER EIGHTEENTH

What thou bidst,
Unargued I obey; so God ordained.

—MILTON

"I HOPE YOU DON'T INTEND to hurry this child away from me, Horace?" remarked Miss Stanhope inquiringly, glancing from him to Elsie, as she poured out the tea.

"I'm afraid I must, Aunt Wealthy," he answered, taking his cup from her hand. "I can't do without her any longer, and mamma and little brother want her almost as badly."

"And what am I to do?" cried Miss Stanhope, setting down the teapot, and dropping her hands into her lap. "It just makes a baby of me to think how lonely the old house will seem when she's gone. You'd get her back soon, for 'tisn't likely I've got long to live, if you'd only give her to me, Horace."

"No, indeed, Aunt Wealthy, she's a treasure I can't spare to anyone. She belongs to me, and I intend to keep her," turning upon his daughter a proud, fond look and smile, which was answered by one of sweet, confiding affection.

"Good-evening!" cried a gay, girlish voice. "Mr. Dinsmore, I'd be delighted to see you, if I didn't know you'd come to rob us of Elsie."

"What, you too ready to abuse me on that score, Miss Lottie?" he said laughingly, as he rose to shake hands with her. "I think I rather deserve thanks for leaving her with you so long."

"Well, I suppose you do. Aunt Wealthy, papa found some remarkably fine peaches in the orchard of one of his patients, and begs you will accept this little basketful."

"Why, they're beautiful, Lottie!" said the old lady, rising and taking the basket from her hand. "You must return my best thanks to your father. I'll set them on the table just so. Take off your hat, child, and sit down with us. There's your chair all ready to your plate, and Phillis's farmer's fresh fruit-cake, to tempt you, and the cream biscuits that you are so fond of, both."

"Thank you," said Lottie, partly in acknowledgment of the invitation, partly of Mr. Travilla's attention, as he rose and gallantly handed her to her seat. "I can't find it in my heart to resist so many temptations."

"Shall I bring a dish for de peaches, mistis?" asked Chloe, who was waiting on the table.

"Yes."

"Oh, let us have them in that old-fashioned china fruit-basket I've always admired so much, Aunt Wealthy!" cried Lottie eagerly. "I don't believe Elsie has seen it at all."

"No, so she hasn't, but she shall now," said the old lady, hastening toward her china-closet. "There, Aunt Chloe, just stand on the dish, and hand down that chair from this top shelf. Or, if you would, Horace, you're taller, and can reach better. I'm always like the sycamore tree that was little of stature, and couldn't see Zaccheus till he climbed into it."

"Rather a new and improved version of the Bible narrative, aunt, isn't it?" asked Mr. Dinsmore, with an amused look, as he came toward her. "And I fear I'm rather heavy to stand on a dish; but will use the chair instead, if you like."

"Ah! I've put the horse before the cart as usual, I see," she said, joining good-humoredly in the laugh the others found it impossible to suppress. "It's an old trick of my age, that increases with my advancing youth, till I sometimes wonder what I'm coming to, the words will tangle themselves up in the most troublesome fashion. But if you know what I mean, I suppose it's all the same."

"Why, Aunt Wealthy, this is really beautiful," said Mr. Dinsmore, stepping from the chair with the basket in his hand.

"Yes, it belonged to your great-grandmother, Horace, and I prize it highly on that account. No, Aunt Chloe, I shall wipe it out and put the peaches into it myself. It will take but a moment, and it's too precious a relic to trust to any other hands than my own."

Lottie was apparently in the gayest spirits, enlivening the little party with many a merry jest and light, silvery laugh, enjoying the good things before her, and gratifying her hostess with praises of their excellence. Yet through it all she was furtively watching her friend, and grieved to notice the unwonted paleness of her cheek, the traces of tears about her eyes, that her cheerfulness was assumed, and that if she ate anything it was only from a desire to please her father, who seemed never to forget her for a moment, and to be a good deal troubled at her want of appetite. In all these signs Lottie read disappointment of Egerton's hopes, and of Elsie's, so far as he was concerned.

"So I suppose her father has commanded her to give him up," she said to herself. "Poor thing! I wonder if she means to be as submissive as she thought she would."

The two presently slipped away together into the garden, leaving the gentlemen conversing in the sitting-room, and Miss Stanhope busied with some household care.

"You poor dear, I am so sorry for you!" whispered Lottie, putting her arm about her friend. "Must you really quite give him up?"

"Papa says so," murmured Elsie, vainly struggling to restrain her tears.

"Is it that he believes Mr. Travilla was not mistaken?"

"Yes, and—and he has heard some other things against him, and thinks his explanation of Mr. Travilla's mistake quite absurd. Oh, Lottie, he will not even allow us one parting interview and says I am never to see Mr. Egerton again, or hold any communication with him in any way. If I should meet him in the street I am not to recognize him, must pass him by as a perfect stranger, not looking at him or permitting him to see my face, if I can avoid doing so."

"And will you really submit to all that? I don't believe I could be so good."

"I must. Papa will always be obeyed."

"But don't you feel that it's very hard? Doesn't it make you feel angry with your father and love him a little less?"

"I was angry for a little while this afternoon," Elsie acknowledged with a blush, "but I am sure I have no right to be. I know papa is acting for my good—doing just what he believes will be most likely to secure my happiness. He says it is to save me from a life of misery, and certainly it would be that to be united to such a man as he believes Mr. Egerton is."

"But you don't believe it, Elsie?"

"No, no, indeed! I have not lost my faith in him yet, and I hope he may someday be able to prove to papa's entire satisfaction that he is really all that is good, noble, and honorable."

"That is right. Hope on, hope ever."

"Ah, I don't know how we could live without hope," Elsie said, smiling faintly through her tears. "But I ought not to be wretched—oh, very far from it, with so many blessings, so many to love me! Papa's love alone would brighten life very much to me. And then," she added in a lower tone, "'that dearer Friend that sticketh closer than a brother,' and who has promised, 'I will never leave thee nor forsake thee.'"

"And he will keep his promise, child," said Aunt Wealthy, joining them in the arbor where they had seated themselves. "I have proved his faithfulness many times, and I know that it never fails. Elsie, dear, your old auntie would save you from every trial, but he is a far wiser and truer friend, and will cause all things to work together for your good, and never allow you to suffer one unneeded pang." She softly stroked her niece's sunny hair, as she spoke, and the kind old face was full of pitying tenderness.

"Come back to the house now, dears," she added. "I think the dew is beginning to fall, and I heard my nephew asking for his daughter."

"How much longer may we hope to keep you, Elsie?" Lottie asked as they wended their way toward the house.

"Papa has set Monday evening for the time of leaving."

"And this is Friday, so we shall have but two more rides together. Oh, dear! how I shall miss you when you're gone."

"And I you. I shall never forget what pleasant times we have had together, Aunt Wealthy and you and I. You mustn't let her miss me too much, Lottie." And Elsie turned an affectionate look upon her aged relative.

"As if I could prevent it! But I'll do my best, you may rest assured of that."

"You are dear girls, both of you," said Miss Stanhope with a very perceptible tremble in her voice, "and you have brightened my home wonderfully. If I could only keep you!"

"Well, auntie, you're not likely to lose me altogether for some time yet," returned Lottie gaily, though the tears shone in her eyes.

Bromly Egerton went out from Mr. Dinsmore's presence with his temper at a white heat, for he had just been treated to some plain truths that were far from palatable, besides which it seemed evident that he had missed the prize he so coveted and had made such strenuous efforts to win. He had learned nothing new in regard to his own character, yet somehow it had never looked so black as now, when seen through the spectacles of an upright, honest, vice-detesting Christian gentleman. He writhed at the very recollection of the disgust, loathing, and contempt expressed in Mr. Dinsmore's voice and countenance as well as in his words.

He scarcely gave a thought to the loss of Elsie herself. He had no feeling for her at all worthy of the name of love—his base, selfish nature was, indeed, hardly capable of such a sentiment, especially toward one so refined, so guileless in her childlike innocence and purity that to be with her gave him an uncomfortable sense of his own moral inferiority.

No, the wounds under which he smarted were all stabs given to his self-love and cupidity. He had learned how honest men looked upon him, and he had failed in the cherished expectation of laying his hands upon a great fortune, which he had fondly hoped to have the opportunity of spending.

Rushing into the street, boiling with rage and shame, he hurried onward, scarcely knowing or caring whither he went. Out into the open country, and on through woods and over hills he tramped, nor thought of turning back till the sun had set, and darkness began to creep about his path.

There was light in Miss Stanhope's parlor and strains of rich melody greeted his ear as he passed. He turned away with a muttered imprecation, crossed the street, and entered Mrs. Schilling's gate. She was sitting on her doorstep, resting after her day's work, and enjoying the cool evening air.

"Why, la me, Mr. Egerton! Is that you?" she cried, starting up, and stepping aside for him to pass in. "I'd really begun to think you was lost. The fire's been out and everything cleared away this two hours. I kep' the table a-waitin' for you a right smart spell, but finally come to the conclusion that you must 'a' stayed to Miss Stanhope's or someone else, to tea."

"No, I've not had supper," he answered gruffly.

"You haint, eh? And I 'spose you're hungry, too. Well, sit down, and I'll hunt up something or 'nother. But I'm afraid you'll get the dyspepsy eatin' so late. Why, it's nigh on to ten o'clock, and I was just a-thinkin' about shuttin' up and going off to bed."

"Well, you'll not be troubled with me long. I shall

leave the place in a few days."

"Leave Lansdale, do you mean?"

"Yes."

"Why, what's up?"

"The time I had appropriated to rest and recreation. Business men can't play forever."

"Well, I shouldn't wonder. And Mr. Dinsmore's come after his daughter, too."

"What's that got to do with it?" he muttered. But she had left the room and was out of hearing.

Before closing his eyes in sleep that night, Egerton resolved to make a moving appeal to Elsie herself. He would write and find some means by which to get the letter into her hands. Directly after breakfast he sat down to his task, placing himself in a position to constantly overlook Miss Stanhope's house and grounds. He was hoping to get sight of Elsie, and anxious to watch Mr. Dinsmore's movements. Mrs. Schilling had informed him that "Miss Stanhope's friends didn't expect to leave till sometime a Monday," so she had learned from Phillis, through Lenwilla Ellawea, who had been sent over "for a little of Phillis's light'ning, to raise some biscuits for breakfast," yet he had some fear that the information might prove unreliable, and Mr. Dinsmore slip away with his daughter that day.

That fear was presently relieved by seeing Simon bringing out the horses for the young ladies and shortly after a livery-stable man leading up two fine steeds, evidently intended for the use of the gentlemen. He now laid down his pen, and kept close watch for a few moments, when he was rewarded by seeing the whole party come out, mount, and ride away—Mr. Dinsmore beside his daughter, Mr. Travilla with Lottie. Elsie, however, was so closely veiled that he could not so much as catch a glimpse of her face.

With a muttered oath, he took up his pen again, feeling more desirous than ever to outwit "that haughty Southerner," and secure the prize in spite of him.

Half an hour afterward Simon, who was at work gathering corn and tomatoes for dinner in the garden behind the house, heard someone calling softly to him from the other side of the fence. Turning his head, he saw Mr. Egerton standing there, motioning to him to draw near.

"Good-mornin', sah. What you want, sah?" inquired the lad, setting down his basket, and approaching the fence that separated them.

"Do you know what this is?" asked Egerton, holding up a small glittering object.

"Yes, sah, five-dollar gold piece, sah," replied the negro, bowing and chuckling. "What de gentleman want dis niggah do for to arn 'em?"

"To put this into Miss Dinsmore's hands," answered Egerton, showing a letter, "into her own hands, now, mind. If you do that, the five dollars are yours, and if you bring me an answer, I'll make it ten. But you are to manage it so that no one else shall see what you do. Do you understand?"

"Yes, sah, and I bet I do it up about right, sah."

Very anxious to win the coveted reward, Simon was careful to be on hand when the riding party returned. He stationed himself near Elsie's horse. Her father assisted her to alight, and as he turned to make a remark to Lottie, Simon, being on the alert, managed to slip the note into Elsie's hand, unperceived by Mr. Dinsmore, or the others.

She gave a start of surprise, turning her eyes inquiringly upon him, the rich color rushing all over her fair face and neck, as he could see, even through the folds of her thick veil.

Simon grinned broadly, as, by a nod and wink toward the opposite side of the street, he indicated whence the missive had come.

She turned and walked quickly toward the house, her heart beating very fast and loud, and her fingers tightly clasping the note underneath the folds of her long riding-skirt, as she held it up. She hurried to her room, shut and locked the door, and, throwing off her hat and veil, dropped into a seat, trembling in every limb with the agitation and excitement of her feelings. She longed intently to know what he had said to her, but she had never deceived or willfully disobeyed her father, and should she begin now? The temptation was very great, and perhaps she would have yielded; but Mr. Dinsmore's step came quickly up the stairs, and the next moment he rapped lightly on the door.

She rose and opened it, at the same time slipping the note into her pocket.

"Why, my darling, what is the matter?" he asked, looking much concerned at the sight of her pale, agitated countenance.

"Oh, papa, if you would let me! If you only would!" she cried, bursting into tears, and putting her arms coaxingly about his neck.

"Let you do what, my child?" he asked, stroking her hair.

"Read this," she said, in a choking voice, taking the note from her pocket. "Oh, if you knew how much I want to! Mayn't I, papa? Do, dear papa, say yes."

"No, Elsie. It grieves me to deny you, but it must go back unopened. Give it to me."

She put it into his hand and turned away with a sob.

"How did it come into your hands?" he inquired, going to her writing-desk for an envelope, pen and ink.

"Must I tell you, papa?" she asked, in a tone that spoke reluctance to give the information he required.

"Certainly."

"Simon gave it to me a few moments since."

He touched the bell, and, Chloe appearing in answer, bade her take that note to the house on the opposite side of the street.

"There is no message," he added. "It is directed to Mr. Egerton, and you have nothing to do but to hand it in at the door."

"Yes, sah." And with a sorrowful, pitying glance at the wet eyes of her young mistress, the faithful old creature left the room.

"My poor little daughter, you feel now that your

father is very cruel," Mr. Dinsmore said tenderly, taking Elsie in his arms again, "but someday you will thank me for all this."

She only laid her face down on his breast and cried bitterly, while he soothed her with caresses and words of fatherly endearment.

"Oh, papa, don't be vexed with me," she murmured at length. "I'm trying not to be rebellious, but it seems so like condemning him unheard."

"No, my child, it is not. I gave him the opportunity to refute the charges against him, but he has no proof to bring."

"Papa, he said it would break his heart to lose me," she cried with a fresh burst of grief.

"My dear child, he has no heart to break. If he could get possession of your property, he would care very little indeed what became of you."

Mr. Dinsmore spoke very decidedly, but, though silenced, Elsie was not convinced.

Egerton, watching through the half-closed blinds of his bed-room, had seen, with a chuckle of delight, the success of Simon's maneuver, and Elsie hurrying into the house, for the purpose—he had scarcely a doubt—of secretly reading and answering his note. He saw Chloe crossing the street, and thought that her young mistress had sent him a hasty line, perhaps to appoint the time and place of a clandestine meeting, for such confidence had he in his own powers of fascination for all the fair sex that he could not think it possible she could give him up without a struggle.

Lenwilla went to the door, and in his eagerness to receive the message he ran out and met her on the landing. What was his disappointment and chagrin at sight of the bold, masculine characters on the outside, and only his own handwriting within!

"Sent back unopened! The girl must be a fool!" he cried, fairly gnashing his teeth with rage. "She could have managed it easily enough; she had the best chance in the world, for he didn't see her take it, I know."

He considered a moment, put on his hat, and, walking over to Dr. King's, inquired for Miss Lottie.

"Jist walk intil the parlor, sir," said Bridget, "an' I'll call the young lady."

Lottie came to him presently, with her kind face full of regret and sympathy.

He told his tale, produced his note, and begged her to be his messenger, saying he supposed Mr. Dinsmore had come upon Elsie before she had time to read it, and he thought it hard for both her and himself that she should not have the chance.

"Yes," said Lottie, "but I am very sure she would not read it without her father's permission, and you may depend upon it, she showed it to him of her own accord."

He shook his head with an incredulous smile. "Do you really think she has so little sense? Or is it that you believe she too has turned against me?"

"No, she has not turned against you, she believes in you still. Nor is she wanting in sense, but she is extremely conscientious about obeying her father, and told me she meant to be entirely submissive, whatever it cost her."

"I can hardly think you are right," he said, with another of his incredulous smiles, "but even supposing she was silly enough to hand my note over to her father, I should like to give her an opportunity to retrieve her error, so won't you undertake"—

"Don't ask me to carry it to her," interrupted Lottie. "It would go against my conscience to tempt Elsie to do violence to hers, I do assure you, though I have no idea I should be successful. So you really must excuse me."

He tried argument and persuasion by turns, but Lottie stood firm in her refusal, and at length he went away, evidently very angry.

Lottie spent the evening with her friend, and when a fitting opportunity offered gave her an account of this interview with Egerton, Elsie telling her in return something of what had passed between her father and herself in regard to the note.

That Egerton had desired to tempt her to disobedience and deception did not tend to increase Elsie's esteem and admiration for him, but quite the reverse.

"I think he'll not prevent me from getting sight of her today," muttered Egerton, stationing himself at the front window the next morning, as the hour for church drew near.

He had not been there long, when he saw Miss Stanhope and Mr. Travilla, then Mr. Dinsmore and Elsie, come out of the house and cross the lawn. He made a hasty exit and was in the act of opening Mrs. Schilling's front gate as the latter couple reached the one opposite.

"Put down your veil Elsie, take my arm, and don't look toward that man at all," commanded her father, and she obeyed.

Egerton kept opposite to them all the way to the church, but without accomplishing his object. He followed them in and placed himself in a pew on the other side of the aisle, and a little nearer the front than Miss Stanhope's, so that, by turning half way round, he could look into the faces of its occupants. But Elsie kept hers partly concealed by her veil, and never once turned her eyes in his direction.

She was seated next her father, who seemed to watch her almost constantly—not with the air of a jailer, but with a sort of tender, protecting care, as one keeping guard over something belonging to him, and which he esteemed very sweet and precious—while now and then her soft eyes were lifted to his for an instant with a look of loving reverence.

"Poor Elsie was well watched today," remarked Nettie King to her sister as they walked home together. "Her father scarcely took his eyes off her for five consecutive minutes, I should think; and Mr. Egerton stared at her from the time he came in till the benediction was pronounced."

"Yes, I thought he was decidedly rude."

"Isn't Mr. Dinsmore excessively strict and exacting?"

"Yes, I think so, yet he dotes on her, and she on him. I never saw a father and daughter so completely wrapped up in each other."

They were now within sight of their own home and Miss Stanhope's.

"Just look!" cried Nettie. "I do believe Egerton means to force himself upon their notice and compel Elsie to speak to him."

He was crossing the street so as to meet them face to face, just at the gate, giving them no chance to avoid the rencontre.

"Good-morning, Miss Dinsmore," he said in a loud, cordial tone of greeting, as they neared each other.

Elsie started and tightened her grasp of her father's arm, but neither looked up nor spoke.

"My daughter acknowledges no acquaintance with you, sir," answered Mr. Dinsmore, haughtily, and Egerton turned and strode angrily away.

"There, Elsie, you see what he is; his behavior is anything but gentlemanly," remarked her father, opening the gate for her to pass in. "But you need not tremble so, child, there is nothing to fear."

Chapter Nineteenth

Oh, what a feeble fort's a woman's heart,
Betrayed by nature, and besieged by art.

—Fane's Love in the Dark

"Dear child, what shall I do without you?" sighed Miss Stanhope, clasping Elsie in her arms, and holding her in a long, tender embrace, for the time of parting had come. "Horace, will you bring her to see me again?"

"Yes, aunt, if she wants to come. But don't ask me to leave her again."

"Well, if you can't stay with me, or trust her yourself, let Mr. Vanilla come and stand guard over us both. I'd be happy, sir, at any time when you can make it convenient for me to see you here, with Horace and the child, or without them."

"Thank you, Miss Stanhope; and mother and I would be delighted to see you at Ion."

"Come, Elsie, we must go. The carriage is waiting and the train nearly due," said Mr. Dinsmore. "Good-bye, Aunt Wealthy. Daughter, put down your veil."

Egerton was at the depot, but could get neither a word with Elsie, nor so much as a sight of her face. Her veil was not once lifted, and her father never left her side for a moment. Mr. Travilla bought the tickets, and Simon attended to the checking of the baggage. Then the train came thundering up, and the fair girl was hurried into it, Mr. Travilla, on one side, and her father on the other, effectually preventing any near approach to her person on the part of the baffled and disappointed fortune-hunter.

He walked back to his boarding-house, cursing his ill luck and Messrs. Dinsmore and Travilla, and gave notice to his landlady that his room would become vacant the next morning.

As the train sped onward, again Elsie laid her head down upon her father's shoulder and wept silently behind her veil. Her feelings had been wrought up to a high pitch of excitement in the struggle to be perfectly submissive and obedient, and now the overstrained nerves claimed this relief. And love's young dream, the first, and sweetest, was over and gone. She could never hope to see again the man she still fondly imagined to be good and noble, and with a heart full of deep, passionate love for her.

Her father understood and sympathized with it all. He passed his arm about her waist, drew her closer to him, and taking her hand in his, held it in a warm, loving clasp.

How it soothed and comforted her. She could never be very wretched while thus tenderly loved and cherished.

And, arrived at her journey's end, there were mamma and little brother to rejoice over her return, as at the recovery of a long-lost, precious treasure.

"You shall never go away again," said the little fellow, hugging her tight. "When a boy has only one sister, he can't spare her to other folks, can he, papa?"

"No, son," answered Mr. Dinsmore, patting his rosy cheek, and softly stroking Elsie's hair, "and it is just the same with a man who has but one daughter."

"You don't look bright and merry, as you did when you went away," said the child, bending a gaze of keen, loving scrutiny upon the sweet face, paler, sadder, and more heavy-eyed than he had ever seen it before.

"Sister is tired with her journey," said mamma tenderly. "We won't tease her tonight."

"Yes," said her father," she must go early to bed, and

have a long night's rest."

"Yes, papa, and then she'll be all right tomorrow, won't she? But, mamma, I wasn't teasing her, not a bit. Was I, Elsie? And if anybody's been making her sorry, I'll kill him. 'Cause she's my sister, and I've got to take care of her."

"But suppose papa was the one who had made her sorry; what then?" asked Mr. Dinsmore.

"But you wouldn't, papa," said the boy, shaking his head with an incredulous smile. "You love her too much a great deal You'd never make her sorry unless she'd be naughty, and she's never one bit naughty—always minds you and mamma the minute you speak."

"That's true, my son, I do love her far too well ever to grieve her if it can be helped. She shall never know a pang a father's love and care can save her from." And again his hand rested caressingly on Elsie's head.

She caught it in both of hers, and laying her cheek lovingly against it, looked up at him with tears trembling in her eyes. "I know it, papa," she murmured. "I know you love your foolish little daughter very dearly, almost as dearly as she loves you."

"Almost, darling? If there were any gauge by which to measure love, I know not whose would be found the greatest."

Mr. Dinsmore and his father-in-law had taken adjoining cottages for the summer, and though "the season" was so nearly over that the hotels and boarding-houses were but thinly populated and would soon close, the two families intended remaining another month. So this was in some sort a home-coming to Elsie.

After tea the Allisons flocked in to bid her welcome. All seemed glad of her coming, Richard, Harold, and Sophy especially so. They were full of plans for giving her pleasure, and crowding the greatest possible amount of enjoyment into the four or five weeks of their expected sojourn on the island.

"It will be moonlight next week," said Sophy, "and we'll have some delightful drives and walks along the beach. The sea does look so lovely by moonlight."

"And we'll have such fun bathing in the mornings," remarked Harold. "You'll go in with us tomorrow, won't you, Elsie?"

"No," said Mr. Dinsmore, speaking for his daughter. "She must be here two or three days before she goes into the water. It will be altogether better for her health."

Elsie looked at him inquiringly.

"You get in the air enough of the salt water for the first few days," he said. "Your system should become used to that before you take more."

"Yes, that is what some of the doctors here, and the oldest inhabitants, tell us," remarked Mr. Allison, "and I believe it is the better plan."

"And in the meantime we can take some rides and drives—down to Diamond Beach, over to the light-house, and elsewhere," said Edward Allison, his brother Richard adding, "And do a little fishing and boating."

Mr. Dinsmore was watching his daughter. She was making an effort to be interested in the conversation, but looking worn, weary, and sad.

"You are greatly fatigued, my child," he said. "We will excuse you and let you retire at once."

She was very glad to avail herself of the permission.

Rose followed her to her room, a pleasant, breezy apartment, opening on a veranda, and looking out upon the sea, whose dark waves, here and there tipped with foam, could be dimly seen roll and tossing beneath the light of the stars and of a young moon that hung like a golden crescent just above the horizon.

Elsie walked to the window and looked out. "How I love the sea," she said, sighing, "but, mamma, tonight it makes me think of a text—'All Thy waves and Thy billows have gone over me.'"

"It is not so bad as that, I hope, dear," said Rose, folding her tenderly in her arms. "Think how we all love you, especially your father. I don't know how we could any of us do without you, darling. I can't tell you how sadly wc have missed you this summer."

"Mamma, I do feel it to be very, very sweet to be so loved and cared for. I could not tell you how dear you and my little brother are to me, and as for papa—sometimes I am more than half afraid I make an idol of him, and yet—oh, mamma," she murmured, hiding her face in Rose's bosom, "why is it that I can no longer be in love with the loves that so fully satisfied me?"

"'Thy desire shall be to thy husband, and he shall rule over thee.' It is part of woman's curse that she must ever crave that sort of love, often yielding to her craving, to her own terrible undoing. Be patient, darling, and try to trust both your heavenly and your earthly father. You know that no trial can come to you without your heavenly Father's will, and that he means this for your good. Look to him and he will help you to bear it, and send relief in his own good time and way. You know he tells us it is through much tribulation we enter the kingdom of God, and that whom the Lord loveth he chasteneth, and scourgeth every son whom he receiveth. 'If ye be without chastisements, whereof all are partakers, then are ye bastards and no sons!'"

"Ah, yes, mamma. Better the hardest of earthly trials, than to be left out of the number of his adopted children. And this seems to be really my only one, while my cup of blessings is full to overflowing. I fear I am very wicked to feel so sad."

"Let us sit down on this couch while we talk. You are too tired to stand," said Rose, drawing her away from the window to a softly-cushioned lounge. "I do not think you can help grieving, darling, though I agree with you that it is your duty to try to be cheerful, as well as patient and submissive, and I trust you will find it easier as the days and weeks move on. You are very young, and have plenty of time to wait. Indeed, if all had gone right, you know your papa would not have allowed you to marry for several years yet."

"You know all, mamma?"

"Yes, dear, papa told me. For you know you are my

darling daughter too, and I have a very deep interest in all that concerns you."

A tender caress accompanied the words, and was returned with equal ardor.

"Thank you, best and kindest of mothers. I should never want anything kept from you."

"Your father tells me you have behaved beautifully, though you evidently felt it very hard to be separated so entirely and at once fr—?"

"Yes, mamma," and Elsie's lip quivered, and her eyes filled, "and oh, I can't believe he is the wicked man papa thinks him. From the first he seemed to be a perfect gentleman, educated, polished, and refined, and afterward he became—at least so I thought from the conversations we had together—truly converted, and a very earnest, devoted Christian. He told me he had been, at one time, a little wild, but surely he ought not to be condemned for that, after he had repented and reformed."

"No, dear, and your father would agree with you in that. But he believes you have been deceived in the man's character. And don't you think, daughter, that he is wiser than yourself, and more capable of finding out the truth about the matter?"

"I know papa is far wiser than I, but, oh, my heart will not believe what they say of—of him!" she cried with sudden, almost passionate vehemence.

"Well, dear, that is perfectly natural, but try to be entirely submissive to your father, and wait patiently, and hopefully too," she added with a smile. "For if Mr. Egerton is really good, no doubt it will be proved in time, and then your father will at once remove his interdict. And if you are mistaken, you will one day discover it, and feel thankful, indeed, to your papa for taking just the course he has."

"There he is now!" Elsie said with a start, as Mr. Dinsmore's step was heard without, and Chloe opened the door in answer to his rap.

"What, Elsie disobeying orders, and mamma conniving at it!" he exclaimed in a tone that might mean either jest or serious reproof. "Did I not bid you go to bed at once, my daughter?"

"I thought it was only permission, papa, not command," she answered, lifting her eyes to his face, and moving to make room for him by her side. "And mamma has been saying such sweet, comforting things to me."

"Has she, darling? Bless her for it! I know you need comfort, my poor little pet," he said, taking the offered seat and passing his arm round her waist. "But you need rest too, and ought not to stay up any longer."

"But surely papa knows I cannot go to bed without my good-night kiss when he is in the same house with me," she said, winding her arms about his neck.

"And didn't like to take it before folks? Well, that was right, but take it now. There, good-night. Now mamma and I will run away, and you must get into bed with all speed. No mistake about the command this time, and disobedience, if ventured on, will have to be punished," he said with playful tenderness, as he returned her embrace, and rose to leave the room.

"The dear child! My heart aches for her," he remarked to his wife as they went out together, "and I find it almost impossible yet to forgive either that scoundrel Jackson or my brother Arthur."

"You have no lingering doubts as to the identity and utter unworthiness of the man?"

"Not one. And if I could only convince Elsie of his true character she would detest him as thoroughly as I do. If he had his deserts, he would be in the State's Prison. And to think of his daring to approach my child, and even aspire to her hand!"

Elsie lay all night in a profound slumber, and awoke at an early hour the next morning, feeling greatly refreshed and invigorated. The gentle murmur of old ocean came pleasantly to her ear, and sweetly in her mind arose the thought of him whom even the winds and the sea obey, of his never failing love to her, and of the many great and precious promises of his word. She remembered how he had said, "Your Father knoweth that ye have need of all these things," and, content to bear the cross he had sent her, and leave her future in his hands, she rose to begin the new day more cheerful and hopeful than she had been since learning her father's decision in regard to Egerton.

Throwing on a dressing-gown over her night dress, she sat down before the open window with her Bible in her hand. She still loved, as of old, to spend the first hour of the day in the study of its pages, and in communion with him whose word it is.

Chloe was just putting the finishing touches to her young lady's toilet when little Horace came running down the hall, and rapping on Elsie's door, called out, "Sister, papa says put on a short dress, and your walking shoes, and come take a stroll on the beach with us before breakfast."

"Yes, tell papa I will. I'll be down in five minutes."

She came down looking sweet and fresh as the morning, a smile on the full red lips, and a faint tinge of rose color on the cheeks that had been so pale the night before.

"Ah, you are something like yourself again," said Rose, greeting her with a motherly caress, as they met in the lower hall. "How nice it is to have you at home once more."

"Thank you, mamma, I am very glad to be here, and I had such a good restful sleep. How well you look."

"And feel too, I am thankful to be able to say. But there, your father is calling to you from the sitting-room."

Elsie hastened to obey the summons, and found him seated at his writing desk.

"Come here, daughter," he said, "and tell me if you obeyed orders last night."

"Yes, papa, I did."

"I am writing a few lines to Aunt Wealthy, to tell her of our safe arrival. Have you any message to send?" and laying down his pen he drew her to his knee.

"Only my love, papa, and—and that she must not be anxious about me, as she said that she should. That I am very safe and happy in the hands of my heavenly Father—and those of the kind earthly one he has given me," she added in a whisper, putting her arms about his neck, and looking in his face with eyes brimful of filial tenderness and love.

"That is right, my darling," he said, "and you shall never want for love while your father lives. How it rejoices my heart to see you looking so bright and well this morning."

"I fear I have not been yielding you the cheerful obedience I ought, papa," she murmured with tears in her eyes, "but I am resolved to try to do so in future, and have been asking help where I know it is to be obtained."

"I have no fault to find with you on that score, my dear child," he said tenderly, "but if you can be cheerful, it will be for your own happiness, as well as ours."

She kept her promise faithfully, and had her reward in much real enjoyment of the many pleasures provided for her.

Mr. and Mrs. Dinsmore were still youthful in their feelings, and joined with great zest in the sports of the young people, going with them in all their excursions, taking an active part in all their pastimes, and contriving so many fresh entertainments, that during those few weeks life seemed like one long gala day.

Mr. Travilla was with them most of the time. He had tarried behind in Philadelphia, as Mr. Dinsmore and his daughter passed through, but followed them to Cape Island a few days later.

The whole party left the shore about the last of September, the Allisons returning to their city residence, Mr. Travilla to his Southern home, and the Dinsmores traveling through Pennsylvania and New York, from one romantic and picturesque spot to another, finishing up with two or three weeks in Philadelphia, during which Rose and Elsie were much occupied with their fall and winter shopping.

Mr. Dinsmore took this opportunity to pay another

flying visit to his two young brothers. He found Arthur nearly recovered, and at once asked a full explanation of the affair of Tom Jackson, alias Bromly Egerton, his designs upon Elsie, and Arthur's participation in them.

"I know nothing about it," was the sullen rejoinder.

"You certainly were acquainted with Tom Jackson, and how, but through you, could he have gained any knowledge of Elsie and her whereabouts?"

"I don't deny that I've had some dealings with Jackson, but your Egerton I know nothing of whatever."

"You may as well speak the truth, sir. It will be much better for you in the end," said Mr. Dinsmore, sternly, his eyes flashing with indignant anger.

"And you may as well remember that it isn't Elsie you are dealing with. I'm not afraid of you."

"Perhaps not, but you may well fear him who has said, 'a lying tongue is but for a moment.' How do you reconcile such an assertion as you have just made with the fact of your having that letter in your possession?"

"I say it's a cowardly piece of business for you to give the lie to a fellow that hasn't the strength to knock you down for it."

"You would hardly attempt that if you were in perfect health, Arthur."

"I would."

"You have not answered my question about the letter."

"I wrote it myself."

"A likely story. It is in a very different hand from yours."

"I can adopt that hand on occasion, as I'll prove to your satisfaction."

He opened his desk, wrote a sentence on a scrap of paper, and handed it to Mr. Dinsmore. The chirography was precisely that of the letter. While slowly convalescing, Arthur had prepared for this expected interview with Horace, by spending many a solitary hour in laboriously teaching himself to imitate Jackson's ordinary hand, in which most of the letters he had received from him were written. The sentence he had first penned was, "I did it merely for my own amusement, and to hoax Wal."

"I don't believe a word of it," said Mr. Dinsmore, looking sternly at him. "Arthur, you had better be frank and open with me. You will gain nothing by denying the hand you have had in this disgraceful business. You can hardly suppose me credulous enough to believe an assertion so perfectly absurd as this. I have no doubt that you sent that villain to Lansdale to try his arts upon Elsie, and for that you are richly deserving of my anger, and of any punishment it might be in my power to deal out to you.

"It has been no easy matter for me to forgive the suffering you have caused my child, Arthur, but I came here today with kind feelings and intentions. I hoped to find you penitent and ready to forsake your evil courses, and in that case, intended to help you to pay off your debts and begin anew, without paining father with the knowledge that his confidence in you has been again so shamefully abused. But I must say that your persistent denial of your complicity with that scoundrel Jackson does not look much like contrition, or intended amendment."

Arthur listened in sullen silence, though his rapidly changing color showed that he felt the cutting rebuke keenly. At one time he had resolved to confess everything, throw himself upon the mercy of his father and brother, and begin to lead an honest, upright life, but a threatening letter received that morning from Jackson had led him to change his purpose, and determine to close his lips for a time.

Mr. Dinsmore paused for a reply, but none came.

Walter looked at Arthur in surprise. "Come, Art, speak, why don't you?" he said. "Horace, don't look so stern and angry. I know he means to turn over a new leaf, for he told me so. And you will help him, won't you?"

"I ask no favors from a man who throws the lie in my teeth," muttered Arthur angrily.

"And I can give none to one who persists in denying his guilt," replied Mr. Dinsmore. "But, Arthur, I give you one more chance, and for our father's sake I hope you will avail yourself of it. If you go on as you have for the last three or four years, you will bring down his gray hairs with sorrow to the grave. I presume you have put yourself in Jackson's power, but if you will now make a full and free confession to me, and promise amendment, I will help you to get rid of the rascal's claims upon you, and start afresh. Will you do it?"

"No, you've called me a liar, and what's the use of my telling you anything? You wouldn't believe it if I did."

CHAPTER TWENTIETH

She is not sad, yet in her gaze appears
Something that makes the gazer think of tears.

—MRS. EMBURY

THE FAMILY AT ROSELANDS were gathered about the breakfast-table—a much smaller party than of yore, since Horace had taken Elsie and set up an establishment of his own, and the other sons were away at college and two daughters married, leaving only Mr. and Mrs. Dinsmore, Adelaide and Enna to occupy the old home.

"I presume you have the lion's share as usual, papa," observed the last named, as her father opened the letter-bag which Pomp had just brought in.

"And who has a better right, Miss Malapert?" retorted the old gentleman. "Yes, here are several letters for me, but as there is one apiece for the rest of you, nobody need complain. Here, Pomp, hand this to your mistress. From Walter, I see."

"Yes," she answered, opening it, "and a few lines from Arthur too. I'm glad he's able to write again, poor fellow!"

"Yes," said Adelaide. "Rose says Horace has been up there and found him nearly recovered. She writes that they are coming home."

"When?" asked Enna.

"Why, today! The letter has been delayed," said her sister, looking at the date. "I shall ride over directly, to see that all is in order for them at the Oaks."

"There is no need," remarked her mother. "Rose will have written to Mrs. Murray."

"I presume so, still I shall go. It will be pleasant to be there to welcome them when they arrive."

"How fond you are of Rose," said Mrs. Dinsmore in a piqued tone. "You wouldn't do more for one of your own sisters, I believe, than for her."

"I wouldn't do less, mamma, and I am very fond of her. We are so perfectly congenial."

"And Elsie's a great pet of yours, too," said Enna sneeringly. "Well, I shall put off my call till tomorrow, when the trunks will have been unpacked, and I shall have a chance to see the fashions. Elsie will have loads of new things. It's perfectly absurd the way Horace heaps presents upon her, and pocket-money too. Such loads of jewelry as she has—two or three gold watches, and everything else in proportion."

"He may as well. She can never spend the half of her income," remarked Mr. Dinsmore. "Unless she takes to gambling," he added, in a tone that seemed to say that his purse had suffered severely from someone's indulgence in that vice.

Mrs. Dinsmore winced, Enna looked vexed and annoyed, and Adelaide sad and troubled. But when she spoke it was in answer to Enna.

"Yes, Elsie will have a great many beautiful things to show us, of course, but, though she wears nothing outré, she has never been, and I think never will be, a mirror of fashion. It would suit neither her own taste nor Horace's, and you know, fond of her as he is, he will never allow her to have a will of her own in dress or anything else. So it is well their tastes harmonize."

"I wouldn't be his child for all her money," said Enna.

"There would be some fighting if you were," said her father, laughing.

"I never could tell whether he tyrannized over Rose in the same style or not," observed Mrs. Dinsmore interrogatively.

"All I know about it is that they seem perfectly happy in each other," answered Adelaide. "But I don't suppose Horace considers a husband's authority by any means equal to father's."

Something delayed Adelaide, and it was nearly two hours after they rose from the table ere she was fairly on her way to the Oaks.

"Why, they are here before me!" she exclaimed half aloud as she came in sight of the house.

There were piles of luggage upon the veranda, and the whole family, including all the house servants, were gathered round a large open trunk from which Mrs. Dinsmore and Elsie were dealing out gifts—dresses, aprons, bonnets, hats, gay handkerchiefs, etc., etc., the darkies receiving them with a delight that was pleasant to see.

Mr. Dinsmore too was taking his part in the distribution, and as Adelaide rode up little Horace was in the act of throwing a gay shawl about the shoulders of his nurse, who caught him in her arms and hugged and kissed him over and over, calling him "honey," and "pet," and "you ole mammy's darlin' ole chil'!"

So much engaged were they all that no one perceived Adelaide's approach till she had reined in her horse close to the veranda, and throwing her bridle to her attendant, sprung lightly to the ground.

But then there was a shout of welcome from little Horace, followed instantly by joyous exclamations and embraces from the others.

"Dear me, what a long stay you made of it!" said Adelaide. "You can have no idea how I missed you all, even down to this little man," patting Horace's rosy cheek. "You look remarkably well, Rose, and the two Horaces also. But Elsie, I think, has grown a little pale, thin, and heavy-eyed. What ails you, child? Pining for your native air—no, home air—I presume. Is that it?"

"Hardly pining for it, auntie, but very glad to get back, nevertheless," Elsie answered, with a blush and a smile.

"And you are not pale now. But don't let me interrupt your pleasant employment. I wish I had been in time to see the whole of it."

"You are in season for your own gifts. Will you accept a trifle from me?" said her brother, putting a jewel-case into her hand.

"Coral! And what a beautiful shade!" she cried. "Thank you. They are just what I wanted."

"I thought they would contrast prettily with this, auntie," said Elsie, laying a dress-pattern of heavy black silk upon her lap.

"And these are to be worn at the same time, if it so pleases you," added Rose, presenting her with collar and undersleeves of point lace.

"Oh, Rose, how lovely! And even little Horace bringing auntie a gift!" as the child slipped something into her hand.

"It's only a card-case, but mamma said you'd like it, Aunt Adie."

"And I do. It's very pretty. And here's a hug and a kiss for the pet boy that remembered his old-maid auntie."

"Old maid, indeed! Adelaide, I'll not have you talking so," said Rose. "There's nothing old maidish about you, not even age yet. A girl of twenty-six to be calling herself that! It's perfectly absurd. Isn't it, my dear?"

"I think so, indeed," replied Mr. Dinsmore. "Here, Jim, Cato, and the rest of you carry in these trunks and boxes, and let us have them unpacked and put out of sight."

"Oh, yes!" said Adelaide. "I want to see all the fine things you have brought, Rose. Mamma, Enna, and I are depending upon you and Elsie for the fashions."

"Yes, we had all our fall and winter dresses made up in Philadelphia. We prefer their styles to the New York. They don't go to such extremes, you know; and besides—hailing from the Quaker city as I do, it's natural I should be partial to her plainer ways—but we brought quantities of patterns from both places, knowing that nothing was likely to be too gay for Enna. We will let Elsie display hers first. I feel in a special hurry, dear, to show your aunt those elegant silks your papa and I helped you to select. I hope you will see them all on her, one of these days, Adelaide.

"That child's complexion is so perfect, that she can wear anything," she added in an aside, as they followed Elsie to her apartments. "There's a pale blue that she looks perfectly lovely in, a pearl-color too, and a delicate pink, and I don't know how many more. One might think we expected her to do nothing but attend parties the coming season."

Elsie seemed to take a lively interest in displaying her pretty things to her aunt, and in looking on for a little, while Rose did the same with hers. But at length, though the two older ladies were still turning over and discussing silks, satins, velvets, laces, ribbons, feathers, and flowers, her father noticed her sitting in the corner of a sofa, in an attitude of weariness and dejection, with a pale cheek, and a dreary, far-off look in her eyes that it pained him to see.

"You are very tired, daughter," he said, going to her side, and smoothing her glossy brown hair with tender caressing motion, as he spoke. "Go and lie down for an hour or two. A nap would do you a great deal of good."

"I don't like to do so while Aunt Adie is here, papa," she said, looking up at him with a smile, and trying to seem fresh and bright.

"Never mind that. You can see her any day now. Come, you must take a rest." And drawing her hand within his arm, he led her to her boudoir and left her there, comfortably established upon a sofa.

"A hat trimmed in that style would be very becoming to Elsie," remarked Adelaide, continuing the conversation with Rose, and turning to look at her niece as she spoke. "Why, she's not here."

"Papa took her away to make her lie down," said little Horace.

"Rose, does anything ail the child?" asked Adelaide, in an undertone.

"She does not seem to be out of health, but you know

- 241 -

we are very careful of her. She is so dear and sweet, and has never looked very strong."

"But there is something wrong with her, is there not? She does not seem to me quite the gay, careless child she was when you went away. Horace," and she turned to him, as he re-entered the room, "may I not know about Elsie? You can hardly love her very much better than I do, I think."

"If that is so, you must love her very much indeed," he answered with a faint smile. "Yes, I will tell you." And he explained the matter, briefly at first, then more in detail as she drew him on by questions and remarks.

Her sympathy for Elsie was deep and sincere, yet she thought her brother's course the only wise and kind one, and her indignation waxed hot against Arthur and Egerton.

"And Elsie still believes in the scoundrel?" she said inquiringly.

"Yes, her loving, trustful nature refuses to credit the proofs of his guilt, and only her sweet, conscientious submission to parental authority has saved her from becoming his victim."

"She is a very good, submissive, obedient child to you, Horace."

"I could not ask a better, Adelaide. I only wish it were in my power to make obedience always easy and pleasant to her, poor darling."

"I hope you have something for me there, my dear," Rose remarked to her husband at the breakfast-table the next morning, as he looked over the mail just brought in by his man John.

"Yes there is one for you, from your mother, I think. And, Elsie, do you know the handwriting of this?"

"No, papa, it is quite strange to me," she answered, taking the letter he held out to her, and which bore her name and address on the back, and examining it critically.

"And the post-mark tells you nothing either?"

"No, sir. I cannot quite make it out, but it doesn't seem to be any place where I have a correspondent."

"Well, open it and see from whom it comes. But finish your breakfast first."

Elsie laid the letter down by her plate, and putting aside, for the present, her curiosity in regard to it, went on with her meal. "From whom can it have come?" she asked herself, while listening half absently to extracts from Mr. Allison's epistle. "Not from him surely, the hand is so very unlike that of the one he sent me in Lansdale."

"You have not looked at that yet," her father said, seeing her take it up as they rose from the table. "You may do so now. I wish to know who the writer is. Don't read it till you have found that out," he added, leading her to a sofa in the next room, and making her sit down there while he stood by her side.

She felt that his eye was upon her as she broke open the envelope and, taking the letter from it, glanced down the page, then in a little flutter of surprise and perplexity turned to the signature. Instantly her face flushed crimson, she trembled visibly, and her eyes were lifted pleadingly to his.

He frowned and held out his hand.

"Oh, papa, let me read it!" she murmured low and tremulously, her eyes still pleading more eloquently than her tongue.

"No," he said, and his look and gesture were imperative.

She silently put the letter into his hand, and turned away with a low sob.

"It is not worth one tear, or even an emotion of regret, my child," he said, sitting down beside her. "I shall send it back at once—unread, unless you prefer to have me read it first."

"No, papa."

"Very well, then I shall not. But, Elsie, do you not see now that he is quite capable of imitating the handwriting of another?"

"Yes, papa, but that does not prove that he did in the case you refer to."

"And he has acted quite fairly and honestly in using

– 243 –

that talent to elude my vigilance and tempt you to deception and disobedience, eh?"

"He is not perfect, papa, but I can't believe him as bad as you think."

"There are none so blind as those that won't see, Elsie. But, remember"—and his tone changed from one of great vexation to another sternly authoritative—"I will be obeyed in this thing."

"Yes, papa," she said, and rising, hastily left the room.

"Try to be very patient with her, dear," said Rose, who had been a silent, but deeply interested spectator of the little scene. "She suffers enough, poor child!"

"Yes, I know it, and my heart bleeds for her. Yet she seems so willfully blind to the strongest proofs of the fellow's abominable rascality that at times I feel as if I could hardly put up with it at all. The very pain of seeing her suffer so makes me out of all patience with her folly."

"Yes, I understand it, but do not be stern with her. She surely does not deserve it while she is so perfectly submissive to your will."

"No, she does not, poor darling," he said with a sigh. "But I must make haste to write some letters that ought to go by the next mail."

He left the room, and Mrs. Dinsmore, longing to comfort Elsie in her trouble, was about to go in search of her, when Mrs. Murray, who was still housekeeper at the Oaks, came to ask advice or direction about some household matters.

Their consultation lasted for half an hour or more, and in the meanwhile Mr. Dinsmore finished his correspondence and went himself to look for his daughter. She was in the act of opening her writing-desk as he entered the room.

"What are you doing, daughter?" he asked.

"I was about to write a letter to Sophy, papa."

"It would be too late for today's mail, so let it wait, and come with me for a little stroll into the grounds. Aunt Chloe, bring a garden hat and sunshade. You would like to go, daughter?"

"Yes, sir. Papa, you are not vexed with me? You don't think I want to be disobedient or wilful?" There were tears in her voice and traces of them on her cheeks.

"No, darling!" he said, drawing her to him. "And you did not in the least deserve to be spoken to in the stern tone that I used. But—can you understand it? My very love for you makes me angry and impatient at your persistent love for that scoundrel."

"Papa, please don't!" she said in a low, pained tone, and turning away her face.

"Ah, you do not like to hear a word against him!" he sighed. "I can't bear to think it, and yet I fear you care more for him than for me, your own father, who almost idolizes you. Is it so?"

"Papa," she murmured, winding her arms about his neck, and laying her head on his breast, "if I may have but one of you, I could never hesitate for a moment to choose to cling here where I have been so long and tenderly cherished. I know what your love is—I might be mistaken and deceived in another. And besides, God commands me to honor and obey you."

He held her close to his heart for a moment, as something too dear and precious ever to be given up to another, then drawing her hand within his arm, while Chloe placed the hat on her head, and gave her the parasol, he led her out into the grounds.

It pained him to notice the sadness of her countenance, sadder than he had seen it for many days, and he exerted himself to entertain her and divert her thoughts, calling her attention to some new plants and flowers, consulting her taste in regard to improvements he designed making, and conversing with her about a book they had been reading.

She understood his thoughtful kindness, was grateful for it, and did her best to be interested and cheerful.

"It is so nice to have you treat me as your companion and friend as well as your daughter, papa," she said, looking up at him with a smile.

"Your companionship is very dear and sweet to me, daughter," he answered. "But I think we had better go in now; the sun is growing hot."

"Oh, here you are!" cried a girlish voice as they turned into a shaded walk leading to the house. "I've been looking everywhere and am glad to have found you at last. Really, if a body didn't know your relationship, he or she might almost imagine you a pair of lovers."

"Don't be silly, Enna. How do you do?" said Mr. Dinsmore, shaking hands with her and giving her a brotherly kiss.

"As usual, thank you," she answered, turning from him to Elsie, whom she embraced with tolerable warmth, saying, "I'm really glad to have you here again. I missed you more than I would have believed. Now come in and show me all your pretty things. I'm dying to see them. Adelaide says you've brought home such quantities of lovely laces, silks, velvets, ribbons, flowers, feathers and what not, that one might imagine you'd nearly bought out the Philadelphia merchants."

"No, they had quite a stock still left," replied Elsie, smiling, "but, as mamma says, papa was very indulgent and liberal to us both, and I shall take pleasure in showing you his gifts."

"How do you like my present to Adelaide?" asked Mr. Dinsmore.

"Oh, very much. But when my turn comes please remember I want amethysts."

"Ah, then I have been fortunate in my selection," he said, quite unsuspicious of the fact that Enna had instructed Elsie beforehand in regard to her wishes, should Horace intend making her a present. Elsie had quietly given the desired hint, but merely as though the idea had originated with herself.

The jewelry was highly approved, as also a rich violet silk from Rose, and a lace set from Elsie.

Adelaide had been intrusted with quite as rich gifts for her father and mother; nor had Lora been forgotten. Elsie had a handsome shawl for her; Mr. Dinsmore a beautiful pair of bracelets, and Rose a costly volume of engravings.

"Do you think Aunt Lora will be pleased?" asked Elsie.

"They're splendid! It must be mighty nice to have so much money to spend. But come now, show me what you got for yourselves."

She spent a long while, first in Rose's apartment, then in Elsie's, turning over and admiring the pretty things, discussing patterns, and styles of trimming, and what colors and modes would be becoming to her, trying on some of the dresses, laces, sacques, shawls, bonnets, and hats—without so much as saying by your leave, when the article in question belonged to her niece—that she might judge of the effect, several times repeating her remark that it must be delightful to have so much money, and that Elsie was exceedingly fortunate in being so enormously wealthy.

"Yes, it is something to be thankful for," Elsie said at length, "but, Enna, it is also a great responsibility. We are only stewards, you know, and sometimes I fear it is hardly right for me to spend so much in personal adornment."

"That wouldn't trouble me in the least. But why do you do it, if you are afraid it's wrong?"

"Papa does not think so. He says the manufacturers of these rich goods must live as well as others, and that for one with my income, it is no more extravagant to wear them than for one with half the means to wear goods only half as expensive."

"And I'm sure he's perfectly right, and of course you have no choice but to obey. Well, I presume I've seen everything now, and I'm actually weary with my labors," she added, throwing herself into an easy-chair. "You've grown a little pale, I think, and your eyes look as if you'd been crying. What ails you?"

"I am not at all ill," returned Elsie, flushing.

"I didn't say you were, but something's wrong with you, and you can't deny it. You don't seem as gay as you used to before you went away."

She paused, but receiving no reply, went on. "Come now, it isn't worth while to be so close-mouthed with me, Miss Dinsmore, for I happen to know pretty much all about it already. You've fallen in love with a man that your father thinks is a scamp and though you don't believe it, you've given him up, in obedience to orders, like the cowardly piece that you are. Dear me, before I'd be so afraid of my father!"

"No, you neither fear nor love your father as I do mine, but fear of papa has very little to do with it. I love him far too well to refuse to submit to him in this, and I fear God, who bids me obey and honor him. But, Enna, how did you learn all this?"

"Ah, that is my secret."

Elsie looked disturbed. "Won't you tell me?"

"Not I."

"Is it generally known in the family?"

"So far as I am aware, no one knows it but myself."

"All!" thought Elsie "I did not believe Aunt Adelaide or Walter would tell her, but I wonder how she did find it out."

"I wouldn't give up the man I loved for anybody," Enna went on in a sneering tone. "I say parents have no business to interfere in such matters, and so I told papa quite plainly when he took it upon him to lecture me about receiving attention from Dick Percival, and threatened to forbid him the house."

"Oh, Enna!"

"You consider it wickedly disrespectful and rebellious no doubt, but I say I'm no longer a child, and so the text, 'Children, obey your parents'—which I know is just on the end of your tongue—doesn't apply to me."

"The Bible doesn't say obey till you are of age, then do as you please. You are not seventeen yet, and Isaac was twenty when he submitted to be bound and laid upon the altar."

"Well, when I go to the altar, it shall be leaning on Dick's arm," said Enna, laughing. "I don't care if he is wild. I like him, and intend to marry him too."

"But are you not afraid?"

"Afraid of what?"

"That he will run through his property in a few years, and perhaps become an habitual drunkard and abusive to his wife."

"I mean to risk it anyhow," replied Enna sharply, "so it is not worth while for my friends to waste their breath in lecturing me on the subject."

"Oh, Enna! You can't expect a blessing, if you persist in being so undutiful. I think it would be well for you if your father were more like mine."

"Indeed! I wouldn't be your father's daughter for anything."

"And I am glad and thankful that I am."

Chapter Twenty-first

The human heart! 'tis a thing that lives
In the light of many a shrine;
And the gem of its own pure feeling gives
Too oft on brows that are false to shine;
It has many a cloud of care and woe
To shadow o'er it springs,
And the One above alone may know
The changing tune of its thousand strings.

—Mrs. L.P. Smith

MR. AND MRS. HORACE DINSMORE were most anxious to promote Elsie's happiness, and in order to that to win her to forgetfulness of her unworthy suitor. Being Christians they did not take her to the ball-room, the Opera, or the theater (nor would she have consented to go had they proposed it), but they provided for her every sort of suitable amusement within their reach. She was allowed to entertain as much company and to pay as many visits to neighbors and friends as she pleased.

But a constant round of gaiety was not to her taste; she loved quiet home pleasures and intellectual pursuits far better. And of these also she might take her fill, nor lack for sympathizing companionship, both parents, but especially her father, being of like mind with herself. They enjoyed many a book together, and she chose to pursue several studies with him.

And thus the weeks and months glided away not

unhappily, though at times she would be possessed with a restless longing for news from Egerton, and for the love that was denied her. Then her eyes would occasionally meet her father's with the old wistful, pleading look that he found so hard to resist.

He well understood their mute petition, yet it was one he could not grant. But he would take her in his arms, and giving her the fondest, tenderest caresses, would say, in a moved tone, "My darling, don't look at me in that way. It almost breaks my heart. Ah, if you could only be satisfied with your father's love!"

"I will try. Papa," was her usual answer, "and oh, your love is very sweet and precious!"

Such a little scene, occurring one morning in Elsie's boudoir, was interrupted by Chloe coming in to say that Miss Carrington had called to see her young mistress and was waiting in the drawing-room.

"Show her in here, mammy," Elsie said, disengaging herself from her father's arms, and smoothing out her dress. "She used to come here in the old times without waiting for an invitation."

The Carringtons had not been able quite to forgive the rejection of Herbert's suit, and since his death there had been a slight coolness between the two families, and the girls had seen much less of each other than in earlier days, their intercourse being confined to an occasional exchange of formal calls, except when they met at the house of some common acquaintance or friend. Still they were mutually attached, and of late had resumed much of their old warmth of manner toward each other.

"Ah, this seems like going back to the dear old times again," Lucy said when their greetings were over, and sending an admiring glance about the luxuriously furnished apartment as she spoke. "I always thought this the most charming of rooms, Elsie, but how many lovely things—perfect gems of art—you have added to it since I saw it last."

"Papa's gifts to his spoiled darling, most of them," answered Elsie, with a loving look and smile directed to him.

"Petted, but not spoiled," he said, returning the smile.

"No, indeed, I should think not," said Lucy. "Mamma says she is the most perfectly obedient, affectionate daughter she ever saw, and I can't tell you how often I have heard her wish I was more like her."

"Ah," said Elsie, "I think Mrs. Carrington has always looked at me through rose-colored spectacles."

After a little more chat Lucy told her errand. Her parents and herself, indeed the whole family, she said, had greatly regretted the falling off of their former intimacy and strongly desired to renew it, and she had come to beg Elsie to go home with her and spend a week at Ashlands in the old familiar way.

Elsie's eye brightened, and her cheek flushed. "Dear Lucy, how kind!" she exclaimed, then turned inquiringly to her father.

"Yes, it is very kind," he said. "Use your own pleasure, daughter. I think perhaps the change might do you good."

"Thanks, papa, then I shall go. Lucy, I accept your invitation with pleasure."

They were soon on their way, cantering briskly along side by side, Lucy in gay, almost wild spirits, and Elsie's depression rapidly vanishing beneath the combined influence of the bracing air and exercise, the brilliant sunshine, and her friend's lively sallies.

Arrived at Ashlands, she found herself received and welcomed with all the old warmth of affection. Mrs. Carrington folded her to her heart and wept over her. "My poor boy!" she whispered. "It seems almost to bring him back again to have you with us once more. But I will not mourn," she added, wiping her eyes; "for our loss has been his great gain."

Tender memories of Herbert, associated with nearly every room in the house, saddened and subdued Elsie's spirit for a time, yet helped to banish thoughts of Egerton from her mind.

But Lucy had a great deal to tell her, and in listening to these girlish confidences, Herbert was again half forgotten. Lucy too had spent the past summer in the North, and had there "met her fate." She was engaged, the course of true love seemed to be running smoothly, and they expected to marry in a year.

Elsie listened with interest, sympathizing warmly in her friend's happiness, but Lucy, who was watching her keenly, noticed a shade of deep sadness steal over her face.

"Now I have told you all my secrets," she said. "Won't you treat me as generously, by trusting me with yours?"

"If I had as happy a tale to tell," replied Elsie, the tears filling her eyes.

"You poor dear, what is wrong? Is it that papa refuses his consent?"

Elsie nodded, her heart was too full for speech.

"What a shame!" cried Lucy. "Does he really mean to keep you single all your life? Is he quite determined to make an old maid of you?"

"No, oh, no! But he does not believe my friend to be a good man. There seems to be some sad mistake, and I cannot blame papa, because if Mr. Egerton really was what he thinks him, it would be folly and sin for me to have anything to do with him, and indeed I could not give either hand or heart to one so vile—a profane swearer, gambler, drunkard, and rake."

"Oh, my, no!" and Lucy looked quite horrified. "But you don't believe him such a villain?"

"No, on the contrary, I think him a truly converted man. I believe he was a little wild at one time, for he told me he had been, but I believe, too, that he has truly repented, and therefore ought to be forgiven."

"Then I wouldn't give him up if I were you, father or no father," remarked Lucy, with spirit.

"But, Lucy, there is the command, 'Children, obey your parents.'"

"But you are not a child."

"Hardly more, not of age for more than two years."

"Well, when you are of age, surely you will consider a

lover's claims before those of a father."

"No," Elsie answered low and sadly. "I shall never marry without papa's consent. I love him far too dearly to grieve him so, and it would be running too fearful a risk."

"Then you have resigned your lover entirely?"

"Unless he can someday succeed in convincing papa that he is not so unworthy."

"Well, you are a model of filial piety! And deserve to be happy, and I am ever so sorry for you," cried Lucy, clasping her in her arms, and kissing her affectionately.

"Thank you, dear," Elsie said, "but oh, I can not bear to have my father blamed. Believing as he does, how could he do otherwise than forbid all intercourse between us? And he is so very, very kind, so tenderly affectionate to me. Ah, I could never do without his dear love!"

After this, the two had frequent talks together on the same subject, and though Lucy did not find any fault with Mr. Dinsmore, she yet pleaded Egerton's cause, urging that it seemed very unfair in Elsie to condemn him unheard, very hard not to allow him even so much as a parting word.

"I had no choice," Elsie said again and again, in a voice full of tears. "It was papa's command, and I could do nothing but obey. Oh, Lucy, it was very, very hard for me, too! And yet my father was doing only his duty, if his judgment of Mr. Egerton's character was correct."

One afternoon, when Elsie had been at Ashlands four or five days, Lucy came flying into her room; "Oh, I'm so glad to find you dressed! You see I'm in the midst of my toilet, and Scip has just brought up word that a gentleman is in the parlor asking for the young ladies—Miss Dinsmore and Miss Carrington. Would you mind going down alone and entertaining him till I come? Do, there's a dear."

"Who is he?"

"Scip didn't seem to have quite understood the name, but it must be someone we both know, and if you don't mind going, it would be a relief to my nerves to know that he's not sitting there with nothing to do but count the minutes, and think, 'What an immense time it takes Miss Carrington to dress. She must be very anxious to make a good impression upon me.' For you see men are so conceited, they are always imagining we're laying ourselves out to secure their admiration."

"I will go down then," Elsie answered, smiling, "and do what I can to keep him from thinking any such unworthy thoughts of you. But please follow me as soon as you can."

The caller had the drawing-room to himself, and as Elsie entered was standing at the centre-table with his back toward her. As she drew near, he turned abruptly, caught her hand in his, threw his arm about her waist, and kissed her passionately, crying in a low tone of rapturous delight, "My darling, I have you at last! Oh, how I have suffered from this cruel separation."

It was Egerton, and for a few moments she forgot everything else, in her glad surprise at the unexpected meeting.

He drew her to a sofa, and still keeping his arm about her, poured out a torrent of fond loverlike words, mingled with tender reproaches that she had given him up so easily, and protestations of his innocence of the vices and crimes laid to his charge.

At first Elsie flushed rosy red, and a sweet light of love and joy shone in the soft eyes, half veiled by their heavy, drooping lashes, but as he went on, her cheek grew deathly pale, and she struggled to free herself from his embrace.

"Let me go!" she cried, in an agitated tone of earnest entreaty. "I must, indeed I must! I can't stay—I ought not, I should not have come in, or allowed you to speak to, or touch me. Papa has forbidden all intercourse between us, and he will be so angry." And she burst into tears.

"Then don't go back to him. Stay with me, and give me a right to protect you from his anger. I can't bear to see you weep, and if you will be mine—my own little wife, you shall never have cause to shed another tear," he said, drawing her closer to him and kissing them away.

"No, no, I cannot, I cannot! You must let me go, indeed you must!" she cried, shrinking from the touch of his lip upon her cheek, and averting her face, "I am doing wrong, very wrong to stay here!"

"No, I shall hold you fast for a few blissful moments at least," he answered, tightening his grasp and repeating his caresses, as she struggled the harder to be free. "You cannot be so cruel as to refuse to hear my defense."

"Oh, I cannot stay another moment—I must not hear another word, for every instant that I linger I am guilty of a fresh act of disobedience to papa. I shall be compelled to call for help if you do not loose your hold."

He took his arm from her waist, but still held fast to her hand. "No, don't do that," he said. "Think what a talk it would make. I shall detain you but a moment, and surely you may as well stay that much longer—'in for a penny, in for a pound,' you know. Oh, Elsie, can't you give me a little hope."

"If you can gain papa's approval, not otherwise."

"But when you come of age."

"I shall never marry without my father's consent."

"Surely you carry your ideas of obedience too far. You owe a duty to yourself and to me, as well as to your father. Excuse my plainness, but in the course of nature we shall both outlive him, and is it right to sacrifice the happiness of our two lives because he has unfortunately imbibed a prejudice against me?"

"I could expect no blessing upon a union entered into in direct opposition to my father's wishes and commands," she answered with sad and gentle firmness.

"That's a hard kind of obedience, and I don't think it would answer to put in practice in all cases," he said bitterly.

"Perhaps not. I do not attempt to decide for others, but I am convinced of my own duty, and know too that I should be wretched indeed, if I had to live under papa's frown. And oh, how I am disobeying him now! I must go this instant! Release my hand, Mr. Egerton." And she tried with all her strength to wrench it free.

"No, no, not yet," he said entreatingly. "I have not given you half the proofs of my innocence that I can bring forward. Do me the simple justice to stay and hear them."

She made no reply but half yielded, ceasing her struggles for a moment. She had no strength to free her hand from his grasp, and could not bear to call others upon the scene. Trembling with agitation and eagerness, she waited for his promised proofs, but instead he only poured forth a continuous stream of protestations, expostulations and entreaties.

"Mr. Egerton, I must, I must go," she repeated. "This is nothing to the purpose, and I cannot stay to hear it."

A step was heard approaching. He hastily drew her toward him, touched his lips again to her cheek, released her, and she darted from the room by one door, as Lucy entered by another.

"Where is she? Gone? What's the matter? Wasn't she pleased to see you? Wouldn't she stay?"

Lucy looked into the disappointed, angry, chagrined face of Egerton, and in her surprise and vexation piled question upon question without giving him time to answer.

"No, the girl's a fool!" he muttered angrily, and turning hastily from her, paced rapidly to and fro for a moment. Then suddenly recollecting himself, "I beg pardon, Miss Carrington," he said, coming back to the sofa on which she sat regarding him with a perturbed, displeased countenance, "I—I forgot myself. But you will perhaps, know how to excuse an almost distracted lover."

"Really, sir," returned Lucy coolly, "your words just now did not sound very lover-like, and would rather lead one to suspect that possibly Mr. Dinsmore may be in the right."

He flushed hotly. "What can you mean, Miss Carrington?"

"That your love is for her fortune rather than for herself."

"Indeed you wrong me. I adore Miss Dinsmore, and would consider myself the happiest of mortals could I but secure her hand, even though she came to me penniless. But she has imbibed the most absurd, ridiculous ideas of filial duty and refuses to give me the smallest encouragement unless I can gain her father's consent and approval, which, seeing he has conceived a violent dislike to me, is a hopeless thing. Now can you not realize that the more ardent my love for her, the more frantically impatient I would feel under such treatment?"

"Perhaps so. Men are so different from women, but nothing could ever make me apply such an epithet to the man I loved."

"Distracted with disappointed hopes, I was hardly a sane man at the moment, Miss Carrington," he said deprecatingly.

"The coveted interview has proved entirely unsatisfactory then?" she said in a tone of inquiry.

"Yes, and yet I am most thankful to have had sight and speech of her once more, truly grateful to you for bringing it about so cleverly. But—oh, Miss Carrington, could you be persuaded to assist me still further, you would lay me under lasting obligations!"

"Please explain yourself, sir," she answered coldly, moving farther from him, as he attempted to take her hand.

"Excuse me," he said. "I am not one inclined to take liberties with ladies, but I am hardly myself today—my overpowering emotion—my half distracted state of mind—"

Breaking off his sentence abruptly, and putting his hand to his head, "I believe I shall go mad if I have to resign all hope of winning the sweet, lovely Elsie," he exclaimed excitedly, "and I see only one way of doing it. If I could carry her off, and get her quite out of her father's reach, so that no fear of him need deter her from following the promptings of her own heart, I am sure I could induce her to consent to marry me at once. Miss Carrington, will you help me?"

"Never! If Elsie chooses to run away with you, and wants any assistance from me, she shall have it, but I will have nothing to do with kidnapping."

He urged, entreated, used every argument he could think of, but with no other effect than rousing Lucy's anger and indignation. "Underhand dealings were not in her line" she told him, and finally—upon his intimating that what she had already done might be thought to come under that head—almost ordered him out of the house.

He went, and hurrying to her friend's room, she found her walking about it in a state of great agitation, and weeping bitterly.

"Oh, Lucy, how could you? How could you?" she cried, wringing her hands and sobbing in pitiable distress. "I had no thought of him when I went down. I did not know you knew him, or that he was in this part of the country at all. I was completely taken by surprise, and have disobeyed papa's most express commands, and he will never forgive me, never! No, not that either, but he will be very, very angry. Oh, what shall I do!"

"Oh, Elsie, dear, don't be so troubled! I am as sorry as I can be," said Lucy, with tears in her eyes. "I meant to do you a kindness, indeed I did. I thought it would be a joyful surprise to you.

"I met him last summer at Saratoga. He came there immediately from Lansdale, and somehow we found out directly that we both knew you, and that I was a near neighbor and very old friend of yours; and he told me the whole story of your love-affair, and quite enlisted me in his cause. He seemed so depressed and melancholy at your loss, and grieved so over the hasty way in which your father had separated you—not even allowing a word of farewell.

"He told me he hoped and believed you were still faithful to him in your heart, but he could not get to see or speak to you, or hold any correspondence with you. And so I arranged this way of bringing you together."

"It was kindly meant, I have no doubt, Lucy, but oh, you don't know what you have done! I tremble at the very thought of papa's anger when he hears it, for I have done and permitted things he said he would not allow for thousands of dollars."

"Well, dear, I don't think you could help it, and I'm so sorry for my share in it," said Lucy, putting her arms round her, and kissing her wet cheek. "But perhaps your father will not be so very angry with you after all, and at any rate you are too old to be whipped, so a scolding will be the worst you will be likely to get."

"He never did whip me, never struck me a blow in his life, but I would prefer the pain of a dozen whippings to what I expect," said Elsie, with a fresh burst of tears.

"What is that, you poor dear?" asked Lucy. "I can't imagine what he could do worse than beat you."

"He may put me away from his arms for weeks or months, and be cold, and stern, and distant to me, never giving me a caress or even so much as a kind word or look. Oh, if he should do that, how can I bear it!"

"Well, don't tell him anything about it. I wouldn't, and I don't see any reason why you should."

Elsie shook her head sorrowfully. "I must. I never conceal anything—any secret of my own—from him, and I should feel like a guilty thing, acting a lie, and could not look him in the face. And he would know from my very look and manner that something was wrong, and would question me, and make me tell him all. Lucy, I must go home at once."

"No, indeed, you must not. Why, you were to stay a week—two days longer than this, and if you were ready to start this minute, it would be quite dark before you could possibly reach the Oaks."

Elsie looked at her watch, and perceiving that her friend was right, gave up the idea of going that day, but said she must leave the next morning. To that Lucy again objected. "I can't bear to lose those two days of your promised visit," she said, "for if you are determined to tell your papa all about this, there's no knowing when he will allow you to come here again."

"Never, I fear," sighed Elsie.

"I haven't been able to help feeling a little hard to him on poor Herbert's account," Lucy went on, "and I believe that had something to do with my readiness to help Egerton to outwit him in obtaining an interview with you. But I'll never do anything of the kind again; so he needn't be afraid to let you come to see us."

She then told Elsie what had passed in the drawing-room between Egerton and herself—his request and her indignant refusal.

It helped to shake Elsie's confidence in the man, and made her still more remorseful in view of that day's dis-obedience, for she could not deceive herself into the belief that she had been altogether blameless. "As I said before, I can't bear the idea of losing you so soon," con-tinued Lucy, "but there is still another reason why I must beg of you to stay till the set time of your leaving. Mamma knows nothing about this affair, and would be exceedingly displeased with me, if she should find it out, as of course she must, if you go tomorrow, as that would naturally call out an explanation. So, dear, do promise me that you will give up the idea."

Elsie hesitated, but not liking to bring Lucy into trou-ble, finally yielded to her urgent entreaties, and con-sented to stay.

All the enjoyment of her visit, however, was over. She felt it impossible to rest till her father knew all, shed many tears in secret, and had much ado to conceal the traces of them, and appear cheerful in the presence of the family.

But the two wretched days were over at last, and declining the urgent invitations of her friends to linger with them a little longer, she bade them an affectionate farewell, and set out for home.

Jim had been sent to escort her, another servant with the wagon for Chloe and the luggage. Struck with a sudden fear that she might meet or be overtaken by Egerton, Elsie ordered Jim to keep up close in the rear, then touching the whip to her horse, started off at a brisk canter. Her thoughts were full of the coming interview with her father, which she dreaded exceedingly, while at the same time she longed to have it over. She drew rein at the great gates leading into the grounds, and the servant dismounted and opened them.

"Jim," she asked, "is your master at home?"

"Dunno, Miss Elsie, but the missus am gone ober to Ion to spend the day, an lef' little Marse Horace at Roselands."

"Why, what's the matter, Jim?"

"De missus at Ion little bit sick, I 'lieve, Miss Elsie."

"And papa didn't go with them?"

"Yes, miss, but he comed right back again, and I 'spect he's in de house now."

"Dear papa! He came back to receive me," murmured Elsie to herself, as she rode on, and a scalding tear fell at the thought of how the loving look and fond caress with which he was sure to greet her, would be quickly exchanged for dark frowns, and stern, cold reproofs.

"Oh, if I were a child again, I believe I should hope he would just whip me at once, and then forgive me, and it would be all over. But now—oh, dear! How long will his displeasure last?"

It was just as she had expected. He was on the veranda, watching for her coming—hastened forward, assisted her to alight, embraced her tenderly, then pushing aside her veil, looked searchingly into her face.

"What is the matter?" he asked, as her eyes met his for an instant with a beseeching, imploring glance, then fell beneath his gaze while her face flushed crimson.

She tried to answer him, but her tongue refused to do its office, there was a choking sensation in her throat and her lips quivered.

He led her into his private study, took off her hat and threw it aside, and seating her on a sofa still keeping his arm about her—for she was trembling very much—asked again, "What is the matter? What has gone wrong with you, my daughter?"

His tone, his look, his manner were very gentle and tender, but that only increased her remorse and self-reproach.

"Papa, don't be so kind," she faltered. "I—I don't deserve it, for I have disobeyed you."

"Is it possible! When? Where? And how? Can it be that you have seen and spoken with that—scoundrel, Elsie?"

"Yes, papa." Her voice was very low and tremulous, her heart throbbed almost to suffocation, her bosom heaved tumultuously, and her color came and went with every breath.

He rose and paced hurriedly across the room two or three times, then coming back to her side, "Tell me all about it," he said sternly—"every action, every word spoken by either, as far as you can recall it."

She obeyed in the same low, tremulous tones in which she had answered him before, her voice now and then broken by a half-smothered sob, and her eyes never once meeting his, which she felt were fixed so severely upon her tearful, downcast face.

He cross-questioned her till he knew all that had passed nearly as well as if he had been present through the whole interview, his tones growing more and more stern and angry.

"And you dared to permit all that, Elsie?" he exclaimed when she had finished. "To allow that vile wretch to put his arm around you, hold your hand in his, for half an hour probably, and even to press his lips again and again to yours or to your cheek, and that after I had told you I would not have him take such a liberty with you for half I am worth, and—"

"Not to my lips, papa."

"Then it is not quite so bad as I thought, but bad enough certainly, and all this after I had positively forbidden you to even so much as exchange the slightest salutation with him. What am I to think of such high-handed rebellion?"

"Papa," she said beseechingly, "is not that too hard a word? I did not disobey deliberately—I don't think anything could have induced me to go into that room knowing that he was there. I was taken by surprise, and when he had got hold of my hand I tried in vain to get it free."

"Don't attempt to excuse yourself, Elsie. You could have escaped from him at once, by simply raising your voice and calling for assistance. I do not believe it would have been impossible to avoid even that first embrace, and it fairly makes my blood boil to think he succeeded in giving it to you. How dared you so disobey me as to submit to it?"

"Papa, at the moment I forgot everything but—but just that he was there."

The last words were spoken in a voice scarcely raised above a whisper, while her head drooped lower and lower and her cheek grew hot with shame.

"Did I ever take forgetfulness of my orders as any excuse of disobedience?" he asked in as stern a tone as he had ever used to her.

"No, papa, but oh, don't be very angry with me!"

"I am exceedingly displeased with you, Elsie! So much so that nothing but your sex saves you from a severe chastisement. And I cannot allow you to escape punishment. You must be taught that though no longer a mere child, you are not yet old enough to disobey me with impunity. Hush!" as she seemed about to speak, "I will not have a word of reply. Go to your own apartments and consider yourself confined to them till you hear further from me. Stay!" he added as she rose to obey. "When did all this occur?"

She told him in her low, tearful tones, her utterance half choked with sobs.

"Two days ago, and yet your confession has been delayed till now. Does that look like penitence for your fault?"

She explained why she had not returned home at

once, but he refused to accept the excuse, and ordered her away as sternly as before.

She obeyed in silence, controlling her feelings by a great effort, until she had gained the privacy of her own apartments, then giving way to a fit of almost hysterical weeping. It was years since her father had been seriously displeased with her, and loving him with such intense affection, his anger and sternness nearly broke her heart.

Her tender conscience pricked her sorely too, adding greatly to her distress by its reproaches on account of her disobedience and her delay in confessing it.

It came to her mind at length that her heavenly Father might be more tender and forbearing with her, more ready to forgive and restore to favor, than her earthly one. She remembered the sweet words, "There is forgiveness with thee, that thou mayest be feared." "If any man sin, we have an advocate with the Father, Jesus Christ the righteous." She went to him with her sin and sorrow, asking pardon for the past and help for the future. She asked, too, that the anger of her earthly parent might be turned away, that the Lord would dispose him to forgive and love her as before.

She rose from her knees with a heart, though still sad and sorrowful, yet lightened of more than half its load.

But the day was a very long one. With a mind so disturbed she could not settle to any employment, or find amusement in anything. She passed the time in wandering restlessly from room to room, starting and trembling as now and then she thought she heard her father's step or voice, then weeping afresh as she found that he did not come near her.

When the dinner-bell rang she hoped he would send, or come to her. But instead he sent her meal to her, such an one as was usual upon their table—both luxurious and abundant—which comforted her with the hope that he was less displeased with her than at other times when he had allowed her little more than prison fare. But excitement and mental distress had brought on a severe headache. She had no appetite, and sent the food away almost untasted.

It was mild, beautiful weather in the early spring, such weather as makes one feel it a trial to be compelled to stay within doors, and Elsie longed for her favorite retreat in the grounds.

In the afternoon some ladies called. Mr. Dinsmore was out, and she dared not go to the drawing room without permission. But her headache furnished sufficient excuse for declining to see them and they went away.

Shortly after, she heard her father's return. He had not been off the estate, or out of sight of the house. He was keeping guard over her, but still did not come near her.

Just at tea-time she again heard the sound of wheels, then her father's, mother's, and little brother's voices.

"Mamma and Horace have come home," she thought with a longing desire to run out and embrace them.

"Oh, papa, has sister come home?" she heard the child's voice ask in eager tones.

"Yes."

"Oh, then I must run into her room and kiss her!"

"No, you must not. Stay here."

"But why mustn't I go to sister, papa?"

"Because I forbid it."

Every word of the short colloquy reached Elsie's ear, adding to her grief and dismay. Was she, then, to be separated from all the rest of the family? Did her father fear that she would exert a bad influence over Horace, teaching him to be disobedient and willful? How deeply humbled and ashamed she felt at the thought.

Rose gave her husband a look of surprised, anxious inquiry. "Is Elsie sick, dear?" she asked.

"No, Rose, but she is in disgrace with me," he answered in an undertone, as he led the way into the house.

"Horace, you astonish me! What can she have done to displease you?"

"Come in here, and I will tell you," he said, throwing open the door of his study.

Rose listened in silence, while he repeated to her the substance of Elsie's confession, mingled with expressions of his own anger and indignation.

"Poor child!" murmured Rose, as he concluded. "Horace, don't be hard with her. She must have suffered a great deal in these last three days."

"Yes," he answered in a moved tone, "when I think of that, I can scarcely refrain from going to her, taking her in my arms, and lavishing caresses and endearments upon her. But then comes the thought of her allowing that scoundrel to do the same, and I am ready almost to whip her for it." His face flushed hotly, and his dark eyes flashed as he spoke.

"Oh, my dear!" exclaimed Rose, half frightened at his vehemence. "You cannot mean it ?"

"Rose," he said, pacing to and fro in increasing excitement, "the fellow is a vile wretch, whose very touch I esteem pollution to a sweet, fair, innocent young creature like my daughter. I told her so, and positively forbade her to so much as look at him, or permit him to see her face, if it could be avoided, or to recognize, or hold the slightest communication with him in and way. Yet in defiance of all this, she allows him to take her hand and hold it for, I don't know how long, put his arm around her waist and kiss her a number of times. Now what does such disobedience deserve?"

"Had she no excuse to offer?"

"Excuse? Yes, she did not disobey deliberately—was taken by surprise—forgot everything but that he was there."

"Well, my dear," and Rose's hand was laid affectionately on his arm, while a tender smile played about her mouth, and her sweet blue eyes looked fondly into his. "You know how it is with lovers, if you will only look back a very few years. I think there were times when you and I forgot that there was anybody in the wide world but just our two selves."

A smile, a tender caress, a few very lover-like words, and resuming his gravity and seriousness, Mr. Dinsmore went on: "But you forget the odious character of the man. If I had objected to him from mere prejudice or whim, it would have been a very different thing."

"But you know Elsie does not believe—"

"She ought to believe what her father tells her," he interrupted hotly. "But believe or not, she must and shall obey me, and if she does not I shall punish her."

"And to do that, you need only look coldly on her, and refrain from giving her caresses and endearing words. Such treatment from her dearly loved father would of itself be sufficient, very soon, to crush her tender, sensitive spirit."

His face softened, the frown left his brow, and the angry fire his eye. "My poor darling!" he murmured, with a sigh, his thoughts going back to a time of estrangement between them long years ago. "Yes, Rose, you are right. She is a very tender, delicate, sensitive plant, and it behooves her father to be exceeding gentle and forbearing with her."

"Then you will forgive her, and take her to your heart again?"

"Yes—if she is penitent—and tell her that she owes it to her mother's intercession, for I had intended to make her feel herself in disgrace for days or weeks."

Chloe was at that moment carrying a large silver waiter, filled with delicacies, into the apartments of her young mistress. "Now, darlin', do try to eat to please your ole mammy," she said coaxingly, as she set it down before her. "I'se taken lots ob pains to fix up dese tings dat my pet chile so fond ob."

Elsie's only answer was a sad sort of smile, but for the sake of the loving heart that had prompted the careful preparation of the tempting meal—the loving eyes that watched her as she ate, she tried to do her best.

Only half satisfied with the result, Chloe bore the waiter away again, while Elsie seated herself in a large easy-chair that was drawn up close to the glass doors opening upon the lawn and laying her head back upon its cushions, turned her eyes toward the outer world, looking longingly upon the shaded alleys and gay parter-res, the lawn with its velvet carpet of emerald green, where a fountain cast up its cool showers of spray, and long shadows slept, alternating with brilliant patches of ruddy light from the slowly sinking sun.

She sighed deeply, and her eyes filled with tears. "How long should she be forbidden to wander there at her own sweet will?"

A soft, cool hand was gently laid upon her aching brow, and looking up she saw her father standing by her side. She had not heard his approach, for his slippered feet made no noise in passing over the rich velvet carpet.

His face was grave, but no longer stern or angry. "Does your head ache, daughter?" he asked almost tenderly.

"Yes, papa, but not half so badly as my heart does," she answered, a tear rolling quickly down her cheek. "I am so sorry for my disobedience. Oh, papa, will you for-give me?" And her eyes sought his with the imploring look he ever found it well-nigh impossible to resist.

"Yes, I will—I do," he said, stooping to press a kiss upon the quivering lips. "I had thought I ought to keep you in disgrace some time longer, but your mamma has pleaded for you, and for her sake—and for the sake of a time, long ago, when I caused my little girl much unde-served suffering," he added, his tones growing tremu-lous with emotion, "I forgive and receive you back into favor at once."

She threw her arm about his neck, and as he drew her to his breast, laid her head down there, weeping tears of joy and thankfulness. "Dear, kind mamma! And you too, best and dearest of fathers! I don't deserve it," she sobbed. "I am afraid I ought to be punished for such disobedience."

"I think you have been" he said pityingly. "The last three days can hardly have been very happy ones to you."

"No, papa, very, very wretched."

"My poor child! Ah, I must take better care of my precious one in future. I shall allow you to go nowhere without either your mother or myself to guard and pro-tect you. Also, I shall break off your intimacy with Lucy

Carrington. She is henceforth to be to you a mere speaking acquaintance. Come, now we will take a little stroll through the grounds. The cool air will, I hope, do your head good."

CHAPTER TWENTY-SECOND

'Twas the doubt that thou wert false,
That wrung my heart with pain;
But now I know thy perfidy,
I shall be well again.

—BRYANT

ELSIE SUBMITTED WITHOUT a murmur to her father's requirements and restrictions, but though there was nothing else to remind her that she had been for one sad day in disgrace with him—his manner toward her having again all the old tender fondness—she did not fully recover her spirits, but, spite of her struggles to be cheerful and hopeful, seemed often depressed, and grew pale and thin day by day.

Her father noticed it with deep concern and anxiety. "Something must be done," he said one day to his wife. "The child is drooping strangely, and I fear will lose her health. I must try what change will do for her. What do you say to a year in Europe?"

"For all of us?"

"Yes, for you and me and our two children."

"It might be very pleasant, and Elsie has never been."

"No, I have always meant to take her, but found home so enjoyable that I have put it off from year to year."

Elsie entered the room as he spoke.

"Come here, daughter," he said, making room for her

on the sofa by his side. "I was just saying to mamma that I think of taking you all to Europe for a year. How should you like that?"

"Oh, very much, papa!" she answered, looking up brightly. "I should so enjoy seeing all the places you have told me of—all the scenes of your adventures when you traveled there before."

"Then I think we will go. Shall we not, mamma?"

"Yes, but I must pay a visit home first, and do some preparatory shopping in Philadelphia. Can we go on in time to spend some weeks there before sailing?"

"You might, my dear, but I shall have to stay behind to arrange matters here, which will take some time, in contemplation of so lengthened an absence from the estate."

"Then I suppose we must have a temporary separation," said Rose, in a jesting tone. "I had better take the children and go home at once, so that Elsie and I can be getting through our shopping, etc., while you are busy here."

"No, Rose. You may go, and take Horace with you, if you like, but Elsie must stay with me. I cannot trust her even with you!"

"Oh, papa!" And the sweet face flushed crimson, the soft eyes filled with tears.

"I think you misunderstand me, daughter," he said kindly. "I do not mean that I fear you would fail in obedience to my commands or my wishes, but that I must keep you under my protection. Besides, I cannot possibly spare all my treasures—wife, son, and daughter—at once. Would you wish to go and leave me quite alone?"

"Oh no, no, indeed, you dear, dearest father!" she cried, putting her arm round his neck, and gazing in his face with eyes beaming with joy and love.

"Yours is the better plan, I believe, my dear," said Rose. "I would rather not have you left alone, and I think I could do what is necessary for Elsie, in the way of shopping and ordering dresses made, if she likes to trust me."

So it was arranged. Three days after this conversation Mrs. Dinsmore left for Philadelphia, taking little Horace with her, and a fortnight later Mr. Dinsmore followed with Elsie.

Dearly as the young girl loved Rose and her little brother, it had yet been an intense pleasure to her to have her father all to herself, and be everything to him for those two weeks, and she was almost sorry to have them came to an end.

It was late at night when they reached the City of Brotherly Love. Mr. Allison's residence was several miles distant from the depot, but his carriage was there in waiting for them.

"Are the family all well, Davis?" inquired Mr. Dinsmore, addressing the coachman, as he placed Elsie in the vehicle.

"All well, sir. Mrs. Dinsmore and the little boy too."

"Ah, I am thankful for that. You may drive on at once. My man John will call a hack and follow us with Aunt Chloe and the baggage."

"Did you give John the checks, papa?" asked Elsie, as he took his seat by her side, and Davis shut the carriage door.

"Yes. How weary you look, my poor child! There, lean on me," and he put his arm about her and made her lay her head on his shoulder.

They drove on rapidly, passing through several comparatively silent and deserted streets, then suddenly the horses slackened their pace, a bright light shone in at the carriage window and the hum of many voices and sound of many feet attracted the attention of the travelers.

Elsie started and raised her head, asking, "What is it, papa?"

"We are passing a theatre, and it seems the play is just over, judging by the crowds that are pouring from its doors."

Davis reined in his horses to avoid running over those who were crossing the street, and Elsie, glancing from the window, caught sight of a face she knew only too well. Its owner was in the act of stepping from the door of the theatre, and staggered as he did so—would have fallen to the ground had he not been held up by his companion, a gaudily dressed, brazen-faced woman, whose character there was no mistaking.

"Ha, ha, Tom!" she cried, with a loud and boisterous laugh. "I saved you from a downfall that time, which I'll be bound is more than that Southern heiress of yours would have done."

"Now don't be throwing her up to me again, Bet," he answered thickly, reeling along so close to our travelers that they caught the scent of his breath. "I tell you again she can't hold a candle to you, and I never cared for her. It was the money I was after."

Mr. Dinsmore saw a deadly pallor suddenly overspread his daughter's face; for a single instant her eyes sought his with an expression of mute despairing agony that wrung his heart, then all was darkness as again the carriage rolled rapidly onward.

"My poor, poor darling!" he murmured, drawing her close to him and folding his arms about her as if he would shield her from every danger and evil, while hers crept around his neck and her head dropped upon his breast.

The carriage rattled on over the rough stones. Elsie clung with death-like grasp to her father, shudder after shudder shaking her whole frame, in utter silence at first, but at length, as they came upon a smoother road and moved with less noise and jolting, "Papa," she whispered, "oh, what a fearful, fearful fate you have saved me from! Thank God for a father's protecting love and care!"

"Thank him that I have my darling safe," he responded in a deeply moved tone, and caressing her with exceeding tenderness.

In another moment they had stopped before Mr. Allison's door, which was thrown wide open almost on the instant, for Rose and Edward were up, waiting and listening for their coming.

"Come at last! Glad to see you!" cried the latter, springing down the steps to greet his brother in-law as he alighted. Then, as Mr. Dinsmore turned, lifted his daughter from the carriage, and half carried her into the house, "But what's the matter? Elsie ill? Hurt? Have you had an accident?"

Rose stood waiting in the hall. "My dear husband!" she exclaimed in a tone of mingled affection, surprise, and alarm. "What is it? What is wrong with our darling? Come this way, into the sitting-room, and lay her on the sofa."

"She has received a heavy blow, Rose, but I think—I hope it will turn out for her good in the end," he said low and tremulously, as he laid her down.

She seemed in a half-fainting condition, and Edward rushed away in search of restoratives.

Rose asked no more questions at the time, nor did her husband give any further information, but in silence, broken only now and then by a subdued whisper, they both devoted their energies to Elsie's restoration.

"Shall I go for a doctor?" asked Edward.

"No, thank you. I think she will be better presently," answered Mr. Dinsmore.

"I am better now," murmured Elsie feebly. "Papa, if you will help me up to bed, I shall do very well."

"Can't you eat something first?" asked Rose. "I have a nice little supper set out in the next room for papa and you."

Elsie shook her head, and sighed, "I don't think I could, mamma. I am not at all hungry."

"I want you to try, though," said her father. "It is some hours now since you tasted food, and I think you need it." And lifting her tenderly in his arms he carried her into the supper-room, where he seated her at the table in an easy-chair which Edward hastily wheeled up for her use.

To please her father she made a determined effort, and succeeded in swallowing a few mouthfuls. After that he helped her to her room and left her in the care of

Rose and Chloe.

Having seen with her own eyes, and heard with her own ears, Elsie could no longer doubt the utter unworthiness of Egerton, or his identity with Tom Jackson, of whose vices and crimes she had heard from both her father and Walter, with whom she still kept up a correspondence. She loved him no longer, nay, she had never loved him: her affection had been bestowed upon the man she believed him to be, not the man that he was. But now the scales had fallen from her eyes, she saw him in all his hideous moral deformity, and shrank with horror and loathing from the recollection that his arm had once encircled her waist, his lip touched her cheek. She could now appreciate her father's feelings of anger and indignation on learning that she had permitted such liberties, and felt more deeply humbled and penitent on account of it than ever before.

She slept little that night, and did not leave her room for several days. The sudden shock had quite unnerved her, but the cause of her illness remained a secret between herself and her parents, who watched over her with the tenderest solicitude, and spared no effort to cheer and comfort her. She seemed at this time to shrink from all companionship but theirs, although she and her mamma's younger brothers and sisters had always entertained a warm friendship for each other.

On the fourth day after their arrival her father took her out for a drive, and returning left her resting on the sofa in her dressing-room, while he and Rose went for a short walk.

The door-bell rang, and presently Chloe came up with a very smiling face to ask if "Marse Walter" might come in.

"Walter?" cried Elsie, starting up. "Yes, indeed!"

She had scarcely spoken the words before he was there beside her, shaking hands, and kissing her, saying with a gay boyish laugh, "I suppose your uncle has a right?"

"Yes, certainly, though I don't know when he ever

claimed it before. But oh, how glad I am to see you! And how you've grown and improved. Sit down, do. There's an easy-chair.

"Excuse my not getting up. Papa bade me lie and rest for an hour."

"Thanks, yes, and I know you always obey orders. And so you're on the sick list? What's the matter?"

An expression of pain crossed her features and the color faded from her cheek. "I have been ailing a little," she said, "but am better now. How is Arthur?"

"H'm! Well enough physically, but—in horrible disgrace with papa. You've no idea, Elsie, to what an extent that Tom Jackson has fleeced him. He's over head and ears in debt, and my father's furious. He has put the whole matter into Horace's hands for settlement. Did he tell you about it?"

"No, he only said he expected to go to Princeton tomorrow to attend to some business. He would have gone sooner, but didn't like to leave me."

"Careful of you as ever! That's right. I say, Elsie, I think Horace has very sensible ideas about matters and things."

"Do you? I own I think so myself," she answered with a quiet smile.

"Yes, you see Arthur is in debt some thousands, a good share of it what they call debts of honor. Papa had some doubt as to whether they ought to be paid, and asked Horace what was his opinion. Adelaide wrote me the whole story, you see. Here, I'll give it to you in his exact words, as she reports them," he added, taking a letter from his pocket and reading aloud, "'Father, don't think of such a thing! Why, surely it would be encouraging gambling, which is a ruinous vice, and paying a man for robbing and cheating. I would, if necessary, part with the last cent to pay an honest debt, but a so-called debt of honor—of dishonor would be more correct—I would not pay if I had more money than I could find other uses for.' And I think he was right. Don't you?" concluded Walter.

"I think papa is always right."

"Yes? Well, I was afraid you didn't think he was in regard to that—fellow you met out in Lansdale. I've been wanting to see you to tell you what I know of the scoundrelism of Tom Jackson, and the proof that they are one and the same."

"Yes, I know, I—I believe it now, Walter, and—But don't let us speak of it again," she faltered, turning deathly pale and almost gasping for breath.

"I won't. I didn't know you'd mind, I—I'm very sorry," he stammered, looking anxious, and vexed with himself.

"Never mind. I shall soon learn not to care. Now tell me about Arthur. Will he stay and finish his course?"

"No, papa says his patience is worn out, and his purse can stand no more such drains as Arthur has put upon it two or three times already. So he is to leave and go home as soon as Horace has settled up his affairs."

"And you?"

"I hope to go on and to graduate in another year."

"Oh, Wal, I'm so glad! So thankful you haven't followed in poor Arthur's footsteps."

"He wouldn't let me, Elsie, he actually wouldn't. I know I'm lacking in self-reliance and firmness, and if Art had chosen to lead me wrong, I'm afraid he'd have succeeded. But he says—poor fellow!—that it's enough for one to be a disgrace to the family, and has tried to keep me out of temptation. And you can't think how much my correspondence with you has helped to keep me straight. Your letters always did me so much good."

"Oh, thank you for telling me that!" she cried, with bright, glad tears glistening in her eyes.

"No, 'tis I that owe thanks to you," he said, looking

down meditatively at the carpet and twirling his watch-key between his finger and thumb.

"Poor Art! This ought to have been his last year, and doubtless would if he had only kept out of bad company."

"Ah, Wal, I hope that you will never forget that 'evil communications corrupt good manners.'"

"I hope not, Elsie. I wish you could stay and attend our commencement. What do you say? Can't you? It comes off in about a fortnight."

"No, Wal. I'm longing to get away, and papa has engaged our passage in the next steamer. But perhaps we may return in time to see you graduate next year."

"What, in such haste to leave America! I'm afraid you're losing your patriotism," he said playfully.

"Ah, it is no want of love for my dear native land that makes me impatient to be gone!" she answered half sadly.

"And are you really to be gone a year?"

"So papa intends, but of course everything in this world is uncertain."

"I shall look anxiously for my European letters, and expect them to be very interesting."

"I'll do my best, Wal," she said languidly, "but I don't feel, just now, as if I could ever write anything worth reading."

"I think I never saw you so blue," he said in a lively, jesting tone. "I must tell you of the fun we fellows have, and if it doesn't make you wish yourself one of us, well—" and he launched out into an animated description of various practical jokes played off by the students upon their professors or on each other.

He succeeded at length in coaxing some of the old brightness into the sweet face, and Mr. and Mrs. Dinsmore, mounting the stairs on their return from their walk, exchanged glances of delighted surprise at the sound of a silvery laugh which had not greeted their ears for days.

Walter received a hearty welcome from both. His visit, though necessarily short, was of real service to Elsie, doing much to rouse her out of herself and her grief, thus beginning the cure which time and change of scene—dulling the keen edge of sorrow and disappointment, and giving pleasant occupation to her thoughts—would at length carry on to completion.

CHAPTER TWENTY-THIRD

The shaken tree grows firmer at the roots;
So love grows firmer for some blasts of doubt.

IT WAS TWO YEARS or more since the Oaks had suffered
the temporary loss of its master and mistress, yet they had
not returned. They still lingered on foreign shores, and
Mrs. Murray, who had been left at the head of household
affairs, looked in vain for news of their home-coming.

She now and then received a short business letter
from Mr. Dinsmore or of directions from Rose, or a
longer one from the latter or Elsie, giving entertaining
bits of travel, etc., and occasionally Adelaide would ride
over from Roselands and delight the old housekeeper's
heart by reading aloud a lively gossipy epistle one or the
other had addressed to her.

How charmed and interested were both reader and
listener, especially when they came upon one of Rose's
graphic accounts of their presentation at court—in
London, Paris, Vienna, or St. Petersburg—wherein she
gave a minute description of Elsie's dress and appearance, and dwelt with motherly pride and delight upon
the admiration everywhere accorded to the beauty and
sweetness of the lovely American heiress.

It was a great gratification to Adelaide's pride in her
niece to learn that more than one coronet had been laid
at her feet, yet she was not sorry to hear that they had
been rejected with the gentle firmness which she knew
Elsie was capable of exercising.

"But what more could the bairn or her father desire?

Would he keep the sweet lassie single a' her days, Miss Dinsmore?" asked Mrs. Murray when Adelaide told her this.

"No," was the smiling rejoinder, "I know he would be very loath to resign her, but this is Elsie's own doing. She says the man for whom she would be willing to give up her native land must be very dear indeed, that her hand shall never be given without her heart, and that it still belongs more to her father than to anyone else."

"Ah, that is well, Miss Adelaide. I hae been sorely troubled aboot my sweet bairn. I never breathed the thoct to ither mortal ear, but when they cam hame frae that summer in the North, she was na the blythe young thing she had been, and there was that in the wistfu' and hungered look o' her sweet een—when she turned them whiles upon her father—that made me think some ane he didna approve had won the innocent young heart."

"Ah, well, Mrs. Murray, whatever may have been amiss then, is all over now. My sister writes me that Elsie seems very happy, and as devotedly attached to her father as ever, insisting that no one ever can be so dear to her as he."

Mrs. Dinsmore's last letter was dated Naples, and there they still lingered.

One bright spring day they were out sight-seeing, and had wandered into a picture-gallery which they had visited once or twice before.

Rose had her husband's arm. Elsie held her little brother's hand in hers.

"Sister," said the child, "look at those ladies and gentlemen. They are English, aren't they?"

"Yes, I think so," Elsie answered, following the direction of his glance, "a party of English tourists. No, one of the gentlemen looks like an American."

"That one nearest this way? I can only see his side face, but I think he is the handsomest. Don't you?"

"Yes, and he has a fine form too, an easy, graceful carriage, and polished manners," she added, as at that moment he stooped to pick up a handkerchief, dropped by one of the ladies of his party, and presented it to its owner.

Elsie was partial to her own countrymen, and unaccountably to herself, felt an unusual interest in this one. She watched him furtively, wondering who he was, and thinking that in appearance and manners he compared very favorably with the counts, lords, and dukes who in the past two years had so frequently hovered about her, and hung upon her smiles.

But her father called her attention to something in the painting he and Rose were examining, and when she turned to look again for the stranger and his companions, she perceived that they were gone.

"Papa," she asked, "did you notice that party of tourists?"

"Not particularly. What about them?"

"I am quite certain one of the gentlemen was an American, and I half fancied there was something familiar in his air and manner."

"Ah, I wish you had spoken of it while he was here, that I might have made sure whether he were an old acquaintance. But come," he added, taking out his watch, "it is time for us to return home."

The Dinsmores were occupying an old palace, the property of a noble family whose decayed fortunes compelled the renting of their ancestral home. In the afternoon of the day of their visit to the picture-gallery Mr. Dinsmore and his daughter were seated in its spacious saloon, she beside a window overlooking the street, he at a little distance from her, and near to a table covered with books, magazines, and newspapers. That day had brought him a heavy mail from America, and he was examining the New York and Philadelphia dailies with keen interest.

Elsie was evidently paying no heed to what might be passing in the street. A bit of fancy work gave employment to her fingers, while her thoughts were busy with the contents of a letter received from her Aunt Adelaide that morning.

It brought ill news. Arthur had been seriously injured by a railroad accident and, it was feared, was crippled for life. But that was not all. Dick Percival—whom Enna had married nearly two years before—had now become utterly bankrupt, having wasted his patrimony in rioting and drunkenness, losing large sums at the gaming-table, and his young wife, left homeless and destitute, had been compelled to return to her father's house with her infant son.

Mr. Dinsmore uttered a slight exclamation.

"What is it, papa?" asked Elsie, lifting her eyes to meet his fixed upon her with an expression of mingled gratitude and tenderness.

"Come here," he said, and as she obeyed he drew her to his knee, passing his arm about her waist, and, holding the paper before her, pointed to a short paragraph which had just caught his eye.

She read it at a glance. Her face flushed, then paled. She put her arm about his neck, and laid her cheek to his, while tears trembled in the sweet eyes, as soft and beautiful as ever.

For a moment neither spoke, then she murmured in low, quivering tones the same words that had fallen from her lips two years ago—"Thank God for a father's protecting love and care!"

"Thank him that I have my daughter safe in my arms," he said, tightening his clasp about her slender waist. "Ah, my own precious child, how could I ever have borne to see you sacrificed to that wretch!"

They had just learned that Tom Jackson had been tried for manslaughter and for forgery, found guilty on both charges, and sentenced to the State's Prison for a long term of years.

They were quiet again for a little. Then Elsie said, "Papa, I want to ask you something."

"Well, daughter, say on."

"I have been thinking how sad it must be for poor Enna to find herself so destitute, and that I should like to settle something upon her—say ten or twenty thousand dollars, if I may—"

"My dear child," he said with a smile, "I have no control over you now as regards the disposal of your property. Do you forget that you passed your majority three weeks ago?"

"No, papa, I have not forgotten, but I don't mean ever to do anything of importance without your approval. So please make up your mind that I'm always to be your own little girl—never more than eighteen or twenty to you. Now won't you answer my question about Enna?"

"I think it would be quite as well, or better, to defer any such action for the present. It won't hurt Enna to be made to feel poor and dependent for a time. She needs the lesson, and her parents will not allow her to suffer privation of any sort. Ah, here comes mamma in walking attire. We are going out for perhaps an hour, leaving house, servants and the little ones in your charge. Horace, be careful to do just as your sister tells you."

"Yes, papa, I will," answered the child, who had come in with his mother, and had a book in his hand. "Will you help me with my lesson, Elsie, and hear me say it when it is learned?"

"Yes that I will. Here's a stool for you close by my side," she said, going back to her seat by the window.

"Good-bye, dears. We won't be gone long," said Rose, taking her husband's arm.

Elsie and Horace watched them till they had passed out of sight far down the street, then returned to their employments, her thoughts now going back, not to Roselands, but to Lansdale, Ashlands, and Philadelphia —memory and imagination bringing vividly before her each scene of her past life in which Egerton had borne a part. Did any of the old love come back? No, for he was not the man who had won her esteem and affection, and even while sending up a silent petition for his final conversion, she shuddered at the thought of her past danger, and was filled with gratitude to God and her father at the remembrance of her narrow escape.

Her brother's voice recalled her from her musings. "Look, sister," he exclaimed, glancing from the window, "there is the very same gentleman we saw this morning! And see, he's crossing the street! I do believe he's coming here."

Elsie looked, recognized the stranger, and perceived, with a slight emotion of surprise and pleasure, that he was approaching their door. That he was her countryman, and perhaps direct from her dear native land, was sufficient to make him a welcome visitor.

The next moment John threw open the door of the salon and announced, "A gentleman from America!"

"One who brings no letter of introduction; yet hopes for an audience of you, fair lady," he said, coming forward with smiling countenance and outstretched hand.

"Mr. Travilla! Can it be possible!" she cried, starting up in joyful astonishment, and hastening to bid him welcome.

"You are not sorry to see me then, my little friend?" he said, taking her offered hand and pressing it in both of his.

"Sorry, my dear sir! What a question! Were you not always a most welcome guest in my father's house? And if welcome at home, how much more so here in a foreign land."

Mr. Travilla looked into the sweet face, more beautiful than ever, and longed to treat her with the affectionate freedom of former days, yet refrained, the gentle dignity of her manner seeming to forbid it, pleased and cordial as was her greeting.

He turned to Horace and shook hands with him, remarking that he had grown very much.

"I am very glad to see you, sir," said the boy.

"You have not forgotten me then?"

"Ah, no, indeed, and I can't think how it was that sister and I did not know you yesterday in the picture-gallery—though we knew you were an American!"

"Ah, were you there? How blind I must have been!" and he turned to Elsie again.

"We were there for but a few minutes before your

party left, and quite at the other end of that long gallery," she said. "But I am surprised that I failed to recognize you, even at that distance. But I had no thought of your being in the country. How delighted papa will be to see you. He has often spoken of the old times when you and he traveled over Europe together, and wished that you were with him on this trip. He and mamma have gone out, but will be in presently."

Elsie had many inquiries to make in regard to the health and welfare of relatives and friends, and the old family servants at the Oaks; Mr. Travilla had numerous questions to ask concerning all that she had seen and done since leaving America.

But in the midst of it all she exclaimed, "Ah, you must see our little Frenchwoman! Such a darling as she is!"

"I'll ring the bell, sister," said Horace, seeing her glance toward it.

John appeared in answer, was ordered to tell the nurse to bring the baby, and a neatly dressed middle-aged woman presently entered the room, carrying a lovely infant a little more than a year old.

"See, is she not a darling?" said Elsie, taking it in her arms. "She has mamma's own sweet pretty blue eyes, and is named for her. Our Rosebud we call her. Papa gave her the name, and he says she is as much like her mother as I am like mine. You don't know, Mr. Travilla, how glad I was when she came to us. It was something so new and delightful to have a sister of my own. Ah, I love her dearly, and she returns my affection. There, see her lay her little head down on my shoulder."

Mr. Travilla admired and caressed the little creature, coaxed her to come to him for a moment, and the nurse carried her away.

"When do you return home, Elsie?" he asked.

"In the fall. Mr. and Mrs. Ferris, mamma's grandparents, have their golden wedding in October. Sophy expects to be married at the same time, and of course we wish to be present on the occasion. We have yet to visit Turin, Venice and Munich. After seeing these places we intend to spend the rest of the summer in Switzerland, sailing for America some time in September. Ah, here are papa and mamma!" she added as the two entered the room together.

"Mr. Travilla! What favorable wind blew you here?" cried Mr. Dinsmore, shaking his friend's hand in almost boyish delight.

"A westerly one, I believe," answered Travilla, laughing and shaking hands with Rose, who looked scarcely less pleased than her husband. "They think at Roselands and the Oaks that your year is a very long one, or that you have lost your reckoning, and were anxious to send a messenger to assist you in recovering it, so I volunteered my services."

"Ah, that was kind! But to be able to do so to advantage you will need to take up your abode with us for the present, and to make one of our party when we start again upon our travels."

"Of course you will," added Rose. "We always consider you one of the family, a sort of brother to us and uncle to the children."

"Thank you, you are most kind," he said, a slight flush suffusing his cheek for an instant, while his eyes involuntarily sought Elsie's face with a wistful, longing look.

Her father turned laughingly to her. "Is this your stranger of the picture-gallery? Ah, are you not ashamed of failing to recognize so old a friend?"

"Yes, papa, but I did not catch sight of his full face, and he was at quite a distance, and I never thinking of the possibility that he could be anywhere out of America."

"And time makes changes in us all—is fast turning me into a quiet middle-aged man."

"You are very kind to furnish another excuse for my stupidity," said Elsie, smiling, "but I really cannot see that you have changed in the least since I saw you last."

"And no stranger would ever think of pronouncing you over thirty," added Rose.

"Ah, you flatter me, fair ladies," returned Mr.

Travilla, smiling and shaking his head.

"No, I can vouch for the truthfulness and honesty of both," said Mr. Dinsmore.

Mr. Travilla did not hesitate to accept his friend's invitation, knowing that it was honestly given, and feeling that he could not decline it without doing violence to his own inclination. He made one of their party during the rest of their stay in Europe and on the voyage to America.

His presence was most welcome to all. He saw no reason to doubt that, and yet Elsie's manner sometimes saddened and depressed him. Not that there was ever in it anything approaching to coolness, but it lacked the old delightful familiarity, instead of which there was now a quiet reserve, a gentle dignity, that kept him at a distance, and while increasing his admiration for the fair girl, made him sigh for the old childish days when she was scarcely under more constraint with him than with her father.

Our little party reached Philadelphia a fortnight before the golden wedding. They found the handsome city residence of the Allisons occupied by the family, and full of the pleasant stir and bustle of preparation for the eventful day which was to witness the celebration of the fiftieth anniversary of the wedding of Mr. and Mrs. Ferris, and the marriage of their granddaughter.

Sophy, while paying a visit to Rose in her Southern home, had won the heart of Harry Carrington, and they had been engaged a year or more. Harry had once indulged in a secret penchant for Elsie, but now he would not have exchanged his merry, blue-eyed Sophy for her, or for any other lady in the land.

The young couple were married at church, very early in the evening, Elsie acting as first bridesmaid. Returning to the house the bridal party were ushered into the drawing-room, which they found richly ornamented with evergreens and flowers. In the centre rose a pyramid of rare and beautiful blossoms, filling the air with their delicious perfume. Above that was a wide arch of evergreens bearing the monograms of Mr. and Mrs. Ferris, placed between the dates of their marriage and of this anniversary.

The old bride and groom sat together beneath the arch on one side of the pyramid, while the newly-married pair took up a similar position upon the other.

Only the family and near connections were present for the first half hour. The eldest son of Mr. and Mrs. Ferris made a short address, thanking his aged parents for their unselfish love and devotion to their offspring, and exhorting the youthful bride and groom to follow in their footsteps. Upon the conclusion of this little speech, gifts were presented by children and grandchildren, and letters of congratulation, in both poetry and prose, from absent friends were read.

After this the doors were thrown open to the invited guests, and for the remainder of the evening the house was thronged with the elite of the city, and with friends and acquaintances from other parts of the country.

Among the latter were Adelaide and Walter Dinsmore, and Mr. Travilla and his mother. The last named was seated in the corner of a sofa, her son standing by her side.

He heard a low-breathed sigh, noted the quivering of her lip and the gathering tears in the gentle eyes, as she turned them upon the gray-haired bride and groom, and he knew that her thoughts were with the early dead, the husband and father whose image he could scarcely recall. His heart swelled with tender pitying, protecting love, as he thought of her long, lonely widowhood, and of all that she had been and still was to him.

But her gaze wandered to the pair standing just upon the threshold of married life, and smiling up at him, "They are a handsome couple," she said. "How proud and happy Harry looks! Ah, Edward, when will your turn come?"

He shook his head with a rather melancholy smile.

"It is your own fault, I am sure," she continued in a playful tone. "There are plenty of pretty girls and charming young widows who would like well to be mistress of Ion, and I am growing old, and sometimes feel that I would be glad to resign the sceptre to younger hands."

He gave her a glance of affectionate concern. "I shall look for a housekeeper immediately. I ought to have thought of it before."

"No, no, it is a daughter I want," she returned still playfully. "I have often wondered how it has come to pass that my warm-hearted boy seems so perfectly invulnerable to Cupid's darts."

"All seeming, mother," he answered lightly, but with a wistful yearning look in his eyes which were fixed upon a little group on the farther side of the room. "To tell you a secret," and he bent down, that the low-breathed words might catch her ear alone, "I have been hopelessly in love for many years."

She started with surprise—for there was the ring of deep, earnest feeling beneath the jesting tone—then following the direction of his glance, and perceiving that the group upon which it rested was composed of Adelaide and Elsie Dinsmore, with some half dozen gentlemen who had gathered about them, she looked greatly pleased.

"And why hopeless?" she asked.

"Ah, the evidences of indifference are so patent that I cannot hope she will ever learn to care for me."

"And pray what may they be?"

"Constraint and reserve, where formerly there was much warmth and cordiality of manner."

"You foolish boy! If that be all, you may take heart. I would not ask for better symptoms. And remember the old proverb—'Faint heart never won fair lady.' You do not fear that she still clings to the old love?"

"No, ah no!"

"I never saw Adelaide look better than she does tonight," was Mrs. Travilla's next remark. "What a queenly presence, and noble face she has, and how very lovely our little Elsie is! She seems to have gained every womanly grace without losing a particle of her sweet childish simplicity and freshness."

Her son assented with a slight sigh, and wandered off in their direction. But before he reached the little group, Elsie had taken Harold Allison's arm and was being led away toward the conservatory. Harold had a rare plant to show her, and was glad of the excuse to get her to himself for a few moments.

For the rest of the evening Mr. Travilla devoted himself to Adelaide, his mother looking on with beaming countenance, and thinking how gladly she would welcome the dear girl to her heart and home.

It was past twelve when the company dispersed, Harry and his bride having started an hour before upon their wedding tour.

"Get to bed as soon as you can, my dear child. You are looking sadly fatigued," Mr. Dinsmore said, putting his arm about his daughter as she came to him for her good-night kiss.

"I will, papa," she answered, clinging to him with more than her usual warmth of affection. "Dear papa, what could I ever do without you to love me?"

"My darling, if it please the Lord, may we be long spared to each other," he whispered, clasping her close. "Now, good-night, and may he bless you, and keep you, and ever cause his face to shine upon you."

Elsie turned away with eyes full of tears, and her pillow was bedewed with them ere she slept that night. But the morning found her apparently her own bright, sunny self again.

She was in her mamma's dressing-room soon after breakfast, chatting with her and Adelaide, Mr. Dinsmore sitting by with Rosebud on his knee. Of course they were discussing the wedding, how lovely the bride and her attendants looked, how handsome the groom, how tasteful and becoming was the dress of this lady and that, how attentive was Mr. Such-an-one to Miss So-and-so, etc., etc. Rose making a little jesting allusion to "the devotion of a certain gentleman to

Adelaide," and saying how delighted she was, nothing could please her better than for them to fancy each other, when in the midst of it all, a servant came up with a message. "Mr. Travilla was in the drawing-room asking for Miss Dinsmore—Miss Adelaide."

She went down at once, and as the door closed upon her, Rose turned to her husband with the laughing remark, "It would be a splendid match! They seem just made for each other. I wonder they didn't find it out long ago, and I begin to quite set my heart upon it."

"Better not, my dear, lest they disappoint you. And allow me to advise you to let match-making alone—'tis a dangerous business. Elsie, my child, you are looking pale this morning. Late hours do not agree with you. I think I shall have to take to sending you to bed at nine o'clock again, when once I get you home."

"Won't ten be early enough, papa?" she answered with a faint smile, a vivid color suddenly suffusing her cheek.

"Well, we will see about it. But I can't have you looking so. Go and put on your hat and shawl, and I will take you and mamma out for an airing."

"Looking so?" said Rose, with an arch glance at the glowing cheeks, as she stooped to take Rosebud in her arms. "She is not pale now."

"No, certainly not," he said. "Come back, daughter," for Elsie had risen to obey his order, and was moving toward the door. "Come here and tell me what ails you?"

"I am quite well, papa, only a little tired from last night, I believe," she answered, as he took her hands in his and looked searchingly into her face.

"I hope that is all," he said a little anxiously. "You must lie down and try to get a nap when we return from our drive, and remember you must be in bed by ten o'clock tonight."

"I shall do just as my father bids me," she said, smiling up at him, "my dear father who is so kindly careful of me." Then as he let go her hands, she tripped lightly from the room.

Mr. Travilla had come on an errand from his mother. She begged Adelaide's advice and assistance in a little shopping.

Adelaide was at leisure, and at once donned bonnet and shawl and went with him to the Girard house, where the old lady awaited their coming, and the three spent the remainder of the morning in attending to Mrs. Travilla's purchases and visiting the Academy of Fine Arts. In driving down Chestnut street, the Dinsmores passed them on their way to the Academy.

Adelaide did not return to Mr. Allison's to dinner, but Mr. Travilla called presently after, to say that she had dined with his mother and himself at the hotel, and would not return until bed-time, as they were all going to hear Gough lecture that evening.

He was speaking to Mrs. Allison. Several of the family were in the room, Elsie among them. She was slipping quietly away, when he turned toward her, saying: "Would you not like to go with us, my little friend? I think you would find it entertaining, and we would be glad to have you."

"Thank you, sir, you are very kind, but a prior engagement compels me to decline," she answered, glancing smilingly at her father.

"She has not been looking well today, and I have ordered her to go early to bed tonight," Mr. Dinsmore said.

"Ah, that is right!" murmured Mr. Travilla, rising to take leave.

The Travillas stayed a week longer in the city. During that time Adelaide went out with them quite frequently, but Elsie saw scarcely anything of her old friend, which was, however, all her own fault, as she studiously avoided him, much to his grief and disturbance. He could not imagine what he had done to so completely estrange her from him.

Mr. Dinsmore felt in some haste to be at home again, but Mrs. Allison pleaded so hard for another week that he consented to delay. Adelaide and Walter went with the Travillas, and wanted to take Elsie with them, but he would not hear of such an arrangement, while she said very decidedly that she could not think of being separated from her father.

She seemed gay and happy when with the family, or alone with him or Rose, but coming upon her unexpectedly in her dressing-room, the day after the others had left, he found her in tears.

"Why, my darling, what can be the matter?" he asked, taking her in his arms.

"Nothing, papa," she said, hastily wiping away her tears and hiding her blushing face on his breast. "I—I believe I'm a little homesick."

"Ah, then, why did you not ask to go with the others?"

"And leave you? Ah, do you not know that my father is more—a great deal more than half of home to me?" she answered, hugging him close. "And you wouldn't have let me go?"

"No, indeed, not I. But I'm afraid I really ought to read you a lecture. I daresay you miss Sophy very much, but still there are young people enough left in the house to keep from feeling very dull and lonely, I should think, and as you have all your dear ones about you, and expect to go home in a few days—"

"I ought to be cheerful and happy. I know it, papa," she said, as he paused, leaving his sentence unfinished, "and I'm afraid I'm very wicked and ungrateful. But please don't be vexed with me, and I will try to banish this feeling of depression."

"I fear you are not well," he said, turning her face to the light and examining it with keen scrutiny. "Tell me, are you ill?"

"No, papa, I think not. Don't be troubled about me."

"I shall send for a doctor if this depression lasts," he said decidedly, "for I shall have to conclude that it must arise from some physical cause, since I know of no other, and it is so foreign to the nature of my sunny-tempered little girl."

He saw no more of it, though he watched her carefully. Great was the rejoicing at the Oaks when at last the family returned. Adelaide was there to welcome them, and Elsie thought she had never seen her look so youthful, pretty, and happy. Chloe remarked upon it while preparing her young mistress for bed, adding that the report in the kitchen was that Miss Adelaide and Mr. Travilla were engaged, and would probably marry very soon.

Elsie made no remark, but her heart seemed to sink like lead in her bosom. "Why am I grieving so? What is there in this news to make me sorry?" she asked herself as she wetted her pillow with her tears. "I'm sure I'm very glad that dear Aunt Adie is so happy, and—and I used often to wish he was my uncle." Yet the tears would not cease their flow till she had wept herself to sleep.

But she seemed bright and gay as usual in the morning, and meeting her parents at the breakfast-table, thought they looked as though something had pleased them greatly.

It was Rose who told her the news, as an hour later they sauntered around the garden together, noting the changes which had taken place there in their absence.

"I have something to tell you, dear," Rose said, as Elsie shivered slightly, knowing what was coming. "Something that pleases your father and me very much, and I think will make you glad too. Can you guess what it is?"

"About Aunt Adelaide, mamma?" Elsie stooped over a plant, thus concealing her face from view, and so controlled her voice that it betrayed no emotion. "Yes, I know. She is engaged."

"And you are pleased with the match, of course. I knew you would be. You used so often to wish that he was your uncle, and now he soon will be. Your papa and I are delighted. We think there could not have been a more suitable match for either."

"I am very glad for her—dear Aunt Adie—and for—for him too," Elsie said, her voice growing a little husky at the last.

But Rose was speaking to the gardener, and did not notice it, and Elsie wandered on, presently turned into the path leading to her arbor and seeking its welcome privacy, there relieved her full heart by a flood of tears.

Mr. Travilla called that day but saw nothing of his "little friend," and in consequence went away very sorrowful, and pondering deeply the question what he could have done to alienate her affections so entirely from him.

The next day he came again, quite resolved to learn in what he had offended, and was overjoyed at hearing that she was alone in her favourite arbor.

He sought her there and found her in tears. She hastily wiped them away on perceiving his approach, but could not remove their traces.

"Good-morning," she said, rising and giving him her hand, but with the reserved manner that had now become habitual, instead of the pleasant ease and familiarity of earlier days. "Were you looking for papa? I think he is somewhere on the plantation."

"No, my dear child, it was you I wished to see."

"Me, Mr. Travilla?" and she cast down her eyes, while her cheek crimsoned, for he was looking straight into them with his, so wistful and tender, so full of earnest, questioning, sorrowful entreaty, that she knew not how to meet their gaze.

"Yes, you, my little friend, for I can no longer endure this torturing anxiety. Will you not tell me, dear child, what I have done to hurt or grieve you so?"

"I—I'm not hurt or gri—you have always been most kind," she stammered, "most—But why should you think I—I was—"

The rest of the sentence was lost in a burst of tears, and covering her burning cheeks with her hands, she sank down upon the seat from which she had risen to greet him.

"My dear child, I did not mean to pain you so. Do not weep. It breaks my heart to see it. I was far from intending to blame you, or complain of your treatment," he said in an agitated tone, and bending over her in tender concern. "I only wanted to understand my error in order that I might retrieve it, and be no longer deprived of your dear society. Oh, little Elsie, if you only knew how I love you, how I have loved you, and only you, all these years—as child and as woman—how I have waited and longed, hoping even against hope, that someday I might be able to win the priceless treasure of your young heart."

Intense, glad surprise made her drop her hands and look up at him. "But are you not—I—I thought—I understood—Aunt Adelaide—"

"Your Aunt Adelaide!" he cried, scarcely less astonished than herself. "Can it be that you do not know—that you have not heard of her engagement to Edward Allison?"

A light broke upon Elsie at that question, and her face grew radiant with happiness. There was one flash of exceeding joy in the soft eyes that met his, and then they sought the ground.

"Oh, my darling, could you? Is it—can it be?"

He took her in his arms, folded her close to his heart, calling her by every tender and endearing name, and she made no effort to escape, or to avoid his caresses, did nothing but hide her blushing face on his breast, and weep tears of deep joy and thankfulness.

It might have been half an hour or an hour afterward (they reckoned nothing of the flight of time) that Mr. Dinsmore, coming in search of his daughter, found them seated side by side, Mr. Travilla with his arm about Elsie's waist, and her hand in his. So absorbed were they in each other that they had not heard the approaching footsteps.

It was a state of affairs Mr. Dinsmore was far from expecting, and pausing upon the threshold, he stood spell-bound with astonishment. "Elsie!" he said at length.

Both started and looked up at the sound of his voice, and Mr. Travilla, still holding fast to his new-found treasure, said in tones tremulous with joy, "Will you give her to me, Dinsmore? She is willing now."

"Ah, is it so, Elsie, my darling?" faltered the father, opening his arms to receive her as she flew to him. "Is it so? Have I lost the first place in my daughter's heart?" he repeated, straining her to his breast, and pressing his lips again and again to her fair brow.

"Dear papa, I never loved you better," she murmured, clinging more closely to him. "I shall never cease to be your own dear daughter, can never have any father but you—my own dear, dear papa. And you will not be left without a little girl to pet and fondle. Darling Rosebud will fill my place."

"She has her own, but neither she nor anyone else can ever fill yours, my darling," he answered with a quivering lip. "How can I—how can I give you up? My first-born, my Elsie's child and mine."

"You will give her to me, my friend?" repeated Travilla. "I will cherish her as the apple of my eye. I shall never take her away from you, you may see her every day. You love her tenderly, but she is dearer to me than my own soul."

"If you have won her heart, I cannot refuse you her hand. Say, Elsie, my daughter, is it so?"

"Yes, papa," she whispered, turning her blushing face away from his keen, searching gaze.

"I can hardly bear to do it. My precious one, I don't know how to resign you to another," he said in a voice low and tremulous with emotion, and holding her close to his heart, "but since it is your wish, I must. Take her, my friend, she is yours. But God do so to you, and more also, if ever you show her aught but love and tenderness."

He put her hand into Travilla's, and turned to go. But

she clung to him with the other. "Yours too, papa," she said, looking up into his sad face with eyes that were full of tears, "always your own daughter who loves you better than life."

"Yes, darling, and who is as dearly loved in return," he said, stooping to press another kiss on the ruby lips. "Let us be happy, for we are not to part." Then walking quickly away, he left them alone together.

The End